D0364481

'AN ABSOLUTE TRIUMPH'
HOLLY SEDDON

'COMPELLING'
T.M. LOGAN

'BRILLIANT'
JO SPAIN

'ORIGINALITY OOZING
OFF EVERY PAGE'
EVA DOLAN

'TENSE RIGHT FROM
THE FIRST PITCH-BLACK
SCENE'
AMY LLOYD

'GRIPPING,
GRITTY AND TIMELY'
HEAT

'DISTURBING'
CHRIS
WHITAKER

'DARK AND
UNPREDICTABLE'
JENNY QUINTANA

'SEARINGLY RELEVANT'
GILLIAN MCALLISTER

'COMPLETELY
UNPUTDOWNABLE'
MARTYN WAITES

'UNNERVING'
DAVID JACKSON

'BOLD AND
TIMELY'
CRIME MONTHLY

PRAISE FOR DEBORAH O'CONNOR

'ADDICTIVE, THRILLING, SHOCKING'
★★★★★

'EXTREMELY TENSE'
★★★★★

'A MUST-READ'
★★★★★

'YOU REALLY DO NEED TO READ THIS'

'THINGS GET MORE AND MORE OH-MY-GOD'
★★★★★
★★★★★

'HAD ME GRIPPED FROM START TO FINISH'
★★★★★

'HARD-HITTING'
★★★★★

'TENSE AND EXCITING'

'A WELL-CONSTRUCTED, COMPULSIVE STORY'
★★★★★
★★★★★

'ABSOLUTELY DEVASTATING . . . SUPERB'
★★★★★

READER REVIEWS FOR *THE DANGEROUS KIND*

THE
CAPTIVE

Deborah O'Connor is a writer and TV producer. She lives in North Yorkshire with her husband and daughter. *The Captive* is her third novel.

Also by Deborah O'Connor

My Husband's Son
The Dangerous Kind

THE CAPTIVE

DEBORAH O'CONNOR

ZAFFRE

First published in the UK in 2021 by
ZAFFRE
An imprint of Bonnier Books UK
80–81 Wimpole St, London W1G 9RE
Owned by Bonnier Books
Sveavägen 56, Stockholm, Sweden

Copyright © Deborah O'Connor, 2021

Epigraph page ix, Pope John Paul II, copyright © Libreria Editrice Vaticana.
Epigraph page ix, from: *A Suitable Amount of Crime*, Nils Christie,
copyright © 2004, Routledge. Reproduced by permission of Taylor & Francis Group.

All rights reserved.
No part of this publication may be reproduced,
stored or transmitted in any form by any means, electronic,
mechanical, photocopying or otherwise, without the
prior written permission of the publisher.

The right of Deborah O'Connor to be identified as Author of this
work has been asserted by her in accordance with the
Copyright, Designs and Patents Act, 1988.

This is a work of fiction. Names, places, events and
incidents are either the products of the author's
imagination or used fictitiously. Any resemblance to
actual persons, living or dead, or actual
events is purely coincidental.

A CIP catalogue record for this book is
available from the British Library.

Hardback ISBN: 978–1– 83877–265–9
Export ISBN: 978–1–83877–266–6

Also available as an ebook and an audiobook

1 3 5 7 9 10 8 6 4 2

Typeset by IDSUK (Data Connection) Ltd
Printed and bound in Great Britain by Clays Ltd, Elcograf S.p.A.

Zaffre is an imprint of Bonnier Books UK
www.bonnierbooks.co.uk

For Dorothy

'The worst prison would be a closed heart'

Pope John Paul II

'Restore is an Old Norse term. It means, literally, to raise once more the wooden stocks, *staur*, that have fallen down ... to rebuild the house'

Professor Nils Christie, *A Suitable Amount of Crime*

Hannah

The man who had murdered Hannah's husband was due to arrive at midday.

Half an hour, and her home would no longer be her own.

She'd tried to keep busy all morning – cleaning, washing up, doing laundry – anything to take her mind off what was about to happen. Now though, she found herself adrift, stranded in a corner of the kitchen with nothing to do but wait.

She curled her hands in on themselves, tightening and squeezing. Still, they trembled.

I do not want him here.

The urge to scream was overwhelming.

Slowly, she approached the barred cage now fixed to the wall in the middle of the room. The cell was small, the same footprint as a shopping centre parking space, and yet they'd managed to cram in a bed, basin, screened toilet, cupboard and a table and chair. A hatch and metal drawer through which to exchange food, dirty dishes, commissary items and any post the prisoner might receive had been incorporated into a section to the left of the cell door.

The prisoner.

No one could be sure why he did it – he'd entered a not guilty plea – but the consensus in court was that it had been a mugging gone wrong.

She ran her fingers across the steel bars. A harsh metallic noise ricocheted around the room. Heart jittering, she considered the door. Despite regular practice, she'd yet to master the lock. It was strange. She was expert at fashioning the tiny sugar-paste flowers and fondant animal figures that sat atop the bespoke cakes she made for a living but this, a key so large it looked like it had been found at the bottom of a prop drawer and a bulky government-issue deadbolt, had her beat. Fear, it turned out, could do that to a person.

She wafted her apron and leaned toward the fan. It was the last week in September but the heat was oppressive, the temperature in the high twenties and set to rise. It had been the same for weeks, London looped into a nightmarish summer that showed no intention of ending any time soon. The cherry blossoms that lined her street had re-bloomed, the flowers pinking their way through crumbly autumn leaves, and everywhere you looked, confused daffodils lurched from the soil.

She steadied her fingers as best she could and grabbed the key. She wanted to try to get it right at least once before the prisoner arrived.

Technically, her ineptitude wasn't a problem. The lock was electromechanical and operated remotely via the device she now had to wear on a rope round her neck. The deadbolt was nothing more than a fail-safe. A backup in the event of a power cut. It didn't matter if it took her two or even ten times to get it right because she would be doing it with the prisoner already secure in his cell. For Hannah though, being able to operate the lock was important. She'd spent time on message boards in preparation for today and one of the things the more experienced Hosts talked about was how critical it was to show the prisoner you were in control right from the off. 'This is your house,' said Malorie21, who'd hosted her burglar in the box room of her 1930s semi for the last nine months, 'your space. Make sure they know it. Take ownership.'

For Hannah ownership meant having the knack. Only she knew how to waggle the handle on the washing machine whenever it refused to open or how long to leave the bathroom tap before it ran hot. She wanted the cell door to be no different.

She lined the key up to the slot and was about to give it another go when she sensed someone behind her.

'You'll be quite safe.'

She jumped and the key clattered to the floor.

Mr Dalgleish. Hannah's Domestic Liaison Officer (DLO). He'd been doing a final survey of the house and must have come back down to the basement without her noticing. Tall with a 'hup-two' posture hardwired during his military service, Mr Dalgleish refused to tell Hannah his first name ('Helps keep things proper') and was working full time despite being two months into chemotherapy for bowel cancer.

He picked up the key and passed it to her.

'Just checking,' she said, trying to keep her voice steady.

He smiled sympathetically as though he knew something about her she had yet to realise, then stopped, noticing the row of sponge cakes on the side. She'd made them the night before.

'You better not have baked a file into one of those,' he said, wagging a finger.

'They're for a client. A christening,' said Hannah, so on edge she failed to register the joke. 'I had to do the bases yesterday otherwise I wouldn't have enough time to ice.'

'I was kidding, obviously.' He sniffed and brushed a piece of lint from his shoulder. 'You're the last person who'd want to help him escape.'

Hannah looked again at the cakes, each one sealed inside a glass cloche. She'd agreed to the job because she couldn't afford to turn down new clients, no matter how inconvenient. John's death in service pay had gone toward what had turned out to be his surprisingly large credit card debt and her police widow's pension amounted to eight grand per annum. Not nearly enough to cover the bills, let alone her rent.

Now though she was struck by a horrible thought. Would the prisoner think she'd made the cakes for him, to welcome him? There'd been some Hosts on the message boards who believed wholeheartedly in the merits of the system. They had talked of preparing a special meal for their inmate's first night. A lasagne, a roast chicken. One person had made a strawberry trifle for dessert.

She took the top of her dungarees between her fingers. At least there was no chance of him thinking she'd gone to any effort with her appearance. The denim was frayed, a hole forming in the right knee, her apron raggedy, its blue and white daisy pattern blotched with stains. The rest of her was no better. Her hair was the kind of white blond that emboldened strangers to come up to her on the Tube, cock their head to one side and say, 'Swedish?' but she hadn't felt much like washing it this last week and so today it was more of a dirty straw colour, tied into a lank bun that lolled from side to side. No, she looked quite plain. The only thing of note was her amber pendant – a gift from John – and she'd tucked it out of sight down the front of her vest.

John was always getting her things, whether it be a daisy he'd found growing in a pavement crack on his way home, the underside of its petals tinged pink, a new Thermomix when her old one broke down, or a pain au chocolat, still warm, from the bakery at the bottom of their street. He always said that the manner of giving was worth more than any gift, that – his offerings to her aside – the most generous thing you could give someone was something they had no idea was a gift in the first place. He was fifteen years older than Hannah and his hair had been thick and white, having gone that way in his twenties, and sometimes when he went without shaving, Hannah would tease that he looked more like Santa Claus than a Met detective.

She felt for the nub of amber beneath her vest. The pendant wasn't to her usual taste; she preferred delicate jewellery – frail strings of gold or thin bracelets of silver, tasselled with tiny charms – but she figured John had chosen it because of the way the stone matched the streak of tannin in her eyes. Like so many objects she'd once paid no mind – the bottle of hot sauce on the top shelf of the fridge that John added to everything from scrambled eggs to shepherd's pie, the Billie Holiday vinyl they'd liked to slow-dance to before bed – the necklace helped her feel as though John was still around, that any minute now he'd walk through the front door and tell her this had all been a terrible mistake.

A beep. Mr Dalgleish's phone. He checked the screen.

'Oh.'

He seemed disappointed.

For a moment Hannah was visited by an impossible hope. There'd been a change of plan. The prisoner wouldn't be coming after all.

'Better finish up.' He smiled reluctantly, as though he'd just conceded a point in an argument. 'They're two minutes away.'

A crush of disappointment and then Hannah's head began to ring with the same questions that had haunted her since the guilty verdict.

What if he gets out?

What if he tries to hurt me?

During her Host training Mr Dalgleish had reassured her again and again that the system was secure, that the protocols would protect her, that she'd soon relax into it. But Hannah had heard the stories; she knew she couldn't let her guard down, not for one second.

He performed a final lap of the kitchen, checking for objects the prisoner might be able to get at through the bars. His hair was black and dead straight, worn in a dashing Clark Gable side-parting. As he walked he rubbed absent-mindedly at a point just above the nape and a clump came loose and drifted to the floor. The first time Hannah had seen this happen they'd been midway through one of their training sessions. Mr Dalgleish's face had crumpled and, after picking it up with a monogrammed hand-kerchief, he'd told her about his cancer and how he'd decided to continue working during the treatment, partly because he wanted to but also because he needed the money. Then he'd parcelled the hair inside the handkerchief and placed it in his pocket, a look of such naked humiliation on his face that Hannah had had to turn away.

Since then, whenever a tuft fell out Hannah would either pretend not to notice or, if *he* didn't see, she would, with a sideswipe of her foot, discreetly shift the hair out of view. She did this now. Later, when he was gone, she'd sweep it into the bin.

Hannah clocked her wedding rings, still on the side by the sink. She'd taken them off to wash up. She replaced her gold band and was about to put on her engagement ring when she heard the growl of a van pulling up outside.

A thump on the front door.

What if he gets out?

What if he tries to hurt me?

'Here we go,' said Mr Dalgleish. He grabbed the white oval round his neck, identical to her own. 'Black button to lock up, red in case he causes you any trouble. Remember, if you press the red one we'll send someone out to check on you within half an hour.' He made eye contact and held it. 'It needs to be second nature, you understand?'

Hannah nodded, then followed him toward the stairs that led from the basement kitchen to the hall. He reached the front door and went to open it but, as usual, the Yale lock refused to play ball. He fudged it twice before Hannah placed a hand on his shoulder.

'This is my house,' she said, loud enough for the people on the other side of the door to hear. She stepped forward. 'Let me.'

The prisoner stood sandwiched between two guards. Hands cuffed behind his back, he kept his head low and his eyes on the ground. Jem Dahlin.

Almost as tall as Mr Dalgleish, he had hair the colour of burnt caramel, undercut and textured at the top, a style favoured by the teenage boys that hung around Gospel Oak after school. Clean-shaven throughout the trial, he now sported the beginnings of a beard. The stubble emphasised his already full mouth. Soft and red, his upper lip was shaped like a mountain range, two peaks with a slight dip in the middle.

Once in her custody he would be allowed to wear clothes of his own choosing, but for now he was in the Holding Centre uniform of white T-shirt, grey jogging bottoms and black plimsolls. Holding Centres, secure compounds with locked rooms and guards, housed those on remand. Jem had remained in one since his arrest and then, once the guilty verdict was delivered, for the fortnight it had taken to construct the cell in Hannah's kitchen.

Jem shifted on his feet and Hannah remembered a moment during the trial's closing statements. At the mention of his name he'd shaken his head, it seemed, in denial of the accusation levelled against him. Examined closely though, the action was something else entirely: a reprimand. He was annoyed at himself. But whether he was disappointed for having done what he'd done or because he'd been careless enough to get caught was anyone's guess.

Hannah had expected that, when faced with him up close, she'd have to fight the urge to cower and hide. But looking at his bowed head she felt like she'd been punched in the throat, hit by a flash of anger so quick and fierce it took her breath away.

This person had killed John and all for what, a few quid?

She stepped aside and motioned for them to come in. They blundered by and Hannah tensed, worried they'd knock something from the thin shelf to the right of the door. Lined with pictures and trinkets, it was dominated by a cube of gold and black marble, an award presented to John after he triumphed at a work darts night. They passed by without incident, but as they cleared the coat rack one of the guards brushed against John's mac, still hung where he'd left it.

'Careful.' Her voice thorned the air. She closed the door and went to check on the coat. 'Down the hall,' she said, smoothing out the sleeves. 'Staircase on your left.'

She watched them go and tried to comfort herself with the fact that Jem's stay was temporary. The minute the verdict had come through she'd lodged an appeal requesting he serve his twenty-year sentence not with her but with one of the city's Foster Hosts, people unconnected to the crime who took prisoners into their home for a fee.

To qualify for Foster Host assistance a victim (or the family that survived them) had to prove they were unable to take on the prisoner because of ill health, disability or acute lack of space.

Hannah didn't fit any of the criteria but her lawyer had said that John's service as a police officer would likely see the request signed off without fuss and Jem transferred within a month, two at most. She'd still be required to visit him at the Foster Host weekly but that would be nothing compared to having to live under the same roof.

Of course she could have just done what so many did and refused to go ahead with the conviction – for there to be a crime there had to be a victim or someone connected to the victim willing to take responsibility – but in the early days of her grief Hannah had been fuelled by a rage and need for justice so visceral that she had given little thought to what it would mean for her in the long term. Then, during the trial, reality had set in and she'd found herself conflicted. She wanted Jem to be punished but was ashamed to admit that she did not want to be the one to bear that burden.

In the kitchen the guards and the prisoner went to wait by the cell. The guards were young, their navy uniforms roomy, like they'd chosen them from a dressing-up box. One wore a gold watch with a scaly dragon carved into the clock face that was either very expensive or very cheap. Too big for him, it slid up and down his arm and when he stood still it slumped heavy against his wrist.

Mr Dalgleish got out his tablet and went to the keypad on the wall. Making sure to shield both from view, he brought up two six-digit codes and tapped them in, activating the electric fence at the front and back of the house. All set, he took a seat by the French doors and got to work signing and dating the custodial forms. He seemed in a hurry all of a sudden.

'Tea? Cake?' said Hannah, trying to delay the moment when she and Jem would be left alone. 'Feel free to use the bathroom.'

'Thanks, but we need to get on,' said Mr Dalgleish. He nodded at the guards. 'They've got another handover after this and I've got an outside session in Finchley at 2 p.m.'

Through the doors she could hear screams of laughter. Her house backed onto one of Hampstead Heath's ponds and she and many of her neighbours had gardens with steps down to the shore. Ordinarily, there was no way Hannah could have afforded to live here – her neighbours' houses were worth millions – but John's job with the Met meant they qualified for the city's key-worker housing scheme. Some of this housing took the form of new-build flats while others, like this property, were old council stock, grand but shabby and situated on streets that had gentrified around them.

Looking out, she saw a couple from down the road messing around on a rowing boat in the middle of the water. Before, on days like this, she would have left the doors open. The breeze cooled as it passed over the pond and into the kitchen. But since John had died she preferred the house sealed, no matter the weather. She wanted to keep the fragments of him that remained.

One of the guards handed her a large brown paper bag, its top closed with blue and white custody tape.

'His things.'

Jem was allowed a small number of items – books, toiletries, photos – in his cell but the contents of this bag – the clothes he'd been wearing and any objects he had on his person when he'd been arrested – would only be released to him once his sentence was complete. The bag was light but when she placed it on the table something clinked in the bottom. Jem's head shot up. He looked from the paper bag to Hannah, eyes narrowed, as though she'd just trashed something precious. This was the first time he'd looked directly at her. It was like having a torch shone in her face. She turned away, but then she was wired with another shot of rage. *You murdered my husband*, she thought. *When it comes to your stuff, I don't give a shit.* Staring right at him, she lifted the bag back into the air, as if to reposition it, and this time she made sure to bring it down even harder. There was a splintering crack, like the sound of a mug breaking, and the tinkle of broken pieces settling.

Jem flinched and Mr Dalgleish looked up, distracted by the noise. Unable to find an explanation, he was about to return to his paperwork when he clocked something outside.

'Is she OK?' he asked, pointing next door.

Hannah followed his gaze.

An elderly lady wearing a cerise Chanel skirt suit was shouting and swearing while waving a draught excluder toward the branches of a plum tree. Having managed to knock a number of plums to the ground, she then set about weaponising the fruit, hurling them toward the people in the rowing boat. The missiles plopped in the water, well short of their target, but the woman was undeterred and, in search of more ammo, grabbed the draught excluder again and went back to swinging at the tree.

'Pru,' said Hannah, by way of explanation. 'She's harmless.'

Mr Dalgleish seemed unconvinced.

'Not all prisons have bars.' He pointed a pen toward the cell door. 'Would you like to do the honours?'

A guard removed Jem's handcuffs and he rubbed at his wrists, soothing the red marks left behind. His hands were strong, the veins and tendons fanning toward his fingers like exposed tree roots.

I am safe, she told herself, *he can't hurt me.*

She pressed the black button on her device and opened the door.

Slowly, Jem stepped inside.

'Against the wall,' said Mr Dalgleish. His tone was brisk but Hannah had never seen him so relaxed. Following protocol seemed to be a comfort to him, like sliding into a pair of well-worn shoes.

The prisoner did as he was told and went and stood against the wall furthest from the door. He moved with fluidity and held himself with such poise – spine erect, neck elongated, chest and abdomen open – that Hannah was sure he must have once been a dancer.

She pressed the black button for a second time, locking the cell, and Jem nodded respectfully. Now for the fail-safe. She lined the key up next to the hole and was about to put it in when she fumbled. It dropped to the floor, bounced through the bars and skidded across the cell toward the prisoner's feet.

In one balletic movement he reached down to pick it up, took a step forward and passed it to her. She reached for it without thinking. He flattened his palm against hers, his skin warm, and as he slid his hand away she felt his forefinger press hard against her wrist.

Mr Dalgleish was on his feet in an instant.

'Inmate, step away.' He placed his thumb over the red button on his device. Hold it down for five seconds and, as well as sounding the alarm, he would administer an electric shock via the corresponding chip in Jem's spine.

Jem held up his hands, mea culpa, and retook his place by the wall.

Rattled, Hannah began to sweat. She'd failed to react and had left herself vulnerable. Mr Dalgleish had been there to back her up, but next time she might not be so lucky.

'Try again,' said Mr Dalgleish.

She took a breath to compose herself. Through the doors she could see the people in the rowing boat. They'd made it to the other side of the pond. Hopping into the shallows, they dragged the vessel to the shore.

She blocked out Jem as best she could and put the key in the lock. After hooking it up to the right, she waited until it was pushing against the underside of the mechanism and turned. A thunk, the feel of something solid dropping, and it was done. She removed the key and placed it on its hook by the sink.

'The spare?' said Mr Dalgleish, nodding at the key.

Hannah picked up an old green and gold Fry's chocolate tin from the windowsill.

'In here.' She gave the tin a shake and the second key clanged inside.

Mr Dalgleish nodded his approval, then he signed the last form with a flourish, tugged the paper from the clipboard and handed it to her.

'We'll leave you to it.'

I am safe, Hannah told herself again. *He can't get out.*

She went to see Mr Dalgleish and the guards to the door.

Jem stayed where he was by the wall.

His eyes followed her every move.

Hannah should have spent the afternoon icing and decorating the sponge cakes from last night but after the guards and Mr Dalgleish had gone, terrified of facing Jem alone, she'd fled to her room. Now, the sun was starting to set, and with time running out (the christening was tomorrow) she had no choice but to return to the kitchen.

She made her way onto the landing and stopped. The house was stifling, and this combined with the hours lying in bed had left her fingers puffy. She pushed her thumb against her wedding rings, trying to relieve the pressure on her swollen flesh, and realised she could only feel her gold band. She looked to check. She was sure she'd put both rings back on after washing up, but maybe she'd got distracted. Her engagement ring, an oval ruby haloed by diamonds, must still be by the sink.

She forced herself down the stairs and made it all the way to the hall before she stopped again. Her body had started to shake. It was as though her blood was moving too fast through her veins, racing around her organs in search of safety.

If she'd had any say in the matter she would have asked for Jem's cell to be constructed in the living room or spare bedroom; both were spaces that she would have been easily able to avoid. But the kitchen. She worked there; she ate there. It was her only access to the back garden. And that, said Mr Dalgleish, was the whole point.

When it came to deciding where to install a cell in someone's home the prison service were guided by three things: available space, enough pre-existing plumbing infrastructure to support a toilet and sink and, most important of all, where would have the most foot traffic. The new system took restorative justice to its logical conclusion. They *wanted* to make seeing and talking to Jem unavoidable.

She could call the client, tell them she was sick and wouldn't be able to make their christening cake after all? Or maybe she should return to her room, and sneak back down in the dead of night to do the construction while Jem was asleep?

No. She grabbed her amber pendant for courage. She couldn't disappoint the client, she wouldn't, and working in the middle of the night was a stupid idea. This was her kitchen, her house. Jem was behind bars with no way out. She needed to finish the cake and so she would.

Still shaking, she made her final descent and turned the corner to see Jem standing by his basin in a pair of jeans, top off. He was halfway through a strip wash and his wet skin shone in the evening light. He was strong, his body lean, but there was something about the pouched muscle crowding his upper arms that reminded Hannah of a puppy's belly, vulnerable and pink.

Seeing her, he startled and, after rinsing the last of the soap from his neck, grabbed a towel. Hannah blushed and turned away but not before she saw the ladder of scars on his back, the keloided flesh rumpled and thick.

It was even hotter down here, the air treacly, and Hannah realised that although she'd left the fan on, it was useless, pointing as it was away from the cell. She redirected it toward Jem and as the breeze hit his face he closed his eyes.

'Thank you,' he said quietly, like he was whispering a secret.

At the sink she searched the area around the taps for her engagement ring but there was no sign of it. Trying not to panic, she checked the other work surfaces and patted the pockets in her dungarees. Had it fallen down the plughole or worse, into the waste disposal?

Since John had died she got upset whenever she misplaced the silliest of things – she'd spent weeks searching for the Paddington Bear travel-card holder he'd got her for Christmas – but if she lost this . . . She didn't want to finish the thought.

She was about to get down on her hands and knees and scour the floor when she realised she was being watched. She turned round, only for Jem to look away, a moment too late.

She decided to search for the ring again later. If it didn't turn up she'd call out a plumber. The waste disposal had been playing up for months, gargling and spitting; if her ring had fallen down there hopefully it wouldn't have got far.

After putting on her daisy apron, she washed her hands and lined up the sponge cakes. The client was a Dartmouth Park couple who'd conceived twin girls after years of trying. Tomorrow they'd christen them at St Michael's on South Grove.

Hannah had never intended to be a baker. As a teenager she'd harboured dreams of graphic design and after completing her course at Falmouth she'd moved to the city, hoping to find work. But staff jobs were non-existent and the freelance gigs she won were paltry and sporadic. She started temping to make ends meet and at weekends would bake the odd birthday or anniversary cake for friends and family, using her love of design to create fantastical, geometric sponges that she populated with tiny, perfectly sculpted animals and people. Word spread and soon friends of friends were commissioning her for jobs that grew in size and ambition. She continued temping and kept at it with the cakes until the demand for her work became such that she could quit the office job and make a go of it with the baking full time.

These days she catered for a north London clientele who paid handsomely for her kooky, out-there aesthetic. She averaged two to three cakes a week, more during wedding season, and although she tried to work Monday to Friday only, she often found herself up to her eyes in fondant of a Saturday night.

The Dartmouth Park couple had had their first date at London Zoo and wanted their daughters' cake to be a replica of the famous Lubetkin Pool, decorated with individualised penguin characters. The girls' names – Isla and Florence – would be spelled out on the interlocking spiral ramps. Taking even more care than usual – Hannah knew what it was to long for a child and wanted to make their celebration extra special – she set about cutting the sponge to size, sliced each section in half and layered on the buttercream and strawberry jam filling. This would form the base or swimming pool part of the structure.

As she worked she was aware of Jem behind her, unpacking. He unrolled a poster and began Blu-tacking it to the wall. It was a picture of a thin strip of beach, edged by trees. The sea a clear turquoise. Her jaw clenched. *Don't get too comfortable*, she thought, *you're not going to be here long.*

Again, she sensed Jem's eyes on her and turned round hoping to catch him out, but when she looked she realised he wasn't staring at her but at the sealed paper bag containing his things. She'd yet to lock it away – she planned on storing it in the old airing cupboard at the top of the stairs; that way it would be secure and out of sight – and had left it on the side next to the bread bin.

Bread.

She'd forgotten to make him lunch.

She made a mental note to be more careful. Prisoner neglect or abuse was a serious offence and, if proven, resulted in a hefty fine.

'You must be starving,' she said, her words high and tight. And then, on reflex, 'Sorry.'

She cringed. Why should she apologise to him for anything?

'It's OK,' he said, looking to the floor. 'Feeding me must have been the last thing on your mind.'

She decided to make pasta and salad and had just set a pan of water to boil when she heard a shriek from outside.

'Your neighbour,' said Jem. He nodded at the French doors. 'She's been out there a while.'

Hannah squinted into the twilight. Pru had changed out of her skirt suit into a bathing costume and cap and was scaling the fence at the bottom of her garden. Teetering on the top slat, she veered wildly back and forth, like a tulip that has grown too tall for its stem.

After plating up one of the cake offcuts Hannah made her way outside. Pru had been a keen swimmer and in her twenties had swum the Channel in a time of fifteen hours and twenty-three minutes. In recent years though she'd lost the ability to tread water, let alone do the front crawl, and so her children – all grown-up and moved away – had built the fence and raised it on both sides to stop her from venturing down the steps.

Hannah approached the barrier that divided their gardens and guided the saucer through the slats. Pru had turned sixty-two in

April but her shoulders were still roped with muscle, her thighs taut and freckled.

'Prudence?'

Pru peered through her glasses at the Heath beyond. The sky was splashed peach and red, the pond carpeted with the thick green algae that ran amok every summer.

'There's someone watching the house.' She scanned the horizon from right to left. 'They were there this afternoon. I've decided to keep an eye out until Ted comes home.'

Hannah looked back toward Pru's open French doors. A picture of Ted, dead these last eight years, sat on the dresser.

'And the swimming costume?'

Pru ignored the question and stuck out her chest, defiant. 'You weren't trying to get over the fence to the water?' she asked gently. Pru tried to climb the barrier on a monthly basis. 'That wasn't what was happening here?'

Nothing.

Hannah decided to try a different tack.

'Victoria sponge with wild strawberry jam,' she said, waving the plate. 'Your favourite.'

Pru lowered her glasses, torn between the cake and maintaining her lookout.

'I saw Ted this morning, on his way to the station,' said Hannah. 'He mentioned something about having to work late.'

Pru let the specs fall against her chest. 'Really?'

'I'm sure he'll be home soon.'

That did it. Knees wobbling, Pru clambered down from her perch and whipped the cake out of Hannah's hand.

'It's getting dark,' said Hannah brightly. 'We should go in.'

Pru walked with her down the garden, Hannah waiting until her neighbour was indoors before venturing into her own kitchen.

At the cooker she turned off the gas and grabbed a sieve.

'How long has she been like that?' asked Jem.

'A while.' She drained the pasta. 'Some days are worse than others.'

While she was outside he'd put on a T-shirt and a red and white baseball cap emblazoned with a rooster kneeling down to release what looked like a bowling ball. This plus the haircut made him look younger than his twenty-eight years.

'It's cruel, when your brain stops working the way it should.' His hand went to the spot at the top of his spine where the chip had been implanted. 'Like you're walking around in a different world to everyone else.' He pressed gently against the vertebrae, as if feeling for the device under the skin. 'Like the rules have changed . . .'

'But no one thought to tell you,' said Hannah and Jem nodded and smiled sadly. She flushed and turned toward the counter. The words had come out of her mouth as a reflex – he'd voiced something she'd often ruminated on since Pru's deterioration – but still, she was annoyed with herself. Agreeing with him felt like a concession of sorts, a weakening, as if she was already starting to forgive what he'd done.

She focused on preparing the food. Once the pasta was ready she divided it and the salad onto two plates. She placed Jem's portion along with the regulation blunt cutlery onto a tray and passed it to him through the hatch. He could draw his own water from the sink in the cell.

'Smells great.' As he took it from her his eyes slid out of focus, distracted by something over her shoulder. He nodded at the fridge. 'Even Mr Claus makes mistakes,' he said, reading the magnetic letters arranged there. 'Reindeer burgers on me?' He frowned. 'What does that mean?'

Hannah considered telling him the words were a nonsense, but she was sick of playing down her loss in order to make other people more comfortable and anyway, wasn't this the whole point of this terrible situation, for Jem to live and breathe the consequences of his crime?

'It was our thing. John and I, I mean. I bought them to remind myself to buy milk and bread, stuff like that. John had other ideas. Before he left for work he'd often use the letters to leave me a message.' Hannah smiled but in truth the memory was bittersweet. John had left these words as an apology after an argument. 'That's the last thing he spelled out. He wrote it a few weeks before he died.'

She expected Jem to cringe, shamed by this mention of the man he had killed, but instead he nodded slowly, as if to acknowledge her pain, then sat down and began to eat.

Hannah wanted to throw the pasta at him but instead she grabbed her kit bag and, after pricking her finger, she put the strip into the machine and waited. Once she had her reading she calculated the carbs in the food she was about to eat, loaded up the pen with insulin and pushed the front of her dungarees to one side. Lifting her vest, she squidged a section of belly fat together and injected.

All done, she picked up her plate and, holding it close, began shovelling in food. The sooner she was fed the sooner she could get on with the cake and get away from the kitchen, from Jem.

Jem finished eating first. He motioned to the half-completed Lubetkin cake.

'You're talented.'

She said nothing, hoping her silence would discourage him, but then a few seconds later he spoke again.

'Did you train as a baker or teach yourself?'

'I taught myself,' she said dully.

'YouTube? You can learn how to do anything these days.'

She slammed her plate onto the worktop.

'Stop it.'

Jem jumped and his cutlery fell to the floor.

'Just making conversation.'

'Conversation?' said Hannah as though she was trying to make sense of a word from another language.

'Isn't that what we're supposed to do, get to know each other?'

Not wanting to be around him a moment longer, she gulped the last of her food and covered the cake with foil. She'd get up early, finish the penguin figures then.

'While you're here, I'll treat you with respect, follow the rules, but make no mistake,' she said, her voice nettled, 'we aren't friends and we never will be.'

She was at the foot of the stairs when he replied.

'I know what they claimed in court, what they decided. But I need you to know. I didn't do it.' He said the words slowly, each syllable as deliberate as a high-wire footstep. 'I didn't kill your husband.'

She turned to face him. The top right corner of the beach picture had fallen down. It flapped in the breeze.

She marched over to the fan and jabbed the switch, turning it off.

Let him sweat.

Upstairs she sat on the edge of the bed, her blood stilled. She was furious but she was also shocked, surprised at herself, at what she had done.

Being mean had come easily.

She could see how a person might do it again.

The next morning, after delivering the christening cake to the family in Dartmouth Park, Hannah scurried home. Leaving Jem alone for the first time, albeit locked in the cell, had been unnerving – it felt like she'd left the gas on, or a tap running – and she was keen to get back and check all was well.

It had only just gone eleven but the sun was hot, the sky blue, and the streets were full of people and dogs on their way to the Heath. The pavement was sludgy with fallen apples and the fruit foamed in the sun. A pair of dog walkers approached, a couple with a white lurcher in tow. As they passed the woman tripped on a broken paving slab and the man reached to catch her fall. She righted herself quickly but his touch lingered and they paused to smile at each other before carrying on their way.

Hannah felt for the smooth spot on her finger where her engagement ring usually sat. She'd searched for it again this morning, but to no avail. Without it she felt untethered, like the rope connecting her to John was starting to fray.

He'd been gone almost six months and the needlessness of his murder had yet to get any easier to bear. He was a detective sergeant in the Metropolitan Police and the night he died had been so painfully ordinary. He'd gone to enjoy a post-work drink with his partner Rupert on the Kingsland Road and at 8.30 p.m. Rupert had left to go and meet friends in another part of town. John had stayed at the bar and then headed home around 10 p.m. Halfway down Shoreditch High Street he entered an alley. It was impossible to know if he took a wrong turn and went in there by mistake or if he'd needed to relieve himself before he got on the Tube, but CCTV showed that he was followed into that alley by Jem, who was working as a glass collector in the same bar from which he'd just come.

The theory went that Jem had noticed John drinking heavily and figured he was someone he could hustle without too much resistance – Jem's colleagues had testified to rumours, never proven, that he sometimes stole from inebriated customers – and that when they ended up leaving the bar at around the same time he saw an opportunity. It was thought that Jem entered the alley to try to mug John, that he threatened him with a knife, and that as John was in the process of handing over his possessions he told Jem he was a police officer in the hope he would get scared and run away. Instead Jem had panicked and stabbed John – twice in the stomach, once in the ribcage and twice in the back – as he lay face-down, helpless and bleeding, before fleeing the scene.

The alley was a dead end. CCTV showed that no one else went in or out until the following morning, when John's body was discovered by a passer-by.

Jem had protested his innocence throughout the trial, despite the fact his fingerprints and DNA had been found on the inside and outside of John's wallet and its contents as well as his phone and keyring – and, most damning of all, that his fingerprints had been found on the murder weapon discarded in a nearby commercial waste-bin.

Clearing the Highgate Road, Hannah decided to take a shortcut and, after nipping across the bottom of Parliament Hill, jogged through an alleyway dense with privet.

She was halfway down the street before she realised her mistake.

This route would take her past the house on the corner.

She decided to retrace her steps and go back the long way round. It would add another twenty minutes to her journey but she didn't care; she couldn't face that house, not today. She was about to double back when her phone rang. Aisling. Her best friend.

'Ash.'

'How are you holding up?' Her voice was slow and nasal. The warm weather must have reignited her hayfever; either that or she was getting a cold.

'I'm scared of being in my own home and I hardly slept a wink.' She spoke fast, like she didn't want to dwell on her new reality. 'I got up at the crack of dawn to finish a cake and he was already awake, just sitting there staring.'

'Any news on the Foster Host?'

'I should hear soon.' Hannah took a breath, and when she next spoke her tone was bright. 'What time are you coming over?'

Hannah was forbidden from having visitors until tonight; they had arranged to get together and order takeout.

'About that.' Aisling's words were pinched. It seemed like an effort for her to speak. 'Something's come up. Last-minute booking.' She forced out the last piece of information. 'I need to be in Belgravia by 7 p.m.'

A masseuse, Aisling worked in a physiotherapy clinic two days a week and supplemented her shifts with mobile jobs, dragging her massage table around the city and treating people's aches and pains in the comfort of their own homes.

'Oh.' Hannah scrambled to hide her disappointment. She knew Aisling needed the money and that she wouldn't ditch her unless she really had to. Still, she'd been looking forward to seeing a friendly face. 'You can't reschedule?'

Aisling was the one person Hannah could not do without and, these last six months, had been her rock. At her side when the police knocked on the door with news of John's murder, having arrived by chance half an hour earlier, that's where she'd stayed through the funeral and the trial and all the grey days and nights in between. She'd made sure Hannah had hot food to eat and clean clothes to wear and had come to comfort her in the bleak twilight hours when she thought she would go mad with grief. At a time when everyone else had tiptoed around the topic, scared to say John's name for fear of causing upset, Aisling had made sure to constantly remind her of all the funny, annoying or special things John had ever said or done.

'It's a ninety-minute session and the client pays premium, so . . .' Aisling faltered. 'Sorry.'

With curly brown hair and pale skin, Aisling had been born and bred on a sheep farm in New Zealand. The only member of her family to ever leave the province, let alone the country, she'd travelled to the UK with dreams of being a zoologist and ended up in the same Deptford houseshare Hannah was living in then. Aisling had grown up on a diet of meat and boiled vegetables and on her first night, not long after she'd unpacked her things, Hannah had blown her mind by cooking her tortellini with Parmesan sprinkled on top. A week later and Aisling had tried to repay the favour by making a recipe she'd found online: stir-fry with noodles. Hannah had her fork raised, ready to dig in, when Aisling had reached across and, with a proud smile, proceeded to shower her plate with Parmesan. Hannah had devoured it without comment. They'd been friends ever since.

'What's it like?' – Aisling sniffed – 'having him there?'

'Weird. Everything in the kitchen is the same, except there's now a whacking great cell where the breakfast bar used to be.' She stepped on a particularly gooey bit of rotten apple and almost lost her footing. 'I keep banging my knee against the bars on the way to the fridge.' She grabbed a wall to anchor herself and, looking around, realised she'd forgotten her plan to change course. She now stood opposite the very place she had so wanted to avoid.

The house in question was situated on the corner of Shirlock Road and had a large front garden, lavish even by NW3 standards, bordered by hip-height brick walls that wrapped around the front and side. The square of grass to the right of the front door was dominated by a sycamore tree and underneath it was pitched a two-man dome tent. Khaki with a brown stripe around the bottom, the tent's roof was spattered with white stains, bombardments from the birds above.

'You're sure you'll be OK?' said Aisling, misinterpreting her silence. 'You're not mad?'

In front of the tent was a camping stove and next to it was a plastic table, a bucket containing metal plates and utensils underneath. Hannah was about to scuttle away when a woman emerged from the tent and checked on the kettle. Laurie Simmons. Immaculate in navy capri pants and a white T-shirt, Laurie was a trader who, until she was raped, had lived inside the house with her husband and three boys. She'd chosen to pursue a conviction, rare these days, and, unwilling to live under the same roof as her rapist and unable to get out of her obligation (she was required by law to reside on the property for the duration of the sentence), when the guilty verdict came through she despatched her family to her in-laws in Crouch End and moved into her front garden. That was four years ago. She'd been there ever since.

Her situation had been covered in depth by the *Ham & High* and had always filled Hannah with horror, but ever since John's murder she'd gone to extreme lengths to avoid the story and the house itself. Laurie's predicament was now a horrible combination of the familiar and the obscene. She found the way the grass and flowers had started to grow up around the tent almost graphic. It was the longevity.

'Hannah?'

Hannah watched as Laurie lifted the kettle off the stove and poured the boiling water into a teapot. Leaving it to brew, she zipped the tent and approached the front door.

'I'll be fine,' said Hannah, unable to take her eyes off Laurie. 'But let's get together soon OK? I need you.'

Standing on the doorstep, head dipped, Laurie reminded Hannah of a high jumper pausing to fortify herself before taking a run-up to the bar. A few moments later and she put the key in the lock. Hannah waited until she was gone and the door closed behind her. Only then did she continue on her way.

Back home, Hannah picked up the post from the mat and headed downstairs. The fresh air and exercise had given her a boost but in the last few minutes she'd started to get the heavy, foggy-headed feeling that meant her blood sugar was low. She needed to drink some juice and fast, otherwise she'd pass out or, worse, have a seizure.

Inside the kitchen the midday sun was dazzling. She recoiled and, without waiting for her eyes to adjust, felt her way to the fridge and poured a glass of orange juice.

It was then she realised.

She'd yet to see Jem.

She turned round and squinted at the cell. The bedcover was smooth, his chair stored neatly under the table. He wasn't there.

Maybe he was on the loo?

She moved in close to the bars.

'Jem?'

Nothing.

Trying not to panic, she got down on her hands and knees and searched for his feet in the gap between the bottom of the toilet cubicle and the floor, but there was no sign of him.

'Jem?' she said, louder this time. 'Where are you?'

She knew it was impossible; still she checked the hook by the sink, making sure the key was where she'd left it. But then maybe there'd been a power cut while she was out and he'd managed to pick the lock? The cell door looked secure, but it was hard to tell. She was about to push on it to check when she heard a noise upstairs. A thump, like someone falling over.

She scrambled back, reached for the red button round her neck and pressed it once, raising the alarm.

Her phone rang a few seconds later.

'This is the Domestic Prison Service.' The woman's voice was blank. 'We received an alert from this address. Who am I speaking to?'

'Hannah, Hannah Cavey.'

She hovered by the mouth of the stairs, adrenalin lashing through her veins. Jem couldn't have gone far. The chip in his neck also corresponded with the invisible electric fence that now surrounded her house. Any breach across it would trigger the implant and administer a mild shock. If, after that first shock, he continued to move away from the boundary then he would be hit by another, much stronger jolt that would increase in intensity until it disabled his nervous system and he collapsed.

Activated by six-digit codes that were reset every four weeks and which only Mr Dalgleish had access to, the fence was divided into two zones, one at the front of the house and one at the back, and was controlled via the keypad on the wall.

All that meant he had to be hiding somewhere in the house, but where? Her instinct was to run, to escape into the street, but what if Jem was lying in wait? He could be anywhere en route to the front door.

'My inmate, he's not in his cell.' Pressing her back against the wall, she began to climb the stairs. 'I went out and when I came back he was gone.' The fog in her head was getting thicker now, seeping deeper into her brain. The orange juice was still on the side, the glass furred with condensation. She could dash back and get it but what if Jem had hid in one of the cupboards? In theory she was supposed to press her red button for five seconds and shock him, but what if she didn't do it in time? What if he beat her to it? 'I know the cell was locked, I *know* it.'

The woman's voice remained flat to the point of sounding bored.

'A team is on their way.'

Hannah hung up and, after broaching the last few steps, she stopped, listening. Nothing. She peered round the corner. It was ten paces to the front door but to get there she'd have to go past the living room.

She blinked, trying to maintain her focus. Her peripheral vision was starting to cave in, the walls like a collapsing hall of mirrors. If she didn't go now she risked passing out here, alone.

Keeping her finger on the device, she sprinted to the door and out to the opposite side of the street. On a gently sloping hill, the road was wide, the pavements spacious, some of the houses so tall you had to crick your neck to see all the way to the top. The sun was brutal but a horse chestnut tree offered shade, its branches heavy with shrivelled conkers. She shuffled toward it and sagged against a wall.

Almost immediately a woman appeared at a nearby bay window, a fat grey cat at her side. She was wearing a mauve and yellow kaftan and her hair was masked by a matching turban that she patted like a frightened pet.

Kiki Masters and her house cat, a Russian Blue named Poobah who regularly made breaks for freedom and who, on more than one occasion, had tried to sneak in through Hannah's front door.

Kiki had no time for Hannah. The problem was her house. Being a key-worker property, it was owned and maintained by the council, which meant it was visibly down at heel compared to the rest of the street. It was widely agreed among Kiki and her neighbours that its practical UPVC windows and lack of Farrow & Ball brought down the tone. Kiki was especially vociferous because her and her surgeon husband Maxwell Masters had had their house on the market for over a year but had yet to secure a decent offer. Kiki blamed this on the fact that her property overlooked Hannah's. And now, to make matters worse, Hannah had the ultimate real-estate deterrent: a prisoner.

Kiki peered out into the street, nose wrinkled, no doubt calculating how much the last forty-eight hours had caused her house to depreciate. Hannah thought she was going to come and shoo her off but then her eyes widened and Hannah turned to see a van with metal grilles on the windows pull up. A team of guards in stab vests and helmets tumbled into the road, followed by Mr Dalgleish. He directed them toward the house and came to join Hannah.

'Tell me,' he said as he guided her back across the street. He moved cautiously, as though it hurt to put one foot in front of the other, and Hannah wondered where he was in his current chemo cycle.

'The cell was secure.'

Mr Dalgleish narrowed his eyes.

'You didn't let him out? Because some do, despite everything. They feel sorry for them or they want to be their friend.'

'No.'

Hannah remembered what he'd said to her in training 'Criminals aren't like us. They will lie to you, they will get you in trouble. They don't care.'

Mr Dalgleish studied her a few moments more, clearly trying to work out if she was telling the truth, then shrugged.

'He'd be fried to a crisp if he went past the perimeter for any length of time so he must be nearby. Still, I've put out an alert.'

The guards reappeared, moving down the path in a smooth formation. She searched for Jem in their midst.

'No sign of the prisoner in the house or back garden.' One of the guards raised his hand. 'We did find a pile of books on the floor in an upstairs bedroom. It looks like they toppled under their own weight.'

Mr Dalgleish raised an eyebrow.

'Oh dear.' He waited until the guards had got back into the van, then turned to Hannah. 'Shall we?' He nodded at the house. 'I need to take your statement.'

Hannah led the way. She was still paranoid Jem might be hiding somewhere inside, but in the last few seconds her lips had started to tingle. If she didn't get some glucose into her system in the next few minutes then her mouth would go numb, and not long after that she'd lose consciousness.

She planned to head straight for the glass of orange juice she'd left on the side but when they emerged into the kitchen they were greeted by the sight of Jem, headphones on, crawling out from under his bed.

Hannah crashed back into Mr Dalgleish and he winced.

Jem got to his feet, turned round and startled, as surprised to see them as they were to see him. His eyes were crusty with sleep, his hair askew.

He removed his headphones.

'You've been there the whole time?' said Hannah, still not sure whether to trust the situation. She ducked up and down, trying to observe the bed from different angles. 'But I couldn't see you, the guards couldn't see you.'

He raised his arms in the air and stretched from side to side. The movement was precise, easy; Hannah was again reminded of a dancer, warming up.

'I hardly slept last night and then today.' He gestured at the glaring sun. 'It's dark under the bed and these are noise-cancelling.' He looked from Hannah to Mr Dalgleish, realisation dawning. 'You thought I'd got out?'

Hannah hid her face in her hands. She felt like a kid who'd told her parents there were monsters in the wardrobe, only for them to turn on the light and show her there was nothing there.

Mr Dalgleish patted her on the arm.

'Always best to err on the side of caution.' He looked from Jem to the bed and chuckled. 'It's natural to be jumpy, especially in the first few weeks.' He went to the keypad on the wall and reset the codes for both the front and back fence, standard procedure after a call-out, false alarm or not.

Hannah knew she should apologise for wasting his time, and she would, but the numbness was spreading down to her throat. She reached for the juice, now warm and gloopy, and necked it in one. Then she poured another and drank that too.

Within a few minutes she started to feel better, like a wilting plant that had perked back up to full height, strong and tall and green.

Jem watched her carefully from behind the bars, fascinated by the transformation. Before the juice she had been so unsteady. Weak. Vulnerable.

The next day and Hannah had to deliver fifty red velvet cupcakes to a press event for a new boutique in Covent Garden. All done, she headed to the river and along the Embankment to New Scotland Yard where she'd arranged to meet John's old boss, Mickey, for a coffee and a catch-up.

Tiny but fierce, Detective Chief Inspector Michaela Coombes headed up one of the Met's twelve Organised Crime Teams. An amateur bodybuilder, she had a tendency to address even the most hardened of criminals by pet names that ranged from lovey to noodle to sweetie pie. She and John had been close and after his murder she'd struggled to cope, her grief compounded by the fact that John was the second person in her team to die in three months; the first was an undercover officer who had committed suicide. Both detectives had been off duty at the time of their deaths but Mickey considered her team to be her responsibility whether they were on the clock or not.

Hannah always enjoyed hanging out with her but after yesterday's drama she was looking forward to it more than usual. Despite her promises, Aisling had yet to come over (she'd had another influx of bookings she couldn't turn down) and Hannah was craving the comfort of an old friend.

She approached the HQ's art deco facade. To the right of the door sat a marble bust of Sir Robert Peel, the founder of the British police service, 'The police are the public and the public are the police' engraved on the plaque beneath. John had been based here for the last three years of his career. He always said the historical artefacts on display made him feel that he – a working-class East End boy – was an imposter, that he was play-acting at being a detective, and that at any moment he could be found out, exposed as a fraud.

Mickey came down to collect her from reception. Wearing a black trouser suit, she carried a stack of files under one arm. Her hair was pulled into a neat bun, her tan a deep mahogany. Her thigh muscles bulged and Hannah saw how they made the lower part of the trousers hang wrong, the fabric veering forward from the knees.

'Petal.' They embraced and Hannah felt herself relax for the first time in days. 'You look exhausted.' She signed her in. 'Canteen?'

Hannah shrugged. She didn't care where they went, she was just glad to be in her company.

They got into a lift and as they began their ascent Mickey seemed to sway a little on her feet. She hooked her arm through Hannah's as if to balance herself and drew her close. The glass gave a view of each floor as they rose through the building and Hannah could see how half the desks were empty, the detectives that were there slouched and pale. It had been the same when John was alive. She figured it was the futility. The knowledge that, no matter how hard they worked to catch the bad guy, often as not, their efforts would be in vain.

Nineteen years earlier, a mix of complaints from opposite ends of the spectrum had set the change to the justice system in motion. On the one hand, the prisons had been at breaking point, the conditions appalling, riots commonplace. Despite jails cramming three and sometimes four inmates into the same tiny space, costs soared. On the other hand there had been a frustration at the supposed lack of justice facing some criminals, tabloid scoops about PlayStations, flat-screen TVs and mobile phones in cells, which made people angry. The authorities were being too soft, the newspapers said, prison was like a holiday camp.

The then government had launched a pilot scheme, the brainchild of a notorious policy wonk, designed to do away with mass incarceration. Its focus was restorative justice and the importance of the rehabilitation, not punishment, of those that broke the law. They argued that situating the prisoner within the home of the victim would ensure they truly faced up to the damage they had done, that they would learn from the experience and come out the other side a better person.

It quickly became apparent the scheme was ripe for abuse.

One case in particular had caused a public outcry. A heavily pregnant shoplifter serving a six-month sentence was left alone for a weekend when her Hosts decided to bend the rules and go and visit family elsewhere. They'd left her with ample rations but food wasn't the issue. The woman had gone into premature labour and delivered her baby alone on the cell floor. The infant had not survived.

The government had immediately announced the end of the programme and had been in the early stages of disbanding the whole thing when a snap general election saw them ousted from power. Everyone assumed the newly anointed government would be glad to see the progressive scheme consigned to the dust heap – they were, after all, the party of law and order – and that they would sign its final death warrant. But during campaigning it transpired that swathes of the electorate weren't concerned about the shoplifter and her baby (after all, stuff like that had happened in actual prisons all the time) and that in fact they really quite liked the idea of being in charge of the severity of punishment a prisoner might receive, that they relished the idea *they* would be the one to decide whether or not to institute a games-console or a more spartan bread-and-water-like regime. Then there was the fact it was so very much cheaper. Before long, the scheme was rolled out en masse.

In the canteen they found a table by the window.

'So,' said Mickey once they were settled. 'How are you?'

Her speech was the tiniest bit off kilter. The circles under her eyes visible even through the fake tan. Grief manifested in many ways and for Mickey it had shown itself in a chronic and debilitating bout of insomnia. She'd told Hannah that in recent months it had started to improve, but looking at her now, Hannah thought it seemed to have returned with a vengeance.

'I feel like I'm trapped in a nightmare,' said Hannah. She fiddled with her pendant, sliding her finger over the cognac-coloured teardrop. 'It was bad enough having to see him every day during the trial. The feelings it brought up. But now I have to have those feelings on repeat. I can't get away. I have to cook for him, make sure he isn't too hot or too cold.' She clucked a breath, stifling a cry. 'I have to do his bloody washing.'

She looked out of the window, across the slab of river to the London Eye and the aquarium, trying to compose herself. John had taken her to the aquarium for their second date. Afterwards, he'd told her he'd wanted to impress her by doing something magical she'd never forget and, at first it had been exactly that, even with the crowds. John's bulk had shielded her from being bumped and shoved, his arms acting like a guard rail. They'd held hands by the flickering blue tanks and giggled into each other's shoulders at the manta rays rising up to be tickled and fed; but then they'd got to the penguins. As soon as John saw them and realised how and where they were kept his smile had evaporated. 'How is that allowed?' he'd said, trying to direct his eyes anywhere but the enclosure. 'They don't even have daylight.'

'Oh, angel. It's shit. The worst,' said Mickey. 'But hopefully you won't have to put up with him for much longer.' She squeezed Hannah's forearm and as she drew her hand back across the table it brushed against her stack of files. 'Almost forgot.' She reached inside the pile and pulled out a clear plastic folder full of paper. 'Someone got assigned John's old desk. They cleared out the drawers.' She pushed the folder across the table. 'I junked the five thousand salt and pepper packets and miniature soy sauce sachets he seemed to have stockpiled. The rest was just takeaway menus and old darts programmes. Still, I thought you might want them.'

There it was again, that slight delay to her speech, like she was concentrating hard on her pronunciation.

Like she was making sure not to slur.

Hannah tensed, wanting to reject the thought even as it formed.

Mickey hadn't. She wouldn't.

She tried to focus on the plastic folder, and tipped the contents onto the table. Mickey was right; it was mainly menus, darts stuff and what looked like property details for a series of flats in Dalston.

She separated out the rental brochures.

'Weird.' She gathered them up and went to hand them back to Mickey. 'Did these have something to do with a case?'

Mickey refused to accept them.

'I considered that but if they were they would have been logged.'

Hannah leaned back, studying Mickey afresh. Now she'd tuned into what was wrong she noticed other things. The DCI's gaze was swimmy, like she was wearing the incorrect glasses prescription, and there was a garrulousness to the way she moved – a lack of precision when she lifted her mug or sat back in her seat – that wasn't usual.

'And you?' said Hannah. Mickey had struggled with booze in the past. Her addiction had led to the breakdown of her marriage to a cheerful Canadian called Laramie. Sober for eight years, she'd channelled her obsessive tendencies into her bodybuilding. 'How are you?'

'Fine. Overworked and underpaid. Same old.'

'It's just . . .' said Hannah, wary of coming straight out with it. Mickey was proud of her sobriety. For Hannah to doubt it, to doubt her, would be hurtful. 'Are you still able to go to meetings, what with everything you have on at work?'

Mickey didn't understand the nature of the question at first but then, as Hannah held her silence, she stiffened and made sure to sit up that bit taller.

'There was a leaving do at lunch,' she said flatly. 'I had half a shandy. That's it.'

Hannah waited a moment before replying, letting the lie sink in.

'I know more than anyone how hard the last six months have been. If you're struggling . . .'

Mickey checked the time and got to her feet. 'I should get back.' Her trousers had creased into folds at the top of her quads and when she tugged the twill loose it retained a thin concertina pattern. 'Meetings.'

Hannah shoved everything back into the plastic folder and followed her to the lift.

In reception she hugged her goodbye but the chief inspector kept her arms muscled to her sides. Still, Hannah stayed where she was, hoping her friend would come round, believing that if only she waited long enough, Mickey would return the embrace.

Three days into his sentence, Jem was allowed access to a phone.

That morning he barely touched his breakfast and after placing his plate and mug in the hatch he began moving around the cell, jerking up and down on his tiptoes the way sprinters do before a race. Fizzing with energy, he turned his baseball cap this way then that, then set about picking up and replacing each of the things on his shelf in turn, for no other reason it seemed than to have something to do with his hands.

Like all prisoners, he had a weekly sixty-minute call allowance, paid for through his commissary. Conversations were conducted on a specially modified mobile that had no internet capability and had been designed so as to be impossible to force apart and access the wiring inside.

Hannah had charged the phone in the living room overnight and, after clearing the breakfast things away, she ran to get it and placed it in the hatch. Black and chunky with square metal buttons, it looked like an ancient Nokia and weighed the same as a bag of sugar.

'All yours,' she said, pushing it inside.

'I'm sorry,' he said quietly. 'About the other day and the sleeping under the bed thing. I didn't mean to frighten you. I was going to try and wake up before you got back but I was more tired than I realised.'

Hannah shrugged. She was still embarrassed and would have preferred to forget it had happened.

'My rooster cap,' he said, holding it out for her to see.

'What?'

'Whenever I sleep under the bed, I'll leave it on my pillow. That way you don't need to worry, you'll know where I am.'

He smiled shyly and pulled at his T-shirt, exposing the dip and rise of his collarbone. She saw how the top of his neck was smudged with stubble, the tiny black hairs like scratches of ink. He tilted his head slightly, catching her eye, and guided her gaze back up. She felt heat rising in her chest and, not wanting to blush in front of him, searched for a distraction. She nodded at the book, face-down on the bed.

'What are you reading?'

He held her gaze a beat and then slowly turned to look.

'Frank O'Hara.' He said the poet's name like he was an old friend. 'My favourite.'

Hannah nodded. She'd studied one of his poems in school.

'How come you worked in a pub?' She'd only been around him for a few days but his intelligence was obvious and she was curious as to how someone like that could end up making their living glass-collecting. 'I mean, was it a temporary thing?'

He smiled.

'One of the guys I worked with had a PhD in astrophysics.' He held his hands out to the side and grinned. 'A pay cheque is a pay cheque.'

She cringed. Of course, he was right. It had been a thoughtless, snobbish thing to say. The job a person did was not necessarily a reflection of intelligence.

'I'll leave you to it,' she said, tapping the side of the hatch and rattling the phone inside, then launched herself up the stairs.

She had planned to go and wait in the living room but before she stepped out into the hall she paused, listening.

She wondered who he'd call first. A girlfriend? His mother? He'd yet to mention any family. Hannah wasn't sure if that was because he had none – she'd not seen anyone in the gallery during the trial – or if, after what he'd done, he'd been disowned.

She heard the beep-beep-beep of him inputting a number and then she couldn't help it; she leaned back, curious, and strained her ears for his opening line.

Silence.

A minute passed, then another. She held her breath, waiting for him to speak.

A beep.

He'd ended the call.

Had he not been able to get through or had he been directed to voicemail and not wanted to leave a message?

She waited for him to call someone else but instead she heard a dull thud, followed by a metallic shunk-shunk, the sound of something being put in the hatch and pushed through to the other side.

The phone.

She checked her watch. There were still fifty-six minutes remaining but, for this week, at least, it seemed he was done.

Saturday morning and the plumber was on his back under the sink.

'Any joy?' said Hannah, hovering by his feet. She felt for the smooth spot on her finger where her engagement ring usually sat. Now someone was here helping look for it she felt calm, hopeful it would soon be back where it belonged.

'How long has it been like this?' he said, his voice flattened by the inside of the cupboard. His calves were huge and hairless, clusters of knotted vein protruding from his skin like sandworm casts on a beach.

'Since the start of the year,' she said, moving closer. 'A month or so before my husband died.'

Hannah remembered how she'd made a Valentine's dinner, beef Wellington and buttered greens, only for John to get stuck at work. She'd given up on him at midnight and thrown the whole lot down the waste disposal, only for it to craw and creak. A few seconds later it had cut out altogether. The mangled beef had been pushed back up to the opening and she'd had to fish it out with her hands, the pastry sticking to her skin like glue.

A squeak and the wet slop of something heavy landing in a bucket. A rotten, almost faecal stench filled the kitchen.

Hannah put her hand over her nose and mouth and retreated to a safe distance. When she looked she saw that Jem had done the same. He flapped at the air, trying to disperse the smell, and, despite everything, she laughed.

They stood next to each other, the bars between them.

'Working in the pub,' he said quietly so the plumber couldn't hear, 'you were right, it was supposed to be temporary. I wanted to go to university. Get a degree.' His voice was thick with regret but there was something else pulling down the edges of his words too, like stones in pockets. Shame. 'But I needed to earn money and then, once you start earning, you need to keep doing it, know what I mean?'

Hannah thought of her bachelors in graphic design, how she'd had to switch to something else to ensure she could make the rent.

'Uni isn't everything it's cracked up to be,' she whispered. 'Take it from me.'

The plumber slid out from the sink and selected a wrench from his toolbox. The kitchen was hot and Hannah saw that the floor tiles were blotched with his sweat.

'How long are you stuck with him?' he said, waving the wrench toward the cell. His eyes scanned Jem top to bottom, like a faulty boiler.

'I've appealed.' Hannah looked to Jem and away. It felt wrong to talk as if he couldn't hear them, as if he didn't matter, especially after their most recent exchange, but then she wasn't sure how to include him either. 'Asked for a transfer.'

The plumber strode over to the cell, gave one of the bars a shake and looked up.

'Does this attach to a frame in the ceiling?'

Hannah nodded. They'd plastered over the worst of the damage and repainted but if you looked hard enough you could still see the odd crack.

'It'll make a mess, ripping all that out. Never mind your walls and floor.'

She shrugged. The damage would not be her concern. Once Jem was gone she would no longer be allowed to live here and the house would be allocated to another key worker. She and Aisling had talked about getting a flat together, somewhere close enough for her to continue to keep an eye on Pru. Still, the prospect of dismantling the stuff she'd worked so hard to preserve since John's death – edging the hoover around the jeans he'd left piled in a corner of the bedroom, guarding the fridge magnets against wandering hands – terrified her. The house and his things were like a spell she had to maintain. She knew it was irrational, mad even, but she worried that to change or tidy away any of these items – to concede he'd gone – would be to remove the possibility he might one day return.

Back at the sink, the plumber sat a black metal cylinder on the worktop and started taking it apart with a screwdriver.

'I was on a job the other day,' he said, placing each bit carefully to one side. 'Harlow Civic Centre. They had two inmates in the cells there, a man and a woman who until recently had been Host and prisoner.' He winked and poked his tongue into the side of his cheek. 'They'd started a relationship. Got caught.' He shook his head at the memory, separated the cylinder in two and peered inside. 'A-ha!'

Hannah ran to him.

'Did you find it?'

He held up a piece of gold.

'SIM card.'

'That?' She squinted from it to the black cylinder. 'It's tiny.'

'It didn't cause the blockage, although it won't have helped.' He fished out a mangled chunk of plastic from the blades. 'This is your culprit.' He pulled it apart and laid it flat on his palm. It looked like a white credit card with a rectangular-shaped hole in the top right-hand corner. 'The holder it came in.' He set to work putting the cylinder back together. 'Looks like a pay-as-you-go.'

'My phone is on contract.' So was John's, she thought. She felt again for the smooth spot on her finger. How could she have lost something so precious?

She paid and went to see him out. Opening the front door, she found John's partner, Rupert, walking down the path, a black Prius pulling away from the kerb.

'Where's the MG?' said Hannah as he and the plumber passed each other. Rupert travelled everywhere in his beloved maroon coupe and was the only person she'd ever met who wore driving gloves as if they were a regular item of clothing, whether he was behind the wheel of a car or not.

'In for a service.' He grimaced. 'I'm having to go everywhere by Uber.'

Rupert Cammish. Full name Rupert St. John Oberon Cammish. A trust fund boy who didn't need to work but did, he had a narrow, whippet-like face and dopey brown eyes that were more Disney than Detective Sergeant and liked to wear yellow wool scarves wrapped round his neck, even though it made it easy for people to tease him about the similarity to Rupert the Bear, his furry namesake. An unlikely copper, he came from a family where it was routine for men to have 'Explorer' as their job title and as a baby he had been encouraged to scale a climbing wall long before he could walk. His father and three brothers were all avid mountaineers. Tragically, Rupert's youngest sibling Hugo had died trying to summit Everest two years earlier.

Despite coming from different ends of the social scale – John had grown up on a Shadwell estate – they'd become good friends after working their first case together in homicide, a gruelling investigation into the murder of nine prostitutes in west London. John had been sceptical of Rupert at first, unhappy at being partnered with some posh boy who was clearly only in the Met to make Daddy mad, but had soon been won over by his tenacity, work ethic and willingness to get his hands dirty. Rupert had always volunteered to take first watch on overnight stake-outs, had done the lion's share of paperwork and had been responsible for catching the monster responsible, thanks to his painstaking analysis of thousands of pages of mobile phone records. He also, much to John's delight, shared his partner's love of darts and for his birthday that year had bought them both tickets for the World Championships. They'd had such a great time that they went again the next year and the year after that, the trip out to Lakeside becoming the highlight of their December.

Hannah remembered the case the pair had bonded over and how only four of the women's families had been willing to press charges. As was the way with a single perpetrator and multiple crimes, once the guilty verdict was delivered they had divided his sentence between them, taking the prisoner into a cell in their home for seven years each.

Rupert gave Hannah a hug. After a few seconds she went to draw away but he lingered, his hand on her lower back. She tensed and patted him firmly on the shoulder and this time, when she retreated, he did the same.

'To what do I owe the pleasure?' she said, as they headed downstairs. She was glad he was here; she wanted to raise the question of Mickey's drinking, see if he'd noticed anything.

'I thought you deserved to know straightaway.' In the kitchen he clocked Jem and his face hardened. He seemed more puzzled than angry, perhaps unable to process how or why this person had killed his friend.

'Know what?' said Hannah, her hand circling her pendant.

He sighed. 'Maybe you should sit down.' He guided her to a chair and then set about removing his driving gloves.

'Rupert?'

'The ruling on your Foster Host request came through.' The gloves gone, he flexed his hands. His fingers and palms were calloused from years of gripping rock. 'I saw it on the system. Your appeal has been denied.'

Hannah frowned. 'There must be some mistake.' She looked from Jem to the freshly painted ceiling. All intentions to discuss Mickey's sobriety gone. 'It was a formality.'

'Word is you're the fourth case they've knocked back today. There's a feeling in Westminster that too many people are dodging their responsibilities. They've issued a crackdown.'

He reached a hand toward her but she wasn't ready to be comforted and shook him off.

'So what, my husband is dead and now I have to spend the rest of my life with the man who killed him?' The more she said, the louder she got. 'How is this fair? Who exactly are they punishing here?'

'You can lodge a second appeal,' he said, low and firm, 'but I have to tell you, they look badly on repeat applications.'

'Twenty years.' She looked to the cell but Jem had hung his head, unable to meet her eye. 'I can't.'

The plumber had left the heap of brown sludge he'd cleared from the waste disposal in a bowl on the side. Already, flies had started to gather on the surface.

Hannah sat on a chair in the middle of the kitchen. Spread out on the floor around her was a mosaic of objects and photographs. Selecting and arranging the items, over a hundred in all, had taken most of the night but now she was done and ready to survey her handiwork.

To her right sat a pair of John's old trainers, the grey laces muddied and tied into double bows; over by the French doors was an auger shell they'd found on a weekend in Filey, its cone speckled brown, and in front of the cell was a row of selfies she'd printed out from John's phone. He'd loved to document himself in the cool and often bizarre parts of London his job took him to and the pictures showed him everywhere from a secret tunnel that ran underneath Downing Street to high atop a city roof to the inside of the tiny black and white house in the middle of Soho Square.

She felt for her amber pendant. Found on him when he died, it had been gift-wrapped with a love note tucked inside. His bank statement showed he'd purchased it that morning. She'd placed the note, black ink on white card, centre stage.

For my love. I know things have been difficult recently but I'm so excited about the future and the adventures that await. I love you. JC x

John had always had his own way of saying sorry. Never one to come right out with it, if they'd had a row he preferred to make up obtusely, to sometimes comic effect. Once, after they'd bickered over chores – Hannah was sick of him not doing his fair share – she'd woken to find him naked but for a pinny and a pair of rubber gloves, scrubbing the bathroom. Seeing her, he'd paused briefly, given her a wink, and got back to it. All the frustration she'd felt dissolved into giggles.

They'd argued more than usual in the months before he'd died. John had been cranky and distracted. But then in the weeks leading up to his murder there'd been a shift. The rows had stopped and he'd shown the same fondness – plaiting her hair in tiny braids as they chatted in bed at night, bringing her tea on a morning, hand-feeding her snacks when her hands were deep in fondant – as at the start of their marriage. The amber necklace had obviously been some kind of peace offering.

She crossed her legs and then uncrossed them, trying to get comfortable on the chair.

Jem had been oblivious to her many comings and goings, asleep under his bed. It was clear the other morning had been far from a one-off and that, for whatever reason, he preferred to sleep with his headphones on, out of sight on the floor. True to his word, he'd left his baseball cap on his pillow so she would know not to worry if she found his cell seemingly empty.

She was wondering why, imagining what might have happened to make being hidden the only way he could feel safe enough to rest, while the sun wearied its way up into the sky and the cell bars were hit with light. Shadows striped her lap.

Twenty years of living like this. Twenty years with him.

She looked at the notecard again. At John's excitement about the future.

Who cared where Jem slept?

He deserved neither sympathy nor concern.

He emerged shortly after, his hand curling around the side of the bed frame. Seeing Hannah, he startled and removed his headphones, surprise changing to confusion as he took in the arrangement on the floor.

'What?' His eyes ran up and down the different items. 'Are you OK?'

'His first day at Hendon,' she said, reaching for a colour snap of a much younger-looking John, sweaty and red-faced. 'They had to run 10k and so he gave it all his might and finished before everyone else. They made him run it again.' She replaced it and picked up a pink silk tie. 'He wore this with a white three-piece suit to our wedding.' She brought it to her nose. 'I can still smell his aftershave.'

Understanding dawned. He blinked slowly, then turned away.

'Look at it,' she said her voice low, 'look.' She held up the tie. 'Isn't that why you're here, for you to understand who you took from me?'

Still, Jem refused to meet her eye. He seemed to have decided that the best thing to do was withdraw from the situation, to pretend she wasn't there.

'I'm sorry you lost your husband,' he said softly, after a moment. 'That you're stuck with me.' His words were thick with regret but there was something else there too, some emotion he was trying hard to keep under control. It strained beneath the surface, a fish in a net, fighting for release. 'But I meant what I said. I'm innocent, I didn't do it.'

Hannah laughed bitterly.

'Were you not listening when they reeled off the evidence against you in court? What do you think I am, an idiot?'

'No, of course not . . .' he said and there it was again, some feeling he was working hard to keep in check.

'John was good, decent, whereas you . . .' She tried to stop herself – despite everything she didn't want to stoop to this – but giving in to her anger felt good, like careening down a hill in a car with no brakes. 'You're nothing.'

Exhausted, she got to her feet.

Jem swallowed. 'You think he was perfect,' he said. 'He wasn't.' It seemed he too had decided to let go. He paused before continuing. 'That evening, when he left the bar, he was on his way to meet someone. A woman.'

It was like she'd been hit. She swayed back on her feet, blinking, unable to believe what she was hearing.

'Seriously? You kill him and then you decide the best way to make reparations is to insult his memory?'

'I'm telling the truth. Before he left I heard them arguing on the phone.'

'Funny,' said Hannah, 'how you omitted to mention any of this at the trial.'

'My lawyer said it was hearsay, that it would harm my defence.'

Jem's version of events had been torn apart by the prosecution. He'd claimed John had dropped his wallet, phone and keys on the floor of the bar and that he'd been about to run after him to return them when he was detained by another customer. That, he'd said, was why he'd had to pursue him at pace, why he'd had no choice but to follow John into the alley and why his fingerprints were on John's things.

He had not been able to offer an explanation as to how his prints had found their way onto the murder weapon.

'Liar,' said Hannah. The police had checked John's phone records; if there'd been any such call they would have investigated. But then she remembered the SIM the plumber had found in the waste disposal.

The doubt wasn't there and then it was, a sinkhole in the middle of the road.

Was it possible John had a secret pay-as-you-go, is that what people did when they had affairs?

'From what I heard, he'd tried to break things off between them but she wasn't having it. Something had happened at a hotel they'd been to, The Wallaby or The Warlaby, something like that. He seemed to want to come clean about the affair but she didn't. He kept saying "we have to tell her", that he was planning to confess to you the next day.' Jem's sentences crashed over each other like waves. 'He had some weird pet name for her, Marzipan Rain, something like that. By the end of the call he'd agreed to meet.'

Hannah's skin prickled.

'Say that again.'

'They arranged to get together.'

'Before that.'

'Marzipan Rain? I remember because I thought it sounded like a great name for a band.'

Her pulse snickered in her neck.

'Marzipan Rain, you're sure?' She'd heard those words once before. Or rather she'd seen them, written down on a piece of paper.

'I'm not lying,' said Jem, mistaking her expression for fury. 'Promise.'

The sun was up. The shadows yawned to nothing and they found themselves paired by the same white light. Hannah went to walk away, only to look down and see John's things dotted across the floor, like booby-traps.

Jem

Late afternoon and Hannah is making cupcakes. Chocolate sponge with yellow buttercream, each cake is topped with a tiny fondant teddy bear.

I'm reading. *We Are All Completely Beside Ourselves*. It's one of my favourite novels, a story of sibling loyalty against all odds, but I keep getting distracted. Watching Hannah sculpt the bears' paws and faces is mesmerising. Her fingers coax the fondant into shape with only the lightest touch. I've always admired dexterity in others but there is something magical about the way she rolls, pats and carves these figures into being. I notice that each bear is slightly different; one has a flower behind its ear, another clutches a green bag, and one wears what looks like a tiny hearing aid.

We haven't exchanged a word since this morning. Hannah is even more furious with me than she was already. She might have dismissed my claims out of hand but they definitely hit a nerve and now, mixed in with her fury, is something else, a softening. I've made a hairline crack in the wall. Tiny now, if I work at it long enough I'll be able to turn it into a fissure, then a gap, big enough to crawl through.

Humming a rock ballad under her breath, she nestles another selection of bears into the buttercream and places the finished cakes in a box. Lunch was hours ago and the candied air is making me hungry. A low growl fills the kitchen. My stomach. I cover my belly with my hand, trying to muffle the sound, but it's no good. The growl gets louder.

Hannah pauses but doesn't turn round and, after putting the box to one side, she sets to work creaming the next batch of butter and sugar.

The kitchen is large, two basement rooms knocked into one, but still my cell dominates. A protrusion of concrete and metal, it sits against the wall in the middle of the space and is the first thing you see as you come down the stairs. I don't know what was here before but at a guess I'd say the dining table, huddled as it is now into the too-small corner by the French doors, and maybe some cupboards; the remaining storage spaces and worktops overflow with crockery and pans that don't seem to have a home.

I'm sure Hannah would rather I was hidden away in some more avoidable part of the house, but I'm glad the cell was put here. It means I get to see her often. To observe.

The kitchen had been filled with sunshine but now it dims. The worktop where Hannah has set out her slabs of fondant and tools is cast in shadow. She turns on the downlight built into the underside of a cupboard but it fails to come on. The gloom slows her down but she takes it in good temper, and when the sun comes back out she nods her thanks toward the heavens.

I know I'm lucky to have her as my Host. She takes care of her neighbour and I've seen how she pretends not to notice when Mr Dalgleish stumbles or when a tuft of hair comes away in his hand.

Could I trust her? Should I?

One of the reasons I've been put here is to make me realise the impact of this crime, to understand its cost first-hand. Already, I know that whenever Hannah smiles her mouth lifts only slightly, as though even the tiniest happiness has a caveat, and I can tell by the way her eyes linger on certain things – a mug on the shelf, a dent in the wall – that she sees the world through a filter of what was and what could have been.

Seeing her like this, it troubles me. Like most people, my biggest fear is losing those I love.

She removes the bowl of buttercream from the mixer and turns to face me. She takes a breath to prepare, like she's about to say something. I sit up, ready, but then she seems to think better of it and turns away.

I wish I could make her realise she has nothing to be scared of. That I regret everything about that night. What happened, what I did. It was all so avoidable.

Still, what's done is done.

My goal remains the same.

It's going to be difficult and there isn't much time, but I'm nothing if not adaptable.

I'll find a way, I always have.

I return to my book and this time I manage to lose myself in the words. I finish the chapter and move on to the next. It feels good to go somewhere else for a while, to be transported to a place I can roam free.

A squeal of metal brings me back to myself.

The hatch. Hannah has pushed the drawer into the cell. I go over to see what's inside and find a single cupcake. A teddy bear sits jaunty atop the yellow buttercream.

I go to thank her but she's already on her way upstairs, humming another ballad.

I don't want to damage the bear and so I place him carefully to one side and take a bite of the cake. The sponge is delicate, the cream sweet. I devour it in seconds.

Hannah

Hannah gave up on sleep around midnight.

Jem's claims were desperate, outlandish even. There'd been a ton of evidence to prove he'd murdered John. And yet. Marzipan Rain. It was such a bizarre phrase, too odd for someone to have plucked out of thin air, and there was no way Jem could have known she'd seen it once before.

Was he telling the truth? Had John been on his way to meet someone before he died?

It had been earlier in the year, a weekend, when she'd stood by the washing machine about to put a load on. As always, she'd checked John's jeans pockets before placing them in the drum, and pulled out his payslip. MARZIPAN RAIN had been written in large capital letters, along with some other stuff she couldn't remember, on the back. Because they were odd words you don't normally see next to each other, she'd read them out loud; a question to herself more than anything. John had been at the kitchen table, engrossed in the newspaper, but as soon as she spoke he'd jumped up and snatched it from her. He'd said it was a tip, the name of a racehorse someone had told him was a sure thing, and that he was glad she'd saved it from being ruined, then stuffed it in his back pocket. At the time she'd thought nothing of it. John liked the odd bet, as did Rupert. They gambled on everything from football matches to the Christmas number one.

She turned on the lamp, tied her hair into a bun and got out of bed. She wanted to look at the slip again, to see what else had been written there. But where to find it?

John had kept important paperwork – P60s, his birth certificate and insurance documents – in an expanding file at the bottom of the wardrobe. Maybe it was in there?

She dragged the folder out onto the carpet and clicked it open, but a rummage through its concertina pockets proved unsuccessful. She considered the rest of the room. John's laptop was still left where he'd wedged it among loose papers and magazines in the bottom cubby of his bedside table. She pulled out the lot and rifled through the various letters and forms. There was one payslip but it was from two years earlier and clean of scribble. She remembered the folder of stuff Mickey had harvested from John's desk and, after digging it out of her bag, tipped the contents onto the floor. Nothing but takeaway menus and those property particulars for a selection of east London flats.

She decided to call it a night. Who knew if John had even kept the payslip she'd seen, let alone put it somewhere she might find it?

Back under the duvet, she turned out the lamp, grabbed her phone and plugged in the headphones. In the blurry weeks that followed the funeral she'd created a compilation of John's old voicemails and whenever she couldn't settle at night she liked to listen to it on repeat. It made it feel like he was still there with her and, if she was lucky, she would fall asleep with the recording going and John would come to her in her dreams.

She clicked on the file and pressed start. John had always preferred voicemail or talking to someone in person. He said he found text or WhatsApp laborious, that he thought hastily typed missives were too easy to misconstrue and that it was quicker and easier to just say the words out loud. The messages spanned two years and, played back to back, ran to one hour and sixteen minutes. Each message was preceded by an electronic notification of the date and time it was recorded.

Monday 6th April, 6.35 p.m.

'I'm in town, about to head home. Want me to pick up some bao buns from that place in Chinatown?'

Saturday 13th June, 7.58 p.m.

'Hey you, it's looking like I have to work late tonight so eat without me, love you, bye.'

Wednesday 2nd September, 10.17 a.m.

'Leaving this message now in case I forget to tell you later. Trish in forensics has a silver wedding anniversary coming up. Wants you to do the cake. Remind me and I'll give you her details.'

She'd always loved his voice. A rich leathery baritone, it had been the first thing she'd noticed about him. Later, she'd learned his timbre was such that whenever he interviewed suspects at work they had to tweak the levels on the machine specially, so as to avoid distortion.

When people used to ask how they'd first met John would tell them he saved her life and, thinking he was joking, they would laugh. But then he'd tell the story and their mouths would slacken, eyes widen, as they realised it was true.

Hannah had been twenty-seven, in London six years, her cake business in its infancy, when John had quite literally crashed his way into her world. She'd been in Soho, a teetering column of gateaux boxes balanced in her arms, on her way to Old Compton Street when an oncoming truck had mounted the kerb at speed, the driver having passed out at the wheel. Hannah had been oblivious, her view of the pavement obscured by the cake boxes, and it was only when John, who'd happened to be walking a few steps behind her, called out that she'd known anything was wrong.

'Watch out!'

His voice had been such that she'd felt it in her solar plexus, a boom, like a cannon going off. She swirled round, trying to locate the threat, and John, realising there was no time, had leapt forward and rugby-tackled her into a nearby doorway. Moments later the truck had crashed into a shop window.

After watching the glass shatter, Hannah had drawn her attention back to her rescuer. His suit was covered in demolished gateaux, a line of cherries epauletting their way down one shoulder, his face cragged with acne scars, his eyes milky blue. He smelled clean, like sheets that have dried on the line.

'You OK?' he said, breathing hard.

'Think so.' She'd later discover that she'd fractured two ribs in the fall. 'Thanks to you.'

Then he'd scooped up a bit of the demolished cake from his knee and licked his finger.

'Delicious,' he said, already searching out a second helping.

And even though her ribs hurt and she was shaky with adrenalin she'd laughed and then he'd kept on making her laugh, while they waited for the ambulance to arrive, in A & E, on their first date and beyond.

The compilation continued to play.

Sunday 11th October, 2.10 p.m.

'Thought I'd catch you before you go off to your thing tonight. Bit hectic here but the good news is Mark still has his eyebrows. Our plane lands around 7 p.m. tomorrow so I should be home by 9 p.m.'

She'd listened to the messages so many times that she knew the words and accompanying sound effects off by heart. There was the tinny melody of an ice-cream van that time he called to tell her he thought he'd left the back door unlocked, there was the thump of a car boot closing when he was on his way home from the supermarket, there was the office chatter when he was apologising for having to work late again.

Thursday 26th November, 6.07 p.m.

'Just calling to tell you not to wait up. This case, I'm going to have to pull an all-nighter.' This voicemail had an annoying sound effect that she knew from past experience would hurt her ears – a high-pitched beep, an alarm of some kind – and so she braced, ready. *BEEEEEEP*. 'I'm trying to think of the overtime.'

The recording finished and Hannah lay there even more wide awake than before, her thoughts going back to what Jem had said.

Marzipan Rain.

What did it mean?

She took off the headphones and turned the light back on. John's laptop and papers lay where she'd left them on the floor.

She knew his password. Maybe his computer was worth a look?

A search of his inbox and Word files threw up zero matches. She moved on to his browser history. Again, there was nothing. Most of the sites he'd spent time on were unsurprising – BBC News, cinema listings, darts scores – but there was one site that stood out. A funeral notice in the *Cambridge Evening News* for a man called Roddy Blessop who had died back in December of last year. She didn't recognise the name or recall John mentioning anything about a friend or relative having passed away and yet, when she counted she saw that he'd looked at the notice on seventeen separate occasions.

She was about to shut the computer when she remembered the hotel Jem said John had mentioned on the phone that night. The Wallaby or The Warlaby. Again, she combed his inbox, Word files and browser history. No match. Finally, she typed both names into the search engine. The top result was for a boutique hotel called The Warlaby in Clerkenwell.

She clicked on the link and the screen was filled with a bland chunk of grey pocketed with small square windows. It looked like your average Travelodge but the entrance, a jazzy affair lit by row upon row of yellow light bulbs gave it something extra. The pictures of the inside showed a reception decorated with old LPs, bicycles fixed sideways to the walls and a long table full of millennials on laptops.

According to Jem's account, John had mentioned having been there with the person he'd talked to on the phone that night.

She looked at the contact number in the top right of the screen. She felt bad for even entertaining the possibility and yet she knew that the only way she'd ever get this out of her system was to prove Jem wrong.

She grabbed her phone and dialled.

'The Warlaby. This is Jakob, how may I help?'

It was only now she was about to speak that Hannah realised just how improbable it was they'd be able to tell her anything.

After introducing herself she launched into her request.

'I'm trying to find out if my husband has ever stayed at your hotel or made a restaurant reservation.'

The receptionist's response was immediate.

'I'm sorry but I can't give out information about our guests, past or present.' He spoke in long, falling vowels and rolled 'r's' that Hannah associated with bad impressions of Count Dracula. 'If that's all?' he said, clearly going to hang up.

'Please, my husband, he died.' Hannah's voice cracked a little. Uttering those words, especially to a stranger, was always hard. In the weeks after John's murder she'd had to say them so many times, to the bank, to his mobile phone operator and to his many credit card companies. She remembered opening bill after bill and seeing the outstanding amounts inside. She'd assumed his cards had been cloned and had gone through the most recent entries one by one, checking it had actually been him. It turned out the debt was longstanding, a prosaic accumulation of overdraft bailouts and end-of-the-month cash withdrawals that had snowballed into tens of thousands. 'His name was John, John Cavey. There's a dispute with our credit card bill,' she lied. 'I don't want to know anything else, I just need to confirm that he was actually a customer otherwise it's a fraudulent charge.'

They took down her name and mobile and then there was a pause.

'John Cavey?'

'Yes, C-A-V-E-Y.'

The receptionist went quiet and Hannah assumed he was busy typing John's name into the system but then he spoke again.

'Let me get the night manager.'

A clunk. The receiver being put down. She heard muffled voices. At first the exchange was monotone, two members of staff on the graveyard shift going through the motions, but then the conversation switched up a pace and the voices became louder, their tone urgent.

Another clunk and the receiver was picked back up.

'We can't help.' It was the receptionist.

'Can I speak to the manager?'

'We cannot breach data protection law. I'm sorry.'

Hannah was crushed. Of course he was right. With nothing to lose she decided to ask one last thing.

'I realise this might sound weird,' she said quickly, 'but do the words Marzipan Rain mean anything to you?'

'It's late. My apologies, but I have guests to deal with.'

The line went dead.

Hannah slumped against the headboard. She felt foolish all of a sudden, as if by making that call she'd fallen for a horrible trick. Of course it was a lie. No doubt Jem had overheard John using the phrase while he was glass-collecting that night and now he was using it against her, trying to spin it into something that might work to his advantage.

She turned out the light, closed her eyes and thought of Jem asleep in his cell downstairs.

The house seemed to pulsate with his presence, a hum that hurt her ears.

She lay like that for hours. Finally, just as dawn was breaking, she found peace. Her bun came loose, her blond hair alluvial across the sheets. She reached for John's pillow and pressed her face into his smell, but her dreams were without him. Blank, endless, sad.

La Porchetta in Muswell Hill. Hannah finished the last of the olives and checked her phone. Mickey was supposed to have been at the restaurant forty minutes ago. Most likely she was stuck at work; still, she was the one who'd asked if they could meet – she'd heard about the Foster Host transfer and wanted to offer her sympathies – plus it wasn't like her not to call.

The restaurant was busy, the staff in and out of the kitchen. Hannah noticed the couple to her right whispering and then, when the waiter retreated behind the bar to sort a drinks order, they got up and legged it toward the door. Abandoning the drinks, the waiter pursued them into the street. He was fast and managed to knock the guy to the floor and hold him there till the manager could be found. Hannah watched through the window as waiter and manager argued. Finally, the waiter let go of the thief and he sprinted off.

'No point,' said the manager as they returned inside. 'Not like we're going to press charges.'

Hannah gave Mickey another five minutes and, after trying and failing to reach the DCI on her phone, got up to leave. Mickey lived nearby, in an Edwardian terrace off the Broadway. She might be wrapped up in something at work, or on the Tube, but Hannah decided to check in on her on her way home.

At the house she found all the curtains closed, the lights on. Standing by the front door, she could hear country music, a ballad, slow and mournful.

Mickey had once lived here with her ex-wife Laramie and had managed to hold on to the property after their divorce. Laramie had since remarried but the pair remained friends and Laramie would often come to whistle and cheer her on whenever she competed in one of her amateur bodybuilding championships.

Hannah rapped on the door and peered through the leaded glass for signs of life. She was soon rewarded by an approaching shadow. Mickey opened the door and Hannah felt a tiny pulse of relief. Then she saw her.

Tottering back and forward, her mascara was smeared, her hair loose.

'Baby doll.'

She slapped her palm against her forehead, the movement sloppy and clownish.

'La Porchetta,' she said, her speech fuzzy. 'I finished early then I must have lost track.' She motioned for Hannah to come inside. 'Give me a minute to get cleaned up and then we'll head out, yeah?'

Hannah took a seat in the living room. An empty bottle of Chablis sat next to another, half-drunk, on the coffee table.

Mickey reappeared soon after, hopping on one foot as she tried to put on her flats.

'Maybe we should call your sponsor?' said Hannah gently. 'Or Laramie? We could take you to a meeting tomorrow, or tonight even?'

'I'll call the restaurant,' said Mickey, ignoring her. 'See if I can get us a later reservation.'

'Mickey,' said Hannah, louder now. 'Sit.'

She fussed a few moments more, obviously still hoping Hannah would play along, before giving in and slumping back onto the sofa.

Hannah motioned to the wine.

'I know there doesn't need to be a reason, there never needs to be a reason . . .'

'Can we not do this now?' She lurched forward and sloshed another measure of white into her glass. Some of it breached the side and she caught it with her finger and licked it clean. 'I'm tired.'

Hannah got to her feet.

'Water?'

Mickey brushed her away with a flutter of fingers but Hannah went to get her some just the same. The kitchen was a mess of cereal bowls and bottles stained with protein shake. She found a clean glass at the back of a cupboard and filled it to the brim.

Back in the living room the country ballad had come to an end. Mickey had fallen asleep, white wine in hand. Hannah took the glass from her and as she covered her with a rug Mickey opened her eyes.

'He was my responsibility,' she said, swallowing hard. 'I knew something was wrong.' Her eyes drooped. 'I let him keep going there, alone.'

Hannah presumed Mickey was talking about the undercover officer who had committed suicide at the back end of last year. It was just like Mickey to blame herself. She shushed her back to sleep and then, once she was settled, set to work emptying the house of booze. She glugged the bottles into the sink and then gathered the empties in a black bag, turned off the lights and let herself out. At Mickey's recycling bin she lifted the lid and dropped the rubbish inside. It landed with a smash, glass on glass, colliding hard with the bags of bottles already there.

Jem

Monday morning.

I have a visitor.

Alina.

I wait inside the cell, my hands gripping the bars, while Mr Dalgleish waves a metal detector wand around her body. It looks like a small black cricket bat and when he swipes it near her hip it makes a high-pitched cheep like a smoke alarm. Alina doesn't need to be told. She empties her trouser pockets, revealing a phone, lipstick and tissue pack.

'You'll get them back at the end,' he says, holding out a plastic tray.

She hands them over and he scans the rest of her without incident.

Hannah hovers by the kettle in a white vest and denim cut-offs. There are flecks of pink icing in her hair and a smear of butter-cream on her cheek. She picks up an empty mug and then puts it down again, as though she's not sure whether to offer everyone a cup of tea.

Mr Dalgleish gives Alina the all-clear and motions for her to take a seat on one of the chairs arranged in front of the cooker. Once she's in position I am let out.

I can cover the length of my cell in just one and a half strides and being able to walk those few extra steps toward the chair is luxurious. My quads and hamstrings twitch in pleasure and I have to fight the urge to keep going, to sprint toward the stairs and take them two at a time.

Mr Dalgleish guides me to the seat opposite and goes to sit by the French doors. He has to observe each visit, to make sure she doesn't try to slip me contraband or break any personal contact rules.

'Hannah,' he says when she shows no sign of moving from her spot by the kettle. 'Some privacy?'

'Oh.' She puts down the mug and grabs hold of the pendant she wears. 'I'll leave you to it.'

Alina watches her go and turns to me with a smile.

'Cute.'

'Seriously?'

'Girl next door meets Swedish exchange student,' she teases. She looks over my shoulder, toward the pond and the Heath beyond. 'You've landed on your feet.'

I nod at the cell.

'Not quite.'

She laughs that bit too loud and I realise she's relieved, that she was more worried about all this than she'd let on.

Alina and I met working the summer season in Majorca. We were based in the port town of Pollença and spent our nights prowling the promenade or hanging out by the enormous sand-castle sculpture that all the tourists stop to photograph. I'd noticed her around but I preferred to keep to myself. Then one night I stumbled across her outside the disco that overlooked the small outcrop at the far edge of the bay. She'd got herself into a spot so I decided to help out. We became friends soon after.

These days Alina is a single mum to a three-year-old called Franklyn, conceived on a one-night stand with one of the yacht workers who flitted in and out of the port, and so she prefers to work closer to home, in the Square Mile. The City is better money and the regular hours mean she gets to spend weekends with her son. She's come here on her way in to Bank and she looks the part. Her hair is bouncy with fat curls, her silk blouse soft underneath her suit. I imagine she blends right in.

When I was arrested it was Alina I called. She was the one person I knew I could trust, who would be able and willing to help.

'I'm a bit ripe, sorry.' I sniff at my armpits. 'I only get two showers per week.'

'I don't mind.' She goes quiet then, a spot of pink on each cheek. 'So.' Her eyes flick to Mr Dalgleish. The DLOs aren't supposed to listen in on prisoner visits but of course they do. 'Any joy?'

'Not yet.'

She appraises the cell.

'I really don't see how—'

'That's my problem,' I say, cutting her off. 'I'll figure it out.'

'Do you even know where it is?'

'No, but give me time.'

Alina came to visit me often in the Holding Centre. Those conversations were largely unsupervised and there I'd been able to tell her everything. We'd come up with a plan.

'You know how it is, I take what I can get.'

This is an old joke of ours and we laugh.

'I heard about the transfer request.'

I smile.

'The universe finally gave me a break.'

She's quiet then, thinking.

'Why not just tell her?'

'You know why.'

She hears the warning in my voice and sits back. She tucks her hair behind her ear and I notice she's wearing the pearl earrings I gave her for her birthday that summer.

'Did you find out anything more?'

I've been wanting to broach this since she arrived, holding the question in like a breath.

Her face changes, a tensing around her lips and cheeks.

'I asked around.'

'How long?' She can't meet my eye. 'Tell me.'

She finds the sleeve of her blouse underneath her jacket and fiddles with the tiny cloth-covered button.

'Six months, maybe more.'

I do the maths. Today is 27th September.

'I have until March.'

'Or it's over,' she says, completing the thought.

I sag, a punctured balloon.

She gets to her feet and smooths down the creases in her skirt. 'I should go. Work.'

'You know, this would be a whole lot simpler if you could just get it for me.'

She looks from the cell to Mr Dalgleish.

'No thanks.'

'I'll send you another visitation order in a few weeks.'

Mr Dalgleish looks up.

'All done?'

He walks me back to the cell, locks the door and then goes to get the tray of confiscated items. He hands it to Alina to empty but she fumbles and the contents flip onto the floor.

'Sorry.'

Mr Dalgleish crouches down to help her. Alina thanks him and once she has everything back in her pocket he goes to see her out. She gets to the bottom of the stairs, stops and turns round.

'Got everything you need?' she asks. Her curls have dropped in the heat and her hair hangs limp against her shoulders. She gives it a beat, making sure I properly understand the question. 'Toiletries, books? I put some money in your commissary.'

'I'm good.'

They leave and I force myself to stand still, to ignore my legs' craving to pace the one and a half steps back and forward. The clock is ticking but I mustn't rush.

I look at the bags of flour and boxes of eggs Hannah has stacked on the worktop, at the green and gold Fry's tin on the windowsill behind the sink, at the calendar on the wall. I know it's an optical illusion, a trick of the brain, but it's amazing how quickly you stop seeing the metal bars. After a few minutes it's as if there's nothing there and I could step forward and go anywhere I liked, into the kitchen, up the stairs, into the house.

Hannah

Friday night at the Southbank Centre. Hannah took the lift to the roof garden at the top of the Queen Elizabeth Hall and searched the grassy expanse for Rupert's angular frame. Disturbed by her encounter with Mickey, she'd asked if they could meet. She wanted to share her concerns, to discuss what, if anything, she should do about the DCI's drinking.

The bar was packed with people basking in the October evening sun, the fruit trees and wildflowers heady with the zing of cold Pimm's and orange. Even at this hour, it was baking. The warm air shimmered. It made the scene before her look like someone had pressed pause on a videotape.

No one could put an exact date on when the weather changed. It was more of a gradual muddying of the seasons, the prolonged heat creeping across the weeks and months like bindweed, the occasional vicious cold snaps and floods brutal anomalies. It was like living with someone who gradually piles on weight. Even as their flesh grows and bulges you remain oblivious. Being that close, seeing them every day, brings on a kind of blindness, an inability to see things how they really are.

She spotted Rupert at a table in the corner. Shirt sleeves rolled to his elbows, he seemed to have already sorted drinks and kept arranging and rearranging the placement of the flutes and the ice bucket.

She came up on him from behind, placed her hands on his shoulders and kissed him on the cheek.

'Hannah.' He fumbled to his feet and, turning round, took in her red and white print maxi dress and milk braids, pinned loosely to the top of her head. He took a breath. 'You look lovely.'

Hannah had presumed he'd suggested they meet here because it was convenient for after work but now, looking at him, she realised he was freshly showered, his hair combed, chinos pressed.

They sat and he reached for the fizz. She tried to refuse – drinking champagne felt odd; there was nothing to celebrate and it turned what she'd thought was a quick catch-up into something else – but he poured her a glass anyway.

'I feel bad I haven't been over more.' He leaned forward on the table. His forearms were strong, the bones packed with muscle. 'It must be awful, having him there.'

He squeezed her hand and then, self-conscious, quickly let go.

'It's Mickey,' said Hannah, getting straight to it. 'She's drinking again.' She relayed the events of the other night and told him how she was sure the DCI had been inebriated when she'd met her at work a few weeks back.

'Shit.' He puffed his cheeks and then blew out the air. 'I had no idea.'

'I was thinking we should call Laramie?'

'I'm not sure Mickey would appreciate that.' He paused, thinking. 'Maybe it's not as bad as you think, maybe she's telling the truth. The other night was a one-off. She has it under control?'

Hannah held her silence.

'OK, you're right,' he said. 'I'll keep an eye on her. If I think she's struggling we'll talk to her direct, not go behind her back to Laramie. Agreed?'

'Agreed.' Hannah smiled grimly, relieved to have an ally.

She was wondering if she should bring up the things Jem had said, if she should tell Rupert about the hotel he'd mentioned, about Marzipan Rain, when they became aware of a crowd forming by the wall that overlooked the river. They were quiet, their heads craned in the same direction.

Curious, they grabbed their drinks and went to join them and were rewarded with the sight of three guys parkouring across the concrete below.

Vaulting, swinging, climbing and rolling, they moved as if weightless from the outer curves of the enclosed staircase to the Royal Festival Hall.

One of the trio completed a particularly daring leap and the roof broke into mass applause.

'Hugo was into that as a kid,' said Rupert. 'Loved it. When he got older Dad made him stop, said he needed to focus all his energy on serious climbing.' He smiled sadly.

'Does it get easier?' she said, alluding to Rupert's grief. 'Tell me it gets easier.' This morning she had found herself calculating how many days it had been since John had died.

One hundred and eighty.

Every twenty-four hours a lifetime.

'When Hugo died it was like falling down a rabbit hole. I'm not sure when you're supposed to stop falling, but it's been two years and it hasn't happened yet.'

His brother's body was still there on top of the mountain. In the past Rupert had explained that it would be impossible for them to ever bring him home.

He reached in his inside pocket and held something red in the flat of his palm.

'His climbing knife.' He angled the handle so she could see the initials – H.C. – embossed in gold. 'This was the only thing of his they brought back from the expedition. Mum let me have it.'

They looked out at the river, the buildings opposite hazy in the dimming sun.

Rupert placed his hand on her hip and brought her close. Ordinarily Hannah would have pulled away, put some distance back between them, but even once the parkour lot were gone and the crowd dispersed, she stayed where she was. Maybe, she thought, if she stood by him for a while, she could help slow his fall.

Hannah rinsed the last of the pans, set them to dry and got to work unloading the dishwasher. Everything inside was covered in the dusty white coating that builds up when things have been washed and rewashed many times.

Pru hovered by the French doors.

'They think I can't see them.' She held the right arm of her glasses between her fingertips, as if to focus her gaze, and peered at the Heath. 'Yesterday there was one by the front of the house. Hanging around for hours. Looking to burgle the place, rob us in our sleep.'

Hannah placed a stack of plates in an overhead cupboard and was hit by a waft of rancid air. She searched the kitchen for the source and soon landed on the bin, overflowing with empty milk cartons. A blast radius of sodden teabags covered the nearby floor.

'How are you for food?' she said, opening the fridge. A packet of bacon sat on the middle shelf, a head of broccoli, limp and sallow, at its side. 'Shall I go to the shops for you later?'

Pru nodded absently, her eyes now trained on a bench on the other side of the pond.

'Ted would know what to do. He'd see them off.' She pushed her glasses up onto her head and looked around the kitchen as if expecting to see her husband appear. 'He's been gone all morning, do you know where he is?'

Hannah stuffed as much of the overflow into the bin bag as she could and drew it shut.

'He went to post a letter.'

Pru waited until Hannah had set the bag by the door, nodded her approval at a job well done and returned to surveying the Heath.

Pru had lived here for decades and her house had a crumbly, faded grandeur that was tolerated by Kiki Masters and her like because it spoke of a Hampstead gone by. Her kitchen had the same footprint and French doors overlooking the pond as Hannah's but that was where the similarity ended. In the spot where Jem's cell sat, a cream Aga sweltered, the splashback covered with colourful tiles collected by Pru and Ted on their travels, and whereas Hannah's units were uniform white MDF topped with grey Formica, Pru's were a higgledy-piggledy collection of scrubbed pine, handcrafted shelves and drawers that got stuck whenever you tried to open them. The walls gleamed with copper pans hung in rows, a set of thirty gifted to the couple on their wedding, and a yellowed newspaper cutting detailing Pru's Channel swim, picturing her limp on the Sangatte shingle, was framed and fixed to the wall above an enormous dining table.

The photo filled Hannah with awe but also fear. She'd never learned to swim, not even the doggy-paddle, and the thought of being alone in open water like that was terrifying. Her parents hadn't been able to swim either and the single term of obligatory once-weekly school sessions had made little impact. She had tried to learn in her first term at Falmouth; the council pool offered cheap lessons to students. But putting her head underwater had given her nightmares and after only three sessions she'd stopped, never to return.

John had encouraged her over and over to give it another shot. He'd swum in the Heath's mixed pond and wanted her to be able to join him. She'd usually refuse but then, when the city boiled, she'd concede and put on her bathing costume underneath her clothes, pack a towel and walk full of good intentions across the scrub to the disc of greeny-brown. She'd be keyed up, certain that this time she was going to go for it, but as soon as she saw the light netted across the water she'd change her mind and by the moment they reached the packed mud she'd have formulated an excuse, a reason, why today wasn't the day after all.

Whenever this happened, John would carefully adjust the rug on the ground, make sure she was comfortable and then dash off into the pond alone. Hannah had loved it when he resurfaced in the shallows, skin twinkling. After shaking the droplets from his hair, he'd slick it back and then come and join her on the rug, the exertion making his chest barrel in and out.

The bin sorted, she set to work wiping down the draining board and emptying the plug of the translucent scraps of onion that had accumulated since the last day she was here.

Pru had always been house-proud and had had help come once a week for as long as Hannah could remember. But then, a month or so after John died, Hannah had popped over and found the worktops piled with dirty crockery. Pru had grown paranoid the cleaner was stealing and so had taken to following her around the house while she worked. The woman had endured it for months before handing in her notice.

She'd had a word with Pru's children, Christopher and Annabel, and they'd organised a replacement and that seemed to be that. Christopher lived in Winchester with his wife and four boys and Annabel worked in Paris as a buyer for a department store. Since Pru's dementia diagnosis she was regularly assessed and, after having the back gate removed and high fences installed to prevent her from getting down to the pond, had been deemed fit to live alone; but then the same thing happened again. After that Christopher and Annabel started making noises about putting their mother into care. Hannah couldn't bear the thought of Pru being made to leave her home and so when the fourth cleaner in as many weeks walked out after only an hour on the job, Hannah had decided to keep quiet and take on the role unpaid for herself. She already had a spare set of keys for whenever Pru locked herself out, she didn't mind the hoovering and dusting and besides, these days, being around her neighbour was a kind of respite.

One of the things Hannah had struggled with most after John died was that, for everyone else, life went on. This horrific thing had happened, this wonderful man had gone and yet the world still turned, people went out for dinner, complained about hangovers, took holidays, tried to get that promotion at work. Hannah felt like Buster Keaton in a black and white movie, dangling from the hands of Big Ben in a bid to try to stop time moving forward. But with Pru there was no dangling. As far as she was concerned, John was alive. To correct her would only be to cause confusion and so, as Hannah saw it, she had no choice but to play along. These days to be around Pru was to pretend so wholeheartedly that John was just next door, taking one of his hour-long baths, or that he was on his way back from work, home just as soon as he'd picked up pizza for dinner, that after a little while it felt almost real.

It was a balm.

After the events of last week she'd come here today craving that feeling more than ever. Still unable to find the offending payslip and unsure what to make of Jem's claims, she was at a loss as to what, if anything, to do next.

The sun had reached the point in the sky where it blasted directly through the French doors. Pru stood her ground against the dazzle for a good minute before giving in.

'You mentioned cake?' she said, searching the worktops.

Hannah produced a tin from her bag.

'Banana bread with a white chocolate ganache.' She got her a plate and grabbed a knife from the drawer.

'I heard someone singing through the wall earlier,' said Pru, accepting a generous slice. 'A man.'

The houses on this row had surprisingly thin connecting walls and Hannah often heard Pru sneeze or the hum of the radio. Hannah hadn't told Pru about Jem (how could she explain the presence of John's murderer when the old lady thought John was still alive?) and had decided to say he was a friend if Pru saw him in the garden during outside time.

'I know you loved John but I'm glad you're seeing new people.'

Hannah froze. Pru was lucid. This happened sometimes. It was disorienting, like being inside a dark house in which the light is suddenly turned on.

'No that's, he's . . .'

'John didn't deserve you.'

'You liked John,' said Hannah, unable to keep the chip of anger from her voice.

'Coming and going all the time.'

'He was a detective,' the past tense still felt alien in her mouth, 'that's the job.'

Pru helped herself to another slice of banana bread.

'I saw him in town once. Up to no good.' She sniffed. 'I know it's wrong to speak ill of the dead but you're better off without him.'

Hannah was trying to figure out how to reply when Pru stopped eating and put down her fork. A cloud seemed to pass over her face. She looked at the clock on the wall and tutted.

'Where has Ted got to?' She finished the last of her banana bread with gusto and licked her lips. 'Tell me, when are you and that husband of yours going to have babies?' A smear of ganache remained on her chin. 'You know what they say,' she looked at Hannah's belly, 'Tick, tock.'

The lights had been turned off, the house was once more in darkness.

Hannah tried to summon the enthusiasm required for a second session of John make-believe. This, after all, was what she'd come here for. But she couldn't do it.

She grabbed the rubbish.

'I should be going, I'll drop some shopping round later.' She reached for Pru's fall alarm, curled in a heap of rope on the side. 'And put this on.' She was forever nagging her to wear it, especially as Pru's only phone was a peach-coloured landline mounted to the wall in the kitchen.

Pru dusted her jacket for crumbs, reached for her glasses and walked with her to the front door. Hannah deposited the bag in the wheelie bin and looked up to see Pru stationed in the bay window. She gave Hannah a wave and then set about scouring the street for burglars, her spectacle lenses flashing in the sun. The living room was dark and the glass circles looked like giant eyes peering out from the gloom.

Thursday lunchtime and Hannah was on her way to see a potential client on Queen's Crescent. Less than a mile from her own
house as the crow flies, some of the crescent's grand mansions
backed onto the far side of the same pond, but, as Hannah was
discovering, it took much longer to get there on foot.

The meeting was with a woman called Maraschino, one of
Aisling's clients. When Aisling had got wind that Maraschino
and her husband were having a tenth-wedding anniversary
party she'd recommended Hannah to do the cake. Hannah
figured the introduction was Aisling's way of saying sorry for
bailing on her this week.

It was even hotter today, the blossom trees studded with
bees out of their minds on unseasonal nectar, and their buzz-
ing filled the air with white noise, constant and oppressive. She
checked the address again – Aisling had stuffed it through her
letter box late last night, her bubble-shaped handwriting taking
up most of the page, her i's topped with fat circles instead of
dots – tucked her portfolio under her arm and jogged the last
few streets, trying to make up time. Maraschino had serious
money – the crescent was one of the most expensive streets in
London – and so, wanting to make a good impression, she'd
worn her mint flowered tea dress and heels. Already though she
could feel a puddle of sweat forming beneath her bust.

At the stretch of tarmac that marked the start of the crescent,
she stopped to catch her breath. The properties ahead were all

detached, vast mini-palaces hidden by high walls and iron gates, the cars stored in private driveways and garages. Looked at on a map, the main body of Hampstead Heath was a solid whole. Protected by heavyweight conservation orders, its grassland was untouchable. Roads curved to fit its geographical idiosyncrasies, houses fitted themselves into the most inconvenient of gaps and utility companies forged pipes and wires into costly circles that kept a respectful distance from its boundary. Queen's Crescent was the one anomaly. Built in the early 1980s, before the heritage society could beat the Greater London Council into submission, developers had hacked a scythe-shaped road into the north-west corner and lined it with some of the city's most ostentatious properties, many of which were immediately bought up by foreign investors.

Famously, several of the investors had never taken up residence and had left their acquisitions empty or stuffed with cars and furniture they never used. These houses now stood like mausoleums, gates chained, their doorways blocked by the same metal fences they use to keep people without tickets out of festivals.

Hannah reached the address she was looking for and rang the intercom. The security gate slid open and she stepped onto a gravel drive bordered by bright green lawns. The house lay three metres ahead, red brick with white window frames. Its frontage spanned the length of an average Victorian terrace and was foregrounded by a stone portico held in place by four pillars.

She made her way to the front door and was about to ring the bell when Aisling appeared. Hannah knew she'd been working long hours but still she was surprised at how tired her friend looked. Her eyes were bloodshot, her face gaunt.

'Where have you been?' she said, pulling Hannah into the marble lobby. 'You better talk quick. Maraschino has Gyrotonic at 1 p.m.'

'Sorry Ash.' She was. This wasn't the first time Aisling had gone above and beyond to help her find work. Since John had died she'd sung her praises to all and sundry. 'I underestimated how long it would take to get here.'

Aisling tutted and hustled her down the hall to the orangery. She was wearing her hair loose and her curls gambolled around her neckline.

'You should have got here early.' She guided Hannah out to the garden and over to an arrangement of cane sofas on the terrace. 'Maraschino is fussy as it is.'

'I know Ash, I'm really sorry, OK.'

Aisling heard the regret in Hannah's voice and caught herself.

'Ignore me.' She softened. 'Hard week.' She bit her lip. 'But then you'd know all about that.' She reached for her hand and squeezed. 'So shit about the Foster Host transfer.'

'He's still going with the whole "I'm innocent" routine,' said Hannah. 'Jem I mean.' She felt weird telling Aisling about the Marzipan Rain thing, embarrassed to admit she'd taken him at all seriously, but she was keen all the same to get her friend's take and summarised it as best she could.

'Ridiculous. Was he not listening when the barrister outlined the mountain of evidence against him?' She was about to go on when a woman emerged from the orangery. Five feet in heels, she wore a black vest and jeans. Brown hair grazed her hips.

Aisling stood to attention.

'Chi-Chi!' She approached and they air-kissed three times. 'This is my friend Hannah.'

Maraschino shook her hand, flopped down onto one of the sofas and started fanning herself with a nearby *Tatler*.

'This heat, when will it end?'

Anywhere from her late twenties to her early fifties, her skin was Profhilo smooth, her nails polished. Every part of her was immaculate, but then Hannah clocked it, a green shadow on her upper arm, a tattoo that had been lasered off. It lurked there below the skin like an ancient sea creature, evidence of some past folly.

'Jane, could you get us some San Pelli?'

Hannah was confused, not sure who she was addressing, but then she saw her: a woman wearing a dusky pink uniform, a white apron tied round her waist. Over by a hedge, she seemed to be peering at a nearby tree but, hearing her name, she snapped to attention and disappeared inside.

'I'll go pack up my table,' said Aisling, backing toward the house. She waited until she was far enough behind Maraschino and gave Hannah a good luck thumbs-up. 'Leave you to it.'

Hannah crossed her arms, trying to hide the oval of sweat beneath her bra, but then, worrying about her body language, dropped them to her side.

'It's our anniversary at the end of this month,' said Maraschino, abandoning the magazine. 'We're having a party. Three hundred of our closest friends.'

Hannah went to reply but was interrupted by her phone ringing.

Maraschino frowned, a tiny wrinkle at the side of her mouth.

'Sorry,' said Hannah, sending the call to voicemail.

'We wanted to have a marquee but then everyone would have to look at that thing.' She gestured to the house next door. 'Eyesore.'

Hannah followed her gaze. Over the wall she could see one of the crescent's famous dilapidated mansions. The roof tiles were dishevelled and plants had sprouted from the brickwork. Hannah's first thought was that it looked like the Heath was trying to reclaim its land leaf by leaf. Her second was that the damage to the house was superficial, that even though its neglect was decades-long, its foundations, the thing that mattered, stood firm. It could be put back. It could be lived in.

'I want to move but Robert won't hear of it.'

The woman in uniform appeared with a tray of sparkling water, bowls of ice and lemon on the side. Once she'd gone Hannah got out her portfolio and opened it to the page she thought would most suit Maraschino's taste.

'I was thinking, maybe something like this?' She showed her a complex geometrical sponge she'd created from a 3-D printer mould.

Maraschino scanned the page. She seemed impressed but then Hannah's phone rang again and she grimaced.

'Or like this?' she said, turning the page and flicking her phone onto silent.

That last call had been the final straw. She put down the folder.

Hannah scrambled for some way to recapture her attention. This would be a highly lucrative contract. Maraschino would have friends, rich friends. If she did a good job it could lead to other things.

'I have an appointment.' She tilted her watch and Hannah saw how its face was decorated with an 'M' made up of tiny diamonds. It looked custom, one of a kind. 'I should be going.'

People like this wanted something unique, a conversation piece, something that money apparently couldn't buy. She thought again of the number of days since John had died. One hundred and eighty. Every twenty-four hours a lifetime.

'You've been married for ten years,' she said, trying to recapture her attention. 'That's what, 3,650 days, give or take a leap year. Each one special, important.' Emboldened by her idea, she spoke loudly, more confident than before. 'How about a simple three-tier centrepiece surrounded by thousands of cupcakes, one for every day you've been married. All of them unique and personal to you in some way. Reflecting how and when you met, your favourite song, your favourite place, the day your husband proposed.'

Maraschino paused. She seemed to be calculating the response of her peers, assessing whether any of them had ever done anything like this before.

'Go on.'

Hannah explained how she would create a colour and flavour scheme for the cakes and then she showed her some examples of the intricate sugar-paste work that would feature on every cupcake.

'I could bring you some samples to try, sketch out how the display might work?'

Her phone continued to buzz but she ignored it.

'Sounds good.' Maraschino got to her feet. 'I'll think about it.'

Hannah thanked her for her time and waited until she had disappeared inside the orangery before walking to the bottom of the garden to decompress.

The back of the crescent couldn't have been more different to her own row of houses. Instead of a gate and steps leading down to a shore there was a high wall and then a sheer concrete drop to deep water below. A wooden platform provided a view over the water and after climbing it she looked out, trying to spot her home in among the others on the other side of the pond.

A Victorian terrace, it was impenetrable, apart from a thin gap at one end where the houses briefly broke ranks before joining up again two metres later. Looking at it from this distance, she could see how every one of her neighbours except Pru had made some kind of complicated addition or accoutrement to their property. Glass lofts jostled for position with tiled balconies and some had even tacked an extra storey to their roof. Her own house was quite plain in comparison. Smothered in ivy, its sash windows were peeling, the brick dirty and she noticed that some of the tiles near the chimney were missing. Her bedroom windows winked in the sun, the glass shiny as jewels.

Again, her phone buzzed. This time she accepted the call.

'You contacted the hotel, The Warlaby,' said a voice she didn't recognise. A man. Not Dracula. This was someone else.

'Can you help? Your colleague didn't think it possible.'

'I'm sorry about John. He was a good man, kind.'

'Wait, what?' Hannah flailed, wrong-footed. 'You knew him?'

'I'm calling to warn you. I owe him that much.'

'Did something else happen that night? Was John on his way to meet someone? Was he coming to meet you?'

'My advice? Walk away.'

'If something else happened . . .' She thought of Jem in his cell. 'If someone else was responsible . . .'

'You have nothing to gain from this. You must understand that.'

'Does this have something to do with that phrase, Marzipan Rain?'

Silence. She thought he'd hung up but then: 'Be careful Hannah.'

'What does that mean?'

This time the line did go dead.

She looked out across the pond again, searching for her house in among the clutter of brick and glass. In the time she'd been talking the sun had shifted. Without light the windows were dull and black. Despite the heat she shivered, her arms knocking against her ribs, bone against bone, sharp and hard.

Jem

I stand in the garden and lift my face to the sun. It's my first time outdoors since I arrived a week ago and the combination of light, colour and smell is overwhelming.

Hannah is in the kitchen pulling out drawers and rootling through cupboards. She's been at it since she got home and is oblivious to all but the task at hand.

Is today the day?

It could be.

'You have one hour,' says Mr Dalgleish, setting a timer on his phone. He's pale and the skin at the sides of his mouth is splintered. He motions to the white line painted on the grass at the sides and bottom of the garden. 'Remember, stay within the perimeter.'

The line marks the electric fence. Any breach across it will trigger the implant in my spine. If after the first shock I continue to move away from the boundary I will be hit by another much stronger shock, then another. In the Holding Centre I heard a story about a Host who had marched their prisoner past the boundary and held them on the spot until they died. They claimed the prisoner had gone there of their own accord, that they committed suicide.

The garden is modest, ten metres by six, and apart from a small decked area by the door it is covered in grass. After being cooped up for so long it feels enormous and I walk a few laps, enjoying the fresh air. I can see people drowsing on picnic blankets on the Heath and the black and white streak of moorhens as they push through the algae fermenting on the pond. Its idyllic and I'm greedy for the view but I only get two outdoor sessions per week; I need to stay in control, to use this time to my advantage.

I move to the middle of the grass and, making sure to face the back of the house, I start my exercise routine. I've worn my navy tracksuit bottoms on purpose; they have deep pockets and let me get into each position – press-up, hip flexor stretch, downward dog – with ease. I study the house as I move, trying to work out its geography. Tall and thin, the brickwork is covered with ivy. It seems to be spread across four floors. There's the basement kitchen where I live, the first floor with the hall and living room, then another two floors.

Where does Hannah sleep?

I get on my back and start a round of sit-ups. The clock is ticking and there'll be limited chances to do what I need to do; still, I've laid the groundwork and now I must pick my moment and be careful not to rush. If the last year has taught me one thing it's the need to stay fluid, to adapt. Opportunities will present themselves. I just need to make sure I'm ready to take them.

I'm halfway through my routine when Hannah appears.

'Can I leave you to lock up?' she asks Mr Dalgleish. Her eyes have a soft, faraway focus. 'There's somewhere I need to be.'

I fall back onto the grass in a heap. If she leaves it might be days before I can try again.

'Unless you have applied for an exemption, the guidelines stipulate the Host be in residence for every outside time and shower.' The protocol seems to fortify him and he sits a little straighter in his chair. 'I can let the prisoner out but it is your responsibility to see to it that he is secured back in his cell.'

'Please, I—'

'Those are the rules.'

Hannah looks like she is going to protest but then she seems to think better of it, closes the door and returns inside.

I pick myself up off the ground, finish my workout and have just reverted to performing laps when Mr Dalgleish gets to his feet. He grips the chair for support.

'Time's up.'

I join him on the decking and he walks me inside.

The kitchen has been ransacked. Drawers gape, their contents spread across the worktops, and cupboard doors swing wide, orphaned pan lids littering the floor. Hannah is standing by the cooker looking at a small rectangle of white paper.

Mr Dalgleish installs me back in the cell, closes the door and stands there waiting. He coughs once, a prompt. When Hannah still fails to notice he bangs on the bars.

'Hannah?' It's the start of October but in his brief time outside he's caught the sun and his nose and cheeks glow in the gloom.

'What?' She's dazed, her thoughts stuck somewhere else. Then she looks at us and seems to come to. 'Yes, sorry.'

She presses the button on the fob round her neck, securing the door electronically, and grabs the fail-safe from the hook by the sink. She puts the key in the lock, turns it without any trouble and is about to walk away when she stops.

'My ring!'

She slips the key into her front dress pocket and bends down to the floor. 'I thought it was gone for good.' She is trying hard not to cry and her voice is thick with unspent tears. She looks at the empty drawers and piles of paper scattered across the worktops. 'It must have been in among all that.' She slips the ruby onto her finger, holds out her hand to admire it and then clutches it to her chest, as if she's afraid it will fall off. She's standing right next to me and when she turns our shoulders brush in the gap between the bars. The contact startles her and she steps back, then she catches sight of her ring again and laughs.

I look her in the eye and smile. I'm also happy. Her gaze is sharp and before long I feel my cheeks redden. When she begins to blush too she lets go of her ring finger. Her hand drops to her side like a stone.

Hannah

The Uber turned off the dual carriageway, took a left and stopped.

Hannah peered out at a scrap of ground filled with ten or so shipping containers.

'Are we here?'

The containers were underneath a railway line and separated from the road by the same metal fences she'd seen outside the abandoned mansions in Queen's Crescent. Canary Wharf's glass towers glared in the distance.

The driver tapped his satnav.

'This is the address you gave.'

Hannah thanked him and got out as a DLR train rumbled overhead. The ground was dusty and scattered with broken bits of concrete, as though a building had recently been demolished here.

She felt for her engagement ring with her thumb, reacquainting herself with its shape and weight, and moved along the fence until she found a gap big enough to slip through. On the other side she stopped and sniffed. The air was ripe with the smell of curry, fried meat and the tang of lemon. She was trying to work out what to do next (should she go from container to container?) when a man appeared on a pushbike. On his back he wore a bag branded with the logo of a food delivery app. He approached the nearest metal box, set the bike on the floor and went inside.

What interest would John have had in this place? What even was it?

The phone call from the hotel had been a spur. As soon as she got home she'd conducted a fresh search for the payslip she'd pulled out of his jeans pocket that day. She was sure there were other words written on it and she wanted to know if they could shed any light on why someone might want to warn her off. John had sometimes left paperwork he couldn't be bothered to take upstairs lying around in the kitchen, stuffed on top of the fridge or next to the bread bin (where it would inevitably fall in the gap between cupboards, never to be seen again) and so she'd turned the place upside down looking for it. Finally, she'd found the payslip in a drawer of takeaway menus slotted inside a leaflet for Korean Fried Chicken. She was right. Underneath the words MARZIPAN RAIN John had also jotted down a postcode and a name. Piotr Nowak.

She was certain John had lied to her, that it wasn't a horse. But why? What did it mean?

She decided the only way to find out if the three bits of information were connected was to go to the postcode and ask around.

She was assessing the different containers, working out which one to try first, when a woman appeared.

She frowned at Hannah, 'You can't keep turning up like this.' She wore a denim shirt tucked into oversize cords and was leaning on a crutch encased in a brown and yellow knitted cover. 'Check your files. Everything is above board. We have a five-star hygiene rating.'

Hannah was confused but then she realised she was still in her dress and heels, and the penny dropped.

'I'm not from environmental health.'

The woman tucked in her chin, unconvinced.

'I'm looking for someone, Piotr Nowak?'

A sigh. She still wasn't happy but the name was like a password. She turned on her heel.

'Follow me.'

A flutter of excitement. John's payslip scribbles weren't random. Maybe Piotr would be able to tell her what the phrase meant?

The woman was surprisingly fast, her crutch throwing dust into the air, and Hannah had to run to keep up.

As they passed the different cabins Hannah saw glimpses of people at work flipping burgers, stirring huge pans and scooping rice into foil containers. The cabins were cramped and windowless. Brand-name restaurant signs denoting sourdough pizza, Thai and sushi were fixed above every door.

The woman led her into a box in the far corner and approached a man slicing chicken.

'Immigration,' she said, cocking her head at Hannah. She lifted her crutch in the air and pressed it against his right shoulder. 'Better not be any trouble.' Then she hobbled out, back the way she had come.

'I'm here legally.' He brushed at the grey circle the woman had left behind and tipped the diced chicken into a tub of buttermilk. 'I can show you my papers.' His accent was faint, like he'd left home a long time ago.

'I'm not from immigration.' Hannah took a breath. She wanted to start from the beginning. 'I'm here because of my husband. He died. Six months ago.'

Piotr cocked his head, waiting for more.

'He was a detective. I found your name in his things.' She stopped, trying to figure out how to explain Jem's place in all this. 'There are rumours about what happened the night he was killed. I'm trying to find out if there's anything to them.'

Piotr scanned the other workers in the room, as if to make sure they weren't listening.

'Detective?' He reached a sieve inside the vat of buttermilk, fished out the meat and dropped it into a nearby fryer. A delicious smell filled the air. 'White hair?'

'You met him?'

Piotr held out his hand, indicating that she should keep it down.

'He came here a while ago,' he said quietly.

'As part of an investigation?' A flicker of hope. Maybe Jem was telling the truth about what he'd heard John say on the phone that night but he'd misinterpreted. There was no woman, no affair. John had argued with someone about a case. Scribbled the details down on a payslip because he didn't have his pocket notebook to hand.

Piotr removed the cooked chicken from the fryer and left it to drain.

'Let's go outside.' He guided her round to the back of the cabin. The floor was covered with mops in buckets, gas cylinders and canisters of vegetable oil. 'It's been a while,' he said, retrieving a vape from his pocket. He nodded at the cabin. 'But you can't be too careful.'

'Did John tell you anything about the case?'

'He was asking about the people I worked for before I started here. The Heppels.' He sucked on the vape and exhaled, his face obscured by white clouds. 'They have places all over town – hotels, bars, restaurants – but they're into everything, drugs, gambling, money-laundering.' His voice blended with the hum of a nearby generator, deep and low. 'He was trying to track down a guy called Slig who'd worked for them around the same time as me. I told him what I knew, which wasn't much, and he went away.'

'The Heppels. Did they have anything to do with a hotel called The Warlaby?'

'Maybe.' He shrugged. 'The whole operation was run by a bloke called Symeon and his two sons, Benton and Bobby. These days it's just Symeon and Bobby. Benton died at the start of the year.' He smiled wryly. 'Car accident.'

'Slig? Why was he trying to find him?'

'He didn't say.'

'When was this?'

'Not long after I'd started working here.' He thought back. 'January?'

Two months before John was killed.

'This is random, but have you ever heard the phrase Marzipan Rain?'

Piotr shook his head.

'If you think of anything else will you please call?' She gave Piotr a business card and he walked her back round to the front of the cabin. She was looking at her phone, trying to sort a taxi, when he spoke.

'I did hear one rumour about Slig, the guy your husband was looking for, but it was a while after he came here.'

A driver accepted her request and she put her phone in her bag.

'He killed someone. Caused a huge fuss. He had to leave town.'

She frowned. 'Why the fuss?'

Another train rumbled overhead. Something was burning in one of the containers and the air stank of singed coconut.

'The person he killed. It was a police officer. A detective.'

Jem

On Saturday, Mum leaves for a night out in a flurry of bangles and lipstick. The next morning there is no sign of her. The flat is quiet, calm. Normally when this happens it's OK. I know how to take care of myself; how to brush my teeth, how to work the telly, what to say to the neighbours. I read my books. Eat at school.

But it's the summer holidays and the fridge is empty.

Two days pass.

I make the cereal last as long as I can. But then a day after finishing it all I can think about is food. I feel like someone has scraped out the inside of my stomach, like it is twisting and turning into knots.

I go to the mini-market at the bottom of our block. I tell myself I just want to look. To sniff the loaves. Hold the fruit in my palm.

The shop is quiet, the man who runs it by the till with his son. The son is older than me. Tall with bleached ear-length hair, he has headphones round his neck and I can hear the tinny tsk-tsk-tsk of dance music coming through them. His younger sister is in my class at school.

I watch as the man chats to a customer, an old lady, and the son packs her groceries inside her trolley. When I'm sure they're not looking I take a packet of chocolate biscuits from the shelf, tuck it into the back of my shorts and cover it with my T-shirt. My mouth is dry and I'm sure the whole world can hear the whomp of my heart. I know it's wrong but I decide that when Mum comes *back I'll ask her for some money, come back and leave what I owe on the counter.*

I walk slowly toward the exit, the biscuits slipping around my waistband. I'm almost there when I see the manager coming toward me. I speed up and so does he. I pull out the biscuits from the back of my shorts and throw them on the floor. Then I run.

Three days later and Mum still isn't back. She's never been gone this long before.

My stomach has stopped hurting but I feel tired and when I walk up the stairs to the flat my head is woozy.

I hover around the burger place on the high street. There are tables outside and sometimes people leave a few fries or a half-eaten cheeseburger on one of the trays when they go. I'm about to swoop in on some abandoned chicken nuggets when I see the son with the bleached hair from the supermarket.

He takes off his headphones and marches over to where I stand. I'm convinced he's remembered me from the other day, that he's going to drag me back to his dad so they can call the police about my stolen biscuit attempt. I try to back away but the road behind me is busy, the pavement clogged with people.

He looks me up and down.

'You live in the flats, above the shop?'

I nod, terrified. He knows where I live. He can send the police to my house. Not only will I get in trouble for shoplifting but they'll realise Mum isn't home. I'll be taken into care again.

'At the shop, it's my job to go through the shelves and remove anything out of date. Most of the stuff is fine, especially if you eat it that day, but still, it's the law we throw it out . . .' He pauses. 'Every Thursday I load up a trolley and wheel it out to the big

metal bins in the cut at the back of the shop. Sometimes I leave the trolley there, have a smoke, listen to my music. If someone were to come and take a few things I doubt I'd even notice.'

He pauses then, wanting to make sure I've understood his meaning.

'Five o'clock?' I say.

'Every Thursday without fail,' he says and then he clamps the headphones back on his ears and off he goes.

Thursday afternoon and I wait at the mouth of the alley. I'm wary, worried this is a trick. The back of the supermarket is marked by metal shutters that run from the ceiling to the floor. Just after 5 p.m. one of the shutters clatters open and the boy appears, pushing a trolley heaped with food. Seeing me, he pauses briefly, then wheels it over to the bin, puts on his headphones and goes to lean against the wall.

Slowly I approach, pick my way through the pile. There are packets of raw chicken and pork I wouldn't know what to do with, but there is also ham, cheese and bread. At the bottom I find a clump of smashed Kinder eggs. I've brought my backpack and I fill it to the brim. Before I leave I go and stand in front of the boy and nod, letting him know I'm done. He pushes himself away from the wall and sets to work disposing of what remains.

Mum came back after a fortnight. Thin and exhausted, her eyes blank. Still, the arrangement with the shop continues. The boy's name is Kenzie. He's fifteen and tells me that when he leaves school he's going to be a dance music producer, that he's going to make songs the whole world will listen to.

One Thursday Kenzie asks if there's anything else I need. If everything is OK at home.

I tell him it's fine. I know better than to admit the truth.

I've just begun my mooch through the trolley when his dad appears at the opening. He looks from the food to my backpack and his face darkens.

'Not this again.' He comes forward and grabs the trolley, drags it back into the loading bay.

'But Dad,' says Kenzie. 'What's the harm?'

His father doesn't reply and so Kenzie goes and tries to wrestle the trolley from him. In the scuffle they dislodge the metal shutter from its holder and it drops a few inches.

'Enough,' says his dad finally and, after pushing Kenzie to the floor, tugs the trolley back inside the bay.

I run to check he's OK, crouch at his side. A click and the shutter is falling, clattering towards us at speed. I lean over Kenzie, trying to shield him from the impact, and the sharp metal scrapes against my spine.

Hannah

The next morning and Hannah was waiting for Aisling outside a house on Savernake Road. Aisling was finishing up with a client and when she was done Hannah was going to walk with her to her next job on the other side of the Heath. Their catch-up would be brief but Hannah had seen so little of her friend of late that she was grateful for all she could get.

She thought again of what she'd learned from her trip to the docklands. She'd messaged Mickey and Rupert as soon as she'd got home, told them she wanted to talk to them about John's murder, that there might be more to it, but they had yet to respond. She decided to try Mickey again now, while she had a moment.

Hearing the DCI's phone ring, she felt hopeful. She'd tell her what she'd learned, see if it chimed with anything John had been investigating in the months before his death, and then the police would take over, decide what to do next.

'Hello.'

A Canadian accent, the vowels clipped.

'Laramie?' Mickey's ex-wife.

'Hannah,' said Laramie. She sounded weary. 'Can I call you later? I've been up all night.'

'Is Mickey there?' asked Hannah, confused. 'Is she OK?'

Laramie paused.

'I thought that was why you were calling, that you'd heard . . .' She stopped and took a breath. 'I just dropped her at The Priory.'

'Rehab?'

'You don't seem surprised?'

'I knew she was drinking again . . .' She tailed off.

'But you didn't think it was that bad?' said Laramie. 'That's the thing about alcoholics, they don't really do moderation.'

'What happened?'

'One of the neighbours called,' said Laramie, 'they thought Mickey was in trouble. I came over and found her on the front step, a pile of vomit on one side, a bottle of Merlot on the other.'

'Sorry.'

'Nothing I haven't seen before.'

'Can I visit? Or maybe I could talk with her on the phone? There's something I want to ask her about, it's kind of urgent.'

Laramie was firm.

'She can't see or talk to anyone, not for a while.'

Hannah wished her well, told her to shout if she could help in any way and hung up. She felt at more of a loss than ever. About John, about Jem, but mostly Mickey. Everything seemed to be disintegrating, dissolving into tiny pieces.

A click and Aisling shot out the front door, pulling her massage table in its bag on wheels behind her. Wearing leggings and a T-shirt branded with the purple and orange RUB logo of the physiotherapy clinic she worked at, she'd fixed her curls into a pair of French braids and tamed the escapee strands at her temples with a complex arrangement of slides and clips.

'Sorry I'm late.' She bumped the table down the steps. 'He wanted a bit extra on his rhomboids.' She gave Hannah a hug. 'We best walk fast, I've got a pinched nerve on the Vale of Health in fifteen minutes.' She charged toward the cut that led to the Heath. 'So, how is life with the convict?'

Aisling had yet to come to the house. Hannah wasn't sure if she was scared to see Jem up close or if there was something else keeping her away.

'Odd,' said Hannah, wondering where to start. She broke into a half-run, trying to keep up, and gave her a summary of everything that had happened in the last few days. Marzipan Rain, the strange warning call, how John had been trying to track down a man who was later rumoured to have killed a police officer. Finally, she told her about her call with Laramie just now, how Mickey had been admitted to rehab.

'There's a chance Jem's telling the truth,' said Hannah once she was done. Then she said the words she'd been wanting to voice for a while. 'Ash, what if they arrested the wrong guy?'

Aisling's eyes widened.

'He murdered John in cold blood. They have his fingerprints, they have him on CCTV.' Hannah was taken aback by her friend's anger, the force of it. 'What other possible explanation could there be?'

They emerged onto the Heath and Aisling surged forward, tackling the slope at speed. The grass stretched for miles, dogs tearing across the open ground like pinballs. Hannah had lived and walked here for years but coming upon the vast stretch of space and sky never failed to surprise her. Living in the city, she wasn't used to being able to look off into any real distance, and it always took a moment for her eye muscles to adjust.

'That night, before John left the bar,' she said when they'd reached the top of the incline. 'Jem said it sounded like he was talking to a woman.' Lolloping hills spread out before them, the grass tufty and yellowed. 'That he was on his way to meet her.' She grabbed her pendant – holding the stone grounded her – and held it in front of her like a compass.

Aisling frowned.

'I'm late.'

She picked up the pace and they soon reached a pocket of woodland. The trees were filled with the luminous green parakeets that populated this part of London, but the prolonged summer had left the birds sluggish and the wood was silent.

'I worry about you.' Hannah gestured at Aisling's table. 'Rubbing naked strangers.'

The ground was rougher here, the stones pushing up through the baked mud like a reptile's back.

'Think of it as Uber, but for injured shoulders,' Aisling said, her face growing red with exertion. 'They book me through the app and so all their details are registered online.' They broached a particularly bumpy bit of ground and the table wobbled, almost tipping over onto its side. Aisling stopped to right it, her breath ragged. 'Plus, there are the things I do on the app to keep myself safe. I use my soap star name so they can't stalk me on social media.'

'Your what?'

'Stacey Tweed. My soap star name. It's your middle name plus the name of the first street you ever lived on.'

Again, the terrain changed. One side of the path was now dense with undergrowth, trees and brambles, the other dropped away to a muddy ravine.

'You could always come back to making cakes. God knows I could use the help.' Aisling's dreams of becoming a zoologist had not panned out. After trying and failing to get on a degree course, she had ended up working at the Vulture Preservation Society as a press assistant and topping up her paltry salary with evening and weekend work assisting Hannah. Even now she loved to regale people with carrion facts and could often be found at parties dazzling some unsuspecting guest with the story of how antibiotic use in cattle almost wiped out the Indian vulture population. But then eighteen months ago, Aisling had decided she'd had enough of vultures and red velvet cupcakes and retrained as a masseuse.

'I've got so much on,' said Hannah, 'I could do with another pair of—' She was cut off by a man sprinting across the path in front of them. Wearing a suit and tie, he passed by so fast and close his elbow almost clipped Aisling's shoulder.

'Where is he off to in such a hurry?' But no sooner had she recovered when three women appeared from the same section of undergrowth and, after scanning the horizon, set off down the ravine at speed in pursuit of the man. The women all had slender Barre-core toned bodies clad in leggings with sheer panels across the calf and thigh.

'What,' said Aisling, putting her hands on her hips, 'was that?'

'Whatever it is, it doesn't seem good.' Hannah made to go but Aisling remained where she was.

The man was zooming toward a cluster of trees at the bottom of the ravine. A streak of grey, every few seconds he turned his head, checking on the women's progress. He reached the copse and disappeared inside, the women following soon after.

'He seemed terrified.' Aisling checked her watch, torn between wanting to find out what was going on and getting to her next client on time.

Aisling had a tendency to get involved. Over the years, Hannah had seen her step in and break up a street fight, talk someone out of throwing themselves in front of a tube and rugby-tackle a mugger trying to make off with a stolen handbag.

'Aisling, no,' Hannah said. But she was already gone, hurtling down the slope toward the trees, her massage table abandoned where it stood.

Hannah stayed where she was, hoping Aisling would change her mind, but when she too was swallowed by the undergrowth, she hid the massage table in a bush and skidded off down the slope to find her. After picking her way through a mass of holly and bramble, she came out onto the edge of a small clearing. There were more green parakeets here. They dozed in clusters, garish in the trees.

Hannah saw Aisling first. Standing off to the right, she was staring at something. Hannah followed her gaze and saw the man, prostrate on the floor, his head rucked against a tree root. In his early thirties, he had a smooth pink head circled by severely cropped hair, and beneath his glasses were dark, pebble eyes. His nose twitched, as though he was resisting a sneeze, and Hannah was put in mind of a dormouse emerging from hibernation.

Two of the Barre-core women were holding him down, one on each arm. Skeletal oak leaves clung to their leggings' sheer panels.

'I don't know what's going on,' said Aisling. 'But you need to let him go.'

The women ignored her and the one who wasn't holding the man down reached into a canvas Hampstead Butcher tote and pulled out a black device that looked like a walkie-talkie. She pressed a button and a bright blue worm danced in the dip at the top.

A taser.

She approached the man from the side. 'This is none of your business.'

'You're not seriously going to use that?' said Aisling.

The woman kneeled on the floor and the man swung his pelvis up in the air and kicked his legs wildly. His toe caught her on the chin and she shrank back.

'You can't just assault someone in broad daylight.'

'This isn't assault,' said the woman. She straddled the man's ankles, pinning his legs with her body weight, and began moving the taser toward his groin. 'We're teaching him a lesson.'

'If he's done something wrong you should go to the police.'

'What and have him as my new housemate?' A hollow laugh. 'No thanks.'

She turned on the taser and the man moved his face to the side. His glasses fell into the dirt.

'Let him go.'

Aisling got out her phone and started taking pictures. The shutter sound gave the woman pause. She turned round. Aisling waited until she had her full attention, then brought up her keypad and dialled 999. She showed the woman the screen, her finger poised over the green call button.

'Let him go or I'll tell the police.'

The woman looked to the other two, asking for guidance.

'Even if she calls them,' said one, 'it's not like he's going to press charges.'

'You really want to take that risk?' said Aisling, her finger still over the button.

They held him captive a few moments more and then, after a last glance at Aisling and her phone, released their grip. The man scrambled sideward.

'You're making a mistake.' The woman replaced the taser in her bag and went to rejoin her pack. 'He'll do it again and when he does it'll be your fault.'

'Do what?'

But they were already retreating, picking their way through the bushes from which they had come.

Aisling collected the man's glasses from the ground and went to help him to his feet. His suit was covered in dirt.

'Thank you,' he said, brushing himself down.

'Here.' Aisling offered him her phone. 'Report them.'

'I don't want any trouble.' He shook Aisling's hand. 'Thank you again though, really.'

His nose twitched one last time and then he sneezed, a long drawn-out staccato.

Before Aisling could say anything more he jogged off in the opposite direction to the three women, and after pushing through the foliage, he was gone.

Hannah took Aisling's hand and went to lead them both back up the ravine.

A cloud appeared, obscuring the sun. The sudden drop in temperature woke the parakeets from their stupor. The wood rang out with a thousand squawks. An alarum.

It sounded like people screaming.

Jem

I'm woken by the smell of coffee and toast. I turn onto my back and my cheek grazes the wall. I'm normally up and about before Hannah comes downstairs but the last few nights have taken their toll. I've slept in.

I slide out from under the bed, grab my red and white baseball cap from the pillow and put it on top of the cupboard.

Hannah places a tray through the hatch.

'Breakfast.'

'Thanks.' I take it to my table and sit. I'm tired but I feel good, hopeful. I'm making progress.

Hannah settles in a dining chair and, after pricking her finger, she blots the blood against a thin test strip and slots it in the meter.

'Looks like another lovely day,' I say, nodding at the sky.

She looks at me carefully, breathes out, then purses her lips. It's like she can't decide how to reply, like she wants to say something, or ask something, but she's worried about making a mistake.

The machine beeps with the result. She checks the number, gives herself a shot of insulin and reaches for her toast.

I realise she's in her pyjamas. Until now she's always been showered and dressed before she makes an appearance. The pyjamas are too big for her and the sleeves hang low over her wrists. I wonder if she prefers them like this or if they once belonged to her husband.

We eat in silence, Hannah working her way through a pile of post. She opens and discards the first two letters but the third envelope gives her pause. She reads it through twice, her face creased into a frown, then she tuts and shoves the piece of paper back into the envelope and down into her handbag on the floor.

Alina was right, she is attractive, but not in the bland girl-next-door way she described. Her reddish brown eyes are fierce, her blond hair startling. It's the kind of beauty that seems to hail from another time or another world.

She pours herself a second coffee and holds the cafetière in the air, asking if I want more. I put my mug through the bars and she comes over and tops me up. Our movements are slow and lazy, the morning light soft, the horizon a smear of yellow and pink.

'How do your family feel?' she says, gesturing at the cell. 'About you being here?'

I pause, trying to work out how best to answer.

'I don't have any,' I say, 'not anymore.'

'Oh.' She considers this. 'Your visitor. She's your girlfriend?'

'An old mate.' I smile. 'I'm single.'

'Oh, right, I thought . . .'

'Afraid not.'

The radio murmurs in the background, the news giving way to an old pop song. The opening bars are full of yearning for a first love and a summer long ago and, hearing them, Hannah comes to.

'It must be boring,' she says, her voice louder than before. She's brisk, businesslike. 'I know you have your books but . . .' She looks around, searching for ideas. 'I could move the TV down?'

'Radio and books are more than fine.' She thinks we're done but just as she turns to sit I speak. 'Although . . .'

'Yes?'

'Maybe one night, if you're not busy, we could play a board game?'

She frowns for a second, before grinning.

'A board game?'

'Yahtzee,' I say, dead serious.

Her eyes widen, her glee growing as she absorbs my request. She shakes her head.

'But I have to warn you,' I say, posturing. 'I'm good.'

'Yahtzee?' she says, still delighting in the unlikely nature of my request.

'The fun game that makes thinking fun!' I say reciting the catchphrase printed on the outside of every box.

She shakes her head and, chuckling, returns her attention to her toast.

I look at the fridge magnets, the letters fixed into the last words John arranged before he died. Even from here I can see their tops are furred with the dust, their edges grimy.

It's strange to think Hannah and I might grow older together. Twenty years.

I've been so focused on the task at hand that I haven't let myself think about what that means. How my prime – the time when I should be getting married and having kids – is going to be spent here, in this cage.

Finished with her breakfast, she takes her plate over to the sink. White boxes sit stacked on the countertop, packed with cupcakes. She lifts each lid in turn, inspecting her handiwork. When she reaches the last box she hovers her finger right to left, then reaches in and pulls out a cupcake. Dark chocolate sponge with a tiny green Frankenstein monster on top. Then she hands it to me through the bars.

'Still a few weeks away but, happy Halloween!'

I turn it left and right. The silver bolts at the sides of the monster's neck are precise and symmetrical.

'What is this made out of?' I hold the cake in the air. 'Him I mean.'

'Three things.' She holds a trio of fingers in the air and smiles. 'Pure. Unadulterated. Sugar,' she says, lowering each digit in turn. 'They should come with a health warning.'

'Are you baking today?' I keep my tone light.

'No, I—'

She stops. Something has caught her eye.

I tense.

What is she looking at?

She reaches for the pile of post on the table.

'Almost forgot.' She hands me an envelope. 'This came.'

A green kangaroo logo sits next to the stamp. It's from Roost, the social storage company I use to house my things. It's an unusual set-up – the website lets people offer their spare garage, attic or cupboard space for a price online – but it's cheap and what with everything, I'm grateful for the fact it's so random. The Brixton loft where I keep my stuff would be the last place someone would think to look.

I turn over the envelope in my hands. I pay the Roost providers, a retired couple called Rita and Winston, by direct debit, so it can't be an invoice. Besides, Roost tend to correspond by email.

When I read what's inside my stomach drops, quick and sudden as a lift whose cables have been cut.

Rita and Winston are moving house and can no longer honour our agreement. Any monies I am owed will be refunded and I have twenty-eight days to remove my things. The small print informs me that if I do not do this by the specified date then the providers have the right to dispose of my stuff however they wish. They've written to me by snail mail as a last resort, having had no response to their digital correspondence and phone calls.

I do the numbers in my head. All post has to be vetted by the prison service and so it gets to me on a delay. The letter is dated two weeks earlier, 2nd October. I've got a fortnight to sort something out.

I feel like I've been at the wheel of a car, navigating it expertly around hairpin bends and up and down steep hills, only for the steering column to sheer. Now, when I turn the wheel there is no resistance. It spins, loose and free.

Hannah grabs an apple from the bowl and heads toward the stairs.

'See you at lunch.'

She takes a bite. The crunch jolts me back to the kitchen, to the cage. I realise I still don't know her plans for the day, whether she's in or out.

Hannah

The Virgin Active was at the bottom of Camden High Street. Set back from the stalls of cherry-red Doc Martens and feathered dreamcatchers, it was all glass and neon and looked more like a nightclub than a gym. John had come here two or three times a week to swim or do circuits.

Inside, Hannah went to the front desk. A final demand requesting she clear John's locker had arrived this morning. The letter had explained that if she did not vacate the unit by the end of the day the gym would donate the contents to charity. She handed over the piece of paper and the man behind the desk typed the details into a computer.

'There's a fine for late collection. Ninety-five pounds.' He smiled brightly. 'How do you want to pay, cash or card?'

Hannah didn't miss a beat.

'My husband died, he was murdered actually, and I couldn't face coming to get his stuff until now.' She made sure to speak loudly enough for the other people in the queue to hear. 'Are you really going to charge me? I mean, do you honestly think that's OK?'

The man held out for a few seconds more, then folded.

At the locker bank Hannah stood to one side as he applied a pair of snippers to the padlock. Snap. The sheared metal looked chewed, like a dog had been at it.

'I'll leave you be,' he said, tucking the snippers under his arm.

Hannah opened the door and peered inside. She'd expected trainers or goggles, a mouldy towel dangling from a hook, but the only item was a large sports holdall, zipped shut.

She went to hoist it out only to realise she'd misjudged how much it might weigh. Her wrist was unprepared and the bag dropped to the floor with a thud as a flurry of post-HIIT class men and women rushed past, chattery with endorphins. She lifted the bag onto her shoulder and headed for the door. She knew it would most likely contain shower gel, maybe some socks and towels. Still, it had been part of John's life and so was precious. She'd open it at home, in private.

Outside, she checked her phone for messages. Still no response from Rupert. She was surprised. She'd thought that, once he heard about Mickey, he'd have called right away, especially after their previous conversation.

She hopped onto the bus and was about to head up to the top deck when she stopped. This route would take her past Chalk Farm Road. From there Primrose Hill was a few minutes' walk. It was Saturday, so Rupert might be home.

'I'm in the neighbourhood and thought I'd stop by,' she said, leaving another voicemail. 'Get the kettle on and I'll see you soon.'

Rupert lived in Chalcot Square. Highly desirable, the houses were all painted different colours. Burnt orange, candy pink and sherbet yellow, they rainbowed around a patch of playground and grass rarely used by the residents but which he and John liked to sit in every Monday to eat their favourite breakfast (a bacon and fried egg roll with brown sauce), which they took it in turns to provide. Just one of many bromantic quirks and traditions that Hannah had liked to tease them about, but which in private she'd thought adorable. They also had a roster of secret spots across the capital they considered 'theirs', which they liked to go and hang out and brainstorm in whenever they hit a roadblock in an investigation. From a bench in the far corner of the Phoenix Garden, a little-known oasis of green near Seven Dials that they accessed through a hidden churchyard gate, to a for-gotten footbridge full of nesting sparrows by Platform 11 on Paddington Station, each spot had been discovered by accident while they were working other unrelated cases.

Their bond was such that Hannah used to joke a lesser woman would feel jealous.

Rupert's house was on a square corner. Wedgwood blue, it had been bought and paid for in full years ago thanks to his hefty trust fund. It took Hannah twenty minutes to get there. Outside his front door, she set the holdall on the ground and rang the bell.

No answer.

She searched the street for his MG but the maroon coupé was nowhere to be seen. Maybe he was out or doing a weekend shift? Coming here had been a long shot – still, walking around Primrose Hill was always a pleasure. Maybe she'd go to the bookshop before she went home. She'd noticed the majority of Jem's possessions were dog-eared paperbacks. She could see if there was something he might like, something new.

She was about to knock again when she heard footsteps.

'Hannah.'

Rupert appeared at the top of the path. Out of breath, he grabbed onto the iron railing for support, his hand nursing a stitch.

'I was running errands in Kentish Town,' he said, panting. 'Wasn't sure if I'd make it back in time.' He smiled. 'Shall we go for coffee?' He beckoned her forward, 'Lemonia?'

They linked arms and set off toward the high street. Despite the heat Rupert was in his usual leisurewear of camel chinos, white shirt and navy blazer. Gold cufflinks twinkled at his wrists.

'Sorry for the radio silence. Especially after the news about Mickey. I wanted to call but work has been crazy.' He yawned. 'Double shifts.'

The historically low crime rate had not, as might have been expected, made things easier for the police. The government saw the declining figures as justification to pare back staffing levels already cut to the bone. John had railed against it. No one, he'd said, had disagreed the old prison system wasn't fit for purpose, but using it as justification to eviscerate an already overstretched Met was perverse.

And as John and every other police officer knew, the crime *rate* might be low, but the actual number of crimes being committed had spiralled as people realised folk were unlikely to press charges. He'd balked at the ethics that were bandied around, the morality, about how the new system was more humane, that the prisoners involved would be less likely to reoffend. 'They can wang on about recidivism and compassion all they like,' he'd used to say, 'but it cost thirty-eight grand a year to keep a prisoner in the old system and now it costs twenty grand. Like everything, it all comes down to money.'

At the restaurant, they settled at an outside table under one of the green awnings and ordered. Women in cotton dresses and leather sandals trudged by carrying groceries and flowers. Wearied by the ongoing heat, their skin was dappled pink, their hairlines damp and curling.

'What's the talk at the Yard?' she said, 'About Mickey.'

He let out a slow breath.

'They were really straightforward. Open, honest. It was refreshing actually. She's taking a leave of absence and then, once she's out the other side of treatment, they'll see where she wants to go from there.'

The waitress set down their coffees and two plastic-covered biscotti.

Rupert grabbed one and squinted at the tiny writing on the wrapper.

'Seventeen grams of carbs,' he said, placing it back down.

'Thanks,' said Hannah, already prick-testing her thumb.

Rupert's father was also a type 1 diabetic and so he was fluent in the disease and the constant plate-spinning calculations it took to keep it in check.

'So,' he said once Hannah had injected. 'Was it just Mickey you wanted to talk about?'

Hannah hesitated. Now she was in front of him she found it hard to find the words. To ask his advice would be to admit that she had taken Jem's claims seriously. She worried she would seem horribly naïve or, worse, that he'd think she was betraying John somehow.

'Back at the start of the year,' she said, 'were you and John investigating a gang. The Heppels? They run a string of hotels and bars.'

'A gang?' He reached for one of his cufflinks and twisted it. 'What's that got do with anything?'

'Jem,' she said, trying to go back to the beginning. 'He said that on the night John was killed, before he left the bar he heard him on the phone. He said it sounded like he was arranging to meet a woman, but the more I look into it, the more I think he was working on a case after hours, that maybe it had something to do with his death.'

'Jem?' Rupert was thunderous. 'Heard him on the phone?' The way he absorbed the information was like pennies falling in one of those coin-pusher machines in an arcade. 'A woman?'

'I've been asking around and there seems to be something to it. One person said John had been looking for a man, Slig. A man who was later rumoured to have killed a copper.'

Rupert cocked his head. This was clearly news to him.

'If John went and talked to these people, he did it alone.'

He took her hand and ran his thumb over her knuckles. 'Everyone deals with grief in their own way, I get it, but listening to that –' he screwed up his face like he had a bad taste in his mouth, 'that criminal is not the answer.'

She withdrew her hand. 'But he knows things he couldn't possibly have known.'

Rupert nodded.

'He's got inside your head. I know you're stuck together, he's in your kitchen for God's sake, but you need to try and keep your distance, mentally I mean.'

He stayed watching her for a few moments more, wanting to be sure she'd understood.

'Shit.' He checked the time. 'I should have left five minutes ago.' He signalled for the bill and, when the waitress appeared, tapped his card against the machine.

'I'll try to drop by at the end of the week.' He tugged at his shirt until the cuffs sat neat against his blazer. 'And remember, don't let him in.' He tapped the side of his temple. 'He's a rat in a cage. Rats will do anything to escape.' Then he was off.

Hannah shifted on her chair and her knee knocked against John's sports holdall. It sat waiting at her feet like a guard dog, loyal and solid.

Jem

Visit day.

I've been awake since dawn, my heart a twitchy animal in my chest. I know Alina will help me come up with a plan to move my stuff, that there'll be a simple fix, but the thing I'm coming to realise about being inside this house, this cell, is that the tiniest bumps in the road can derail you. When you are so absolutely reliant on others for your most basic needs – food, bathing, heat – when someone else decides what time you go to bed, what time you wake up, what you listen to, it's hard not to become a cog, to remember you still have agency.

The clock turns 11 a.m. and there is no sign of her. 11.05 a.m. – still nothing.

She's never late.

At 11.15 a.m. Mr Dalgliesh goes to the sink and peers up through the window, to the street above.

'Maybe there's a problem with the Tube?' he offers and I get the sense he's been in this situation before.

I stand up and sit back down. My muscles push against my skin. I want to move, to pace, to run. The pressure builds.

At 11.30 a.m. the doorbell goes.

A rush, like air being let out of a balloon, but also impatience. I stand by the cell door transferring my weight from foot to foot, waiting to be let out.

Mr Dalgliesh brings Alina down to the kitchen and scans her with the wand. She doesn't look at me and when the wand beeps she jumps. Her suit jacket is creased and there is a smudge of mascara on her right eyelid.

Hannah comes to let me out and disappears upstairs. Mr Dalgliesh takes his place by the French doors.

'I need your help,' I say before I've sat down. 'My stuff. I need to move it and soon.'

Alina doesn't seem to hear me.

'I got burgled.' She pulls her jacket close. 'I'm late because I was with the locksmith.'

'What?' I'm so consumed with my own problems that it takes me a moment to change track. 'Are you OK? Is Franklyn OK?'

'We weren't home.'

Her lips are pressed. There's something she's not saying.

'Alina?'

'They tossed the whole place, every cupboard, every drawer. They even went through Frankie's toy box.'

'What did they take?'

'That's just it.' The words seem hard for her to say. 'Nothing is missing.' For the first time since she arrived she meets my eye. 'I think they were looking for something specific.'

She waits for me to understand her meaning.

'No.' I lean back in my chair, as if to distance myself from her words. 'No way.'

'They must have seen me at the Holding Centre.' She shudders, pulls her jacket even tighter. 'Followed me home.'

My hand goes to the tiny scar on the back of my neck. The chip is deep, close to my spine. Still, I rub at the skin, searching for it under the surface.

'I can't help you anymore.' She says it quietly, like a confession.

'Alina, please,' I say, panicking. 'I'm so close.'

Already, I'm trying to figure out a fix. My next phone call isn't for another two days and I can't even begin to try to find an alternative solution till then.

'What if they'd broken in when I was there with Frankie?'

I slump. She's right. I'm ashamed that I've put her and her son at risk. And yet. I need her.

'I've made real progress, please don't do this now. I'm so close,' I say, glancing over at Mr Dalgliesh. 'Log into my Roost account, find another space,' I add, scrambling for a compromise. 'It will be online, no one will know. I'll get someone else to do the actual move.'

She gets to her feet.

'Please?' I say as she retrieves her things from the tray.

'Take care, Jeremiah.'

She heads for the stairs. Before she disappears out of sight she releases her jacket from her grip. The material defaults into its lines and creases.

'Chin up,' says Mr Dalgliesh as he locks me back in the cell. 'Happens all the time.' He nods at the bars. 'You being in here. It's too much. They walk away.'

Hannah

Thursday morning and Shoreditch High Street was just starting to come to. Hannah got off the bus and headed north, toward Kingsland Road and Fleece, the bar where John had spent the last night of his life. She was here to retrace his steps, to see for the first time where her husband had met his death.

This part of town was in a constant state of redevelopment and judging by the contrast between now and the crime scene photographs presented during the trial, the last six months had seen a huge number of buildings constructed or torn down. Over the road she could see a Georgian storefront that had had its guts ripped away, a phalanx of steel and glass already being poured into the gap. It reminded her of a child's mouth, the way emerging adult molars would crowd themselves against baby teeth, edging behind the original white pearls long before they were ready to fall out.

The last week had been spent stewing over her conversation with Rupert. She knew he meant well, that when he'd told her to leave things alone he'd done so out of concern, but she also knew there was too much that didn't make sense for her to walk away.

Jem had been convicted beyond a reasonable doubt but now she had doubts, plenty of them. Putting aside the strange calls and conversations, he *seemed* considerate. Kind even.

Not capable of murder.

In the end she'd decided she had no choice but to keep going, to try to find out if someone else might have been responsible for John's death. If Jem was telling the truth, if he was innocent, then she needed to know, and not just because it would mean he had been wrongfully imprisoned. He would be released from her custody. She'd no longer have to share her home with a stranger. And as for the true culprit waiting to take his place, well, now Hannah knew better. She thought of the man sprawled in the scrub on the heath the other day, how the taser had crackled blue in the dim light. There were other ways to exact justice.

Outside the bar she stopped and took in its gilt and grey facade. The window, designed to look like a Victorian drapery, was stacked with oak and glass-fronted haberdashery drawers, burlap mannequins and flat rolls of fruit-print cloth. Her conversation with Rupert had been useful in one way. It had made her realise that she needed to adopt a more methodical approach, to do what John used to do: start at the beginning and follow through every lead from there. Rupert was a detective, a man of evidence, and she'd come to him with stories of mysterious phone calls and hearsay. Of course he'd dismissed her. If she went to him again it would have to be with something substantial, something he couldn't ignore.

Her first act was this, her scouting mission to the bar, and then, once she was done here, she planned on taking a train to Cambridge and seeing if she could find any more on the man whose funeral notice John had looked at all those times, then it was home by 4 p.m. for Jem's outside session.

Being tied to another person's schedule, having to organise your day around them in the same way you would a child or a pet, was bizarre (a whole industry of people had sprung up to provide cover for Hosts when they went on holiday or away for the weekend but that didn't help with the day-to-day errands), and yet she was starting to realise there was a comfort to being relied upon too, that it felt good to be needed.

Inside, the bar was empty, the tables stacked with chairs. Looking at the bottles of spirits racked to the wall and the white wine ready to be shelved, her thoughts went to Mickey and the night she'd found her drunk, their dinner date forgotten. She got out her phone and sent Laramie a text asking how the DCI was getting on and if she could pass on her love. She wondered when she'd next see her again, when they might be able to talk on the phone.

French rap played quietly in the background and she could hear the bang and clatter of someone at work out back. She wasn't expecting to stumble on some key piece of evidence the police had missed, she wasn't naïve, but she did know that whenever John had got stuck on a case he would return to the scene of the crime and walk around. He said he did it not to try to see things differently but to look at them as they actually were; to notice how the mud attached itself to your feet or how a bus rumbled by every half an hour or how the roof leaked when it rained.

She did a quick circuit of the space, trying to imagine John here. He usually drank near his office on the Embankment or in one of the few proper pubs still left in Soho. Getting to this part of town would have been an effort. In court Rupert had explained that central London had been heaving, everyone out celebrating the start of the Easter weekend, and so they'd decided to head east in search of a change of scene.

'Hello?'

Hannah jumped and banged her hip against a table corner. She turned to see a guy wearing mirrored wraparound sunglasses hefting a box of mixers under his arm.

'Are you open?' She rubbed at her side and gestured at the deserted space. 'I wasn't sure.'

'Not for ten minutes.' He looked her up and down, jawing a wad of pink gum. 'But I can make an exception.'

Hannah ordered a lime and soda and took a seat at the bar. He served her and then got back to stocking the fridges.

'Worked here long?'

'A while.' He didn't look up.

'Ever work with a guy called Jem?'

He paused and Hannah couldn't tell if it was because he'd lost his grip on one of the bottles or something else.

'I work with lots of people.'

'My husband,' she said, trying a different tack. 'He drank here the night he died. He was stabbed.'

He wedged the last two bottles into position, got to his feet and began winding the gum onto his finger.

'The detective?'

Hannah nodded.

'Sorry for your loss.' He pulled his hand away from his mouth, stretching the gum perilously thin.

'I wanted to see what it was like, to try and imagine him in the space.' She swirled the ice around her glass. 'Jem, the person that did it, he worked here. He's living in my house now, in my kitchen.'

The guy twisted another loop of gum round his finger but it was pulled too thin. It snapped and fell to his T-shirt, like a rope bridge slamming against a cliff.

'Better get back to it,' he said, stuffing the gum back into his mouth.

Hannah finished her drink, took one last look around and headed outside, in the direction of the alley.

In court they'd shown CCTV of John leaving the bar over and over, so she knew the route well. Cross the street at the traffic lights, then keep going another three to four hundred metres until the alley appeared on the right.

It had been assumed that John had been headed toward Liverpool Street to get the Tube home but if Jem was telling the truth, and he had been on his way to meet someone, then his direction of travel could have been a red herring; maybe he was going somewhere else entirely?

The CCTV had been a huge part of the prosecution's case against Jem but his lawyer had got them to concede that they didn't have definitive coverage of the entrance to the alleyway. There were gaps: a small area to the right of the opening and a patch a few metres from the left side. In theory, someone other than Jem could have got in or out, but footage from the other parts of the pavement suggested this was highly unlikely. Besides, the presence of Jem's DNA on the murder weapon was damning. His lawyer could have nit-picked all she liked. It would have made no difference.

She reached the opening to the alley and stopped, trying to summon the courage to move forward. The air was saturated with urine and rice-flecked takeaway cartons littered the floor. Above she could hear the pneumatic squeal of drills and the rhythmic thump of a hammer, hard at work in the carcass of a building that already reached six storeys high.

John had died here in the dark, alone and frightened.

Grabbing her amber pendant for comfort, she kicked the takeaway cartons into the street and began walking the alley's perimeter. The width of a car, it stretched a hundred metres back and was used primarily by local businesses to store waste-bins. John had been found halfway down, lying on his front.

Again, she knew the chance of the police failing to spot some hidden doorway was ridiculous, but she checked anyway. The walls were solid, a combination of brick and concrete, and reached at least twenty feet high. Beyond them were the walls of other buildings, a mix of old and new. A stretch of pebble-dash to her right was branded with a ghost sign for Bovril, yellow capital letters on a faded blue background.

She videoed the whole scene on her phone, lifting it high and low so as to cover every possible angle, and then, after lapping the alley once more, she headed back onto the street.

She looked left and right, trying to get her bearings, and was about to set off toward the Tube when she saw someone who made her pause. Directly opposite her, on the other side of the road, was the guy from the bar. Leant against a stack of hire bikes, he was talking on the phone, another length of chewing gum wrapped round his finger.

It made no sense for him to have followed her here. It must be coincidence.

She stared directly at him but he didn't flinch. The sunglasses made it hard to tell whether he was looking at her or at some other random point.

She decided she was being paranoid and set off at pace toward Liverpool Street. But when she turned round to check she saw he'd stepped away from the bikes and was now facing toward her, his sunglasses focused squarely on her progress. She picked up speed, walking faster and faster, and then she was running. Pneumatic drills pealed through the air, drowning out her footsteps with their din.

Jem

'Abracadabra!'

A small boy stands in the doorway holding a baguette. He snaps it toward me like a wand and the bread breaks in two. The top half falls and hangs limp in the plastic.

The social worker pushes me forward and I flinch. My back is almost healed but still sore to touch.

'Jem, this is Lucas.' She holds my bag in the air, shows it to him. 'Lucas, Jem has come to stay for a while.'

Lucas laughs and turns on his heel, the fractured baguette bouncing at his side.

A woman and a man appear. The man is wiping his hands with a tea towel.

They look at me and smile. 'We didn't hear the door.'

'Mr Tarker,' says the social worker. She nods at the woman. 'Mrs Tarker.'

Mrs Tarker holds out her hand, palm flat.

'Would you like to see your room?' Her chin, cheeks, forehead – even her earlobes – are covered with freckles, her reddy-brown hair a coarse bob. 'We have bunk beds.'

When I don't reply we go inside to the living room. The social worker chats to Mr and Mrs Tarker about our journey.

The house is warm and through the doorway that leads to the kitchen I can see a pan steaming on the hob and a bowl of fruit. The apples are shiny, the bananas yellow.

I wonder where Mum is, what she's doing. If she's thinking of me.

Lucas reappears, a chunk of baguette in his mouth. He gnashes his teeth against the dough and white crumbs fall to the carpet like snow. He's much younger than me, maybe four or five, and his face is round with puppy fat, his hair the same reddy-brown as his mum's.

He lifts his hand and I think he's going to perform another imaginary magic trick but then I see he's torn a piece of bread for me. I stuff the lot in my mouth and he gives me a thumbs-up.

For the first time today I smile.

'Allakazam!' he says and toddles back to the kitchen for more.

Hannah

It was an hour from King's Cross to Cambridge. Hannah got off the train and made her way out to the taxi rank.

Roddy Blessop. Forty-two years old.

John's browser history showed he'd searched for his funeral announcement on seventeen different occasions.

Why?

She didn't have much to go on, just the man's name and St Laurence's, the Catholic church where his funeral had taken place. She hoped it would be enough.

The car crept along Milton Road, past streets crumbed with fallen leaves and pavements flaky with dust. The university town was cooler than London but the air was still toffee-thick and people moved through it slowly.

Hannah hadn't been inside a church since John's funeral and as they neared their destination she thought back to that day and how it had marked a watershed.

She'd once moved through the world freely. Put one foot in front of the other and just expected the ground to be there. She'd go to a wedding and assume the marriage would last, she'd hear about a friend's pregnancy and start talking baby names, she'd go on holiday and have no doubt the plane would land in one piece. After John was taken from her though it was like she'd had a membrane of skin removed, like she could see and feel life and its random horrors more truly, no longer oblivious to the tragedy waiting round every corner. She'd see a mother

walking her kids home from school and imagine a car mount-
ing the pavement, crushing them against the wall, she'd look
at a house with a fairy-lighted tree in the window and see the
plug overheat, the sparks turning the place to ash. She'd refuse
invites to baby showers, scared the event was a jinx, hubris she
wanted no part of.

In the end, seeing the world through that filter became too
overwhelming. She'd had to find a way to lock it down and separated from reality, just a little, imagine herself as a pond-skater,
gliding across the surface, able to observe everything going on
beneath the water but never getting wet.

It had made life more bearable but it had also made her less.

Had made her life less.

She arrived at the church to find the priest locking the her-
ringbone door. The entrance was sheltered by a wooden porch
and, seeing her, he stepped out from under it, into the light.

'Mass was at twelve thirty,' he said, smiling kindly.

'No.' She stopped, not sure how to explain. 'Last year,' she
gestured at the church's modern red brick. 'There was a funeral.'

The priest half-closed his eyes, squinting against the harsh
light.

'We have many funerals sadly, but also many happy occasions.'
His tone was benign but wary. 'Weddings, christenings, first holy
communion.' He wasn't sure of her, what she wanted, and reciting the list seemed to be a way of buying himself time.

'It was in December,' she said, angling her body so that his
face was shielded from the sun. 'Roddy Blessop?'

'Ah.' He pocketed the keys in his cassock. 'Sad business.'

'This is going to sound weird,' said Hannah, 'but my husband,
he was a Met detective. Earlier this year he was killed.'

At this the priest seemed to relax. He rocked back on his heels and once again found himself back in the sun's firing line.

'He'd looked at Mr Blessop's death notice online,' she went on, 'many times. I'm trying to find out why.'

The priest nodded, now squinting so hard his eyes were almost sealed shut.

'Maybe they were colleagues?' said the clergyman. 'Roddy was also a detective. Cambridgeshire police.'

Jem

Later, the social worker has gone and Mr and Mrs Tarker are in the kitchen, preparing dinner. Lucas is on the floor, watching TV, one sock on, one sock off.

I sit on the edge of the sofa and think about Mum. I want her to be worried about me, to miss me, but I know that she won't, not for a while anyway.

The sofa is full of cushions and a blanket sits folded on one arm. It's cosy, the air fogged with simmering Bolognese.

I don't want to like it here.

I get up and skirt my way around the edges of the room. A shelving unit stacked with books and board games sits next to an armchair and an airer, heavy with wet clothes, hugs the radiator.

Lucas looks away from the film, observing my progress.

'How old are you?' he says, swinging his feet back and forward.

'Ten.'

'I'm four. In one month I'll be five.' He inserts a finger into his right nostril and begins to dig. 'I'm in reception. My teacher is called Miss Yewande.'

School.

Come Monday I'll have to start again.

I continue my circuit. I want to take a closer look at the picture over the fireplace. It's a black and white print of an old-fashioned-looking woman in a white dress floating horizontal in mid-air. A man in a suit stands behind her, hands outstretched. It seems like he has pulled her off the floor with invisible strings and is using *all his might to keep her hovering. I move forward and my knee bashes against something solid.*

I look down and see a black case with steel edges. Tucked between the recliner and the lamp, it's like an oversized briefcase and has silver stars stuck to its edges. Blue glitter smears each corner.

I kneel down and run my finger across the stars. It doesn't fit with the rest of the room. It's solid, dense, like a rock.

I smooth my hand across the top and down the side. My pinkie snags against a lever, inset into the bottom right corner of the case. Without thinking, I press down.

The top lid of the case springs up and bashes my chin. I fall back in shock.

Lucas is at my side in an instant.

'Don't cry,' he says, taking my hand.

I look back at the case, now standing tall, the top half forming a kind of small table. Silk handkerchiefs and playing cards litter the carpet.

I look toward the kitchen, checking they haven't noticed. I don't want to get in trouble on my first day.

'Help me,' I say trying to stuff everything back inside. Lucas does as I say, his chubby hands bunching the cards into the gaps at the bottom.

I'm fiddling with the lever, trying to get the case to retract, when Mr Tarker enters the room.

'What are you doing?'

My mouth opens and closes. Just tell the truth. That's what the social worker said. Tell the truth and nothing can go wrong.

But now looking at Mr Tarker's face I'm not so sure.

Lucas steps forward and places his stumpy body between me and the case.

'It was my fault Daddy,' he says, pushing his socked foot against his inner calf. 'I wanted to show him your magic.'

Mr Tarker looks from me to him, unconvinced.

In the intervening silence Lucas manages to inch off the sock and, with a little shake, discards it on the carpet. He stands there barefoot, his nostril caked with drying bogey, and stares until finally Mr Tarker turns back to the kitchen.

'Spaghetti will be ready in five minutes,' he says. 'Both of you, go wash your hands.'

Hannah

That night, Hannah sat at the kitchen table. Balanced on her finger was the gold SIM card the plumber had found. She examined it up close. It might have sustained too much damage. On the other hand.

Follow through on every lead, no matter how ordinary or extraordinary. That's what John had always said.

On her way home from Cambridge she'd done two things: emailed her contact at COPS (Care Of Police Survivors) and asked if they could pass on a message to Roddy Blessop's widow requesting she get in touch (it was standard practice for the charity to reach out to the partner of a police officer after their death); and two, bought a pay-as-you-go mobile.

Now she placed the SIM inside the phone and turned it on.

Jem was engrossed in the copy of *All The Light We Cannot See* she'd bought for him that day in Primrose Hill and paid her no attention.

The phone screen lit up and began searching for a signal. She had no idea if the card had belonged to John or what need he might have had for a second phone but she couldn't figure out where else it could have come from – who other than he might have been in the house and thrown it down the waste disposal?

Jem's assertion that John had been on his way to meet a lover flicked back into her head. She planned to call any and all of the numbers recorded on the card. What would she do if a woman were to answer?

Finally, the signal stabilised and she was able to access the log. There were no texts to speak of but there were two numbers listed. Both mobiles had been called multiple times a day over a period of months. The last registered call had been made in February, four weeks before John's murder.

She brought up the number and dialled.

The line was dead.

She moved onto the second number. This time the phone connected.

She braced, willing someone to pick up or at the very least for it to go through to voicemail. It rang and rang.

After a few more tries she hung up.

She sat there in the quiet, the silence punctuated by the occasional papery lisp as Jem turned a page, then went to the countertop and opened one of the Tupperwares. Before going into town this morning she'd experimented with a new fondant and made a batch of cupcakes each with a tiny figure from history on top. Looking down she saw Frida Kahlo sitting alongside Martin Luther King, Emmeline Pankhurst and Alan Turing. She selected the most intricate of the batch – a particularly accurate rendering of Winston Churchill – and took it over to the cell.

'I went to Shoreditch today,' she said, handing it to him through the bars. 'To Fleece, where you used to work.'

'You did?' He accepted the cake dozily, his brain still straddled between the book and the real world.

'I needed to see it for myself.' She wanted to tell him what she'd uncovered so far – that there was merit to the things he claimed to have overheard John say that night – but she was still scared this was some awful set-up on his part, that he was playing her, out of cruelty or because he thought it might make his life easier somehow. 'I talked to the guy behind the bar.'

Jem swung his feet off the bed and came to stand by the cell bars

'Don't go there again,' he said, then stopped. When he spoke next his words were measured, but he couldn't shake off his initial urgency and it lingered like an echo. 'Or, if you do, take someone with you.'

'Nothing happened,' she said, thinking of the way the bartender had watched her from the other side of the street.

'Just promise me?' he said, his voice strained.

'OK,' she said, 'I promise.'

She waited for him to sit back down before continuing with the next part of her story.

'I also went to the alley.'

Jem looked to the floor.

'I know what you said in court, but I want you to tell me again. That night. What happened?'

He blinked slowly and took a breath, as if to prepare himself.

'Look, I don't know how to prove to you or anyone that I didn't do it.' He gestured at the cell. 'Obviously, or I wouldn't be here. All I can say is I have no history of violence, I've never laid a finger on anyone and I never would.'

His face was so open, his eyes so kind, and yet Hannah was sure he was holding back, that there was something he wasn't saying.

'It's late.' She got to her feet. 'Want anything before I turn in?'

'I'm good.'

She switched off the light and headed up, only to notice her wedding picture on the staircase wall. The frame was listing to one side, the glass cracked. She'd had no idea it was damaged or when it might have happened. She was trying to right it when the phone rang. On reflex she reached for her mobile inside her jeans pocket, but then she realised – it wasn't her phone it was the pay-as-you-go. She'd left it on the kitchen table. Its screen glowed in the dark, a tiny square of green. She retraced her steps and picked it up.

'Hello?'

There was the sound of machinery, the wail of a truck reversing, then a man spoke.

'Who is this,' he said, his voice mired with catarrh, 'and how do you have this number?'

She took a breath. 'My husband John, I found a SIM I think belonged to him.' Before continuing, she glanced at Jem, worried he was listening in, but he had his back turned and seemed to be focused on adjusting his ear plugs. He'd told her they were noise cancelling. 'Did you know him?'

The man coughed and drew the phone away from his mouth. She heard him hack, but he couldn't seem to clear his throat of the obstruction.

'This SIM,' he said once he was finished. 'Destroy it.'

'What, why?' She scrambled to get a hold on the situation. 'Who are you? Did you know John?'

'I know he had a golden reputation. A top-notch copper, loved and respected by all.' He said the last sentence in a pretend hoity-toity accent, like he was reading from a report. 'I also know that if you want that reputation to remain intact you need to get rid of any evidence to the contrary.'

'Who are you?' she said, trying again.

'I made sure John did what we needed him to do and then I made sure he got paid.'

'Paid?'

'John was on the take,' he said. His words had a flint to them now. Nasty and sharp. 'He was dirty, dirty as fuck.' He coughed again, a thick, liquid sound that turned Hannah's stomach.

'Why are you telling me this?'

'The fact you bothered to call this number. It means you're digging around in our business.' Again, he moved the phone away from his mouth and hacked. This time she heard him spit. 'Now you know. Doing that is not in your interest, not in your *husband's* interest.' Another wail of a truck in the background and the hiss of brakes being applied. 'John was in deep. It's no wonder he ended up dead.'

Hannah went to protest, wanting to defend her husband's honour, to ask more questions, but before she could say another word the man ended the call. She dropped the phone from her ear and balanced the device on the flat of her palm, staring at it for a moment, before tossing it down onto the table. Clatter, thud.

Hannah was woken by knocking. Rat-a-tats that morphed into a rhythmic thud. She checked the time and saw it was already gone ten.

Downstairs she opened the door to find Mr Dalgleish, clipboard in hand.

'Good morning.' He fished a monogrammed hanky from his pocket, the initials W.D. embroidered on the corner in navy copperplate, and wiped his nose.

Hannah blinked, trying to remember why he was here.

'Inmate shower,' he said before she could ask. He nodded toward the hall. 'Shall we?'

He stepped inside, his movements slow. He was always weaker in the days following a chemo session but this was different; he seemed smaller somehow, his complexion like dishwater.

She was about to shut the door when Aisling appeared at the gate.

'Morning!' Clutching coffees and pastries, she bundled down the path toward Hannah, her curls kept in check by a ruby hairband. 'You OK?' Her movements were stuttery, her voice high and brittle. 'I came as soon as I could.'

After the phone call last night Hannah had been too wired to sleep and in the early hours had texted Aisling asking to see her. She wanted to tell her friend what she'd learned, to seek her advice.

'It's about John.'

'Oh?'

'I'll tell you inside.'

Crossing the threshold, Hannah almost tripped over a blur of grey sneaking past her ankles. Poobah. She looked up to see Kiki Masters following in his wake.

'I don't know why he's so intent on getting into your house,' she said, scowling. She fished a packet of Dreamies from her pocket and shook it vigorously until Poobah advanced cautiously back onto the path, then she grabbed him and tucked him under her arm. 'Maybe he's attracted to some kind of smell? How often do you empty your bins?'

Before Hannah could reply Aisling closed the door in Kiki's face and Hannah remembered how Poobah had performed the exact same escape-artist routine through Aisling's ankles the morning she learned John had died.

Aisling had always shown up at random hours – whenever she had a free spot in between clients she'd pop round for caffeine and a gossip – but that day she'd seemed to have a sixth sense that Hannah would be needing her and had arrived on her doorstep half an hour before the police had knocked with the news.

She'd been wired then too, unable to sit still, her hands flitting from her mouth to her ears to her neck, like she was searching for something. It was the same when she'd told Hannah she wouldn't be able to help her with the cake business anymore. She'd held the news in like a breath she was too scared to exhale.

Hannah had been gutted but it turned out to be exactly what their friendship needed. In the months that led up to the break they'd started bickering, just the odd snip at the start or end of the day, and Hannah had noticed the occasional eye-roll whenever she'd asked Aisling to do something she didn't want to do. Afterward, things had got better; they'd gone back to relishing each other's company, to nights out at the cinema and walks on the Heath and comfort-scrolling on the sofa together, glasses of wine in hand.

They were about to head down to the kitchen when Jem and Mr Dalgleish appeared, on their way up to the bathroom, clutching a towel and toiletries.

This was Aisling's first time at the house since Jem's arrival and seeing him there she stiffened. A strange mix of embarrassed and scared, she reminded Hannah of someone bumping into an ex after a nasty break-up.

Mr Dalgleish stopped and put out his hand, holding Jem in place to let her pass, but Aisling didn't move. He waited a few more seconds and then, when she still didn't budge, he motioned for Jem to squeeze past her toward the stairs. Then he did the same.

It had been four days since Jem's last shower and although he'd been strip-washing his upper half he'd failed to keep his natural scent at bay. Aisling wrinkled her nose in disgust.

'As always, you'll have twenty minutes to bathe and get dressed,' said Mr Dalgliesh, reciting his usual spiel. 'Then Hannah will return you to your cell.' Jem moved slowly, his eyes darting from the living room to the ceiling to the front door, like he was committing the upper geography of the house to memory. 'If you are not finished after twenty minutes I'll knock and give you a verbal warning, if another minute passes and you are still not ready I will come inside.' They reached the landing. 'I'll have my hand on this button the whole time, so don't try anything.'

Prisoners were allowed two showers a week, both of which were supervised by the DLO. Upon learning this Hannah had been appalled but when she'd queried it with Mr Dalgliesh he'd pointed out that it was exactly the same allocation they'd had in communal jails. 'People just notice it more,' he'd said with a smirk, 'when it's happening right under their nose.'

Her bathroom had been made inmate-proof at the same time as they'd installed the cell. Bars were placed on the outside window and any objects that could be used or modified into weapons had been removed or replaced to ensure Jem could not use them to harm himself or others.

Hannah waited until she heard the door shut and the hum of the shower before continuing down to the kitchen.

'Had a slightly paranoid journey here,' said Aisling as they hit the stairs. 'Yesterday I saw that guy we saved. The dormouse.'

'The one from the Heath?'

'Him.'

'You know Hampstead. Small place.'

'That's just it, I was in Walthamstow, seeing a client.'

Hannah heard the worry in her voice.

'You think he's following you? How would he even know who you are?'

'He wouldn't,' said Aisling, once they were sitting at the table. She shook her head, as if to dismiss the thought. 'Like I said, I'm being paranoid.'

She pulled up her sleeve to scratch her elbow and Hannah caught a glimpse of the balloon tattoo on her bicep. It was supposed to have been a Forever Friends bear but she'd found the pain so unbearable she'd made them stop and turn it into something else that wouldn't take as long. Hannah remembered a story she'd heard about a girl getting her best friend's name tattooed on her ankle. At the time she'd thought it extreme, ridiculous almost, but that had been before she'd met Aisling. Now it seemed like an entirely reasonable thing to do.

'Last night when you texted me,' said Aisling, 'what happened? You said it was something about John?'

'This is going to sound mad,' said Hannah, taking a sip of coffee. 'But it turns out he had a secret phone.'

'What?' Aisling said, her face paling. 'Seriously?'

'I know you didn't think there was anything to the stuff I told you, about Marzipan Rain and that guy John was looking into, but I kept digging.' Hannah gave her a summary of everything that had happened in the last few days. Her trip to Cambridge and how she'd used the SIM the plumber found in the waste disposal.

'There's more to John's death than everyone realises, I'm sure of it.' She took a breath. 'And I know I haven't lived with Jem long, but I don't think he would hurt anyone.'

Aisling was quiet then. She studied Hannah carefully.

'You like him.'

'What?' The blush hit her hard. She could feel the heat coming off her neck. 'Don't be ridiculous.' She felt for her pendant and pressed it against the skin, trying to cool it. 'I just want the right person punished, don't you?'

Aisling nodded, cowed.

'There were only two numbers on the SIM card,' said Hannah, continuing with her story. 'I called them both. One was dead and one rang out. Then the second number called me back.'

'Who was it? What did they say?'

Hannah remembered how her hands had fumbled with the device, how in her eagerness to answer she'd almost dropped it on the floor.

The words were hard to repeat.

'They said John was dirty,' she said, still smarting from the slur. 'That he'd been taking bribes.'

A clatter of footsteps on the stairs. They looked up to see Jem and Mr Dalgliesh returning to the kitchen. Jem's hair was wet, a towel round his neck. He'd shaved off his beard and his jawbone was sharp. As he walked by Hannah smelled the air and recoiled at the tang. Shower gel.

She hadn't realised how accustomed she'd grown to his own smell. How she only missed it now it was gone.

'They're wrong,' said Aisling, whispering so the others couldn't hear. She took Hannah's hands in hers and brought her face in close. 'John was a good man. The best.'

'He was,' said Hannah, trying to match her friend's conviction. 'I keep trying to remember that.'

Jem

Hannah places the phone in the hatch and thumps upstairs, leaving me to it.

I could only hear one side of the call she received last night and so it made little sense, but she's been out of sorts ever since, banging around the house in a dazed huff.

I'm worried about her, what I've started. Doubt is good. I wanted doubt. A crack, a fissure. But this. I never expected her to go to the bar and although I've made her promise not to return I'm scared of where else she might end up, who she might talk to.

I lift out the phone and type in Kenzie's number. Alina won't help me anymore but maybe he will. He doesn't need to know the details. Just that my stuff needs to be moved and I can't do it because I'm stuck in here.

The dial tone is a low burr with long spaces in between. The noise you get when you call someone abroad.

He picks up after one ring.

'Hola.'

Kenzie never did become a dance music producer but he managed the next best thing. Club DJ. He spends most of the year in the Balearics, working the circuit, and although these days he has a paunch and much less hair he still dresses like a teenager in jeans that ride down his backside and oversize sport tees.

'Kenzie, it's Jem.'

'The convict.' He laughs. 'How's porridge? Remember to keep your back to the wall in the shower.'

Kenzie is one of the only people (apart from Alina) who didn't cut me off after I was charged. The cheerful, accepting philosophy he had as a kid has never changed. Kenzie viewed the trial and its outcome as just another bump in the road, something that could happen to any of us.

'Where are you?'

'I'm gigging in Ibiza, back in London on the thirtieth.'

October 30th. The day before Rita and Winston are within their rights to dump my stuff on the street. Not ideal, but it'll have to do.

'Feeling lonely? Want me to come visit?'

'I'm in a bit of a fix.' I tell him about my predicament. 'Can you help?'

'Course.' He coughs and I hear the rasp of a lighter followed by the high-pitched squeal that happens when someone sucks on a newly lit cigarette. 'Tell me what you need.'

I stay on the line while he opens his laptop and logs into my Roost account. It doesn't take him long to find me another space. An old airing cupboard in Stockwell. He reserves it for the day after he lands. He'll collect my stuff from Brixton and transport it there in a cab. I don't have much; it should all fit.

The phone beeps, warning me I have only two minutes left.

Stomping on the stairs. Hannah. She wants me to know she's coming.

'Thanks,' I say, trying to finish up. 'I'll find some way to repay the favour.'

'Any time,' he says, lighting up again, then laughing, 'and remember what I said about those showers.'

Hannah

Hannah stood outside Maraschino's front door holding three plastic boxes, one balanced on top of the other. Inside were samples, a variety of cupcake designs and flavours, for her to consider.

The woman from her last visit let her in.

'Maraschino had to go out,' she said, guiding her through to the kitchen. 'Last-minute gong bath.' She motioned to the table. 'She said she'll try them later.' She was in the same pink uniform and pristine white apron as before but, Hannah was curious to note, she now had a set of mini binoculars round her neck.

'Will she be back soon?' Hannah said, placing the boxes down. 'I'm happy to wait.' She wanted to take Maraschino through the samples in person; it was more likely to lead to a commission that way.

'She should be back around 2 p.m.'

Forty minutes from now.

'OK if I hang on?' she said. 'I promise not to get in your way.'

The woman laughed.

'Of course.' She motioned to the sofa in the orangery and offered her hand. 'I'm Jane.'

'Hannah.' They shook hands and she took a seat.

Jane hesitated. 'Aisling,' she said shyly. 'She mentioned you have a prisoner.'

Hannah nodded and prepared to accept the commiserations she was sure would follow but instead Jane beamed and moved closer, like she'd just discovered they were both fans of the same obscure podcast. Hannah saw a flash of gold near her neckline. A crucifix on a chain.

'Such a positive thing to do,' she said, gushing, 'commendable.' She inched nearer. 'A pensioner in our congregation, she said she was so lonely before her mugger came to stay. She helped him learn how to read and write. They became friends. Once his sentence was finished they both decided it would be best if he stayed on in the spare room as a lodger, just until he could get back on his feet. Last week he asked her to be godmother to his kid.' She smiled again and Hannah saw she had tiny, toddler-size teeth. 'Best thing that ever happened to her, to both of them.'

Hannah didn't know what to say and searched the room for a change of subject.

The glass ceiling offered a prime view of the crumbling mansion next door.

'It's so weird,' she said, nodding toward the shambling roof. 'Buying a pile like that and leaving it to rot.'

Jane fingered her crucifix, pulling it right and left on the chain.

'It's even crazier inside,' she said, eyes twinkling. 'Want to see?'

'What? How?' said Hannah. 'Do you have a key?'

'We don't need a key,' she said, moving toward the orangery door.

Hannah followed her out to the garden and over to a gap in the trees.

'I like to come here on my break.' She lifted a slat in the fence and motioned for Hannah to slide through. 'The garden is so overgrown, it attracts all kinds of birds. Last week, I saw a black redstart.'

Hannah looked again at the mini binoculars and remembered how Jane had been standing staring at the trees on her first visit.

She thought she'd been daydreaming but now she realised – she'd been looking at the wildlife.

They stepped out into a tangled wilderness. What had once been a vast lawn was now a meadow thick with wildflowers and dozing insects. Trees and bushes encroached from all sides, the garden walls strangled with ivy.

'This is nuts,' said Hannah, as a fox streaked across the meadow and disappeared into an explosion of privet in the bottom right corner.

'You haven't seen anything yet,' said Jane, heading toward the mansion.

A set of steps led down to the basement and a door crackled with green paint.

'How long has it been empty?' asked Hannah as Jane gave the door a shove.

'Twenty-five years. It was bought by the Saudi royal family for a million or so and then forgotten.'

'A million quid.'

'Pocket change to them.' Inside the air was dank, the walls peeling. 'They shipped their Bentleys here but never got round to the furniture. The cars are just sitting there in the garage.'

The skin of the house – the plaster covering the walls and ceilings – was mostly gone, exposing wooden rafters and dirty insulation.

'There are so many empty on this road. Has anyone ever moved back in?'

'One was sold last year but they didn't bother to renovate. It's much easier to tear the whole mess down and start again.'

They made their way up a set of stairs, through a door hanging askew from a single hinge, and came out into the mansion's entrance hall.

It was enormous, fifty feet wide and a hundred feet high, a giant rectangular window stretched above the front door. To their right was a staircase, its balustrade gilded with bird droppings. Every stair was lush with ferns, the leaves so shiny that Hannah found herself wanting to reach out and rub her thumb across their surface.

She took a step forward and something crunched underfoot. The floor was littered with pigeon skeletons and rubble from half-collapsed ceilings.

It was surprising how much damage *not* touching something could do.

'Want to see the bedrooms?'

Hannah nodded and they broached the staircase, pushing past the lurid foliage to get to the top.

They reached the first floor and Jane pulled her into a room with a giant chandelier.

'The master suite.'

Hannah edged past an arrangement of wooden crates resting against the wall. The words BULLET PROOF GLASS were scrawled on the side in black marker.

'Seriously?' said Hannah.

'I know, right?' said Jane, moving toward a huge window framed by ragged curtains, the pelmet ruched with moss. 'Where did they plan to install it? The living room?' She laughed. 'The toilet?'

Below they could see the garden and beyond it, the pond.

'That's my house,' said Hannah, pointing to the terrace on the other side of the water. 'There.'

'Where?' said Jane, lifting her binoculars.

'The one covered with ivy in the middle,' said Hannah, 'see?'

'Got it,' said Jane and clicked her tongue approvingly. She tilted the binoculars up a fraction and laughed. 'I see your husband.'

'Not possible,' said Hannah. 'You must be looking at the wrong one.'

'See for yourself.' She handed her the binoculars.

It took a few seconds to single out her property and then a few seconds more to focus. The view of the kitchen was blocked by the trees at the bottom of the garden but she could see into all the other windows. She scanned each one in turn. Nothing.

'You were definitely looking at the wrong house,' she said, about to hand the binoculars back, then stopped. It wasn't much, a flash of colour streaking across her bedroom, but it belonged to a figure. She was sure of it.

She wanted to shout, to blare a megaphone across the pond and order them out.

Her heart bolstered against her ribs.

'I need to call the police,' she said, picking her way back through the pigeon bones. 'I'm being burgled.'

Hannah called 999 while she was still in the mansion, and arrived home to find an officer waiting by the front gate.

'Thanks for coming,' said Hannah, looking past her toward the front door. She'd expected to find it open, the lock splintered. It was shut, no sign of forced entry.

'You reported a break-in?' said the policewoman, following her down the path.

'I was on the other side of the pond,' said Hannah, opening the door. 'I saw someone in my bedroom.'

Inside, they checked every room in turn but the house was empty and nothing seemed to be missing.

They saved the kitchen till last. Jem was lying on his bed, reading. Seeing the police officer, he sat up.

'Everything OK?'

Hannah went to the French doors and rattled them. Locked. The officer tugged at the cell door. It too was secure.

'Hear anything strange,' said Hannah, 'while I was out?'

Jem shook his head.

'And you haven't had your headphones in?'

'Nope.' He put down his book.

Hannah turned to the policewoman.

'My neighbour,' said Hannah, 'she keeps seeing someone hanging around. She thought they were sizing the place up. Maybe it was them?'

The officer unlocked the French doors, walked to the bottom of the garden and squinted across the pond.

'How far away was this house you were at?' she asked once Hannah had caught up.

'There,' said Hannah, pointing at the broken-down mansion. 'I was on the first floor.'

The policewoman looked from Queen's Crescent to Hannah's place and back again. Sunshine bounced against the windows, rippling the glass with light.

'Maybe it was a trick of the eye?' she said, returning inside. 'A false alarm.'

The Warlaby hotel, Clerkenwell. Hannah stepped into the lobby and swerved to miss a rich-looking couple, all hair and sunglasses, sashaying toward the street. She felt for the picture of John in her back jeans pocket and, dazzled by the bulbs lining the wall and ceiling, moved toward reception.

Piotr Nowak had said the Heppels, the family John had been looking into, owned and ran various hotels in the city. Piotr hadn't known whether this place belonged to them or not, but regardless, her phoning here and mentioning John's name had led directly to a call warning her off. Whatever stuff John had been involved in, that warning had left her sure of one thing: it had something to do with this place.

Today she wanted to find out what kind of reaction her turning up and asking questions in person might unleash.

She flashed John's picture to the staff behind the front desk, then the bellboy and concierge. None of them recognised him and although some reacted oddly she sensed their discomfort was more down to the weirdness of the situation – having a strange woman ask if they knew her deceased husband – than to them trying to mask any criminal connection.

She retreated to the bar, took a seat at one of the tables near the back, and placed John's picture down. His face looked out at her, his eyes kind, his white hair ruffled.

She still couldn't get her head around the idea of him as a dirty cop. He'd cared so deeply about the Met, what it stood for, his colleagues, Mickey. He would never betray that, no way. Reluctant to confide in anyone other than Aisling about the accusation – the thought of repeating those words to Rupert, false as they may be, felt like she would be sullying John's memory – she'd decided that she'd keep it to herself until she knew more.

A waiter came to take her order, a young guy with cropped neon-pink hair. She waggled John's picture in his face.

'Do you recognise him? His name was John, he was a detective? Do you remember him ever being here?'

The waiter took his time looking at the photograph and then handed it back to her.

'Sorry.'

'How about Slig? Know anyone by that name on the staff?' She was about to press him further when the lift dinged open and out stepped someone she knew.

Curls bouncing, she wore a black T-shirt and leggings, a chunky turquoise stone on a chain round her neck.

Aisling.

Hannah sprang to her feet, almost upending the table, and shouted her friend's name. Aisling startled and as they locked eyes her face fell. She stepped back a fraction, as though she was about to retreat into the lift, then seemed to decide against it and crossed the bar to where Hannah sat.

'What are you doing here?' she said when she reached her.

'I could ask you the same question,' laughed Hannah and they hugged.

'I cover the odd shift in the spa when they're short-staffed,' said Aisling as they drew apart. Her gaze twitched between the bar and reception.

Hannah patted the chair for her to sit down.

'This is the hotel I told you about, remember, the one Jem said John mentioned on the phone that night.' She gestured at the milling staff. 'I wanted to ask about him in person, see if I could find anyone he knew.'

'And,' Aisling tried to brush her curls out of her eyes and failed, 'any joy?'

'Nope. Nobody remembers him.' She paused. 'Or at least they say they don't.'

Aisling nodded and let out a breath.

'Ash, are you all right?' Hannah took her hand. 'You seem on edge.'

The question seemed to drain Aisling of her nervous energy and she collapsed back into the chair.

'On the way here I saw that bloke from the Heath again, the dormouse.' She shuddered. 'The whole time I've been on shift I've been scared he was downstairs waiting for me.' She nodded at the lift. 'When you called my name I freaked.'

Hannah squeezed her hand.

'You should go to the police.'

'And tell them what?' Her hands jittered around her throat. 'I don't even know his name.'

'Talk to Rupert. Maybe he could find out who he is, have a quiet word.' Hannah gathered her things. She'd learned nothing new by coming here, but it was another thing ticked off her list. Looking up, she saw Aisling was staring through the glass lobby to the street outside, her face ashen.

Hannah followed her gaze and soon located the source of her dismay.

The dormouse.

Leaning against a tree, he was wearing the same grey suit as the first time she'd seen him, his black eyes narrowed against the sun. Hannah was struck by his brazenness. He was so nearby and so obviously watching the hotel entrance. She thought again about the women with the taser. What had he done to deserve their wrath? No wonder Aisling was scared.

Hannah marched toward the doors, intending to go outside and confront him, but as he clocked her approach he stepped away from the tree and, pretending to check something on his phone, scurried off into the crowds. Still, Hannah stayed there by the glass a few minutes more, watching and waiting. When she was sure he wasn't coming back she returned to Aisling.

'What a creep,' she said and took her hand. 'We'll leave together. Make sure you get home OK.'

'Thank you for being my friend,' said Aisling as they headed for the lobby. 'I don't deserve you.'

Jem

'Boiled eggs for breakfast?'

I put down my book and pretend to think seriously about the question.

'Sounds good.' I pause and lift my eyebrows. 'And soldiers?'

A smile.

'You're a grown man.'

I shrug.

'They make the toast taste better. Everyone knows that.'

She rolls her eyes, fills a pan with water and sets it on the gas. Then she turns on Magic Radio. A power ballad fills the room. It's one of those songs that manage to tell an epic love story in three minutes. Hannah knows all the words and is singing along under her breath and popping bread in the toaster when the doorbell goes.

She runs upstairs and returns with the post and a parcel. She drops one of the envelopes in the hatch and sets to work opening the box of what look to be baking supplies.

I pull the drawer through and reach for the letter.

So far, the only correspondence I've had has been the edict from Roost telling me I need to move my stuff. Kenzie would never write and besides, he has no need, we sorted everything over the phone.

The handwriting is small and blockish, the biro smudged.

It's from Alina.

My heart lifts.

Maybe she's had a change of heart? Has she decided to help after all?

But when I open it I see she has bad news.

'Things have got worse,' she writes. 'There is less time than we thought. I realise things are hard, impossible even, but you need to act quicker. You've got till Christmas, then it's over.'

Christmas. Three months from now.

A clang. Hannah places a tray in the hatch. A boiled egg, its shell speckled brown, and two slices of buttered toast cut into soldiers.

'Breakfast is served,' she says and I see she's set an identical meal on the table so we can eat together. Her toast is also shaped into long thin slices, ready for dipping.

She sits and begins to eat.

'Who knew?' she says, once the first soldier is gone. 'They do taste better.'

We share a smile and I can tell she wants me to tease her some more, for us to banter back and forth, but I'm too floored by this latest development to say anything and so she shrinks down into her chair.

I take the tray to my table but my appetite is gone. I bite into the toast and chew. It's like swallowing sludge. I make sure to give Hannah a big thumbs-up and then I keep going until the shell is clean and my plate empty.

Hannah

Thursday evening and Hannah had invited Aisling over for shepherd's pie and Rioja. Jem made Aisling uncomfortable and so she'd asked if they could hang out in the living room while they waited for the pie to cook.

'Bad news,' said Aisling as Hannah handed her a goblet-size glass of wine. 'Maraschino has decided to go with someone else for the anniversary cake. She loved the samples but they decided to go for a more traditional approach.'

'Shame,' said Hannah, 'I could have done with the money.'

'Rich people.' Aisling shrugged and rolled her eyes. 'No taste.'

Hannah had put olives and focaccia out for them to nibble on and before she reached for a piece of bread she pricked her finger and placed the strip in the meter.

'Ever get sick of that?' said Aisling, spitting out an olive stone. She mimed her hands exploding out of her brain. Pow. 'The maths alone.'

'It's easier now,' said Hannah, holding up her clicker pen. She'd switched from bottled insulin and single-use syringes a year earlier. 'Still. Thirteen prick tests a day, plus the same number of injections. Then there's all the kit. Test meter, sharps bin, test strips, lancets.' A doctor had once told Hannah about a computer game that had been developed to help teenagers better understand their glucose levels. Based on the Tower Defense genre, it involved the player being holed up in a castle they had to defend from a constant onslaught of enemy fire while at the same time trying to earn enough points to maintain the castle's energy levels. Hannah had thought the analogy perfect but what had really struck her was the never-ending nature of the game, how, no matter how long or well you played, it could never be won or completed, how you had to remain vigilant forever. 'Then there's the fact that every-thing – sleep, stress, exercise, if I'm on my period – messes with my sugars.' Hannah took a breath. 'It's shit.'

'So,' said Aisling, flipping open her laptop. 'What shall we look at to soothe your troubled soul? Choose your poison. DILFS of Disneyland or Hot Dudes Reading?'

Hannah chose the Insta feed and they settled in, readying to oooh and aaah. There was a dad pushing a double stroller, wearing the same mouse ears as his toddler daughters, his fore-arms strong and tanned, there was the dad rocking a baby in a papoose, baseball cap on backwards, while he queued with his under-5 for the Teacups ride, there was a dad with his son on his shoulders, both transfixed by the Princess Parade.

The stream was mainly old favourites, but there was one pic-ture Hannah hadn't seen before. It showed a dad on the grass in front of the Magical Kingdom with his young daughter. Sitting cross-legged, he was holding her to him and their foreheads were pressed together, their smiles scrunched. The foliage behind them was a deep green, the flowers tropical.

There was something about the pose that took her breath away and for a moment she had to avert her gaze, to steel herself against the arm of the sofa.

She wondered if the wanting ever went away, if the need – so primal as to be obscene – would ever leave her.

She and John had tried for years to have kids. They'd gone it alone at first and then, when it became clear there was an issue, had consulted a doctor. Age wasn't thought to be a factor, Hannah had been thirty-one at the time, and while John was older at forty-six, his sperm count had been more than decent. Tests had been done and although there was nothing obviously wrong, there was a theory that Hannah's diabetes might be compromising her fertility. Four rounds of IVF had followed, the first funded by the NHS, the rest by John's work health insurance. Hannah remembered seeing one of the invoices the hospital sent out after each appointment, agog at the thousands involved.

The scans, blood draws and follicle tracking had been relentless. Every cycle had been disastrous in different ways but the moment that stuck in her mind was the morning a peppy Italian embryologist had called to tell them that none of the eggs they'd retrieved the previous day had fertilised. She'd been so cheerful, so bright, so oblivious to their devastation.

When, at the end of their fourth fruitless cycle, John had told her meekly that his health insurance would not fund any more treatment, she'd felt relieved.

Hannah decided to sit out the rest of this scroll session and was about to say as much, when she saw that Aisling had already done the same and was staring off to the right of the computer, her thumb autopiloting the mouse.

'Ash?'

She came to.

'What? Sorry.'

Clocking Hannah's distress, she flipped the laptop shut and they sat there in silence, Aisling nodding and gripping Hannah's hand – she understood how much Hannah had wanted a child and how, even if she were to meet someone new, her age, diabetes and fertility history meant it was probably never going to be. Then Hannah caught sight of the time and jumped to her feet.

'Food.' She motioned for Aisling to stay on the sofa. 'Stay put. I'll bring it up. We can eat off our laps.'

Downstairs, she was sorting cutlery for them both when the doorbell went. She went to run upstairs but Aisling was already in motion.

'I'll get it,' she shouted.

Hannah was serving up the pie, broccoli and carrots when Aisling appeared holding a white carrier bag like a prize, its top stapled together.

'Deliveroo?'

Jem looked up from his book and he and Aisling locked eyes. Then, like enemies who have realised they've both turned up at the same party, they turned away, each of them pretending the other person wasn't there.

'Must be a mistake,' said Hannah.

'Your name and address are on the ticket.' She ripped off the receipt and handed it to her. 'Look.'

There were three containers. Pad Thai, fried chicken and sushi. A folded piece of paper with her name on it was at the bottom of the bag. She fished it out and opened it. A few lines of blocky handwriting were printed inside.

> WARREN STREET TUBE
> TURN LEFT AT THE TOP OF THE ESCALATORS
> GET THERE BEFORE 8 AM
> ASK FOR JAMAL
> P.

Hannah reread it a few more times and then searched the bag in case there was anything else.

'What is it Han?'

'Not sure.'

She opened one of the containers and breathed in the buttermilk chicken. It was the same dish she'd seen Piotr cooking that day in the industrial kitchen. The note must be from him.

But what did it mean? He was telling her to go to Warren Street but when, tomorrow? Was someone going to be there waiting for her? Who was Jamal?

Aisling hovered by the stairs, food in hand, not wanting to be around Jem a moment longer than necessary, before retreating to the living room.

Hannah took his plate over to the hatch and slid it through, then returned to the counter, her mind fogged with questions.

When she finally brought a forkful of mince and potato to her mouth it was cold.

Jem

Moving day and I'm up at dawn. Hannah appears soon after.

I ask if I can have my phone call early and she agrees. I want to speak to Kenzie, make sure he's all set. This is too important to leave to chance.

The dial tone is the same low burr as before. I hold my breath. He was supposed to fly in from Ibiza yesterday.

'Hola?' He sounds groggy, like I've woken him.

'Kenzie.' I breathe, my words a jumbled rush. 'It's Jem.'

'Jem.' He perks up.

'Where are you?'

He pauses and in that moment I know. He's not coming.

'About that.' He grunts and I imagine him hauling himself upright. 'Something came up. Hotel gig. I'll be there tomorrow for sure.'

'You said you could do it.' My voice is shrill. 'It's organised.'

'Calm down. It's one day. Your stuff will be fine.'

I try to contain my panic but all I can think about is my things being left on the pavement, my photo albums kicked around by the wind, my microwave looted by strangers, passers-by mooching through my books.

'If someone isn't there by noon they're going to chuck everything out.'

I hang up and phone Alina, only to end the call after two rings. There's no point. She won't help and, even if she did, she might be followed. I don't want to put her at that kind of risk.

I look around, at the bars, at my cage.

Twenty years of this, and for nothing.

I'm scrabbling for a solution when Hannah slides breakfast through the hatch.

'Everything OK?'

I'm too at sea to pretend.

'My stuff, it's in storage but the lease has run out.' I relay the information calmly but inside I feel like I'm in a collapsing building, slowly smothered by rubble. 'A friend organised another place for me online. They were supposed to move everything today but they've let me down at the last minute. If no one shows up they've every right to bin it all.'

Hannah chews on a corner of toast, thinking.

'Where's the storage space?'

'A house, Brixton. The new place is in Stockwell, ten minutes away.'

'What time?'

'Deadline is midday.'

She finishes the toast and slaps her hand free of crumbs.

'I could do it?'

'What? No.' I speak without thinking, wrong-footed by her kindness. What if she looks inside the boxes, what if she sees? Then I stop. I'm being ridiculous. Even if she saw it, she wouldn't understand. 'I mean,' I say, trying to back-pedal. 'You'd do that?'

She smiles.

'I would.'

Hannah

Hannah emerged from Warren Street tube and turned left, toward Marylebone Road, as the note had instructed.

She wasn't sure what she was looking for: a shop, a cafe?

She soon discovered this stretch of pavement had neither. The few units that were here were either long shuttered, rusty cans and rotten leaves wedged against their doorways, or specialist outlets with bizarre opening hours.

She continued forward past the bus stop, the roar of traffic like the sea on a stormy day. London was already baking hot but the tall buildings on either side of the road had turned this strip of pavement into a wind tunnel. Hannah crossed her arms over her chest, trying to keep warm, her vest and thin cotton maxi skirt no match for the chilly squall.

She had a busy day ahead. Once she was done here she needed to go to Mornington Crescent to collect stock from Rahnak, the woman who supplied her with the delicate hand-stitched silk flowers she liked to use on wedding cakes (she felt for the envelope in her bag; Rahnak operated on a cash-only basis) and from there to Brixton, to pick up Jem's things.

She thought about the look on his face when she'd offered to help. He'd been relieved but not entirely so – a tiny wrinkle in his chin, a pressing of the mouth – the prospect of her handling his stuff worried him. She remembered the day he'd arrived, the way she'd purposely slammed his custody bag onto the table, breaking something inside, and was hit by a rush of shame.

Ahead she could see an overhang, a long concrete lip that fed out from an office building and provided shelter for twenty or thirty people sleeping rough.

Is this where Piotr had meant for her to go?

Moving closer she saw that each sleeping area was clearly demarcated by a cardboard box, folded and shaped into a kind of futon, and that instead of sleeping bags, everyone had white double duvets. Kerosene stoves, bottles of water, half-eaten packets of croissants and large wheelie suitcases sat next to their beds. One man had an alarm clock by his pillow.

Most of the camp were sleeping soundly despite the traffic and chattering pedestrians, but one person was awake, a woman. Sitting with her back against the wall, she'd wrapped the duvet around the lower part of her body and was watching the world go by, smoking.

Hannah came to stand at the foot of her bed.

'Sorry to intrude,' she shouted, competing against the blare of cars.

The woman put out her cigarette and drew the duvet up to her chin. Her face was stained orange by the sun, her eyes black.

'We are not moving,' she said. Her accent was Baltic, her voice low. 'We don't want to go to your shelter or your church, we stay here.'

The couple in the next bed along stirred, the man cricking his eyes to the morning.

'I'm not from a charity,' said Hannah. 'I'm looking for some-one. Jamal? Do you know him?'

The woman said nothing but Hannah saw how her eyes flicked toward the duvet at the farthermost part of the row.

'We can't help you,' said the man in the next bed, his eyes now wide open. 'Fuck off.'

But Hannah was already on her way.

The edge of the camp was bleak. Those who slept here were buffeted by the worst of the wind and vulnerable to everything from rain to those who might want to steal from them while they slept. The final bed was occupied by a woman wearing a puffa jacket zipped to her chin and a paisley scarf in her hair. She looked no more than twenty. As Hannah approached she reached for something and sat bolt upright, a screwdriver in hand.

'Sorry,' said Hannah, taking a step back. 'Didn't mean to frighten you.'

The woman eyed Hannah's clothes and bag and, reassured, dropped the screwdriver on the bed.

'I'm looking for someone,' said Hannah. 'Jamal?'

'Jamal? Don't know anyone with that name,' she said and shook her head, but the slight change in her face, a breeze rippling across a pond, told Hannah otherwise.

'My husband,' said Hannah. 'He was killed. I was told Jamal might know something about the person that did it.' She got out a business card. 'Please, if you see him, ask him to call.'

As the woman took it from her the duvet slipped, exposing her rounded belly.

Hannah startled.

'How many months?'

A flicker of shame.

'Seven.'

Hannah looked at the pavement next to where the woman lay, the concrete pocked with gum, and wondered what she'd do, where she'd sleep, once she'd given birth.

She felt for the envelope of cash in her bag. Rahnak would have to wait.

'For the baby,' she said and handed it to her.

The woman hesitated, caught off guard, then snatched it and pushed it inside her jacket.

Hannah went to walk away.

'Jamal was a cleaner,' she shouted after her. She gestured at the row. 'We all are. But now he doesn't answer his phone, no one knows where he is.' She shrugged. 'Even if I wanted to, I couldn't ask him to call.'

More people were awake now. They sat up in their beds, heads craned toward the intruder at the end of the row.

'You are making everyone nervous,' said the woman. 'They see me talking to you and they won't trust me. I am already at the edge of the group. Please go.'

Jem

It's just before 2 p.m. when I hear the key in the front door. I get to my feet, ready to greet her, ready to thank her.

Minutes pass and she has still not appeared.

I strain my ears and catch what sound like footsteps and the occasional metallic clank. Then she says something I can't make out and the door slams shut.

Quick thuds on the stairs and she's there.

'That was eventful,' she says, going to the sink for a glass of water. She is red-faced and sweaty, hair tied back, but she doesn't seem concerned; if anything she's chipper. A spring in her step.

'Were Rita and Winston difficult?' I'm not sure if she's talking about what happened at Warren Street or with the move. 'They can be grumpy.'

'They were fine,' she says gulping the water down in one. 'It was the new place that was the problem.' She refills her glass. 'They wouldn't let me in. Said they'd messaged you last night to say they'd changed their mind, that your money would be refunded.'

I grip the steel bars and squeeze. Kenzie should have been on top of this, he had access to the account, to my messages.

'So what happened to my stuff?'

'I didn't know what else to do, so I brought it here.'

'Here?' The word is more of an accusation than a question. 'In this house?'

Hannah cocks her head to one side, her expression flitting from confused to insulted and back again. She thought she'd done me a favour and she has, her intentions were good, but she's also put us both in danger.

'I'll put the boxes in the spare room for now,' she says coolly, 'then I'll move them into the loft.'

I see a chance and take it.

'Or you could put them with my custody bag,' I say, trying to keep my voice light, 'store all my things in the one place?'

'More like I'd have to put the bag with them,' she says, mooching through the fridge. 'It's in the old airing cupboard at the top of the stairs.' She emerges with a packet of sliced chicken and a punnet of tomatoes. 'Not exactly roomy.' She dumps the food on the counter. 'Enough storage chat for one day. You ready for lunch?'

Hannah

Early evening Wednesday, Jem's phone time. Hannah left the device in the hatch and retreated to the living room. She'd just hit the top stair when she heard him hang up. This was usual – from what she could tell there'd only been two occasions on which he'd actually talked to someone – still, until now, she'd always made sure to keep her distance for the full hour in case he decided to use his minutes on someone else. Tonight though, as soon as she heard the hatch clank she came back down. He'd been living with her for nearly two months and she was curious as to why he rarely spoke to anyone, why his visitors were so few and far between.

Turning the corner into the kitchen she realised that, when it came to a spontaneous getting-to-know-you chat, she couldn't have picked a more inappropriate moment. He sat on the bed, head in hands; she'd never seen him with his guard so down.

It was a private moment, intensely so.

She turned round, hoping to double back before he realised she was there. She wasn't quick enough.

'Hannah?'

'Sorry. Didn't mean to intrude. I'll go.'

'No.' His response was immediate, his voice thick with some emotion she couldn't place. 'Please, I don't want to be alone.'

Hannah came and stood by the cell. Her instinct was to ask what was bothering him, to tell him he could confide in her, that she was here to listen, but she sensed that to acknowledge his upset would be to embarrass him. That he would close off completely.

She grabbed a bottle of red from the rack. She decided that, if she wanted to put him at ease, her best bet would be to change tack completely.

'So.' She unscrewed the lid, poured two glasses and handed one to him through the bars. 'Your name. Who was the Harper Lee fan?'

Jem took a few beats to catch up. Then, as he understood what she was doing, he smiled, grateful.

'Mum,' he said, accepting the drink. 'She taught literature.'

They both took a sip of wine.

'Funny,' said Hannah, cocking her head left and right as if she was marking him for size, 'you seem more like a Scout to me.'

Jem laughed and then, as the break in tension rolled over him, threw back his head and laughed some more.

Hannah pulled a chair close.

'Where did she teach?'

'Anywhere that would have her.' He pressed his lips against the outer side of the goblet, as if in a kiss. 'Sixth form, university. She was bipolar, never stayed in any one place too long.'

'And your dad?'

Jem shrugged.

'Off the scene before I was born. Mum was vague on the details.'

They drank their wine in silence.

'I can't be bothered to cook tonight,' said Hannah once she'd drained her glass. 'Shall we order in? Pizza or Indian?'

Jem laughed, not sure if this was another joke, and then again once he realised she was serious.

'Either.'

'Indian it is. Do you like poppadoms? Because if you do I'm going to order double.'

She went to the drawers, rifling for menus, and had just found the one she was looking for when her phone rang. It wasn't a number she recognised.

'You asked me to let you know if I heard from Jamal,' said a woman. In the background Hannah could hear the roar of traffic. 'He called this morning, asking about the baby.' She took a slow breath, like she was still weighing up whether or not to share what she'd learned. 'Afterward I googled the number he'd called from.' Her voice was edged with triumph now, delighted at her ingenuity. 'It was for a hotel.'

Parade sat on the outer reaches of Margate's Marine Drive. Its Victorian frontage and stained-glass windows were still intact, the woodwork painted racing green. The woman said Jamal had called her from a number that matched this hotel and that, although he wouldn't tell her as much, she was sure this must be his new place of employ.

Hannah looked to the beach twinkling with broken glass, sniffed and covered her nose. The tide was going out and the air was ripe with rotten seaweed. For a brief moment she thought she saw a person in the water but when she looked again she realised it was the head and shoulders of an Antony Gormley, the iron statue facing out to sea.

She pushed against the hotel's swing door and flinched at a loud, electronic hee-haw above her head. An alarm. The noise was familiar, like an old radio jingle you're surprised to find you still know the words to. She was trying to figure out where she might have heard it before when the man behind reception said hello.

'Do you have a reservation?' Hunched over the computer, he was already swishing the mouse, ready to input her details.

The entrance area was all pristine white leather and sheep-skin, a large leather-bound guestbook on the counter. Looking closer though she saw that the floor was littered with dust balls and that a glass bowl of what she guessed were supposed to be crisp green apples was on the turn, the fruit mottled brown.

'I'm looking for someone that works here,' she said. 'Jamal?'

He withdrew his hand from the mouse and came to standing.

'That would be me,' he said slowly. His manner was still bright but there was a new strain to his voice, a pinch around the cheeks, like he wasn't sure whether to be wary or open to some wonderful impending surprise. His hair was cropped close to the scalp and Hannah noticed a long white scar lintelled above his right ear.

'I've been told you might know something about my husband's death,' she said, watching him carefully. 'He was a Met detective.'

His smile hardened.

'Can't help you.' His eyes went from the black CCTV orb above the door to the one behind the counter.

'Please,' she said. 'Tell me what you know and I'll leave you in peace.'

He crossed his arms, thinking.

'How did you find me?' he said eventually. Then he looked at her again, reassessing. 'Wait, are you the one who gave Martina money?'

'She needed it.'

His hand went to the scar above his ear, his fingers ley-lining back and forward across his skull. He seemed to be softening.

'Did you know him?' said Hannah, trying to capitalise on the moment. 'John?'

He looked again at the security camera.

'I need this job,' he said, pleading. 'Please, I can't be seen talking to you.'

Hannah considered threatening him somehow, saying she would make trouble unless he told her what he knew, then immediately dismissed the idea. She wasn't that person. Getting someone fired would be a nasty, abhorrent thing to do. Then he said it.

'I used to work as a cleaner. It's only recently I've been given the chance to come into the hospitality side.' He motioned to the leather guestbook and mouldy apples. 'I get a room thrown in.'

Hannah thought of his girlfriend. Pregnant under a duvet in Warren Street.

She wouldn't play fair after all. He didn't deserve it.

'This job,' she said carefully. 'I take it all your papers are in order? National Insurance, tax.' She paused. 'Work visa?' She let the implication hang.

His posture slackened, the threat landing exactly where she'd intended, but then he shifted and smartened up again, shoulders back, chin out. He'd underestimated her but now he'd recalibrated and was ready to face her on different terms.

'Did you know John?' she asked again slowly.

He hesitated.

'I knew *of* him.'

'How about the Heppels or a guy called Slig? Does the phrase Marzipan Rain mean anything?' she said, bombarding him with questions.

'Slow down,' he said, tensing against the onslaught.

She thought he was going to hold out on her some more but then he gestured at the hotel lobby.

'I work for the Heppels.'

Hannah stopped.

'This place, it's theirs?'

He nodded.

'You know about the family?'

'There's a dad and two sons,' she said, recounting what Piotr had told her. 'One died earlier this year, car accident.'

'Benton,' said Jamal. He dropped his voice to a whisper, as if afraid the CCTV could hear him. 'What most people don't know is that Benton died because of a copper.'

'What?' This she hadn't expected.

'They have police on the payroll. Their job is to turn a blind eye, tip off the family when a raid's coming, that kind of thing. The night Benton died there was a big deal happening, a trade. It was supposed to be off the radar but then CID turned up. Benton fled the scene, they made pursuit. He flipped his car on the A11. His brother Bobby blamed the copper, he didn't feed them the right information.'

Was Jamal saying John was the bent copper?

'You know all this and you were a cleaner?'

'We don't matter,' he said, swiping his hand in front of his face, 'we're invisible. They forget we're there.'

'What does any of this have to do with John?'

'Bobby has a temper at the best of times,' he went on. 'Things were already tense and then, to make matters worse, the week after the accident a load of money went missing.'

'Are you saying this brother, Bobby, he killed my husband?'

He took a breath.

'I'm saying Bobby might have organised for it to happen.' And then, when Hannah still seemed unconvinced. 'The night your husband died, everyone was on and off the phone for hours in a panic, like someone had done something they shouldn't. They kept talking about this bloke, Slig. Said he'd killed a copper and now it was all turning to shit and they had no idea what to do about it.'

A young couple entered the lobby, the woman burying her giggles in the man's neck as they headed toward the tiny bar. The door alarm sounded again, the frequency so high it needled her ears.

Jamal paused then, looked Hannah up and down as if reappraising her.

'How does she look?' he asked, and she got the feeling he'd been waiting to ask this all along. 'Martina?'

'She's about to have a baby and sleeping rough.' Hannah left this statement of fact hanging. It was enough.

She decided to get the next train back to London. She needed to order her thoughts, to figure out if there was any merit to what she had discovered. More and more it seemed that Jem was telling the truth, that he was innocent, imprisoned for a crime he didn't commit.

Who should she tell? Mickey, once she was out of rehab? His lawyer?

The postman appeared, clutching envelopes and a large parcel. Once more the door alarm sounded. Hee-Haw. Hannah startled. She'd remembered where she'd heard it before.

Wanting to be sure, she searched her phone for John's voice-mail compilation and put in her headphones, stepping back from the reception desk. The message in question was three quarters of the way through.

Thursday 26th November, 6.07 p.m.

'Just calling to tell you not to wait up. This case, I'm going to have to pull an all-nighter.' Then there it was, a high-pitched *BEEEEEEP*, like an alarm. A frequency that made her want to clap her hands over her ears. 'I'm trying to think of the overtime.'

There was no doubt it was the exact same sound, but John had said he was in London. No doubt the alarm was standard, used on countless doors up and down the country. Still, the last few weeks had taught her to question everything. This place was owned by the Heppels; maybe John had some business here he hadn't wanted her to know about?

She placed her arms on the counter.

'One last favour,' she said and Jamal sank back. She pointed at the black orb in the corner. 'The CCTV. Does the hotel keep the recordings it makes?'

'No, no way,' he said, backing away from the computer on the desk, hands up. 'I told you what you wanted to know, we're done.'

She looked from him to the computer, how he was now treating it like it was radioactive.

'Can you access the files on there?' She leaned forward, over the counter, trying to see the screen. 'How far back do they go?'

Still, he refused to move.

'You said you get your accommodation here thrown in. Sweet deal. Would be a shame to lose it.' She gave him the date. 'Do this one last thing and I'll go.'

Still he held out, but then, realising this might be the only way to get rid of her, he caved.

'Fine,' he huffed, approaching the keyboard. 'What was the date again?' Hannah told him and, after typing something into the computer, he scrolled through a list of entries and clicked twice. 'Here it is, 26th November,' he said, turning to show her the video.

'Fast forward to 5.45 p.m.,' she said. John had left the message at 6.07 p.m.

John appeared in shot at 5.59 p.m. She watched as he walked over to the desk. After chatting to the receptionist, he got out his phone and made a call; presumably this was him leaving the voicemail she'd been using to help her fall asleep these last six months. Hannah was about to look away – John had lied, now she needed to figure out why – when another person appeared in shot, dragging a suitcase. John held up his hand as if to silence them and they busied themselves at the desk, flipping through the guestbook and reaching for a pen.

Hannah didn't want to believe it. She couldn't.

'Stop,' she said to Jamal, 'I've seen enough.'

She reached for that very same guestbook and flipped back through the pages. When she reached the date in question, she slid her finger down the page, searching for the name. It wasn't there. Maybe she'd got it wrong – but the figure was so familiar. She checked again and this time she made sure to scroll through the entries slowly.

A name halfway down the page made her take pause. The handwriting was oversized and bubble-shaped. The i's topped with fat circles instead of dots.

Stacey Tweed.

Your middle name plus the name of the first road you ever lived on.

Aisling's soap star name.

She managed to keep it together until she got outside.

Across the road the tide was receding fast, the iron figure fully exposed, rusty and carbuncled. This time she didn't need to look at it twice. She breathed deep on the kelpy air. The stench seared the back of her throat, rancid and sour.

Hannah walked down the street to her house, head pulsing with everything she'd seen and heard. The journey back along the promenade to the station had been a blur, the train a hazy collection of stops and passengers, now though, back in the blowsy city air, she licked the sea salt from her lips and tried to focus.

Despite everything, she was having a hard time accepting what she'd learned. She felt like she was in a fort under siege, her back braced against the marauders hammering on the other side of the gate.

John had been a good man. Honest, faithful, decent.

He would never have taken money from criminals.

Aisling was her best friend.

She would never have betrayed her.

She was almost home when she noticed Kiki Masters coming toward her from across the road. Wearing a yellow and brown striped kaftan, she carried a plastic pet carrier and kept lifting the meshed front up to her face to reassure the cat inside.

Hannah pretended not to see her and picked up the pace.

Kiki hailed from the same kind of old money as Rupert. The two of them weren't friends but their families moved within the same golden circles – Rupert and Kiki's brother Totty had boarded together at Harrow – and whenever Rupert stopped by they would exchange polite nods and the occasional small talk. Still, this cordiality didn't usually extend to Hannah; in fact Kiki – Poobah's attempts to inveigle his way into her house aside – usually behaved as though Hannah didn't exist. And so it was a surprise when she inserted herself in front of Hannah's garden gate.

'I'm on my way to the vet,' she said, lifting the carrier up and making kissing noises. 'Poobah needs his prescription renewed.' She lowered her voice. 'Antidepressants.'

'Isn't it against their nature,' said Hannah, 'to keep a cat locked indoors?'

Kiki startled. She was used to Hannah playing nice. Once she'd recovered her face sharked into a high grin. 'I'm actually glad I caught you. I've been doing research and it turns out there are grants key-worker tenants can apply for to have the front of their house revamped.'

Hannah looked past Kiki, across the street to the FOR SALE board in her front garden. It had been there so long that the estate agent's burgundy and gold logo had started to fade.

'I've printed out the forms,' she said, the grin starting to slouch back down her face. 'All you have to do is fill them in.'

Poobah began to meow. Strange pitiful cries that sounded more baby than cat. Kiki lifted the box up to her face to comfort him and Hannah took her chance. She sidestepped round her, but she wasn't fast enough and Kiki blocked the way.

'You need to do something,' she said, any pretence at neighbourly philanthropy now gone. 'The place is an eyesore. No one wants to pay three million for a house that's going to look out onto that.' She pointed at Hannah's basement window. 'Never mind the thought of living cheek by jowl with your new guest.'

'I'm not feeling well,' said Hannah, pushing up close to Kiki's face and breathing hard. 'Tummy bug. It's this weather, the bacteria thrives.' She moved again to navigate her way round the kaftan to the garden gate, and this time Kiki didn't try to stop her.

Inside, she went upstairs to her room and sank onto the edge of the bed. Jem would be hungry but she needed to be alone with her thoughts a little while longer, to try to arrange them into some kind of order.

So John *had* been on the phone to another woman the night he died. Aisling.

What was it they'd argued about? Had John wanted to come clean about their affair and Aisling disagreed? And then what happened? John had headed off to meet her and at some point, before or after he went into that alley, he'd been intercepted by Slig and killed in revenge for the death of Benton Heppel?

She imagined going to Rupert and Mickey with what she'd discovered. Telling them John had been corrupt. Saying those words out loud was a huge deal, and then what if there turned out to be no truth in any of it? It wasn't like she had any real proof. She'd have tarnished his reputation for nothing.

She looked at the array of John's stuff still spread around the room: his dressing gown on the back of the door, the electric razor on the chest of drawers, his shoes in a heap by the wardrobe.

Her eyes landed on the bag she'd retrieved from his gym locker. She'd brought it home, dumped it next to the shoes and forgotten about it. Now she considered it afresh. She couldn't remember having ever seen it before that day. Why? Had it been his overnight bag for overnights with Aisling, had he taken it with him on their Margate mini-break?

She'd forgotten how heavy it was and as she lifted it onto the bed she was struck by another even more horrible thought. If

John had been planning to leave her then maybe he'd packed it with enough stuff to keep him going until he could come back with a removal van? She imagined him ferrying clothes, shoes and personal artefacts out of the house without her knowing, secreting them away in his locker for some future date.

But when she opened the zip she saw neither clothes nor toiletries.

Instead, stacked on top of each other in neat bricks was money. Lots and lots of money. Hannah pulled out a brick and placed it on the bed. Secured by a plastic band, it was made up of used ten- and twenty-pound notes. She rummaged in the bag, calculating, and realised there were tens if not hundreds of thousands of pounds.

It was like a knob had been twisted on a microscope. Every shape and line in the room seemed to sharpen.

This was proof, surely, that John was not the police officer she and his colleagues had thought him to be.

The fort gate she'd imagined herself pressed against began to splinter and crack. She loosened her knees and surrendered to the charge. Before long the whole place was overrun.

A week went by and Hannah still hadn't done anything about the bag of money, or Aisling.

She had counted the cash. Sixty grand. That was how much John had kept hidden in his gym locker. Most likely the fruit of his work with the Heppels. And yet he'd died up to his neck in credit card debt. Why hadn't he used the funds to clear it? Was it because he was looking for some way to launder the bricks of used notes without drawing attention, or was the debt untouched because he'd only recently acquired the cash as a lump sum? Jamal had said a large amount of money had gone missing from the Heppels in the week before John was murdered. Had he stolen it from them?

As for Aisling. On the one hand she wanted to have it all out, to rage and yell and press her for details she could torture herself with later. How long had it been going on? Had she and John ever had sex in her bed? Did he love her? On the other hand she wanted to pretend it wasn't true for as long as possible. Every day she kept those grainy CCTV images to herself was another day she could squint at her wedding ring or the message John had written with the fridge magnets and not feel like her life was burning down. To this end she'd decided to avoid Aisling completely, fobbing off any requests to get together with lies.

This morning she'd messaged suggesting they meet for lunch and Hannah had replied saying she was sick in bed with flu. In fact she had a day of errands ahead.

She gave Jem breakfast, went over to Pru's to clean and then walked to the high street to stock up on groceries.

She was coming out of the mini-supermarket when she saw her. Pulling her massage table along Hampstead High Street, her curls tied into a jaunty ponytail, her purple and orange RUB T-shirt straining at her chest.

It was like someone had let off a grenade in her stomach.

Her first instinct was to run back inside the shop and wait till Aisling had gone. She wasn't prepared to face her, not now.

Aisling waved.

There was no escape.

'Han!' She huffed the bed toward her, smiling, then as she got near she frowned. 'Should you be out and about?' She scanned her for signs of fever. 'If you needed food I could have got it for you.'

Hannah decided she would keep up the pretence that everything was fine for a little while longer. She'd make small talk, confront Aisling some other time when they weren't in the middle of a busy street. And so it was a surprise when something else entirely came out of her mouth.

'How long?'

The bags she was carrying were heavy, the plastic handles cutting into her palms. She shifted them around, trying to relieve the pressure.

'What?' Aisling peered at her and raised the back of her hand, as if to press it against her forehead for a temperature check. 'Are you OK?'

'You and John?' said Hannah, her voice flat. 'How long was it going on?'

Aisling's whole face went slack, her skin and muscle like mud sliding down a hill, then it tightened back up. Hannah thought she was going to feign ignorance but after a moment, she nodded.

'We wanted to tell you.'

'We?' Aisling had uttered the word so casually, like their pairing was a simple fact and not the annihilation of all Hannah had once held dear.

'How did you find out? Did your neighbour say something, Pru? She saw us in town together once. I knew she'd tell you eventually.'

'It wasn't Pru,' said Hannah, remembering what she'd said about John that day, what she'd implied. The bags seemed to be getting heavier, the thin plastic slicing her skin. She placed them on the pavement and rubbed at her welted palms.

She thought of the property particulars Mickey had found when they cleared John's desk. The thought hit her like a truck.

'Were you looking at flats? In Dalston? Was John getting ready to leave me?'

Aisling hung her head.

'That's why I showed up on your doorstep that morning. The day after he died. We were going to tell you together.'

'And The Warlaby? Why did you argue about it?'

Aisling shrugged. In the grand scheme of things, this was minor.

'He wasn't keen on my working there, not that he ever said why.'

'And he used to call you from a pay-as-you-go?'

A nod.

'But we didn't argue about it that night,' she said, catching up with Hannah's meaning. 'The night he was killed. If he was talking to someone on the phone, it wasn't me.'

Hannah cocked her head, sceptical.

'You work at The Warlaby.' She remembered how on edge Aisling had been when Hannah had run into her there, how she'd tried to blame it on the strange guy outside. 'He took you to stay at Parade. Both Heppels' hotels. So you knew then, about him being on the take?'

'What? No. I mean, he would never have done that. He was a good copper. No way.'

'Who is Slig? Did you know him? And Roddy Blessop, why was John so obsessed with him? And who was the guy that called me that night on the SIM?'

Aisling shook her head, trying to absorb the bombardment of names and questions. Then she moved closer, wanting to change tack. 'I'm sorry Hannah, really I am. But you guys hadn't been happy for years.'

'Years?' Hannah stopped, railroaded by a new and awful thought. 'Was this why you quit, why you stopped working with me?'

Her eyelids fluttered, like Hannah had thrown something at her face.

'It became a bit much. We worked together, socialised together—'

'You mean it made it harder for you to sneak around?'

Aisling flinched but then she stood a little taller. Hannah's dig seemed to have emboldened her.

'Were you ever happy with John? Truly? I think you wanted to be, I think you liked the idea of him but that's all it was, an idea. John always said—'

'Stop.'

Hannah held up her hand, the gesture as much a warning as a capitulation.

Aisling pointed at the amber pendant round Hannah's neck. 'That was supposed to be mine. I'd noticed it in a shop window when we were out together, said how much I liked it. He must have gone back to get it for me as a surprise.'

Hannah clutched the stone in case Aisling should try to take it from her, and began to walk away.

'Please,' said Aisling, trying to pursue her with the massage table in tow. 'Can we still be friends?'

But Hannah kept going, barging through the crowds of people, her shopping thudding against her thighs.

'I was pregnant,' shouted Aisling, abandoning the table in the street. Free of her cumbersome load, she soon managed to catch up. 'I lost it, a few weeks after he died.'

Hannah stopped and turned round. The world switched and flipped, like a picture being turned this way and that.

'The Thursday they installed Jem in your house. It would have been my due date. That's why I wasn't around those first few days, why I didn't come over. It hit me hard.'

Hannah remembered the circles under her eyes, her voice bunged with what she'd thought was hayfever but now realised was probably from crying.

She put down her bags and took off the pendant.

'Take it.' She placed the necklace over Aisling's head. 'It's yours.'

'I've been grieving too,' said Aisling, grabbing hold of the stone. 'I just haven't been allowed to show it.'

This time Aisling didn't try to stop Hannah when she walked away. She reached the end of the high street and strode down the small slope toward home. She'd email Laramie as soon as she got back. Find out when she thought Mickey might be released. Once the DCI was doing better, she'd tell her what she'd learned about John's connection to the Heppels and ask her advice about what to do next. So what if she impugned his good name? He'd lied to her over and over, he'd been planning to leave her. She owed him nothing.

She hadn't gone far when the grocery bags split open, dumping their contents onto the pavement.

The following afternoon and London was twenty-seven degrees in the shade. Despite the heat, Hannah was hard at work on a sixtieth birthday cake. It was a berry-almond tart topped with an Escher staircase that went up and down in a continuous loop, and she'd been dreading having to make it ever since she'd agreed the design with the client, a composer from Tufnell Park. Technically complex, the interconnected staircase was such that if she made even the slightest mistake she'd have to scrap the whole thing and start again. In actual fact the cake had turned out to be a lifesaver. The intricate construction demanded all her attention and left no room for the roil of thoughts and images that plagued her.

It was the recalibration she found hardest. Her life as she remembered it had been a fraud. She kept trawling the last few years for moments to reassess on the basis of what she now knew. The Valentine's night John had to work late, his habit of leaving the room whenever Aisling came round (she'd always thought it was because he found her irritating), the way he'd stopped kissing her on the mouth. She reconsidered it all afresh.

Then there was Aisling.

Hannah had thought her tendency to turn up at the house at all hours a lovable quirk, but now she wondered if she'd actually been showing up for some prearranged tryst only to have Hannah's presence scupper it at the last minute. The conversations they'd had in the wake of John's death were also ruined.

Hannah had felt so grateful to have a friend who got that she still wanted to talk and think and laugh about her husband. She'd loved the way Aisling had made sure to remind her of the funny things he'd said, how she'd taken such care to sketch out moments from their past. Now though she saw them for what they really were: a way for Aisling to grieve by stealth.

She lifted the final staircase into position and had just finished smoothing the fondant when her phone rang.

Aisling.

It was the fourth time she'd called today.

Jem looked up from his book. The kitchen was stifling, the fan no match for the temperature, and so he was lying on his bed in just his jeans, his upper body sheened with sweat.

'Someone really wants to talk to you,' he said as she let it go through to voicemail.

Hannah shrugged, stepped back from the cake and slapped her hands. She'd told Jem nothing of the affair. She could lie to herself and say she'd kept quiet because it was a personal matter, none of his business, but in truth she hadn't said anything because she was ashamed. In some deep, dark part of her she worried that he and others would think it her fault, that John had strayed because she had been defective in some way. Worse, she feared they'd think her a fool.

She stretched, grabbed a glass of water and wandered over to the French doors. There was a light breeze and every now and again a ripple would fan out across the pond, like someone blowing at a bowl of hot soup.

'What we need,' said Hannah, reaching to flip up the locks at the top of each door, 'is a bit of fresh air.' She pressed down on the handles and pulled them open. A breeze filled the kitchen, ruffling the pile of papers on the table and sending a pen rolling toward the edge.

'Nice,' said Jem, standing up.

For a few moments it was wonderful, but then grit and broken leaves began to blow inside. They swirled around her feet in a dusty ring-a-roses before continuing on their way into the heart of the room.

She closed her eyes, enjoying the flurry against her face. She could smell the Heath, all loam and grass, and hear the splosh of oars, one of her neighbours out in a rowing boat. But the wind was stronger than she'd realised and they were soon hit by a warm gust that sent the contents of the kitchen table flying.

Her glass of water crashed onto the floor and the pile of papers scattered.

She grabbed a dustpan and brush and after sweeping up the worst of it she gathered the paper. In among the mix of bills and fliers she found the photo printouts she'd arranged on the floor that morning for Jem. She scooped them together and was about to put them back on the table when she stopped. There was something about one of the pictures, a selfie John had taken somewhere up high in the city, that jarred.

Wearing a suit and sunglasses, he'd framed the shot so that his head and shoulders were only a small part of the left-hand corner of the image. He'd wanted to show off his location, which meant he thought it unusual or cool in some way.

She studied the shot in more detail, trying to work out what it was that had caught her eye. He wasn't up terribly high, four or five floors at most, but his position was such that you could see the city skyline and a row of cranes, dipped like fishing rods. The foreground was less exciting, all blackened brick walls and grimy air conditioning units tacked under windows, the tip of an old ghost sign peeping over the roof of a beige 1970s block. But there was something about these buildings or their architecture that was familiar. She scanned the picture again, her eyes roaming over the slate, glass and metal.

Then she realised.

She scrambled for her phone and brought up the video she'd shot the day she'd gone to look around the alley where John died. Scrolling to the bit where she'd lifted the device in the air to capture the nearby buildings, she hit pause and compared it against the selfie.

It had changed in the months since John had captured it on camera. The beige block had been demolished to reveal the ghost sign in full: the word BOVRIL spelled out in yellow capital letters, the background a faded blue. But it was definitely the same view. There must be a roof terrace or balcony somewhere in between the wall with the sign and the alley. For some reason John had been there and documented the spot where months later he would meet his death.

Aisling continued to call every day.

At first Hannah listened to the long, teary messages she left begging for forgiveness. She hated to admit it but she missed her and found she wanted to hear her voice. Then the messages grew more desperate. Aisling entered into a bizarre dialogue with herself, veering from profuse apology to a bolshy defence of the affair and all her actions since. In the last voicemail Hannah listened as Aisling told her she kept bumping into the guy from the Heath, the dormouse, that she was worried he might be stalking her and could she please call her back because she wasn't sure what to do. It had felt like bait, as though Aisling were trying to manipulate her into getting back in touch.

Every message that came after that Hannah deleted. Her eyes barely grazed the screen as she swiped left toward the trash.

Now it was Sunday, a week later, and Hannah sat cross-legged on the floor eating breakfast with Jem settled across from her on the other side of the bars. They were both in pyjamas, toast, papers and coffee spread out between them, French doors open, radio on.

'I've been thinking,' she said, as they swapped magazines. 'You should meet with your lawyer, ask about appealing your conviction.'

After realising John had taken a picture near the alley where he'd later met his death, she'd gone to his laptop and scrolled through the photostream to see if he'd taken any other shots that might be able to explain what he'd been doing there. There was nothing from that day but as she'd flicked back through the reel she saw more snaps of him on that same roof. He'd been there a total of six times that she could see. But why? Maybe it was another bar or a hotel belonging to the Heppels? She'd looked on a map but she couldn't figure out which street it was on, never mind which building the roof belonged to.

Jem took a swig of orange juice.

'Appeal? On what grounds?'

She chose her words carefully.

'The more I look into it, the more there is to John's murder than everyone first realised.'

'So you believe me?' he said, sitting up straight. 'That I didn't do it?'

'I think there's reasonable doubt.' She decided against telling him about the bag of cash for now. It was such a big deal and she needed to be absolutely sure she could trust him. 'John was involved in some bad stuff. He may have taken bribes, from a gang. The Heppels. I can't prove anything but there's a rumour they were involved in his death.'

'Have you mentioned any of this to John's partner, the bear?'

'The bear?'

'Rupert the Bear, that's his name isn't it?'

Hannah smiled.

'He certainly looks the part,' he teased.

'I tried but he wasn't exactly receptive. He says I shouldn't believe a word you say.'

Jem was about to reply when the bell went upstairs.

Hannah worried it might be Aisling, here to collar her in person, but when she opened the door she found Rupert, a coffee in each driving-gloved hand, a bag of what looked like his and John's favourite bacon and fried egg rolls between his teeth. Noting the yellow scarf round his neck, she covered her mouth, hiding her smile.

'Breakfast?' he said as best he could without dropping the rolls.

Hannah stood to one side to let him in.

'Did we have plans?'

He slid past her and down the stairs.

'Thought I'd surprise you,' he said, his gnashed teeth making him sound like a bad ventriloquist. 'Sunday morning treat.'

In the kitchen he deposited his offerings on the table and stopped, taking in the scene on the floor.

Jem got to his feet and brushed the crumbs from his shorts.

'Looks like you've already eaten,' said Rupert, his eyes lingering on the plates and glasses at either side of the bars. 'Wouldn't want to intrude.'

He headed back up to the hall.

'Rupert, wait,' said Hannah, running after him. 'Stay. I wasn't expecting you, that's all.'

He stopped at the front door, assessing her pyjamas and the slops of hair that had escaped her braid.

'What's going on?' He was as concerned as he was annoyed, his face flushed.

'What do you mean?' Hannah said, though she knew what he was getting at. Following him down to the kitchen, she'd seen the breakfast tableau through his eyes. The scattered papers and plates, the radio station playing in the background. It reminded her of going to the bathroom at a friend's house and catching a glimpse of the marital bed as she'd crossed the landing. The grub and tangle of the sheets made her feel like she'd seen something she shouldn't and when she'd gone back downstairs she'd struggled to look her friend in the eye.

'Are you two friends now?' he said, not even trying to disguise his hurt. 'Is that it?'

Hannah moved closer and put her hand on his shoulder.

'I don't think he did it, Ru.'

He shook her off, his anger quick and raw, but then he relaxed, soothed by some new thought.

'He's messed with your head,' he said and she could tell this explanation was a comfort. 'I told you before, you can't believe a word he says. He'll say and do anything to get you on side.'

Hannah had planned to hold off telling Rupert what else she'd learned until Mickey was better, but now, desperate to defend herself, the words came tumbling out.

'John wasn't the man you thought he was,' she said, a new grit to her tone. 'He was on the take. He got in over his head. It cost him his life.'

She thought of the money upstairs. Should she bring it down and show it to him, prove that what she was saying had merit?

'You've lost your mind.'

He reached for the latch.

'He was having an affair, with Aisling,' she said before he could open the door. 'It went on for years.'

'*Aisling?* Your Aisling?'

She'd wondered if he'd known, if he'd covered for John in that way partners did, but looking at his face now she realised he'd had no idea.

'He wasn't the man we thought he was,' she said again, gentler this time. 'I'm struggling to come to terms with that too.'

But Rupert didn't want to hear it. Leaving the house, he reached the end of the path, turned round and pointed a gloved finger at the basement kitchen window.

'He murdered John,' he said, his words crisp and clear. 'Never forget it. You're living with a killer.'

Hannah picked up her insulin prescription from the chemist and set off back home. Her phone had been blissfully silent all day, Aisling seemed finally to have accepted she wanted to be left alone, and so she walked a little slower than usual, relishing this time with her thoughts.

Jem had done as she suggested and put a call in to his lawyer, Missy Cunningham, asking how he might go about appealing his conviction. The lawyer had told him that as it was now more than twenty-eight days since he had first been sentenced he would need to get leave to appeal from the Crown Court, to convince them that the new evidence he was putting forward was compelling and credible. If he didn't get this then his case would not be heard. He'd asked her to come to see him at the house so they could discuss it further, and arranged a visitation order in her name.

She was at the top of her street when her phone rang. She flinched and, expecting it to be Aisling, went to reject the call. But it wasn't a number she recognised and so she brought the phone to her ear.

'Hannah, it's Jane, Maraschino's housekeeper.' She sounded overly bright, like an actress performing in a breakfast cereal commercial. 'Maraschino asked me to call.' She paused and Hannah guessed that Maraschino was probably in the room with her, directing the conversation with frowns and nods that Jane was trying to respond to in real time. 'The person they booked to do the cake for the party next week has pulled out.

It's all very last-minute but she wondered if you might be able to step in? The party is Wednesday.'

'Wednesday? But that's four days from now,' said Hannah, already calculating the baking schedule. There was no way she could come up with and then model that many individualised cupcakes by then. 'I'd have to go back on my initial pitch. Most of the cakes would be generic with a few hundred personalised ones mixed in.'

'She said she'll make it worth your while,' said Jane slowly, and Hannah imagined Maraschino mouthing the line and then nodding, pleased, when Jane carried it off. Jane paused and when she spoke again her voice was back to normal. 'Please?'

Just over three and a half thousand cupcakes. Plus a three-tier centrepiece to match. Could she do it? Should she? It would be a nightmare, but the money was good and who knew how many word-of-mouth recommendations it would lead to. Maraschino's circle of friends could be a gold mine.

She decided to go for it and after agreeing a price and morning delivery time she quick-marched the rest of the way home, keen to get back and draw up a shopping list of ingredients.

Opening the front door, though, she was derailed by a postcard on the mat. A picture of a tiny ginger kitten with huge eyes, and the back scrawled with Aisling's huge bubble-shaped handwriting.

I'm sorry. I love you. I miss you. A x

It was like her heart was being squeezed.

What were you supposed to do, she thought, when the person you most wanted to be around, the person who made you happy, was also the person who had betrayed you?

Her phone rang. She thought it might be Jane again, calling to discuss some extra forgotten detail, but when she looked it was an international number.

'Is this Hannah?' said a woman with a Kiwi accent. 'Aisling's friend?' A tannoy screeched in the background. 'This is Heather, Aisling's mum.'

Hannah's first thought was that Aisling had asked her to call on her behalf, that this was some desperate last-ditch attempt at reconciliation. Hannah had never met either of Aisling's parents but she'd seen pictures of them. Bespectacled and smiley, they tended to wear matching green fleece jackets and could usually be seen flanked by their beloved Alsatians, Bernie and Clive.

'The British police called this morning.' Aisling's mum spoke as though on autopilot, her words flattened. 'We're about to board for Heathrow.'

'Police?'

'Aisling's dead,' she said, her words hollow with disbelief. 'Murdered.' The airport tannoy sniped again, louder than before. 'Our girl, she's gone.'

Hannah

Hannah opened the oven, hauled out four trays of cupcakes and placed them on the side.

Two thousand nine hundred down, seven hundred and fifty to go.

She'd been at it for three days straight and, with the deadline closing in, had got up this morning when it was still dark to try to make sure she got them all finished in time.

She knew that, under the circumstances, most people would have walked away, told Maraschino to find someone else. She had considered it. But she also knew that baking was the one thing that would get her through this first nightmarish part of her grief. That she would be able to cling to it like a raft in the blackest of seas.

Aisling had been found in a hotel room in Southwark. Strangled. Her massage table set up in the corner, towels laid out. Early investigations suggested that someone using a false name and stolen credit card had booked her via an app but they had yet to track down a suspect and CCTV had revealed nothing. Hannah had given the police a description of the guy from the Heath, told them how Aisling was sure he was stalking her. They were looking into it, but they didn't have much to go on. Hannah didn't even know his name.

The guilt was devastating.

Aisling had said in her voicemails that she was frightened, that the dormouse was following her, and Hannah had ignored them all. Last night she'd finally plucked up the courage to listen to the messages she'd deleted. They were mostly the same, pleas for Hannah to call her as soon as possible, but then the final voicemail she'd left was a little odd. In it she'd said she'd remembered something about the events leading up to John's death. 'Please call, Hannah, I think this might be important.'

She iced the cakes with buttercream and set to work on the individualised decorations. A tiny white yacht to symbolise the couple's honeymoon island-hopping the Ionian Sea, a rectangular reproduction of the logo from Boujis, the Chelsea nightclub where they'd first met, a fondant Maraschino figure in a red dress to represent the song they'd first danced to at their wedding.

In the garden Mr Dalgleish was sitting on a chair, supervising Jem's outside session. Jem usually used this hour to work out but when Hannah looked she saw that he was chatting to Pru over the fence. Pru was in her swimming costume and cap and, from what Hannah could surmise, was currently lying flat on her lawn, demonstrating her backstroke technique.

Once his time was up, Mr Dagliesh escorted Jem inside. Hannah grabbed the key and was about to lock the door when Mr Dalgleish stumbled against a stray cake box and grabbed the cell bars.

'Mr D?' Hannah went to help him but he shook her off.

'I'm fine,' he said gruffly and nodded at the door. 'Get on with it.'

'Where are you in your treatment?' she asked, turning the key. 'Have they said how many more cycles they think you'll need?'

He shrugged, as if this was not his concern.

'See you in two days for his shower,' he said, signing and dating the form. He glanced at the chaotic worktops and stacks of white boxes littering the floor. 'Try to have the place cleaned up by then. It's a health hazard.'

In recent weeks she'd let him see himself out but today, wanting to make sure he was OK, she followed him up the stairs.

At the door she watched him go. Once he'd cleared the garden gate, she was about to return inside when she saw something move on the other side of the street.

She stepped onto the path, squinting into the sun. Someone seemed to be standing by the wall in the shade of the horse chestnut. She moved closer and had just reached the pavement when the figure shifted and she glimpsed the lower portion of their face. A man.

There was something about his build, wiry with long legs, that gave her pause. He shifted again and this time she saw his glasses, the eyes behind them black and small. The dormouse? Was he watching her house, or was she being paranoid, her brain strung out from the stress and sleep deprivation of the last few days? He couldn't possibly know where she lived – could he?

She went to cross the street, wanting to be sure, but as soon as she stepped out onto the road he took off, half-walking, half-running.

'Wait!' she shouted, still not sure. 'Hey, you.' But the man ignored her and, picking up his pace, launched into a sprint.

Hannah stood in the middle of the tarmac, watching him go, already doubting herself.

9 p.m. and by Hannah's calculation, even if she worked through the night she was going to miss the deadline. Maraschino would be furious.

She stepped back from the counter, head in hands.

'You OK?' said Jem.

'My wrists are killing me and all I can think about is Aisling.' She'd told Jem of her friend's murder the same day she'd learned the news. He'd comforted her as best he could from behind bars. She rotated her fingers left and right, trying to release the muscles. 'I keep imagining what it might have been like for her, at the end. How frightened she must have been, how alone, but even though I'm thinking all that it's like my brain hasn't got it yet, like it can't process the fact she's gone.'

'Come here,' he said, placing his hands through the bars.

Hannah hesitated. They'd never touched on purpose before.

'Come,' he said, opening his palms out flat.

She did as he said. Gently, he took her hands in his, then he circled his grip so that her hands were resting on top of his.

'Sometimes,' he said, sliding his thumbs towards her wrists, 'the body knows first, the body understands first. How you're feeling. What's happened. It just takes the head a little while to catch up.' The pressure was firm but good. Again and again, he pushed at her aching ligaments, shifting his thumb across the arc of her wrist like he was searching for something beneath the skin.

'I'm no baker but maybe I could help with the basics,' he said, changing to a slow circular motion in the spot just above her pulse. 'Show me what to do and I'll do it.'

'Maybe the icing?' She bit her lip. 'That's the easiest part.'

Slowly, he released her wrists from his hold. The pain was gone and her hands felt light, like she'd been carrying something heavy and had just put it down.

'OK then.' He clapped, ready. 'Let's do it.'

Hannah dragged the dining table alongside the cell and Jem did the same with his small table. Once they were sitting side by side she passed a selection of bowls, trays and ingredients through the hatch and after she had demonstrated how to smooth the buttercream on with the spatula they were set.

Every time Jem filled a tray he placed it in the hatch, then Hannah would pull it out and set to work populating the icing with another collection of tiny figures and objects.

'I am sorry,' he said once the third batch was complete. 'About your friend.'

Hannah nodded, her throat dry. She'd seen Aisling's parents a number of times over the last few days but that had been more about helping with practical arrangements and, although Rupert had texted to say he'd heard the news and was very sorry, she'd yet to speak to anyone about her grief.

'We fell out,' she said, shaping a nub of blue fondant into a diamond choker, 'before she was killed.' It felt good to tell someone, to confide. 'I discovered she and John had had an affair.'

'John was cheating on you?'

'For years.'

'So that night,' he paused, trying to understand, 'he was going to meet her?'

'I don't know. She said not, but it seems that way.'

They didn't speak again till dawn, when Jem lifted his arms in the air and stretched, his T-shirt riding up over the flat of his stomach.

'We make a good team,' he said and smiled, and for the first time since she'd heard about Aisling, Hannah felt like she could keep her head above the waves, that something was buoying her up toward the air and the sun.

Hannah delivered the cakes to Queen's Crescent with five minutes to spare. Exhausted, she returned home and got in the shower. She wanted nothing more than to put on a clean pair of pyjamas, eat breakfast with Jem and then spend the rest of the day in bed.

First John, now Aisling. She thought it strange, how no one warns you about the physicality of mourning, how it can rifle through your insides, like a rat through a bin, the way it can make you feel like you're trapped on a waltzer, spinning and sickly, the way it can make you have to concentrate on the simple action of breathing in and out.

Not long after John had died she'd been reading an article about losing someone you love and had learned of a Portuguese word, an equivalent to which did not exist in the English language. *Saudade.* It described a deep emotional state of unmet longing; a yearning, a kind of homesickness, for something or someone you can no longer have. She remembered telling Aisling about it and how Aisling had smiled sadly and told her she thought it beautiful, perfect even.

She stepped onto the bathmat, wrapped herself in a towel and had just started combing out her hair when she realised that, in all the chaos, she'd forgotten to tell Jane how to operate the lazy Susan at the heart of the cupcake display. It would be a disaster without it. She'd call and talk her through it now, before it was too late.

Her phone was in the living room and so, hair dripping, she dashed downstairs and grabbed it from the mantelpiece.

It took her a few seconds to notice him.

Standing by the sofa, he was examining a framed picture of her and John.

'There you are,' he said, placing it carefully back down. His eyes travelled from her shoulders to the bottom of the towel and her still-wet thighs. He nodded at the sofa. 'Sit.'

Hannah tried to speak but her ribs had pinioned themselves around her lungs, squeezing so hard against the soft meat that no air could get in or out. She felt for the red button round her neck – if she pressed it she could alert the prison service, they'd send someone out to check on her – only to remember she'd taken it off to shower.

Her best option was to make a bolt for it, to get out of the house into the street and shout for help.

She pretended to do as he'd said and moved toward the sofa, then sprinted toward the door, but she hadn't gone two steps when he moved in front of her, blocking the way. She cried out and he clamped his hand over her mouth.

Her scream died in his palm.

He pulled her to him, her damp hair blotting his shirt.

'I'm not going to hurt you,' he said, his mouth in her ear, 'I just want to talk.' He took a breath as if to continue, but then he stopped, his body jerking back and forward as he emitted a loud sneeze.

The dormouse. Aisling's stalker and, Hannah was certain, the man responsible for her murder.

'Sorry to descend on you unannounced,' he said once he'd recovered from the sneeze. He walked her over to the sofa and, after positioning her there like a doll, removed his hand from her mouth. 'I've been hanging around for days trying to catch you at home.' Hannah remembered the man she'd spotted across the road the day before. 'Then this morning the door was open so I let myself in.' Open? Hannah thought back to when she got home from dropping off the cakes; she was tired but had she really forgotten to shut the door properly? Registering her horror, his hand went to his chest in a gesture that was half-apology, half-hurt feelings at the insinuation he might have done something wrong. 'I did knock. There was no answer.'

Hannah became aware of a noise, low and urgent. It sounded like someone shouting further down the street. She didn't dare turn her head to the window to look.

'It's about Aisling,' said the dormouse and stopped. Saying her name out loud seemed to upset him. He flexed his hand, stretching his fingers out wide, and examined the blanched palm. He kept going until the skin was pulled as taut as it could go, the ligaments buckling, and then he curled them back in again, into a fat balled fist. 'The night she died I was there, at the hotel. I saw everyone who went in and out, front and back. I think I know who did it.'

'Then go to the police,' said Hannah, 'tell them.'

'I can't, they won't believe a thing I say.' He smiled to himself and shrugged. 'My history.' Hannah thought of the vigilante women and their taser. 'That's why I wanted to talk to you, to tell you, then you can pass on the information. The person who did this can be brought to justice.'

'How did you even know who Aisling was?' said Hannah, then stopped, listening. There it was again. Someone outside, shouting. 'That day, we didn't tell you our names.'

He smiled and tapped his nose.

'Her T-shirt. It had the logo of the clinic where she worked.' He lifted his hand in the air. 'I googled it, scrolled through the staff list, found her name.' Each time he listed a new step he released a finger. 'Called up, asked what shifts she worked, went from there.' He brought his hands together, proud of a job well done. 'Easy.'

Hannah made no attempt to hide her disgust.

'You followed her around for weeks. You stalked her.'

'I wanted to get to know her better,' he said, a new bite to his tone. 'I'm shy, it takes time to build up the courage to ask someone out.'

'What kind of freak are you?' she said, hoping to provoke him. Anger often put people on the back foot. If she could disarm him, even a little, she might be able to get away. She got to her feet and, making sure to hold on to her towel, prepared to make another run for it. 'I wish we'd left you to get your balls fried.'

As soon as the last word left her mouth he brought the back of his hand down hard against her cheek. Crunch. He lunged forward, wrapping his fingers round her throat.

'I loved Aisling, I would never have hurt her.' Up close she could see how his glasses were smattered with greasy fingerprints. Behind them his eyes were bloodshot, the pupils black seeds. 'Why won't you listen to me? I saw the guy that did it, I can give you a description.'

She tried to struggle free but he had her held fast. His grip seemed to be getting stronger, his fingers squeezing and pressing against bone and cartilage. She opened and closed her mouth, straining for air. Her arms grew limp, then her legs. She felt herself melting into the grey, and had just closed her eyes when his hands loosened, then fell. He staggered back, the smooth part of his head crinkled in surprise, then toppled to the floor with a thump.

Hannah coughed and wheezed, blinking, trying to understand what she was seeing.

A red and white baseball cap. A kneeling rooster, bowling ball in hand.

A mouth, curved like a mountain range.

Jem.

'I heard you scream,' he said, his voice hoarse. 'I wanted to make sure you were OK.'

'You're out of the cell?' She pulled her towel higher, cowering against the cushions.

'I shouted and shouted.' He put down the hunk of marble, John's darts trophy from the shelf in the hall, and held up his hands to show he meant no harm. 'Then I pulled at the cell door, out of frustration more than anything, and it opened.' He looked to the floor, uncomfortable with the accusation he was about to make. 'Last night, you must have left it unlocked?'

The cell, and the front door. Hannah remembered how tired she'd been, how Mr Dalgleish had stumbled, taking her attention elsewhere. But still, how could she have been so careless?

She started to shiver.

Jem grabbed a blanket from the sofa and covered her with it.

'Are you hurt?'

'My neck's bruised but I'm OK.'

'Who is he?' He crouched down next to the prone man and rolled him into the recovery position. 'A burglar?'

'Aisling's stalker. We used to call him the dormouse.'

'The dormouse?'

'His eyes. We both thought he looked like one. He wanted to tell me he didn't do it, he didn't kill her. I saw someone hanging around over the other side of the road last night. I thought it was him but I couldn't be sure.'

'And he thought he'd convince you he was innocent by breaking into your house and attacking you?' He picked up her phone and handed it to her. 'Call the police.'

She did as he said and once they'd told her someone was on their way they sat back to wait.

It was strange without bars between them. Hannah realised that although her security button was upstairs, although right now Jem could do anything, she wasn't afraid.

Sometimes, the body knows first, it just takes the head a little time to catch up.

They stared at each other, Jem's gaze steadfast. It was like he was trying to tell her something and ask her a question, all at the same time. The room was quiet but Hannah's ears bellowed with blood and she pulled the blanket higher to hide the bloom she could feel spreading from her neck to her face.

The scream of an approaching siren brought them to.

'You need to go back downstairs,' said Hannah, looking out of the window.

'No way. What if he comes round?'

'The police are pulling up, I'll be fine. Go,' she said, ushering him toward the stairs. 'They mustn't find you out of your cell. How would we explain? We'd both be in trouble.'

Jem was about to protest some more but then he seemed to think better of it.

'Pull the door to,' she shouted after him. 'I'll come and lock it after they've gone.'

Outside she could hear voices and the beep and crackle of a radio as the uniforms made their way down the path.

She waited for the metallic clank of the cell closing and then, drawing the blanket around her shoulders, she went to let them in.

It was late afternoon when Hannah finished giving her statement. An officer dropped her home and after dumping her bag and coat in the hall she went down to the kitchen.

The dormouse's name was Harry Gascoigne. The desk sergeant had taken her to one side and had a word with her on the quiet, told her about his history of stalking and sexual assault. An estate agent from Highbury, he was now under arrest for ABH. He was also being questioned about his involvement in Aisling's murder.

Hannah had already decided not to press charges for her own attack but she was comforted by the thought that, were he to be found responsible for Aisling's death, her family would not have to agonise over whether to carry that burden. New Zealand, who still operated a traditional prison system, would fund a place with a Foster Host and he would serve his time there.

Jem was lying on his bed, reading. Seeing Hannah, he put down the book and came to stand behind the cell door.

'You OK?'

Hannah mirrored his position.

So close they were almost touching. In the real world it would have been odd for them to stand like this, but the bars seemed to legitimate the proximity, to let them pretend there was nothing out of the ordinary.

'I didn't have the security necklace on,' she said, voicing the thought that had troubled her all afternoon. 'You could have done anything, but you didn't.'

'I would never hurt you.' His words were scratchy, sandpapered by his earlier shouts up the stairs.

'If you hadn't come up when you did . . .' She shook her head, trying to rid herself of the image, and grabbed one of the bars for support.

Jem cocooned his hand over hers.

'It's OK, you're OK.'

His skin was warm, his hand heavy. She looked up and there it was again, the roar of blood in her ears. Heat in her chest.

A beat and she dropped her hand to her side.

His face crumpled. Embarrassed, he was about to turn away, to make out like the moment had never happened, when Hannah pressed the button on her necklace and, after retrieving the manual key from its hook, unlocked the cell.

The door swung open.

Jem didn't move.

'What are you doing?'

'Come here,' she said quietly, 'please.'

He searched her face, only stepping forward once he was sure of her meaning.

Hannah brought his mouth to hers.

They kissed slowly at first, Hannah circling her arms round his waist, but as her fingers grazed the stripe of skin between his T-shirt and jeans he pulled away.

'Wait.' He raked his hands through his hair and puffed out his cheeks, stepping forward and then retreating, in some battle with himself.

Now it was Hannah's turn to cringe. She'd thrown herself at him only to be rebuffed. How could she have been so foolish? But then he was coming toward her, taking her hands in his, smiling shyly. They kissed again and then he was lifting her up, wrapping her legs round his waist and carrying her over to the table.

Over his shoulder she could see the empty cell, the door still hanging open.

Morning and Hannah lay in bed half-asleep, unspooling the events of the night before. The shame came in waves. Images crashed over her, relentless and cold.

She knew that, in theory, John's affair with Aisling had given her permission to do what she liked. That, even if she hadn't learned of his infidelity, she was a widow, free to be with who she liked.

In reality though she was nauseated by what she saw as her betrayal of John and his memory. He'd been dead less than a year and she'd slept with someone else. Developed feelings for them. She'd thought more of herself than that, more of her marriage.

It was scary to realise maybe you weren't the person you thought you were, that sometimes you weren't in control of who you loved and when you loved them.

She recalled the moment Jem had pressed his mouth against the soft hollow of her inner thigh and hid her face with her hand, overcome by another wave. When her brain raced ahead, to what happened next, she found a hand over her face was not enough and muffled her blushes under the pillow instead.

Being intimate with a prisoner was dangerous, too.

What if he thought what they'd done was a mistake?

What if he told someone?

Afterwards, they'd fallen asleep together on the floor. Hannah had stirred around 2 a.m. and nudged Jem awake. They hadn't spoken, there hadn't seemed any need. He'd known he had to go back into his cell and Hannah to her room.

It had all seemed fine, normal even.

Now though, fear began to creep in.

Jem was a convicted criminal in her custody. She was his Host.

What they did had felt consensual – she was *sure* it had been consensual – but he was her prisoner. In theory, she had all the power. The thought came like a brick through a window. Last night had meant something to her but what if he'd done it because he felt like he'd had to, or for entertainment, just another way to relieve his boredom and isolation?

She checked the time and after getting dressed headed downstairs. Mr Dalgleish would be arriving soon to supervise Jem's biweekly shower. She needed to talk to Jem before then, to find out where his head was at, to reassure herself he was OK.

He greeted her with a careful smile.

'Morning.' He seemed nervous but happy and kept meeting her gaze and then looking away, only to look at her again.

'About last night,' said Hannah, 'I want to make sure, I mean, I realise that maybe you felt like—' She was interrupted by a knock on the door. Mr Dalgleish.

She huffed hard, loosening the tension in her body.

'Let's talk later?'

Jem gestured at the cell and smiled.

'I'll be here.'

Mr Dalgleish followed her down to the kitchen, fussing with his forms and clipboard. She'd seen him only two days ago but today he was noticeably thinner, his eyes sunken. White crop circles of skin were now visible on his skull and his mouth was cracked and dry. He crossed his arms.

'Something you need to tell me,' he said, his words loaded with meaning. Hannah watched Jem's face drop and realised hers had done the same. 'About yesterday?'

She blinked fast, her throat dry.

How could he possibly know?

Had someone seen them through the window and reported them? Unlikely. Her mind raced to ever more ridiculous scenarios. Had the prison service installed CCTV at the same time as the cell and omitted to mention it?

Although notoriously hard to prove, the penalty for sexual contact with a prisoner was serious. A crime against the state, the Ministry of Justice in this case, it was dealt with in exactly the same way as crimes perpetrated against individuals. If someone was found guilty, the state would take them into custody – in one of the prison cells that now existed in the nearest civic centre or relevant government building – and the workers in that office would be responsible for them for the duration of their ten-year sentence. Were Hannah and Jem to be caught, Jem's sentence would be paused while the pair of them went off to serve their time elsewhere and then, once it was complete, they would return and pick up where they'd left off.

'I heard you had an intruder?' he went on when she failed to speak. 'The prison service gets a notification as a matter of course whenever the police are called out to anything in connection with the Host or their property.'

The reprieve was fierce.

'Yes, that,' she said, her voice high. 'All very frightening.'

While she recounted what had taken place Jem gathered his washbag, towel and clean clothes.

'Well done on fighting him off by yourself,' said Mr Dalgleish, giving her a double thumbs-up. 'Very brave.' He opened the cell and then they were gone upstairs.

Friday was sheet changeover day. Normally, Jem left his dirty linen in a pile by the door for Hannah to take away and then leave a clean set in a pile on his mattress. Now though she saw he'd forgotten, and so set about stripping the bed for him. After freeing the duvet and pillowcase from their covers she tugged at the fitted sheet, but it had got stuck around the bottom corner of the bed and so she lifted up the mattress to unhook it.

She smiled. There, lined up neatly on the skirting board, was a collection of her sugar figurines. She realised that although Jem ate the cakes she sometimes gave him, for whatever reason he'd decided to preserve the sculpted figures. He would see them before he went to sleep and then again when he woke up.

She decided not to mention it – she didn't want to embarrass him – and was about to drop the mattress back into position when she saw something that gave her pause.

A clear plastic bag filled with objects had been tied to one of the slats.

Her first thought was drugs. She had no idea how Jem could have smuggled them in but she also knew that people often found a way.

Emptying the bag out onto the mattress, though, she saw no evidence of narcotics. It was just a random, seemingly nonsensical collection of items: a small piece of fabric, a gold watch, a hair scrunchie. She had no idea why Jem would feel the need to keep such things hidden and was about to reattach the bag to the slat when her eye caught a flash of navy in the fabric. Opening it out flat, she saw it wasn't a scrap of material but a square hanky monogrammed with a set of navy, copperplate initials she'd seen before.

W.D. The hanky belonged to Mr Dalgliesh.

With a growing sense of unease, she turned over each object in turn, trying to make sense of how and why Jem would have these things in his possession.

And then in the clutter she saw something that made her heart lurch.

A business card. Pink with grey text, it spelled out a name, number and occupation.

Aisling Finton

Massage Therapist

07791 299350

Hannah had seen them in Aisling's wallet many times. She'd carried them with her to hand out to prospective clients. But how and why would Jem have one in his possession?

Was it possible he knew her before he came here, before the trial?

She gathered the items back into the bag, shoved it in her pocket and stumbled out of the cell. In her haste she collided with the kitchen table, and stopped to steady herself. Looking around the room, she felt sick at the thought of what she'd done here the night before. How she'd lain back on the scrubbed pine. How she'd fallen asleep on the floor.

It was like seeing things in negative.

The shapes were the same but that which had been light was now dark.

Jem

I've been here a month when I see Mr Tarker perform for the first time. It's a Saturday afternoon, and Mrs Tarker has coaxed me and Lucas along with the promise of a free buffet and a play on the fruit machine in the hotel bar.

We sit at the back on gilt and velvet chairs lined flush against the wall and watch him work the room. He's here to keep the diners entertained in between their prawn cocktail and filet mignon. Most people ignore him, but I am transfixed.

His stage name is The Great Saqisto.

While Lucas swings his legs back and forth, I watch my foster-father circle the tables, performing card tricks and dangling necklaces and wallets in front of shocked faces.

Hands reach toward empty necks and pat pockets as they try to fathom how he could have taken these things without them noticing.

I smooth my thumb across the bevelled glass of my Pokémon watch. A gift from my mum. I know I'm a bit old for it now but I don't care.

That night, before bed, I go to where Mr Tarker's drying up in the kitchen. He's always on drying duty. He says the washing-up liquid irritates his hands.

'How do you do that?' I say, my brain fizzing with images of playing cards zooming from palm to palm, disappearing coins and the slither of handkerchiefs through a shirt cuff.

'Close your eyes,' he says, and flips the tea towel over his shoulder.
'What?'

'Just close your eyes,' he says gently, 'I won't hurt you.'

I hold out a few seconds more and then I do what he says.

'What am I wearing?'

'What? Wearing? I . . .'

'You were just looking right at me, so tell me.'

I try to remember, to visualise him in my mind's eye.

'Jeans and a T-shirt,' I say, but it's a guess.

'Open your eyes.'

I blink and focus. He's wearing a plaid shirt, red, white and grey, and jogging bottoms that hover around his ankles.

I huff, annoyed at my mistake.

He smiles, pleased.

'Your attention is a limited resource. A resource that can be controlled.' He darts his hand up toward his ear and then down to his waist. My eyes follow. 'If you can control a person's attention then you can do anything.'

He dangles my Pokémon watch in front of my face.

I try to snatch it from him but before I can get close he whisks his hand away.

'I'll teach you,' he says, nodding at my right jeans pocket. Reaching inside, I discover my watch. 'If you want?'

Hannah

When Jem and Mr Dalgleish came back downstairs from the shower Hannah had her shoes on and keys ready. She refused to meet Jem's eye and, after locking him in the cell, she saw Mr Dalgleish out and then she was gone, the slam of the front door like a clap of thunder.

She spent the rest of the morning walking the Heath, trying to understand what she'd found. She had a good idea where most of the things came from but she couldn't fathom why or how he'd come to have them in his possession. The watch with the dragon design had belonged to one of the guards who had delivered him into the cell that first day, she was sure of it; the hair scrunchie was hers, lost weeks earlier.

The watch aside, most of the objects weren't valuable and even if they were, it wasn't like he could trot off to the nearest pawn shop. So what did he want with them?

She returned just after midday, went down to the kitchen and laid each item on the table one by one.

'Whatever you do,' she said, 'don't lie.'

He paled, then steepled his hands through his hair, pulling hard on the roots. He seemed to be weighing up his options, wrestling with how best to respond.

'I stole them,' he said finally.

Hannah looked again at the objects.

'No.' She shook her head. It wasn't possible.

'I take things from people without them noticing,' he said. 'I'm good at it.' He looked to the floor. 'Once a thief, always a thief.'

'You're locked up, you couldn't get near someone if you tried.'

'There are always opportunities,' he said, 'you just need to look for them.'

'Opportunities?'

'It's hard to explain,' he said, coming close to the bars. 'When I'm in a difficult situation . . .' He gave up on that train of thought and tried again. 'It's about survival. That stuff might look like junk but for me, in here,' he gestured at his cage, 'it could be useful.'

Hannah got to her feet and squared up to the cell.

'Tell me,' she said, 'that night with John. What happened? Really.'

He reached through the bars to touch her hand and when she recoiled he nodded, chastened, as if to say she had every right.

'I didn't find John's wallet on the floor,' he said eventually. 'I stole it. I stole from lots of people that night. Had my hand in and out of their pockets, their bags, feeling for valuables. I've thought about it and that's the only way I can explain my DNA being on the knife that killed him, that I must have touched it or brushed up against it while it was still on the owner somehow.'

Hannah shook her head, trying to understand.

'You're saying someone in the bar that night killed John?'

'That's the only explanation I have.'

'So you stole his wallet, then what happened?'

'When I opened it and saw his police badge I panicked. That's why I ran after him, to give it back.'

She considered this for a moment.

'That makes no sense. He didn't know it was you that had taken it. You would have been fine.'

'Not necessarily. Once he'd realised it was gone he might have come back to the bar. Caused a fuss.'

'So you didn't mention anything about hearing John on the phone at the trial and you also didn't mention this?'

'Ask my lawyer. She thought it would have made my story worse.'

Again he reached for her hand.

'Last night,' he said, stroking her wrist with his thumb.

'A mistake,' she said, shaking him off. 'It won't happen again.'

His whole body had been leaning toward her, pressed against the bars, but now he straightened up and put his hands in his pockets.

'Right.' He nodded his agreement.

'Right,' said Hannah, and she meant it, but the syllable wavered, the sound puttering through the air.

Jem

I've been back with Mum for three months when she stops taking her medication. She says she doesn't need it anymore, that it makes it hard to think. If she can't think she can't read and, for her, reading is everything. She tells me again about her PhD in literature. How, one day, she is going to be a professor.

I miss the Tarkers, especially Lucas. But I go to watch him at football practice every Sunday and then afterward we go for hot chocolate. He's clever. Top of his class.

Mum stops sleeping. She stays up all night reading and insists on keeping all the lights in the flat on, her music loud. She has an idea for a paper she wants to write. She says that, when people read it, every university in the land will want her on their faculty, that she'll be invited to speak at conferences all over the world. I put my pillow over my head but it's no good. Eventually, I seek out the dark underneath my bed. Stuff my ears with toilet roll.

The fridge is empty. Books litter the floor, pages splayed. Mum is tired. She goes to bed for a week. On Sunday after football I ask if I can have two croissants with my hot chocolate. Mr Tarker takes me to one side. He wants to know if everything is OK. I lie. I don't want to be taken into care again. I won't.

I'm hungry. I look in her purse but it's empty. She lies in bed all day. Stops showering. Her room smells bad.

I don't want to ask Kenzie for help, to get him in trouble again. I figure that, this time, I can look after myself.

I decide on the Waitrose in Wandsworth for two reasons: it's busy and full of rich people. Rich people have insurance; losing their wallet won't break the bank.

I walk the aisles and stop people with silly questions. 'Do you have the time?', 'Did you drop this?', 'Which way to the cheese counter?'

I perform my little dance and then I take what I can.

What I need.

Mum is up and then she's down. Sometimes the flat is spotless, the bedsheets clean, the cupboards full. She gets a job a few hours a week lecturing at Birkbeck. Sometimes she doesn't come home for three nights in a row.

Pickpocketing becomes routine. Necessary.

Lucas and I remain close.

He's ten now. I'm fifteen.

We go to the cinema together. The football.

His cleverness pays off. He wins a scholarship to some fancy school, everything paid for, and so I decide to take him out bowling to celebrate.

We go to the All Star Lanes in Whiteleys. They sell Americana merchandise – T-shirts, varsity jackets, shirts – at the counter. I buy us matching baseball caps. Red and white, they have a rooster bending down to throw a bowling ball on the front. We put them on.

'Cock-a-doodle-do!' says Lucas and pulls the peak low.

We play. He wins.

We're back at the counter, waiting to exchange our shoes, when I decide to skim the pocket of the woman to my right. It's a habit now, a reflex no longer confined to the wealthy of south London, and as soon as I clock her elbows resting on the counter I take the opportunity to remove the phone and travelcard from her right pocket.

When I look round I see Lucas, staring.

'What did you just do?'

Our shoes arrive and I hustle him away, toward the toilets.

'Did you take something from that lady?'

I say nothing but I can feel the red creeping up my neck. I can't bear for him to think less of me.

'Give it back.'

'What?' The lie is futile, but there's no way I'm going to own up. 'I didn't do anything.'

'Jem.'

'OK, OK.'

The woman is still at the counter. I pick up a scorecard from the floor and hand it to her.

'This yours?'

She takes it from me and while she examines the scribbles on the front, I replace everything.

Lucas waits until I'm done and then we leave. Before we can get outside he's taken off his baseball cap. He wedges it in his back jeans pocket but the cap isn't designed to be bent out of shape like that and so the stitching around the peak starts to come away at the seams, the thread frayed.

Hannah

One month later

Tuesday morning and Hannah was loitering in the kitchen, waiting for Jem and Mr Dalgleish to go upstairs to the shower.

Jem had spent the past month trying to reassure her that she had nothing to worry about, that he wouldn't steal anything from anyone again. Still, on the two days he went to wash, she had taken to searching his cell, checking there was nothing else he might be hiding. She'd yet to find anything, and although she knew each clean sweep was a flimsy reassurance, it was something and when you're desperate to trust someone, to believe the things they say, then something can go a long way.

Aisling's murder investigation rumbled on. They'd released the dormouse without charge but had declared him still very much a person of interest. Hannah hoped it was just a matter of time before they had enough evidence to prosecute. Meanwhile the sadness she felt at losing her friend became ever more gnarled and confusing, mixed as it was with her guilt at having ignored her in those crucial final days and her rage at having been betrayed. Feeling those three things at once was disorientating, like listening to different songs at the same time. Then there was the fact that her brain didn't seem able to accept that Aisling was gone. On more than one occasion she'd found herself in a kind of daydream, halfway through the act of leaving a voicemail, before realising her error and hanging up.

Her grief for John was equally complicated. Now, as well as missing her husband she found herself in mourning for the man she thought she'd known and the illusion that their marriage had turned out to be. How do you grieve a fiction?

London was balmy, more late May than December, and the French doors were thrown wide. She and Jem welcomed the morning breeze but Mr Dalgleish, sitting at the table signing and dating paperwork, felt otherwise. Shivery and pale, he held the pen in one hand and used the other to pull his jacket close.

'Cold?' she said, going over to pull the doors shut.

The question was an affront. He released his jacket and sat up tall.

'Perfectly fine.' Most of his hair was gone now, the smatter that remained around his ears and back of his scalp like the fuzz on a newborn. He cleared his throat, wanting to change the subject. 'Hear about that Host a few streets from here?' He grimaced. 'The one in the tent.'

'Laurie Simmons?' Hannah hadn't been by the house on the corner since that day she'd ended up there by mistake.

'Poisoned her prisoner. Gave him apple pie and custard laced with antifreeze.' Mr Dalgleish motioned for Hannah to unlock the cell. 'Two months left on his sentence and she killed him.'

Hannah thought of the way Laurie had paused by her front door, how she'd had to fortify herself before she went to tend to her rapist inside. What torment must she have endured over the years? What fear?

'Where is she now?'

'Holding Centre. The guy's family want to press charges.'

The thought of Laurie being found guilty, of having to spend the next however many years in the custody of her rapist's relatives, was chilling.

She pushed her black button, turned the manual key and pulled the door open. Jem stepped into the kitchen, towel and washbag at the ready. They were almost at the stairs when there was a noise.

A strangled yelp, like a dog being kicked.

It was coming from out the back.

Hannah went to look. There was someone in the middle of the pond. Splashing and coughing, their hair was plastered thickly over glasses that hung low on the bridge of their nose.

Pru.

She must have finally found a way to scale the fence.

Hannah spun round to find that Mr Dalgleish and Jem had joined her in the garden.

'She can't swim,' she said, the realisation a quick one-two punch that made her heart spasm. 'Not anymore. Her dementia. Neither can I.'

Pru's cries were getting louder, her arms bashing at the water. She disappeared for a second and then resurfaced, spluttering and hacking.

Another spasm, this one more brutal than the last, and Hannah clutched her chest, trying to slow her breathing.

'She'll drown.'

'I'll go,' said Mr Dalgleish, taking off his jacket. He beelined for the steps, kicking off his shoes as he went, then slowed. Hannah thought he'd gone over on his ankle or that one of his laces had got stuck, but then his legs gave out from under him and he buckled to the floor.

'Mr D?' said Hannah, rushing to his side.

His teeth clacked behind grey lips. He was freezing but his face was glossed with sweat.

'Should we call an ambulance?' said Jem from his spot behind the white painted line.

'Chemo,' said Mr Dalgleish. He wrapped his arms round his chest as if to warm himself, but his muscles were weak and his arms fell back to his side. 'This last session . . .' He tailed off, no match for his juddering teeth.

Hannah helped him to his feet and, trying to keep one eye on Pru, placed his arm across her shoulders. She scanned neighbouring gardens for signs of life. Should she go out front, knock on doors and ask for help? Would there be enough time? Or should she jump in the boat at the bottom of the steps, row out to her, would that be quicker?

'If you come closer I can help you get him inside,' said Jem, from behind the line.

Jem.

'Stay where you are,' she said, guiding Mr Dalgleish to the house. 'Mr D, you're going to turn off the fence, then Jem can swim out to get Pru.'

'What? No,' said Mr Dalgleish, the suggestion re-energising him briefly. 'Absolutely not.'

Hannah took him over to the keypad on the wall.

'Turn off the fence or she'll die,' she said, flipping open the white cover. 'We have no choice.' She leaned back and shouted outside. 'Jem, get ready.'

While Jem began shucking off his jeans and T-shirt Hannah turned her attention back to Mr Dalgleish.

'He won't run,' she said, trying to convince herself more than anyone. 'He can be trusted. Please, save my friend.'

He shook his head and closed his eyes. Hannah sagged. He wasn't going to do it.

Another shout from the pond. Quieter this time.

He reached for the tablet in his pocket.

'If he escapes,' he said, bringing up the code for the back fence, 'I'll say it was your fault, that you threatened me, that you made me do it.'

Hannah nodded her agreement and, taking care to shield the screen, Mr Dalgleish pulled himself up to standing and typed in the six-digit number. As soon as the zone flashed green she ran outside to give Jem the thumbs-up and he was off, scrambling down the steps to the shore. She sprinted to the end of the garden to watch his progress. Pru was trying unsuccessfully to float on her back and kept tipping onto her front, arms flapping.

Jem ran the first few metres, lifting his knees to reduce resistance, and then he stretched up his hands, arced his body and dived. He resurfaced a few metres away and began front-crawling toward Pru.

He was halfway there when she flailed and sank. He sped up, arms curving through the air, and as soon as he reached the spot where they'd last seen her he took a breath and dived.

The water would be murky, impossible to see more than a few inches ahead. What if he couldn't find her?

The surface stilled, the ripples deadening to nothing. Hannah dug her nails into her palms, pleading under her breath, 'Come on.'

Jem reappeared and Hannah's heart lifted, but when she looked she saw that he was empty-handed. He took another gulp of air and dived again.

A minute passed, then another.

Hannah had given up all hope but then he resurfaced with Pru in his arms. He turned onto his back and, after positioning

Pru on top of his chest, he hooked an arm under her shoulders and kicked back toward the shore.

Watching him drag her onto dry land, Hannah tensed. Jem had done the right thing and Pru was safe but the fence was still turned off. If he wanted, he could get back in the water and swim away, disappear into the Heath, to freedom.

He hoisted Pru over his shoulder and carried her up the stairs and into the garden. Hannah waited until they'd cleared the white line, then ran inside.

'You can turn it back on,' she said, giddy with relief, that Pru was OK, that Jem hadn't run. 'Mr D?'

He was passed out in a heap, the tablet next to him, the six-digit code still on the screen.

00-73-21

The numbers made her think of James Bond and school sports days. 007, licence to kill, and teachers at the start of the egg and spoon race counting down the kids, 3-2-1, before starting them off with a sharp blow of their whistle.

She typed the numbers in and pressed the button and the light flashed red. The fence was live again.

Then she got down next to him and cradled his head in her lap. His skin was feverish, his neck wet with sweat.

Jem appeared soon after, breath ragged. He placed Pru carefully on the floor, water dripping everywhere, and began performing CPR.

Two chest compressions and she coughed, her head rearing up to vomit a puddle of brown water. He waited, making sure her breathing was OK, then grabbed his duvet from the cell and covered her with it.

He looked at Hannah and the unconscious Mr Dalgleish.

'He fainted,' she said, scanning the kitchen for her phone. 'I'm going to call an ambulance.'

'Not necessary.' Looking down, she saw he'd opened his eyes. 'Give me a moment, I'll be fine.' He tried to push himself up to sitting, only to collapse back.

'Someone was watching the house,' Pru murmured under her duvet. 'I was trying to get away.'

'That was the other day,' said Hannah. No doubt she'd heard what had happened with Aisling's stalker, how he'd broken into Hannah's place, and had got it confused with the here and now. 'You're safe.'

They sat there like that for a while. Hannah holding Mr Dalgleish, Jem holding Pru.

Jem's stomach was smeared with pond mud and droplets of water hung from the tip of his nose, earlobes and lashes. Every time he shifted on his hips one of the drops would fall to his thigh with a tiny splosh and Hannah would think about how he had had the chance to run and didn't. How he could have gone and left her but he came back.

He came back.

It was something.

Jem

Lucas has been at his fancy school a year and is doing brilliantly. I'm halfway through my A levels and while Mum is still up and down, at least now, no matter how bad things get, I can provide. The flat will stay warm, our bellies will be full.

It's a Saturday night when she goes out with friends. I stay home and work on an essay, due Monday. I'm in bed asleep when she comes in. I hear a man's voice through the wall and then music. The bass makes the floor vibrate. I crawl under my bed and stuff my ears with tissue.

Sunday morning and Mum and the man are still up. Mum is kneeling on the sofa, the soles of her tights dirty and laddered. A glass of red in hand, she's talking fast, one of her spooling monologues that goes on and on. The man is older. Thick-thighed and paunchy, he wears his shirt tucked into his jeans. He's smiling but it's forced, like he's waiting for something he thought should have happened already.

'My boy,' says Mum as I open the curtains. 'Jeremiah. Got a big brain, like me.'

The man appraises my wrinkled T-shirt and boxers and his pretend smile dissolves. He's realised he's waited all night for nothing.

I turn off the music, get a bowl and cereal from the cupboard. I'm meeting the Tarkers at 10.30 a.m. Lucas has a football match. He's been picked for the first team, centre forward.

I settle at the table with my breakfast and grab my book and half-written essay, read over what I wrote the night before.

The man gets to his feet.

'I should be going.'

Mum doesn't break stride. She continues talking, an endless cheery babble.

I keep my head down and assume he's on his way out of the flat, but then I feel him next to me. He swigs the last of his wine and puts down the glass.

'People who read books.' He sneers at my mum, then hacks and reaches back to spit in the sink. 'Think they're so much better than everyone else.'

Slowly, I turn the page.

'Don't ignore me.' He bashes the edge of my spoon. Milk and cereal fly up and hit me in the face. 'It's rude.'

I wipe my cheek with the back of my arm and get to my feet. I'll go to my room, stay there till he's gone.

'I said, don't ignore me.'

He shoves me toward the fridge and I can't help but bounce back into him.

It's all the justification he needs.

I feel his fingers in my hair, his nails digging into the roots, and then my head is moving fast toward the corner of the table and I ricochet back, onto the floor.

Mum stops talking and for a moment there's silence.

'No,' she says. 'I told you, he's my boy.'

His boot meets my stomach, then my ribs, then my face.

When I come round they're both gone. My ear is wet, my hair stuck to the carpet.

I hear banging. Someone at the door. I think it's Mum, she's forgotten her keys, and limp down the hallway. But when I open the door I find Lucas shivering in his football kit, socks bunched around his calves.

'You weren't at the match,' he says, eyes roving across my swollen cheek. His voice hasn't quite broken and his words are squeaky. He can go up and down an entire octave in the space of one word.

I'm trying to come up with an excuse, some explanation for my current state, when I start to list toward the wall. My vision blurs, my legs liquid. As I slump Lucas steps forward and catches me. My face smushes against his football shirt, the material thin. He smells of sweat.

When I open my eyes again I'm under a duvet on the sofa, a pillow beneath my head.

Lucas is sitting cross-legged on the floor. His reddish brown hair is cut short, close to his head, and as he rakes his fingers through the spikes and down, toward the back of his skull, it makes a shushing sound.

I push myself up to sitting and realise my face is clear of blood, the cut under my right eye covered with a plaster.

'I found a box in the cupboard,' he says, as my hand finds the dressing. 'Thought it was important to stop the bleeding.'

'What was the score?' I say. My voice is hoarse and, hearing it, he runs to get me a glass of water. I try to take it from him but my hand is shaky and so he holds it to my lips and tilts it gently till I'm done.

'We got beat. 5–0.'

'Brutal.'

He shrugs.

I notice the flecks of mud spattered on his cheeks and ears. He is covered in freckles, just like his mum, and they make it hard to tell what's earth and what's skin.

'You need to go to hospital.'

'No.' I'm seventeen, still a minor. The minute they tap my name into the system there'll be trouble, my history with social services. At the very least they'll send someone round.

'Your head. You need to get checked over.'

I don't reply and we sit there quietly. Every now and again Lucas checks my cuts, ices my bruising and brings me water.

'Please don't tell anyone,' I say eventually. The shame of him having seen me like this is worse than the throb in my kidneys. 'Not your mum and dad . . .'

'Not nobody,' he says and this time his voice is deep, his tone unwavering. He hears himself and startles.

A month later and my bruises have healed. Mum hasn't brought anyone home since and has yet to mention what happened.

Its Lucas's thirteenth birthday at the weekend and so tonight I'm taking him for food and then to see a film. To mark the occasion I've chosen somewhere nicer than our usual chicken-shop fare. The food isn't posh – just your standard burger and chips – but they have metal cutlery and staff who come and take your order at the table.

Waiting for him outside the restaurant I see him approach, and tense. This is the first time we've seen each other since my beating and I'm worried he'll want to talk about it, that things between us will be different.

He greets me with a smile.

'All right?'

'All right.'

We're quiet then, looking at each other.

'Shall we go in,' he says eventually. 'I'm starving.'

We're in the queue waiting to be seated when I notice the man in front. Chatting to the woman next to him. The wallet in his inside pocket is fat with notes, his watch designer.

I'm tempted, but the way our bodies are angled makes it risky and it would be too weird for me to try to engage him in conversation. I've just decided not to bother when a waitress drops a pile of plates on her way to the kitchen. The man turns sharply to address the smash and his jacket gapes. I take my chance. The wallet comes easily but as I free his watch from its clasp I fumble and my elbow knocks against his paunchy middle.

The man looks around. Pats himself. He knows something is wrong.

'Come on Lucas,' I whisper, 'this queue is taking too long. Let's go.'

The man puts out his hand, blocking the way. He's realised what's missing.

'You,' he shouts to a passing waiter. 'Call the police.' He jabs a finger in my face. 'I've been robbed.'

I'm not worried. This has happened before and I've always managed to offload the stuff before I can be searched. I slip the wallet into Lucas's front jacket pocket and am about to do the same with the watch when the waiter claps me on the arm.

'It was him,' says the man. 'I know it was him.'

'Empty your pockets,' says the waiter. He sounds bored, like a parent being called in to referee warring children.

I refuse.

'Empty your pockets,' he says, his boredom fading a little, 'or I'm calling the police.'

I do as he says.

The designer watch sits heavy in my palm.

I'm scared about what's going to happen next. Still, this is my first offence, I'm only seventeen, maybe I'll get off with a caution?

But then the manager turns to Lucas.

'And you.' He gestures at his coat. 'Empty them.'

Lucas is horrified but he does as he says. When his hand lands on the wallet he's confused. He looks up, mouth open, searching for an explanation. Then his eyes land on me. A beat and he understands. His shoulders slump and for a moment he does nothing, paralysed by my betrayal, then he brings the wallet out into the open.

The waiter looks at it and sighs, like we are all a terrible inconvenience.

'I'll call the police.' He signals to the man. 'Keep an eye on them till then.'

I stand outside the Tarker house and ring the bell. I want to say sorry, to them and to Lucas, try to explain.

Mrs Tarker answers the door. When she sees me her lips cinch into a thin line.

'Jeremiah.'

'I wondered if I could come in,' I say, waiting for her to step to one side, 'if we could talk?'

That day at the restaurant, I tried to take all the blame. Told the police over and over that Lucas had nothing to do with it. They wouldn't believe me.

'That's not going to be possible.' Her voice is firm but kind. She's still angry but she did all her shouting last week, at the police station.

'Please, I miss him,' I say, and she registers the catch in my voice as I try not to cry. 'I'm sorry.'

Her hand falls away from the door and I think she's wavering, that she's going to invite me in, when Mr Tarker appears.

'You.' He comes out onto the step and I have to retreat onto the path to give him room. 'Do you know how hard it was to get into that school? How hard he worked? What impact it would have had on the rest of his life, on the opportunities that came his way?'

I stare blankly, not understanding.

'Lucas breached the terms of his scholarship. He broke the law. The school kicked him out.' He bunches his hands into fists and then releases them, fingers spread wide, and for a moment all I can see is The Great Saqisto at the end of a coin trick. 'His whole future. Gone. Just like that.'

Hannah

Two days after Jem had rescued Pru, a Thursday morning, and Hannah emerged from the bathroom, mouth agape, shoulders tense.

She smiled, a crescent of pink and white, but no sooner had her cheeks turned upward than her lips gave way and she found herself once more slack-jawed and staring. She hid her face with her hand and closed her eyes.

She'd imagined this moment so many times, but not like this.

She didn't know what to think, what to feel.

To her left was the tall thin case where John had displayed his small vintage dart collection. She looked at the arrangement of brass Kroflites, Unicorn Tungstens and 1960s Dorwins, snug in their pouch, their feathers golden, the tips razor-sharp, and remembered his delight the day he'd won them at auction. How she'd berated him for spending so much money on something so silly, how he'd laughed and told her they were an investment, priceless heirlooms he would one day pass down to their kids.

That had been back when he could still say things like that, before the years of trying, before they'd developed the habit of flinching every time they passed a pram on the street.

She wanted to feel joy, to access the whoop and pelt of surprised laughter she imagined this news could bring; instead, she felt the cold loop of fear, like a rope round her neck.

If anyone were to find out the truth – about what she'd done, how this had happened – her life would be over. This thing she'd wanted for so long, taken from her.

She turned away from the display case and her eye landed on the old airing cupboard where she'd padlocked Jem's custody bag.

Could she trust him? Should she?

Before she said anything she wanted, no she *needed,* to see if there were any clues, good or bad, as to what type of person Jem really was. The bag was tempting but it was sealed with tape and she couldn't look inside without anyone knowing. On the other hand, his boxes in the spare room were there for the taking.

Upstairs, she stood at the doorway.

His possessions didn't amount to much: four cardboard boxes, a microwave and a bin bag of clothes. She knew going through them was wrong, an invasion of privacy that would ordinarily make her cringe with shame, but this was no longer just about her.

Starting with the closest box, she unsealed the brown packing tape, lifted up the flaps and peered inside. She'd hoped to find a photo album or letters, maybe a certificate of some kind, but the contents were unremarkable. Pots and pans mixed in with books, a squash racquet and various pairs of trainers and shoes. The fourth box did deliver one thing – a small framed picture of what looked like Jem as a teenager and another younger boy with reddy-brown hair sitting on a wall, their arms resting on each other's shoulders. It was the only photo he had and so it must have been important to him, and yet he hadn't asked for it in his cell.

None the wiser, she re-taped the boxes and returned to the bathroom. She'd known it was unlikely she'd uncover anything definitive; still, she'd hoped.

The white stick was still on top of the cistern where she'd left it, the word she'd spent years longing for, that she never thought she'd see, contained in its tiny grey screen.

Pregnant.

It was like a spell.

Jem

I stop stealing. Without the income I have to get a job. I find one in a warehouse, picking and packing. Fitting shifts around my lessons is impossible and after a few weeks I drop out of college.

The Tarkers won't see me, and refuse to answer my calls. I miss them, especially Lucas, but they haven't set any of their social media to private and every now and again I take a look to see how they're doing. Sometimes their feed is full of pictures from their favourite holiday cottage in Wales – the three of them bobble-hatted on beaches and taking muddy walks – other times they'll share a clip from a birthday party or a prize-giving at Lucas's new school. I try to read through the lines, to figure out how he's getting on. It's hard to tell.

Mum dies two weeks after my eighteenth birthday. Pills.

Kenzie sorts me out with a bar job in Palma. He's established himself in the club scene over there.

After Mum the sun and change of scene is exactly what I need. I end up staying in Majorca for years, going from resort to resort. I still keep tabs on the Tarkers online. Mr Tarker creates an Official Great Saqisto page and I revel in the blurry shots of him in action at weddings and bat mitzvahs.

The summer I meet Alina is fun. We hang out, sometimes more. But as the months pass I realise the time we spend together means more to her than to me. That perhaps she thinks this is more serious than it actually is. I pull back, make sure she sees me with other women, but we remain friends. Still, every now and again *when we drink a little too much she tries to kiss me, to take things back to how they used to be.*

Eventually I decide to come home. I want to go back to college, finish my A levels.

I find a room in a houseshare and flit between bar jobs. My house is in a ropey part of Tooting (there are two attempted break-ins in my first week alone) but the rent is seven hundred a month. My A level plans come to nothing. Still, I read as much as I can.

I get a job glass-collecting in a bar on the Kingsland Road. It's not ideal. My boss is a bully called Monty. A squib of a man, his teeth are tracked with metal braces to correct a fierce overbite. They make him lisp and spit when he talks. He greets everyone the same way, 'Hello sailor.'

I become friends with his on–off girlfriend, Maya, who works behind the bar, and another member of staff, a skinny Aussie boy called Chickie.

My plan is to get into some kind of a routine, put a little money in the bank, then enrol in college. But the job is a zero-hours contract and some weeks I barely make rent.

I start stealing again, from customers, just a little here and there to make ends meet.

The Tarkers post less and less on social media, then they stop completely. Still, I make sure to check their accounts every week.

I wonder if I will ever stop missing them, if I will ever not wonder where they are and what they're doing.

Hannah

December 21st and Hannah was sitting by her bedroom window with the lights off and curtains open. The sky was clear, the moon a white circle on the pond. A neighbour was having a Christmas party and every now and again, when someone nipped out for a smoke, she heard a snatch of Bing Crosby or John Lennon.

This morning had been spent at the GP, making her booking-in appointment with the midwife. The doctor had prescribed the high-strength folic acid all type 1s were recommended to take while pregnant and advised her to keep a careful eye on her blood sugar. Diabetes could play havoc with her levels, he'd said, and make her more at risk of miscarriage and other complications.

Still at a loss as to whether or not to tell Jem her news, for the last few days she'd been quieter than usual, scared she might give something away. Her biggest fear was that someone would find out the baby was his, that they'd entered into an illegal relationship. If she didn't tell him she could guarantee it would remain a secret, hers alone to nurture and protect. Of course once she started to show Jem might suspect, but she could lie, come up with a make-believe encounter.

Telling him the truth also brought other, more complicated worries. She wanted his involvement in their child's life to be entered into happily, of his own volition, not forced upon him by circumstance and the fact he literally couldn't get away.

The person she really wanted to talk to about all this was Aisling. The last few nights she'd dreamed about her, nightmares, about how and where she'd died. In them she was running down hotel corridors, all the doors the same, trying to figure out which room Aisling was in so that she could break inside and save her. The hallways stretched for miles, every door she tried locked. She'd called for her and called for her.

She looked again at the pond and thought of Jem at the centre of it, diving down through the silt for Pru. Mr Dalgleish had been ordered to take compulsory sick leave and a wave of temporary DLO officers had followed in his wake. They were told they'd be assigned a permanent replacement in the new year.

She could still remember the code for the back fence she'd seen on Mr Dalgleish's tablet. James Bond and the start of a race on school sports day. 00-73-21. They'd only recently changed it, so it would be valid for just under four more weeks, till 8th January, and then it would change automatically, to another randomly generated set of figures she'd have no access to.

Pulling a cardigan over her pyjamas, she slipped on some shoes, grabbed a torch and made her way down to the kitchen. Without turning on the lights, she went to the keypad and inputted the code. The light blinked green. The fence at the back of the house now off, she opened his cell door.

His red and white baseball cap sat on the pillow as usual and so she crouched down, felt underneath the bed and touched his side. He startled and then, realising it was her, shuffled out and removed his headphones.

'Hannah?'

She put a finger to her lips, reached forward and took his hand. He looked at her, questioning. She'd told him what they did was a mistake. Sensing his confusion, she smiled, trying to tell him she'd changed her mind, and led him toward the French doors.

Outside the garden was balmy, the plants limp, everything drugged by the continued heat. She guided him toward the bottom of the garden but as they neared the white line he started to pull back.

'That day with Pru,' she said, 'I saw the code for the fence.' They reached the perimeter and stopped. 'I've turned it off.'

'What, why?'

'Because I think I can trust you.'

'You can,' he said.

'Then come with me,' she said, offering her hand.

He was wary as he crossed the line, conditioned to brace for the shock, and then when everything was OK he laughed.

Hannah opened the gate and they climbed down to the shore.

The rowing boat was under the tree, the bow full of old leaves. She swept the seats clean, pushed it into the shallows and hopped in.

'Early Christmas present,' she said, motioning for him to join her.

'What if someone sees us? They could report you.'

When she didn't answer he made his way into the pond and, water lapping at his calves, pulled himself into the boat. Hannah took hold of the oars and began to row, only stopping once they reached the middle.

'See those houses.' She nodded at Maraschino's mansion. 'That's who the cupcakes were for, the ones you helped me with. The ones that are dark, they're empty. Left to rack and ruin.'

They sat looking at the Heath and the glare of the city beyond. The water's surface was burred with moonlight and it cast everything in a milky glow.

'I thought you didn't want to,' said Jem. 'I mean, before, you seemed to have wished we'd never . . .'

'Things change.'

Hannah leaned forward, the boat rocking gently, and kissed him, then drew back a little, checking this was OK. A beat, his breath fast on hers, then he kissed her back, his hands gripping her waist.

'The other week with Pru, why didn't you run?' she said when they drew apart.

He didn't miss a beat.

'Because it would have been wrong, it would have got you in trouble.'

She picked up the oars and rowed over to the Queen's Crescent side of the pond and the back of Maraschino's house. There was no shore here; instead the water slapped against a high wall.

'Look,' said Jem as they floated toward the back of the ruined mansion. Metal rungs had been fixed into the stone. 'A ladder.'

Looking up, they saw the rungs led to a wooden gate.

'There's something else you need to tell your lawyer,' she said rowing closer. 'That might help with the appeal.' She reached for the rope attached to the boat's prow and tied it to the lowest part of the ladder. 'I found a bag of money. In John's gym locker. It could be proof, that he was taking bribes. That someone else might have had a motive to kill him.'

'Money? How much?'

'Sixty grand.'

'Shit.' He whistled.

She reached out and tested the strength of the topmost rung, curling her hands round the rusted iron.

'What are you doing?'

'This leads to one of those empty mansions I told you about. My client's housekeeper showed me inside one time. You have to see it.'

'No. We should go back.'

But she was already climbing up toward the gate. She reached the top and gave it a shove. It was unlocked.

'Please, let's go home,' said Jem from the boat as she disappeared inside.

In the garden, Hannah waited. She guessed Jem was hoping she'd have second thoughts and return. A few seconds more and she heard him climb the steps. She turned on the torch, grabbed his hand and pulled him toward the back of the house and the basement.

The door was thick with damp, harder to open than that day with Jane, but a few heaves of her shoulder and it gave way. Inside they were greeted by the same smell of animal droppings and dust. She showed him the garage with the Bentleys – both of them aghast at the tinted windows and the discovery of the cars' keys under the sun visors – she showed him the staircase of ferns and their leaves all rolled up for the night, and the empty swimming pool, the rainwater plinking into its mosaic bottom.

In the ballroom, she turned to him and took his hand.

'Why didn't you run?' she asked again. She gestured toward the pond. 'Why aren't you running now?'

He leaned forward to kiss her but Hannah turned her cheek. She needed to hear him say it.

'I would miss you,' he said eventually. 'Seeing you every day. I would miss that.'

She had her answer.

'Now please, can we go back to the house,' he said, taking her hand. 'Being out here, it's making me nervous.'

'I'm having a baby.' The words spilled from her. 'We're having a baby,' she said, slower now.

She braced, trying to read his face, but the torchlight was meagre, his expression in shadow.

'We?' he said, and even though it was only one word, two letters, she could hear his smile, a tiny inflection at the end, like a cresting wave. 'Parents. Us?'

'Us,' she said, quietly. She wanted to share in his apparent happiness but she was too preoccupied by the thoughts of what would happen to the three of them were their affair uncovered. Jem had yet to work through the consequences, to understand the potential horror awaiting them.

'Us.' He took her in his arms and went to waltz her around the broken ballroom. Hannah was going to resist but then she decided to move with him, that for now, for this moment, she would pretend it was all going to be OK. He danced her slowly at first and then faster, their feet crunching through the debris. She closed her eyes and let him carry her through the dark.

Jem

Missy Cunningham. My lawyer. Broad and blond, with cheeks permanently covered with rosacea that looks sore to the touch.

I haven't seen her since the trial.

'So,' she says, settling on the chair opposite. 'You want to apply for leave to appeal?'

The temp DLO in the corner doesn't bat an eyelid, they're not interested and I'm glad because I feel like I can speak more freely than when Mr Dalgleish was here.

'Fresh evidence has come to light,' pipes up Hannah from her spot by the cooker. 'Someone else killed John. We think we might have a case.'

'We?' Missy raises her eyebrows. 'Well,' she says, looking from me to Hannah, reading the situation perfectly, 'isn't this unexpected?'

Hannah pinks, embarrassed, and so I smile and mouth to her that it's OK and then, on reflex, I look at her belly.

I'm going to be a father. Me.

After we got back from the mansion last night I didn't sleep.

They're surprising, my feelings.

Still, I mustn't lose focus. I need to keep going, to do what I came here to do.

'Why don't we start at the beginning?' says Missy, taking out her notepad and pen. 'Tell me what you know.'

Hannah goes through the phone calls and the SIM card and the Heppels. She tells her about the money she found in John's locker and this guy called Slig, how he was rumoured to have murdered a detective.

'Jem said you advised him not to admit the pickpocketing,' says Hannah, 'in court, I mean. Or that he heard John on the phone?'

Missy looks to me for confirmation it was OK to answer.

'The prosecution had already painted John's murder as a mugging gone wrong,' she says when I nod my permission. 'It wouldn't have helped matters one bit if Jem had volunteered the fact that he was a thief, that he was stealing from people that night. It would have made it even easier for the jury to convict.' She shifts on her chair. 'As for the purported call he overheard, it's like everything you've just told me. Hearsay. Especially your late husband's alleged corruption. Not enough to merit an appeal.'

Hannah goes to protest and Missy holds out a hand to stop her.

'Still, I'll file an application later today.' She puts on her coat. 'You never know.' She looks again from me to Hannah. Smirks. 'Stranger things have happened at sea.'

Hannah

Hannah was the one who suggested Jem spend Christmas Day and Boxing Day outside the cell. The holiday, with its break from DLO visits, outside sessions and shower time, offered a rare chance for them to be together like a normal couple, for them to be free.

Jem wasn't sure, but Hannah was persuasive. They'd be hyper-careful. No one would ever know. In case someone from the service did decide to randomly come knocking, she would keep the front door locked and bolted, the curtains closed, so they'd have ample time for Jem to return to his cell before anyone could come inside.

She got her wish.

Her parents had asked if she wanted to come to them for the holidays. They'd expected her to hire a carer to tend to Jem's needs while she was gone. How could she tell them that she'd bought a chicken to roast and crackers to pull and collected stories of Grace Paley for Jem to open on Christmas morning? In the end she'd lied, told them she had too much work on to leave London, that she'd catch up with them in the new year.

Free rein. At first Jem found it bewildering. He moved through the house slowly, not sure where to sit or stand. It was like he'd forgotten how to be outside the confines of his seven metres square; he no longer knew how to inhabit the space available to him. Once, he found himself in a different room to Hannah and panicked, calling for her and banging his shoulders against walls in his haste to locate her in the house.

Gradually he began to relax.

On Christmas morning she presented him with his gifts.

'I didn't get you anything,' he said, tearing the paper on the Grace Paley. And then, when he moved on to her second gift: 'You didn't.'

He set the board game on the table, smoothed his fingers across the picture on the front.

YAHTZEE! THE FUN GAME THAT MAKES THINKING FUN!

They spent the rest of the day nesting under blankets on the sofa, playing the game, eating and watching movies. That night they bathed together. Their conversation was dominated by one topic: their future as a family of three.

Sexual relationships with prisoners were forbidden. If anyone were to discover their secret, they'd both be sentenced and imprisoned in the cells inside Islington's civic centre. Hannah had spent ages researching online and had discovered that she would be allowed to keep the baby for the first few months of its life but then it would be taken from her and placed into care.

They decided that their utmost priority was to protect their secret at all costs, to make sure they stayed together, in this house.

When it came to their relationship they agreed that, so as not to arouse suspicion, once the holidays were over Hannah would start mentioning to the DLO that she had started dating. Eventually she would attribute her emerging baby bump to a fictional lover, a one-night stand she never heard from again.

As for the day-to-day mechanics of how they would live as a family, things were a bit less clear. His lawyer thought it unlikely Jem would get leave to appeal, that his conviction would be quashed, and so the most probable scenario was that they'd have to figure out a way to live like this.

Who, they wondered, should they tell the baby Jem was? What should the baby call him? Should they ever allow the baby in the cell?

Despite their fears, there was joy. Every time they caught each other's eye they shared small, secret smiles, Jem asking Hannah almost every hour how she was feeling until she asked him to please stop.

Due to her diabetes, Hannah wanted to see a specialist who could offer some guidance on these crucial early months and, frustrated with the wait time outlined by her GP, she'd put in a call to Dr Hess, the obstetrician she'd been referred to before embarking on IVF all those years earlier. Dr Hess was a private consultant and so she'd have to pay, but she didn't care; she wanted to see someone now, before any problems might arise.

The thing Hannah had been most looking forward to was sleeping next to Jem in bed, but on Christmas night she woke in the early hours to find him gone. She discovered him staring out at the pond from the landing window. The next night she woke to find him asleep on the floor next to where she lay. He said he was struggling to adjust to life outside bars, that even with the front door locked he was terrified they would be caught.

They'd agreed that Jem would return to his cell the day after Boxing Day. But when the time came Hannah found she wasn't ready to revert to business as usual just yet and suggested they have one last breakfast together. Jem said he would make pancakes and after turning on the radio, he set to work. The kitchen bin was overflowing and so while he cracked eggs Hannah took the rubbish bag up to the wheelie bins out front.

She had intended to scuttle out and in as quickly as possible, to have the door re-bolted in a flash, but then she made the mistake of looking around.

On the other side of the road, Kiki Masters was in her garden, hands clutched to her chest. She was crying, her lips moving quickly, like she was mouthing the same prayer over and over, her eyes fixed on a spot somewhere near the top of her house.

Hannah followed the trajectory of her gaze and was greeted by the sight of Rupert, two storeys up, his limbs spreadeagled against the building. He glanced right, assessing the brick, and stretched a hand and a foot toward some invisible hold. Then he did it over and over again, his fingers and toes intuiting the tiniest of gaps in the mortar, until he reached a point below the third floor.

Was Kiki locked out? Had she asked him to break in through an open upstairs window?

Then she saw it. A flit of grey in the horse chestnut tree. Poobah, Kiki's cat. He must have escaped again but instead of sneaking into Hannah's house, this time he'd clambered onto the highest branch he could and now, judging by his pitiful meowing, was at a loss as to how to get back down.

Rupert steadied himself against the wall and, once he was sure of his hold, reached one arm back and grabbed Poobah by the scruff. Kiki was waiting to catch him and as he dropped the cat into her arms she bellowed and buried her face in his fur.

Rupert made his way down and, after accepting Kiki's thanks, crossed the street to Hannah.

'Rupert Cammish, feline rescuer extraordinaire,' he said, and performed an exaggerated bow. 'At your service.'

Hannah forced a laugh but all she could think about was Jem. If Rupert caught him out of the cell he'd be obliged to report it. They'd be done for. She considered her options and decided her best bet would be to try to keep him talking and hope Jem would hear them and know he needed to get back behind bars.

'He'd been up there for hours,' Rupert said, brushing the dirt from his suit. 'Kiki was about to call the fire brigade. Then I arrived.' He grinned. 'And now for my second good deed of the day.'

Hannah remembered the radio. They'd had it on loud. Would Jem even be able to hear them talking over the noise?

'In a fortnight's time you will no longer have a prisoner.' Rupert let out the words at the same time as his breath, then fixed his expression – eyes wide, smile high – and held it, ready for the response he seemed sure would come.

'What?'

Rupert kept his face frozen, holding out for a reaction, but when a few more seconds had elapsed and she still hadn't understood his meaning his face sagged.

'I lodged another Foster Host transfer request on your behalf. Pulled in a few favours. I didn't tell you because I didn't want to get your hopes up, but this morning I got the call.' Another smile, even bigger than the last. 'It's been approved. They move him on 7th January. As of next Friday you're free.'

The street seemed to tilt and sway.

'I thought you'd be happy?'

'I am, I am,' she said, scrambling for the right words. 'It's a shock, that's all.'

He sank back on his heels.

'I guess it is a bit out of the blue,' he said, clearly meaning the words as a comfort to himself as much as her.

Hannah nodded weakly.

'Right,' he said, trying to disguise his hurt. He'd clearly been excited to finally be able to tell her. 'I'm on my way to work, can't stay.'

She should have been relieved – he wasn't going to come inside, she and Jem were safe. But the information barely registered and after she'd watched him go she stood there a moment, trying to process the news.

Back indoors, she stepped into the kitchen to find Jem placing the pancakes on the table. Seeing her, he smiled.

Hannah kept her face still.

'Ask me how I'm feeling,' she said.

Jem

I've been working at the bar a few months when I find out not all is as it seems.

It's Wednesday night and me, Chickie and Maya are busy setting up – unstacking chairs, stocking fridges, mopping hallways – when a man I presume to be the bar's owner arrives to see Monty. Shiny-suited with black, slicked-back hair, he comes at the same time every week, stays ten minutes, then leaves. He and Monty always go into the back office together and until tonight I'd thought he was in there to check over the books, sign his name against any necessary paperwork.

I think he's been and gone and so after I'm done mopping the corridor, I push on the office door and drag my bucket inside.

Monty is on me in an instant.

'What the fuck?' He pushes me back out into the corridor, then he gives the bucket a kick. It tips over, dirty suds flooding the stretch I've just finished.

Chickie sees and, after grabbing another mop, comes to help me clean up.

'Don't take it personal,' he says, soaking up the worst of the spill, 'he's always tense on collection night.'

I cock my head to one side, confused.

'You know,' he nods toward the office door, 'when the grand fromage comes to get their cash.'

I stop and lean on my mop, waiting for more.

'You really have no idea?' He gestures toward the bar. 'This place is a front. Money-laundering. It comes in here, they scrub it nice and clean, it goes back out again.' He nods at the office door. 'What do you think they do in there every week?'

I only caught a brief glance of the desk but I saw no piles of cash, just a laptop and one of the silver hard drives Monty keeps lying around.

'There was no money.'

'Of course there was.' He laughs. 'What? You think they still deal in used twenties? It's cryptocurrency. Bitcoin. The police can't trace that shit.'

Chickie worked it all out ages ago.

'Bitcoin isn't an actual, tangible thing,' he tells me later as we walk to get the night tube home. 'It exists in the digital world. But most people don't like to leave that stuff lying around online – too easy to steal. So they store it offline, on a USB or, if you have a <u>lot</u> of currency, on a hard drive.'

'So what, if someone were to nick one of those drives they could just plug it into their computer and be rich?'

'If only.' He laughs. 'The only way you can access what's on the drive is with a PIN number, but because Monty and his overlords are so super-paranoid, they have this whole multi-factor authentication shit going on.'

'Multi-what?'

'It's like paying someone with your online banking for the first time, that way they text a number to your phone? When they want to access the currency they plug the drive into the computer, type in the PIN Monty keeps on this metal card thing in *his wallet and then a one-time passcode is pinged to that pager round Monty's neck. Type that in and bingo.'*

'How much do you think is on there?' I ask Chickie as we part ways at the bottom of the escalator.

'To go to all that effort?' He whistles. 'It's not going to be small change now, is it?'

Hannah

They sat at the table, eyes anywhere but on each other, the quiet devastation of an untouched breakfast before them.

The last forty-eight hours felt like a cruel joke. A taste of what might have been. Hannah wondered if it would have been better not to have experienced it at all; that way they wouldn't know what they were missing.

'Two weeks,' said Jem eventually. 'You're sure?' Slouched in the chair, his usual poise was gone. He seemed smaller, his spine squashed.

'I need to call and get the finer details, but that's what he said.'

'So we'll only see each other . . . ?'

'Once a week. It's a mandatory part of the restorative justice programme, but you'll have visiting orders on top of that.'

'And the baby?'

'I'll bring them with me of course.'

'Maybe Missy will come good on the appeal? How long do these things take? We might only be apart a matter of months.'

Again, they reverted to silence, both conjuring the next twenty years in their heads.

The silence was broken by Hannah's phone. Dr Hess's secretary calling to book her in for an appointment.

'I see here we already have your details on the system. You've seen Dr Hess before?'

'He consulted on my IVF treatment, years ago now.'

The woman was quiet and Hannah could hear the clack of a keyboard.

'Yes, I see that.' She typed some more. 'And can I ask, will you be self-paying again or will your health insurance cover it?'

'I'll be paying.' She went to grab her purse and credit card to secure the appointment, then stopped. 'What do you mean, again? When I saw Dr Hess the first time it was covered by my husband's insurance, as was our IVF.'

The woman clacked the keys some more.

'Not according to my records. All bills were self-paying, settled in full each time by a Mr John Cavey.'

'Self-paying?' She thought of the final bill for their IVF. It had run into the tens of thousands. 'He paid for all the appointments, all the procedures himself. You're sure?'

'I have the receipts here on my screen,' the secretary said, chippy now. She didn't like being questioned. 'It's all there in black and white.'

After ending the call, Hannah steadied herself against the counter.

The most generous gift you could give someone was one they had no idea was a gift in the first place.

John had known how badly she'd wanted a baby. Him too. And so when he'd discovered his health insurance didn't cover their IVF he must have decided not to tell her, to swallow the cost himself and fall deeper and deeper into debt.

She picked up the plates and dumped the pancakes in the waste disposal.

'Suppose I should head back in there,' said Jem and went over to the cell.

Hannah grabbed the key from the hook.

Only once he was behind bars, door locked, did they look at each other.

Their stares were punctuated by the soft, slow blinks of those who know when they are beaten.

Jem

I check in on the Tarkers every week. For months there is nothing and then one night I click on Mrs Tarker's Facebook and there it is, a picture of Lucas in a hospital bed. He's thin, his reddy-brown hair gone. A link to a GoFundMe page below.

He's sick.

Aggressive advanced sarcoma that has spread to various parts of his body including his liver.

He is twenty-three years old.

They're raising money to take him to a hospital in San Diego for specialist gene therapy treatment not available on the NHS. The cost of the treatment including travel is £80,000. So far, they've raised nearly £17,000.

They finish off the post with a plea for people to help in any way they can.

Every morning as soon as I wake up I click on Lucas's GoFundMe page.

The donations are trickling in but after ten days they've only managed to raise another £400.

The donations stall. Ten quid here, five quid there. Then nothing for days. Another ten quid.

After a few weeks of watching the total barely move I make a decision.

I'm going to steal one of the bar's bitcoin drives.

I'll take it and then I'll funnel however much money is on there into Lucas's GoFundMe. Keep the whole thing anonymous. The Tarkers never need to know where the cash came from.

Hopefully it will be enough to help him on his way to America, to the treatment he needs.

Hannah

The next few days passed slowly. Hannah spent less and less time in the kitchen. Meals were eaten in silence or with the smallest of talk and they ceased all physical contact. She knew she should be making the most of what they had left, that she should treasure these last private moments, but she was also trying to protect herself, hoping that if she started the process of letting go now it would be less of a shock when the time came for him to actually leave.

She had tried to reverse the Foster Host request. Surely, she had asked her lawyer, it was up to her as to whether the prisoner should be transferred? Their response was firm. It was too late, everything was in motion, there was nothing they could do. Besides, they wondered, wasn't this what she'd wanted right from the beginning?

With eleven days to go, Hannah cleared away the breakfast things and set about rustling up a batch of brownies to take next door to Pru.

She was about to pop them in the oven when her phone rang. Missy Cunningham.

'I've just heard,' she said, her voice low. 'Could you put Jem on?'

Hannah handed the phone through the bars.

'Your lawyer.'

He took a breath and put the mobile to his ear.

'Missy?'

At first his eyebrows were high, his eyes wide, but then as she told him the news his features dropped and he put his hand over his face.

'Thanks for trying, I appreciate it.'

He handed Hannah back the phone.

'They denied you leave to appeal,' she said, beating him to the punch.

'They did.' His words were flat and quiet.

Next door Hannah was surprised to be greeted not by Pru but by Annabel, her daughter.

Pristine in a white cashmere cowl-necked sweater and grey wide-legged trousers, Annabel spoke a weird hybrid of French and English that Hannah was sure must irritate most people (Annabel was English, she only lived in Paris) but which she herself found extremely charming.

'*Salut!* Come on in,' she said, leaving Hannah to close the door. 'I've got a pan of milk on the boil.'

Hannah had called Annabel and Christopher after the pond incident and let them know what had happened. They'd been concerned and Annabel had said she would organise for the fence to be made higher and harder to scale when she came to stay for the holidays. Hannah had thought she would have gone by now.

In the kitchen, Annabel poured the hot milk into a bowl, sprinkled in a handful of grated chocolate and whisked.

Through the wall they heard the dull falsetto of Jem singing along to the radio. They looked at each other, Annabel waiting for Hannah to acknowledge the sound.

'How's it going?' she said, when Hannah kept her silence.

'He's being transferred to a Foster Host. Next Friday.'

'You must be relieved?' The chocolate melted, she lifted the bowl to her mouth with both hands.

'Yep,' said Hannah, her voice hollow. 'I'm very lucky.'

The song reached its crescendo and they heard Jem try to match it note for note, then it ended and the low DJ burble took over.

'I was supposed to go back to Paris tomorrow,' Annabel said, wiping her mouth. 'But Mum is worse than I thought so I've asked for a few more weeks off work. Just until I can get things sorted.'

'Oh?'

'She's going to have me locked up.' Hannah turned to see Pru in a dressing gown and slippers, swimming goggles atop her head. 'She thinks I can't hear her, on the phone, asking about meal plans and the size of the grounds.'

Annabel finished the last of her *chocolat chaud*. Her upper lip was moustachioed brown but she seemed not to have realised.

'No one is locking anyone up,' she said, and Hannah got the sense they'd had this argument many times before. 'We just want to make sure you're safe.'

Pru narrowed her eyes and humphed, unconvinced. She turned to Hannah.

'Cake?'

Hannah held out the tin of brownies.

'Your dad won't stand for it,' she said, helping herself to the biggest square she could find. 'Just you wait.'

'I'm going out for a bit,' said Annabel, reaching for Pru's panic alarm. 'Put this on, please?' She wiped her top lip clean and as her arm swung down to her hip her wrist left a brown smear on her white cashmere. '*Au revoir*, Hannah,' she said, heading for the door, 'nice seeing you.'

Pru waited, listening for a good minute, and then, once she was certain Annabel wasn't coming back, she went to the French doors and tried to open them. They were locked. She pressed down on the handle and rattled it, then stepped back, defeated. Hannah caught a flash of swimsuit under her dressing gown.

'I can't even go and look at the water anymore.'

'Is that all you want,' said Hannah, smiling, 'to look?'

Pru tried to maintain her grump but a tiny smirk showed through, like sun behind a cloud, and she came to console herself with another brownie.

'Ted had a favourite poem,' she said through a mouth of chocolate rubble. 'It was written by a Greek, I can't recall his name. It's about how some people come to a point when they have to decide on a great Yes or a great No.' Hannah frowned. She couldn't tell if Pru was lucid. She was talking about Ted in the past tense but she also seemed paranoid, whispering and glancing toward the doorway in case Annabel should return. 'The final few lines talk about saying No to something, even if it's the right thing to do. The right No can drag a person down for the rest of their life.'

She stopped, waiting to make sure Hannah had understood.

'If I can't be near the water I don't want to be here. As soon as Ted comes home I'm going to tell him, we need to go now, while we still can.'

Hannah noted the shift back to the present tense.

'Yes?'

'Yes,' said Hannah.

Jem

I watch and wait.

Chickie is right. Every Wednesday the slicked-back hair boss guy arrives around 6 p.m., stays for ten minutes and when he leaves he has Monty's fob round his neck and the drive is gone from the office, presumably in his bag along with the PIN.

Then a day later Monty will appear wearing a fresh fob and the whole process starts again.

The fact Monty keeps the PIN and the fob on his person at all times – Maya told us he even keeps the fob on to sleep – is to my advantage. It means that, when his boss realises the money is not there, everyone else will be above suspicion.

That there can only be one possible culprit.

Monty.

I source a hard drive identical to the ones Monty uses, then I buy the same type of pager as he wears round his neck. Both are standard and so easy to find. Then every Wednesday, when I know there's going to be a drive full of bitcoin ready for collection, I make sure to bring them into work.

I'm ready. All I need now is opportunity.

It comes toward the end of the month. It's been raining all day and the roof is leaking. Monty is distracted. Up and down stepladders, on the phone to builders.

I switch the drives first.

Cleaning the office is one of my duties and so no one bats an eyelid when I go in there to mop. Monty keeps the drive in open view, next to the laptop on the desk. The size of a paperback, its metal sides are stickered with barcodes and numbers. It's worthless without the corresponding codes and so he sees no need to lock it away. I substitute the one on the desk for the drive in my apron pocket, deposit it in my backpack, and then I move onto the hard part.

Getting the PIN and the fob from Monty.

I take his wallet first. Slip it out from his back pocket while he's at the till behind the bar. Then I go to the toilets and lock the door. The code – a twelve-digit sequence of numbers and letters – is embossed on a kind of metal dog-tag he keeps wedged next to his debit card. I copy down the code onto a Post-it and stash it inside my travelcard in my back jeans pocket. When I come out, Monty is still by the till, jabbing at the screen. I squeeze past him, a crate of Britvic under one arm, and then I pretend to stumble. When he turns to catch the crate I slip the wallet back in his front trouser pocket.

Finally, I steal the fob.

I wait until he's up a stepladder, squinting at a yellow water stain in the ceiling, then I set to work taking the chairs down off the nearby tables. His phone rings, a roofer getting back to him with a quote, and he retreats to ground level. As soon as he's off the phone I pounce, asking about my rota for the following week, and then when he's halfway through his reply I pretend to see another damp patch in the ceiling.

'I think I see a second leak?'

'Where?' he says, squinting, and so I reach across his body and point and with my other hand I unclip the little plastic clasp at the

back of the rope and slip the fob away and into my apron. Then I point to the floor where I've dropped an identical replacement.

'Is that yours?' I say, already moving away.

He squints into the gloom.

I finish my shift as normal and head home on the Tube. I'm excited, hopeful. As soon as I get in I'll plug the drive into my laptop, type in the passcodes and set about funnelling money into Lucas's GoFundMe page.

Monty has no clue anything is amiss. The boss arrived around 6 p.m. as usual. They went into the office, he handed everything over, he left.

But when I get back to my house in Tooting the front door is open, the brick awash with the blue swoop of a police siren.

Panic. Monty knows what I did and has sent them here to arrest me. I'm about to turn and run when one of my housemates appears. The police are here because there's been a break in. The burglars finally found a way.

Upstairs I find my room ransacked. Living in a houseshare with people I hardly know I keep my valuables hidden, and so even though the place is a mess I'm optimistic.

I go to the shelf where my rent money lies hidden inside the pages of a Murakami, only to realise they've tipped all my books onto the floor and that the envelope of cash I've been accruing for this month's rent, due Friday, is gone. My mattress is pulled out a little from the wall, seesawing up and down on the divan. Still I search my hiding spot underneath, hoping to feel the slim metal of my laptop. Nothing.

Comparing notes with my housemates I discover we're in the same boat, that all our respective hiding places proved useless, *that everyone except for Suhail, who kept his weed stashed inside one of the loose ceiling tiles in his box room, has been thoroughly cleaned out.*

Once the police have left I sit on the edge of my bed with the drive in my hands. I can't transfer the money tonight; I have no computer and I won't be able to get another one sorted for a few days (there's no way I want to risk doing this in an internet cafe or on a borrowed machine), so where am I going to keep it? I can't take it with me to work. Once Monty finds out about the missing money he'll be on the warpath and I wouldn't put it past him to search our bags, and there's no way I feel comfortable leaving the drive in the house when we could get burgled again.

My room is small, so I've had to put most of my stuff in social storage, which is a fraction of the price of those big warehouses. My things are currently holed up in the loft of a Brixton terrace. I'll go there first thing, stash the drive in the boxes.

As for the PIN inside my travelcard holder and the fob – Monty might get away with searching our bags but even he couldn't get away with a strip search. I'll keep them both on me at all times; that way they'll be safe, secure.

Hannah

Hannah returned home and charged down the stairs to the kitchen. Jem was lying on his bed, reading, but as she entered the room he sensed the change in her and quickly got to his feet.

She hovered there a moment, her breath quick, eyes flicking, calculating, then she ran outside to the bottom of the garden. At the top of the steps she looked down to the shore and across the water.

Yes or No?

While we still can.

She imagined going to Aisling with her idea. Even now, her reflex was to tell her friend everything, to ask her advice. She knew Aisling would have told her to go for it, to seize the day.

Back in the kitchen she stood facing Jem on the other side of the bars, close enough to kiss. She reached through and took his hands in hers.

'The code for the back fence is valid till next Wednesday.'

Jem took a tiny step back.

'It was fun, being out there in the boat, but I don't think we should do it again.' He nodded at her stomach. 'Too much at stake.'

'Exactly,' she said, her eyes shining. 'Everything is at stake. Our whole lives.'

Jem shook his head, trying to recalibrate his understanding of the last few minutes.

'Hannah, what's going on?'

'We're going to take the chance while we still can.' Her eyes glittered, her pupils glossy, but her breath had slowed and the words that followed were low and constant, like a prayer. 'We can't appeal your conviction, so we're going to get you out of here another way. Before the code expires we're going to turn off the fence, get in the boat and row across the pond. Then we're going to keep going.' She pulled him closer and their wrists banged against the steel bars. 'We're going to escape.'

Jem was dead against it. He said they'd get caught, that they'd both end up in prison, their baby taken away.

Hannah spent the next twenty-four hours trying to persuade him. She told him it was their only option, that they had no choice.

They argued.

When, on Thursday morning, Hannah had to go into town to deliver a cake, she placed the prison phone in the hatch for his weekly allowance and left without saying goodbye.

She knew Jem was right and his reluctance was entirely sensible, but she also knew that if they didn't try, if they just sat back and accepted that this was how it was going to be for the next twenty years, then it would be as if they had entered willingly into a kind of death.

Still, if he wasn't in agreement, what could she do?

She dropped off the cake – a spherical sponge, iced and painted in red and peach food colouring to look like the planet Mars – to a private members' club on Endell Street and was headed for the Tube when her phone pinged. It was a message from Colleen Blessop, the widow of Roddy Blessop, the Cambridgeshire detective whose funeral notice John had looked up again and again online. She said the charity had passed on her details and that she knew it was short notice, but she was in London for the day seeing friends and did Hannah want to meet, otherwise they could speak some other time on the phone.

Hannah replied immediately. After everything she'd learned she was now fairly confident that John's interest in Roddy was unconnected to his death, but she remained curious as to how the men might have known each other.

They arranged to meet that afternoon at a cafe in Fitzrovia and Hannah decided to kill the two hours while she waited wandering the shops. In John Lewis she rode the escalators past the post-Christmas sales madness to the top floor and the baby department with its rows of prams and rails of tiny sleepsuits. Most of the women browsing had bulging stomachs, and their narrowed eyes assessed the merits of the different cots with impunity, but Hannah, with her as yet unchanged body, felt shy and waited till she was sure no one was looking to grip buggy handles or run her fingers across the tops of the fleece booties. She wondered if Aisling had done this in the early stages of her pregnancy, if she and John had ever come here together. She imagined Aisling pointing out the hangers of impossibly small dungarees and checked shirts, John smiling shyly, and then, as they headed back out onto the street, John surprising Aisling with a plush teddy for the crib, purchased while she was looking the other way.

She got to Fitzrovia well ahead of time and went into the cafe to discover it empty except for a woman nursing a baby in a chair by the window.

'Hannah?' she said, giving her a wave.

Tall with cropped hair, she wore a powder-blue shirt and jeans. A brown stain, coffee or food, covered the opposite side of the shirt to the suckling baby and as she reached out her hand to say hello she caught sight of it and tutted.

Hannah came to join her, her eyes drawn to the soft, chick-like hair at the back of the infant's head.

'How old?'

'Six months,' said Colleen. She used her pinkie to break the baby's latch on the nipple and, after hooking her bra back onto the strap, placed the child against her shoulder and gently rubbed its back. 'Roddy never got to meet him.'

The baby kicked his legs and batted his hand against Colleen's mouth. She took his wrist and kissed his palm, one, two, three times. His fingernails were tiny crescents, the skin on his feet soft and smooth.

'Your husband was in the Met?' said Colleen loudly and Hannah realised she must have been staring at the baby longer than she'd realised.

'He was murdered. Back at the start of the year.'

'I'm sorry,' said Colleen and Hannah was reminded of the shared looks between the pregnant women browsing John Lewis. Colleen and she were in the same club.

'I know John and Roddy served in different forces, but I'm trying to find out if they knew each other.'

'I don't remember Rod ever mentioning him,' Colleen said, 'but he worked with so many people. Did he come to the funeral?'

'I don't know.' She showed her a picture of John on her phone. 'Is he familiar?'

Colleen squinted at the image, thinking, and then once she was sure she nodded.

'They didn't know each other and I don't remember him at the funeral. But I have seen him before.' The baby winded, she brought him down to sit on her lap and once more clocked the stain on her shirt. 'He got in touch a month or so after Rod died,' she said, going at the mark with a tissue. 'Said he was on the board of some new police charity.'

John had had nothing to do with any charity but Hannah did not correct her.

'What did he want?'

'To give us money. We hadn't applied for it, we thought Roddy's death in service payout was it, but he said the committee automatically made donations to families of deceased officers.' The tissue was useless against the stain and so Colleen dipped it in a glass of water on the table, clearly hoping the liquid would make a difference. 'I was grateful of course, but it was odd.'

'How so?'

'I would have expected a cheque, maybe a bank transfer. But when the money came it was in cash. Ten grand in a padded envelope he brought direct to my door.'

Hannah thought of the bag of money still hidden at the bottom of her wardrobe.

'Dealing with him was a bit unpleasant, to be honest.' Her hand flew to her mouth. 'I'm sorry, God, he was your husband.'

'It's OK. Go on.'

'He kept asking about the suicide. Wanted to know how and where Roddy had been found. He was fixated on it.'

'Roddy killed himself?'

'He'd been working undercover for months.' The dampened tissue started to disintegrate, littering Colleen's shirt with tiny white balls that clung to the fabric like snow. 'It's a lot, living like that, pretending to be someone else. He'd suffered with depression in the past, not that he ever disclosed that to his DCI. Clearly it came back with a vengeance.'

The baby wriggled in her lap and let out a yelp of protest.

Hannah remembered Mickey's grief for the undercover she'd lost a few months before John. Could it be the same man?

'Which force was he attached to? Who was his superior?'

'He was never allowed to tell us anything and the Cambridgeshire constabulary certainly didn't give us any details, even after he died. He hanged himself at a hotel in London but we still don't know if he was based in the city or just passing through.' She curled her mouth into disdain. 'The Warlaby. Not Rod's style at all. Too pretentious.'

Hannah stiffened.

'The Warlaby, in Clerkenwell?'

'That's the one.' The baby grizzled again, louder this time, and she jiggled him up and down, trying to soothe him. 'I'm sorry, I have to go. He needs a nap and he'll only sleep if I walk him in the buggy.' She got to her feet and a tiny avalanche of tissue cascaded from her shoulder to the floor. The brown stain was still there. It looked worse than before.

'Hope that clears things up?'

She clipped the baby into his pram. He was wailing now, his back arched against the sheepskin liner, his tiny hands balled into fists.

'It does and it doesn't,' said Hannah, trying to fit the pieces together.

Colleen pressed her lips into a thin line and nodded.

'After Roddy died I looked for answers everywhere, still do.'

Hannah closed the front door, walked to the middle of the hall and stopped. She was clutching a plastic bag, its contents so slight it felt like there was nothing inside.

She'd spent the journey home trying to incorporate the things Colleen had told her into what she already knew. She was still unclear as to the source of John's interest in Roddy Blessop, but the cash he'd given her under what were obviously false pretences spoke of guilt. Or was he repaying some kind of debt?

There was one thing she was sure of: Roddy's having killed himself in The Warlaby couldn't be simple coincidence. How this might connect to John's murder though was beyond her. Mickey was the one person who might be able to help join the dots, but who knew when she'd next be allowed calls or visitors.

Hannah broached the top of the stairs, the bag swinging at her thigh. She'd bought what it contained as a peace offering, but now she saw how Jem might see it as a dig, a continuation of their argument.

In the kitchen she went over to the hatch, retrieved the prison phone and, reaching through the bars, handed Jem the bag.

The babygrow was white and patterned with fat grey elephants, the fabric soft. When Hannah had taken it to the till she'd been furtive, scared in case the cashier might ask who it was for but also eager to tell someone, anyone, that this was for her newborn, that she was going to be a mother.

He held it up with both hands. The garment so tiny as to be improbable. The booteed feet swinging. He looked at it for some time and then came to stand opposite her. His fingers curled around the steel bars.

'OK,' he said. 'Let's try. Let's get away.'

They spent the rest of the night planning their escape.

Timing, they decided, was a priority. The fence code was valid till Wednesday, so it had to happen before then, and they wanted to choose a day that meant there was as much time as possible between them getting away and the alarm being raised. Their best window of opportunity was Tuesday, five days from now. Jem's DLO would arrive for his shower in the morning and, as Jem had no visitor planned, the officer wouldn't be back until two days later, on Thursday, for his outside session. If they went that night as soon as it got dark, they'd have forty-eight hours in which no one would realise they were missing.

Hannah only knew the code for the back fence and so that decided their exit route.

The rowing boat would see them across the pond, but to where?

'We get to the Heath and then what, make our way to a train station, hop in a cab?'

They were sitting cross-legged on the floor opposite each other, holding hands through the bars.

'Too much CCTV,' said Hannah. 'They'll track us.'

'So what, we walk?'

Hannah turned her head toward the French doors. Across the water she could see the Heath's hills bunched against the purply sky, trees spreading toward the stars. She tilted her gaze slightly, to the palaces of Queen's Crescent.

'The broken-down mansion,' she said excitedly. 'No one knows about it and they certainly wouldn't expect us to go there. We can climb the ladder, push through the hole in the fence. You saw the garage – the cars all have their keys right there, underneath the sun visors.'

Jem laughed.

'You're suggesting we make our getaway in a stolen Bentley?'

'Think about it. They have tinted windows, plus the police won't know to have an alert out for those number plates. They're perfect.'

Jem considered this for a moment.

'OK,' he said, a smile forming. 'That could work.'

After that, everything fell into place.

They realised the car batteries would be dead, that the Bentleys might be low on petrol or empty of it altogether. Tomorrow Hannah would go and buy a new battery and row it to the mansion. A YouTube tutorial would show her how to switch them over. She would fill a jerrycan with fuel.

'What will we do for money?' said Jem, reluctantly. Questions like this punctured the fantasy.

'The holdall,' she said, thinking of the bricks of cash inside. 'That should be more than enough to see us on our way.'

Around 8 p.m. they ordered pizza and moved onto the wider details.

'So we get to the mansion, we start the car and we drive,' she said. 'Then where do we go?'

'We need to leave the country,' said Jem. 'We could head for the Balearics. Hide out till things calm down.'

'But won't the police know to look for us there?'

'Not if we use false passports. Different names. And if we keep moving, stay in each place for no more than a few months. If they don't know the identity we're travelling under they can't track us.'

'False documents,' said Hannah. 'And there lies the rub. It's not like we can order them online.'

All their previous energy fizzled away. On this final thing, it seemed, they were defeated.

The pizzas still hadn't arrived.

'Where are they?' said Hannah, testing her blood. Her sugars were all out of whack, an increasingly common occurrence thanks to her pregnancy. She was drinking some juice to stabilise when the doorbell went.

'Finally,' she said and ran upstairs.

She emerged with the food in hand and passed one of the boxes through to Jem. After testing her blood, she calculated the carbs she was about to consume and gave herself a shot.

They were onto their third slice when Jem spoke.

'Alina might be able to help with the passports,' he said. 'She knows people.'

'You trust her? We'd have to tell her our plans.'

He pursed his lips.

'Who else is there?'

The next day Hannah took the Tube to Bank. Inside the Royal Exchange she sat down at a table in the Grand Cafe – the restaurant dominated the shopping centre's glass-covered courtyard – ordered a mint tea and scanned the surroundings for Alina.

Jem had tried phoning but as soon as she'd heard his voice she'd hung up. All further calls were put through to voicemail. They'd decided they had no choice but for Hannah to come here and ask her for help with the passports in person.

The space was loud and echoey, the chink of cutlery and boorish chatter ricocheting off the stone walls and up to the bulbous glass roof. The shops that lined the outer edge of the courtyard were not your average lunchtime retail fare – Hermès, Boodles and Tiffany & Co. were among some of the boutiques on offer – but still the traders and their EAs paused by windows and weaved in and out of doorways, as if they were doing nothing more than having a quick wander around Marks & Spencer.

She'd been there over an hour when she saw her. Standing next to a group of people peering at the Fortnum & Mason display, Alina was dressed in a grey skirt suit, cream pussy-bow blouse and pearl earrings. An oxblood Mulberry Bayswater hooked over her wrist completed her look. She blended in perfectly. No one would think her any cause for concern.

Jem had told Hannah the cafe would offer the best vantage point from which to observe Alina at work.

He was right.

Her movements were subtle, her hand sliding in and out of bags and pockets with the grace of a mime artist, her trajectory through the crowd punctuated by the odd intentional bump. An embarrassed apology would follow soon after, the distraction buying her a few vital seconds to take what she wanted.

She was circling another potential victim, a pinstriped chunk of a man, when she looked up and caught Hannah's eye.

She stalled, trying to place her, and then as realisation dawned Hannah waved and beckoned her over.

Heels clicking on the tiled mosaic, she approached, her face arranged into a polite smile.

Hannah gestured to the swarming crowds.

'Rich pickings?'

Alina tried to maintain her composure but the question had disarmed her and the smile changed to a frown.

'We need your help.'

'We?'

'Sit down.'

Alina didn't move.

Hannah pushed out the chair opposite with her foot.

'Please,' she said, her voice hard, 'or I'll call over that nice City of London policeman and tell him to have a look through your bag.'

All pretence gone, Alina huffed and did what she was told.

'So what, you and Jem are friends now?'

When Hannah didn't answer Alina blinked.

'No way, you're together?'

Hannah nodded. Talking about their relationship felt strange, like being seen without her clothes on.

'That man,' said Alina, twisting one of her pearl earrings. 'It never ceases to amaze me what he can talk his way into or out of.' She shook her head, suddenly all business. 'What do you want?'

'Passports.'

Alina threw back her head and laughed. The harsh sound bounced off the walls.

'You're going to escape?'

Hannah nodded and Alina laughed again. This time though it felt forced, like she was using it to hide some other feeling, grudging admiration or perhaps even jealousy, Hannah couldn't work out which.

'I already told Jem. I can't help him anymore, I won't.'

She got up to leave.

'I'm pregnant,' said Hannah.

Alina stopped and, after looking Hannah up and down, retook her seat.

'We want to be together.'

Alina rolled her eyes but the gesture was too caricatured and once more Hannah felt like the woman was trying to hide some other feeling, a sadness, that she didn't want her to see.

'So he's told you everything?'

'I know about the stealing. That he pickpocketed John.' She breathed out. The courtyard was quieter now, the lunchtime rush almost over. 'Will you help or won't you?'

'If I don't?'

Hannah gestured toward the policeman in the corner.

'I'll report you.'

Alina blinked slowly.

'I'll need pictures of you both. There's an app you can use to make sure you get the correct framing.' Her words were rote, the blank surrender of someone who feels like they have no choice but to comply. 'Once I have the photos it takes a week, sometimes more.'

'We need them by Tuesday at the latest.'

'Four days?' She shook her head. 'Not possible.'

'You're a resourceful lady,' said Hannah, nodding at the Mulberry full of stolen goods. She got to her feet. 'I'm sure you'll find a way.'

All done with Alina, Hannah walked to St Paul's and set about acquiring the things on the shopping list she and Jem had created. After purchasing two pay-as-you-go mobile phones and a tub of prenatal vitamins, she caught a tube to Halfords in Tottenham, which sold the rest of the stuff they'd need.

She'd googled the car battery in advance and after putting it in her trolley she selected two backpacks big enough to carry their stuff and a couple of torches. She was halfway down the tools aisle, headed for the till, when she stopped.

The front gates to the mansion were secured with a chain. They'd need something to sever it. She shuddered – imagine having gone through all that and got so far only to find themselves trapped in the grounds – then set about searching out the biggest bolt cutter she could find, jittery with good fortune at having solved the problem before it could materialise but also afraid. What else hadn't they thought of?

She paid in cash (Jem had rightly pointed out that the authorities would pore over all her recent card transactions for clues) and took the Tube home. She'd row the battery and the bolt cutters over to the mansion tonight and leave them in the garage, ready for Tuesday. After that they had three whole days to sort a jerrycan of petrol and anything else they might need to prepare.

Weighed down with bags, she staggered out of the station, turned onto Rona Road and was struggling up its shallow incline when a car pulled up and beeped its horn.

She didn't recognise it and so she ignored it at first, but then the driver leaned across to push open the passenger door. She saw a hand ringed with bracelets and a sliver of purple turban.

Kiki Masters.

'Lift?'

Hannah hesitated. Kiki had never offered her so much as a smile.

'Well?' said Kiki.

Hannah weighed the bags in her arms and her biceps screamed in protest. She got in.

'Thanks.'

A yowl, like a tiny air-raid siren going off in the back. Hannah turned round and saw Poobah. He glared out of the meshed front of his carrier, street-light bouncing off his whiskers.

'Shopping spree?' said Kiki. She pulled away from the kerb and, bracelets jangling, guided the car down the street.

'Cake supplies,' said Hannah. 'Client wants a big installation.' Kiki would find out what had happened soon enough and then there'd be the inevitable onslaught of protest and speculation about how many more tens of thousands an escaped convict would knock off the value of her house.

Kiki screwed up her mouth and nodded, as if the prospect of having to earn money was distasteful.

'We took down our FOR SALE sign today.'

'Oh?' Hannah braced. So this was why Kiki had wanted to get her in the car, so she could spend the next five minutes berating her.

'We were mortgaged to the hilt and since your . . .' she paused, searching for an appropriate term of derision, 'little addition to the street our house has depreciated significantly. We can't afford to sell, we're stuck.'

They turned onto Shirlock Road. Nearly there. She'd only have to put up with this for two more minutes max.

'Do you know what it's like having to stay living with someone who doesn't want to be with you anymore?'

It was more of a declaration than a question and had a false brightness that suggested Kiki had been left both scared and liberated at having finally spoken it out loud.

'Maxwell wants a divorce. But until we can turn a profit on the house . . .'

Hannah turned to look at her side-on.

'He's started bringing women home.' She pressed on the accelerator and took a corner too fast. An oncoming car beeped angrily. 'The first time was last month,' she said, guiding the car across the roundabout. 'I sleep in the loft but I could hear them. She called him Maxie.' She grimaced like she'd tasted something bad. 'Since then, whenever he brings one home I put Poobah in his carrier, get in the car and drive.'

As they approached the top of their street Kiki slowed and peered out to the spot where the FOR SALE sign had stood.

'I'm glad we can't move house,' she said. 'It's not ideal, him bringing women back, but at least we're still together under the same roof.' She laughed, as though she'd just realised something for the first time. 'You've done me a favour in a way.'

Hannah nodded. She got out of the car and as she grabbed her things from the footwell she saw Kiki, downlit by the pearl of light in the roof. It made her face look like a skull.

'Tell Rupes I said hello and to stay away from the gee-gees.' She shook her head. 'Bad business.'

Hannah nodded again vaguely, not sure what she was talking about.

A hiss. Wet and long.

Hannah looked to the back seat and saw Poobah, mouth stretched wide, the skin inside nubbled and pink.

She leaned forward across the seat and hissed back.

Inside, she picked up the post from the mat and headed down to the basement. Jem was at the bars, baseball cap pulled low.

'So?' he said, lifting the peak of the cap up and down, a nervous tic she'd never seen before.

'She agreed to help.'

He let go of the cap and sagged forward against the steel.

'We're really doing this?' He smiled, and Hannah felt like she had been hit by a ray of sun.

'We are.'

After turning on the kettle, she gave Jem the mobile phone packs to open and flicked through the post. There were two bills and one envelope postmarked with the Domestic Prison Service logo. Probably more Foster Host paperwork. She slit it open with a knife, already intending to dump whatever it was on the side with the other soon-to-be redundant transfer forms, but on seeing the first few lines she pulled it taut and held it so close that it obscured her face.

Jem sensed her concern.

'Hannah?'

The kettle had boiled. It clicked off, steam gurgling toward the ceiling.

'We have now found a permanent replacement for Mr Dalgleish,' she said, reading from the letter, 'as of Monday 3rd January your new DLO will be Miss Biggins. Miss Biggins will be along to introduce herself in due course. Because of

Miss Biggins' pre-existing prisoner commitments your weekly schedule will transition to the below timetable.'

Hannah scanned the sheet. Shower and outside time sessions were switching days. Not a big deal. On the morning of the Tuesday they planned to leave Jem would have time in the garden with the DLO as opposed to a shower. But then, underneath the table she saw an asterisk and next to it a small line of text: 'Please note, regardless of where you currently are in the four-weekly cycle, fence codes will be reset on the first day your new DLO comes into post.'

Hannah dropped the piece of paper to her side.

The fence codes would switch the day before their designated escape day.

'Once the code changes, that's it,' said Jem, fiddling with his baseball cap again. 'I can't go anywhere.' He shifted the peak up and down and Hannah saw how the friction had reddened the skin on his forehead.

'Then we'll go when the code still works,' said Hannah. 'Move the plan forward.' She tried to sound braver than she felt. 'Forty-eight hours and we have to be ready.'

Compressing their preparations from three days to two meant compromising on certain things, most importantly the passports. When Jem called Alina to tell her the new deadline she laughed and told him she'd ask, but not to hold his breath.

Still, they ploughed on in good faith.

Hannah spent Friday and Saturday night rowing over to the mansion to switch the car batteries in the Bentley and to fill the tank with petrol. Her first attempt at the battery was disastrous; trying to work by torchlight was impossible and the signal in the garage was so weak that the video tutorial she was using to walk her through it kept cutting out. Eventually though she'd managed it, and when she put the key in the ignition it had started first time.

Now it was Sunday, the night before they were due to leave, and there was nothing more to do except preprogramme their respective numbers into each other's burner phones and go over their plans again, trying to identify the points where they might come unstuck.

They both agreed they couldn't leave until at least 4 p.m. Rowing across the pond and climbing the ladder would be best performed under the cover of darkness. If a neighbour saw them it might scupper their escape and then, if they were to get away, there'd be witnesses, people who could alert the police to their route; not good when they were counting on no one being able to figure out which way they had actually gone.

In their discussions they had imagined how the DLO would turn up for Jem's outside session the day after they'd escaped. How he'd knock on the door and then, when there was no answer, call for assistance. The guards would break down the door, find them both missing and realise the back fence had been deactivated. Sniffer dogs wouldn't be able to track them across such an expanse of water and so they'd be left to draw their own assumptions. The most logical being that they'd rowed to the Heath and gone on foot from there. The police would waste hours, if not days (they hoped) on this scenario, by which point they'd be long gone.

From the mansion, they'd drive to Dover and board a ferry to Calais. Then they'd motor across France and down to the bottom-most nub of Spain to Valencia, where they'd board another ferry to Palma. The last ferry left Dover at 11.45 p.m., which gave them more than enough time – almost eight hours – from the moment Hannah unlocked the cell to get there, buy a ticket and board.

If Alina didn't come good they'd have no option but to try to get out of the country with their actual passports. It was risky and it would provide a marker for the authorities on where and when they'd left the country but the alternative, staying in the UK to be hunted by the police, was far worse.

'Let's go through it one more time,' said Jem, as Hannah cleared away the dishes.

'OK, and then bed. I'm shattered.'

'It's 8.30 p.m?!'

'In case you've forgotten, I'm growing another human.' She patted her stomach. She was now ten weeks along. 'It's tiring.'

Jem grinned.

Hannah's phone rang. Seeing the caller ID, she gasped and immediately picked up.

'Mickey?'

'The one and only,' said the detective chief inspector. 'I'm home.' She was jovial but there was a hesitancy to her words, a careful navigation of the vowels and consonants, like she was finding her way across a tightrope.

'How are you? I mean, are you OK?'

'Don't know about that, but I'm sober. For now, at least.' She laughed wearily. 'Laramie mentioned you were keen to talk to me about something?'

Hannah hesitated. It didn't feel right or fair to lay everything on Mickey now, in this the first, fragile part of her recovery. And in theory, it no longer mattered what Mickey did or didn't say. Jem had been refused leave to appeal. They were escaping tomorrow. Nothing would change that.

'I'm an alcoholic,' said Mickey, sensing her reluctance. 'That's my burden. Doesn't mean you need to wrap me in cotton wool. Whatever it is, I can handle it.'

Even with her reassurances, it took Hannah a moment to speak.

'Some stuff has come to light, about the night John died.' Jem had been sitting on his bed but now he came up close to where she stood on the other side of the bars, eager to hear more. 'It might all be a nonsense but does the phrase Marzipan Rain mean anything to you?'

Silence. Hannah thought Mickey was making her way across the tightrope again, trying to find the words.

'What did you say?'

But as soon as Hannah heard her friend's tone she realised it was more than that. She'd struck a nerve.

'Marzipan Rain. John might have been on his way to meet someone on the night he died. Before he left the bar he was heard arguing with them on the phone and he used that phrase.'

She decided not to bring up the claims that John was a dirty cop, and she certainly wasn't going to mention the bag of money upstairs, not now she needed it to start a new life elsewhere.

'Marzipan Rain is a codename,' said Mickey. 'A few months before John died I lost another officer, a UC. They committed suicide.'

It was like she'd been staring down a blurry camera lens only for it to suddenly pull focus.

'Roddy Blessop?'

'How do you know that?' Mickey was suddenly cold. 'That's confidential. Even in death we try to keep actual names under wraps in case it jeopardises an ongoing investigation.'

'Did John know him, this UC?'

'He came from another force. John would have had no idea there was an undercover working on his turf. We keep it that way on purpose.' She stopped, distracted by something at her end. 'One minute.' She covered the phone with her hand and shouted something. 'Laramie,' she said once she was done. 'She's staying with me for a few weeks.' Again, she muffled the phone with her hand and shouted something, and when she came back on she sounded distracted. 'Dinner is ready. I have to go but let's talk more when we see each other. Lunch soon?'

'Sure,' said Hannah, the lie catching in her throat. 'Can't wait.'

'And Hannah,' said Mickey before she signed off. 'This thing about the UC. Knowing that codename is serious. Keep it to yourself for now.'

Off the phone, Hannah relayed Mickey's revelation to Jem.

'Why was John arguing about a dead undercover whose code-name he couldn't possibly have known?'

'I don't know, but if it's true that he *was* dirty then maybe it had something to do with that?'

Any further discussion was interrupted by the doorbell.

Hannah ran upstairs to find Alina, a brown A4 envelope in her hand.

'Not the finest work,' she said, handing them over. 'But they should do.'

The passports.

Her posture was different to the other day; her shoulders sagging, her chest concave.

She looked Hannah up and down, as if she was trying to see her through fresh eyes, in search of an answer to some unspoken question.

'Do you want to see him?' Hannah stood back to let her in. 'Say goodbye?'

Alina pressed forward, then stopped and retreated, fighting some hidden impulse. She pressed her lips together.

'I should get back.' She nodded toward the street. 'My son.'

She went to walk away and Hannah called after her.

'Thank you. So much. We wouldn't be able to do this without you.'

Alina paused and Hannah thought she was going to turn round and say something more, but then she was gone, slinking down the path and away into the night.

Monday morning and Hannah woke shivering, her breath white on the morning air. After months of heat and humidity the seasons had finally changed and, judging by the temperature, they'd decided to skip autumn and hurtle straight into the bleak midwinter. She pulled the duvet up around her neck and then she reached for her belly, as if to stop the baby from getting cold.

This was it.

If all went to plan then tonight she and Jem would be gone from here. Tomorrow they'd start a new life in a new country, live together like a normal couple. She imagined what it might feel like to wake up next to him in bed, his hips pressed against hers, his mouth soft against her shoulder blades.

If all went to plan.

All night she'd dreamed the same dream. In it she was a guy, sitting high atop a bonfire that had just been lit. As long as she didn't look at the fire, as long as she kept her head up and her gaze forward, she could keep the flames at bay. But if she looked down, even a glance, then the fire would start to build. The dream ended with it engulfing her completely.

Teeth clacking, she got out of bed and pulled on some jogging bottoms, socks, slippers, a T-shirt and two jumpers. She checked her blood and, finding it high, gave herself an insulin shot. She resolved to test more often. The further she got in her pregnancy the more unpredictable her sugars were likely to become.

Downstairs she found Jem on the bed, knees hugged to his chest. He too had layered on T-shirts and jumpers to keep warm and his upper half looked bulky and misshapen.

'I know, right?' She turned on the heating and went over to the cell. 'I'd forgotten what it feels like to be cold.' She put her face up close to the bars to kiss him good morning but he didn't move. For a horrible moment she thought he'd changed his mind, that he didn't want them to go after all. Then he nodded toward the garden.

'Look.'

Hannah followed his gaze. Everything on the other side of the French doors had been smothered with frost, the fence filigreed with ice.

Then she saw it. The pond.

Overnight the water had been rinked white.

'No.'

She stumbled outside and crunched through the grass to the back fence. Eyes watering, she peered at the mud, peaked and glittering in the morning sun. A moorhen emerged from the reeds and headed for the centre of the pond, its webbed feet skidding across the ice.

After braving her way down the steps to the water's edge she grabbed a stick and prodded at the floe. It was thick and solid, the wood splintering against its surface.

She ran back inside.

'How bad?' he said, still huddled on the bed.

'It's frozen solid. No way we can row through it.'

'Shit.'

He rubbed the hair on the back of his head, forcing the nap one way then the other.

'What are we going to do?' said Hannah. 'It doesn't look like it's going to thaw any time soon.'

Again, he rubbed his head.

'We could walk,' he said finally.

'Across the ice?' Her hand went to her belly. 'What if we fell in?'

'You're right, it's too dangerous.' He shook his head, annoyed at his own thoughtlessness.

They were quiet then, both of them lost in desperate thought.

Hannah looked out of the French doors, to the ice-crusted Heath beyond.

'The ice seemed thick. We could take it slow. You lead, I'll follow a few steps behind. Make sure it can support our weight.'

He got to his feet and came to face her on the other side of the bars. 'No.'

'We have no choice,' she said, trying to ignore the panic gnawing at her throat.

The central heating had kicked in and this plus her many layers was making her armpits clammy. She looked down. Her slippers were covered with melting frost but inside her feet felt like they were burning. She thought of her dream, the flames roaring high and hot around her calves.

'OK,' he said, 'we walk, but the rest of the plan stays the same. Agreed?'

He reached his hand through the bars and placed it next to hers on her abdomen.

'Agreed.'

Hannah went through the house turning off lights, pulling out plugs and closing curtains. In the kitchen she cleared the fridge and set the rubbish outside. She knew it was unnecessary, that in a few hours this place would no longer be her concern, but putting it to rest felt good, like she was drawing a line between it and the life she was about to live. All done, she went and stood by the cell. While she and Jem waited for the sun to slide behind the trees she imagined crouching on all fours, haunches raised, her fingertips brinking a starting line, ready for the clap of the gun.

Darkness.

She went to the keypad first. Inputted the code. It flashed green. She turned to him with a smile. The back fence was off.

Next she pressed the black button on the fob round her neck, slicked the key in the lock and, in one easy movement, opened the cell door. Jem stepped forward and they hugged.

There was something final about the embrace, like he was saying goodbye for the last time, and Hannah knew that, in a way, he was. If this didn't work then they'd likely not see each other again for decades.

They pulled apart and Hannah went to grab her coat, but Jem brought her back to him and cupped her chin, his fingers light against her jawbone.

'Are you sure?'

She smiled and covered his hands with her own.

'I am.'

Jem opened his mouth as if to say something more but then seemed to decide against it, and they broke apart.

Hannah had laid the matching backpacks she'd bought and their twinned essentials – one change of clothes, thirty grand in cash, a torch, a fake passport and a pay-as-you-go smartphone and charger – on the table.

Standing side by side, they began to pack, Hannah saying the name of the object out loud and Jem repeating it in a kind of call and answer, before placing it inside their respective bags. They had decided to split Hannah's diabetes stuff – a fortnight's supply of needles and insulin – between them and Hannah took responsibility for her prenatal vitamins and dextrose tablets.

After grabbing his baseball cap, Jem zipped up his rucksack, strapped it on and headed for the stairs.

'I need the bathroom,' he said, taking them two at a time. 'Won't be long.'

'Use the cell,' said Hannah. But he was already gone and her words tailed to nothing.

She placed her backpack at her feet and zipped up her coat. Standing still, she became aware of a tittering sensation deep up inside. It was coming from the part of her body that usually only made itself known with monthly cramps. She held her breath, not sure if she'd imagined it, but then there it was again, a pulsing, fluttering feeling, sporadic, like corn kernels popping in the pan. She imagined the baby somersaulting in the dark and then the sensation seemed to spread, branching and splitting through the dormant circuitry of her stomach, heart and lungs, until finally it reached her face and, twitching and flickering, pushed her cheeks up into a smile.

Jem reappeared and took her hand. Hannah frowned and stepped back, looking him up and down.

'Are you going to be warm enough?'

He considered his windbreaker's meagre padding as if for the first time.

'Good point.' He smiled, dropped his bag to the floor and reached for one of the jumpers he'd left in the cell.

All set, they went to the French doors and were about to step outside when there was a noise.

'What was that?' said Jem.

'Nothing,' said Hannah. 'Let's go.'

But then the noise happened again, louder than before. A low, muffled moan.

Next door. It was coming through the wall.

They strained their ears and were rewarded with a single word.

'Help.'

Pru.

'She has her daughter staying,' said Hannah. She released her fingers from the door handle only to grab it again. 'But maybe she's out.'

They looked toward the pond and the yellow glow of Queen's Crescent, buttery in the distance.

'You should go check,' said Jem. 'We've got time.'

She let go of the door and kissed him.

'I'll be quick,' she said, grabbing Pru's keys from the drawer.

Jem watched her go and then he turned back to the pond and the mansions' yellow glow. Blood pounded in his ears.

Hannah let herself into Pru's house and stopped, listening. Silence and then a whimper, slight, like a child murmuring in its sleep. She followed the sound through to the kitchen and found Pru lying on her side in the middle of the floor. Her eyes were closed and a heart-shaped bruise bloomed purple on her cheek.

'Pru?' she said, kneeling beside her. She realised the old lady's toes were pointed and that she was moving her feet up and down in a scissoring motion, as if swimming. She remembered that Pru had once told her that at times during her journey across the Channel, the rowing boat accompanying her had dropped back out of sight and that those minutes alone, legs kicking through the black with no speck of land in sight, still gave her nightmares to this day.

Hannah took her hand and squeezed it.

I'm here.

Someone's here.

'I was looking out the window to see Ted coming home,' said Pru, opening her eyes. 'That man was hanging around the front again.' It was as if she'd misplaced something and was now recounting the details, walking back through the steps to the moment she'd last seen it. 'He saw me looking and then he came up close and banged on the glass. I ran to call the police.'

Hannah clocked the usual blast radius of food scraps and sodden teabags around the bin. No doubt Pru had slipped, fallen and possibly passed out. How long she'd been on the floor was anyone's guess. She fetched her a cushion and a rug and, once she was comfortable, used the wall-mounted landline to call for an ambulance. The operator told her that help was on its way and instructed her to leave the front door open.

She did as they asked and returned to the kitchen to see Jem peering over the fence.

'Hannah?' The glass in the French doors made it sound like he was underwater.

After giving Pru's hand another squeeze she went outside. The flagstones were scratchy with frost and the temperature made her eyes water.

'Pru's had a fall,' she said, trying to still the tremor in her voice. 'I've called for help. I'll stay with her till they arrive.'

Jem nodded.

Again, she was grateful that he didn't question this, that even now, his instinct was to do the right thing.

When she returned to Pru she found her shivering, the rug having slipped from her shoulder.

'Don't worry,' she said, leaning over to tuck it back in. 'Help is coming.'

Pru groaned.

'I should wear my button, but I forget.' She grabbed hold of the oval round Hannah's neck, so similar to the device everyone was always nagging her to wear. Looking at it, Hannah realised she'd been so focused on the last stage of their leaving preparations that she'd forgotten to take it off.

'Press in case of emergency,' said Pru, parroting the phrase Hannah had drilled into her. Then she placed her finger on the red button and pushed down hard.

'No,' said Hannah, pulling away. But it was too late.

Staggering to her feet, she ripped off the device, placed it on the counter and retreated to the other side of the kitchen, as if it was a bomb about to explode. Then under her breath she began to beg. 'Please,' she said, hoping Pru hadn't pressed it all the way down, 'please, please, please.' It felt like she was falling off the side of a building. She knew she was going to hit the ground, but still there was a moment, this moment, when her feet had first left the ledge that was like an opening in time, a fraction of a second where it still seemed possible that she might grab onto something, claw her way back up and collapse onto the roof's dusty tarmac, heart yammering.

Jem appeared at the fence holding her regular phone, the screen lit blue with an incoming call.

Impact.

Hannah went out to join him. The ringtone nagged through the night air and Hannah had to stop herself from covering her ears.

'Why would they be phoning?' he said, showing her the caller ID.

The Domestic Prison Service.

Hannah knew the protocol. If the red button was activated they'd send someone out to check on her within half an hour, whether she answered or not.

'You need to go,' she said, letting the call ring out. 'Now, before the guards arrive.'

Jem was confused at first and then, once Hannah had relayed what had happened, resolute.

'No,' he said, and for the first time she heard the crackle of fear in his voice. 'We leave together or not at all.'

She pushed back on her heels, her mind scrambling for another solution. Maybe they should deal with the guards head-on? Have Jem get back inside the cell and then, when they arrived, tell them she'd pressed the button by mistake. Pretend everything was normal. They could set off across the ice as soon as they'd gone. But no, it was protocol for them to reset the fence codes after any call-out, false alarm or not.

'This is our only chance.' She reached up on her tiptoes to kiss him. 'You're wasting time. Go. I'll follow after.' A few streets away they heard a siren scream. The ambulance. 'Please,' said Hannah. 'I won't be far behind.'

He didn't move. Desperate, Hannah was trying to figure some other way out when he hooked his thumbs through his rucksack and stepped back.

'I'll meet you in the garage?'

Hannah nodded and he set off toward the bottom of the garden at pace, baseball cap pulled low.

Her relief was momentary. They were meant to be doing this as a couple, melting away into the night, and now they were separated, about to be tracked like game.

She waited until he disappeared through the gate and down the steps to the shore and then she returned inside to Pru and the sound of people knocking on the open front door.

Paramedics.

'In here,' she shouted. Then quietly to Pru, 'The doctors.'

A man and a woman came through to the kitchen, capable in uniforms of bottle green. They shouldered heavy bags and were full of 'hello's' and 'what have we here's' that made Pru's fall feel jolly and manageable and like they'd all been friends for years.

Hannah explained the situation and they set to work. Annabel arrived soon after, shopping in hand.

'Mum!' she said, rushing to Pru's side.

With Pru taken care of Hannah slunk away, down the hall and out the still open door. No sooner had she stepped onto the front path than she was greeted by a van pulling up on the other side of the road.

Guards.

Heart bouncing, she foxholed back inside before they could see her. In the living room she turned off the lights and took up a position by the bay window just in time to see six guards and one of their temp DLOs tumble out of the van. The DLO knocked on her front door and when no one answered, a battering ram was produced.

Three thumps and they were in.

Hannah tugged at the straps on her backpack. It seemed heavier somehow, harder to carry. She tried to regulate her breathing but her lungs were sieged with panic, the blood vessels small and tight. There was no way she could chance it across the pond now, even via Pru's garden; there was too much risk of being seen. She wondered if she should wait it out, make a break for it once they'd been and gone, but who knew how long they'd stick around once they discovered she and Jem were missing.

She looked at the street. It was empty, the cars shadowed by brittle light.

Maybe being separated wasn't such a bad thing?

Jem might not have been able to go out the front but she could. Alone, she could skip the pond completely, get to the crescent the long way, on foot.

Back in the hall she peeped out the door, checking for guards or passers-by. Once she was sure there was no one around she took her chance.

She wanted to run but the pavement was slithery with ice and so she had to marionette her way forward, her steps jerky. She hadn't gone far when she heard the fizz and beep of a radio back near the house. One of the guards had come outside. A van door slammed shut.

Not looking back, she continued her way down the street, toward the Crescent, toward Jem.

She'd experienced love before with John, she was sure of it, no matter how flawed their marriage had turned out to be; but she'd never realised it could make you this brave, that it could give you the courage to do anything: stroll barefoot through fire, open your arms to a bullet, leap high across a deep ravine with nothing to catch your fall but the jag of distant boulders.

Jem

I thought I was home and dry. No one had a clue I was to blame for the missing bitcoin. Lucas was going to get the treatment he needed. Everything was fine.

Then I did something stupid.

After that everything went terribly, terribly wrong.

Once I've stored the hard drive with the rest of my stuff in Brixton I go to work. I need the job – besides, not turning up would mark me out as a suspect.

On my way to the staffroom I see Monty in the office. Trussed in a too-small shirt and trousers, his mouth is open. His braces twinkle and every now and again his tongue reaches up and sweeps across the tangle of metal and teeth. He's torn the place apart. The desk is full of holes where the drawers once were and every shelf is empty, the floor spread with boxes and papers.

In the staffroom Chickie is putting on his apron while Maya hangs up her coat. I smile hello but Maya looks away, her hand over her mouth, and as she reaches down to pick up her bag she flinches, as if she's pulled a muscle.

'Don't mind her,' says Chickie once she's gone, 'rough day.' He nods at the sound of banging and swearing coming from the office down the hall. 'A ton of cash has gone missing. Or he's misplaced it.' He heads off to start his shift. 'Either way, his head is on the block.'

'How much?' I call after him. Until I hook the drive up to a laptop I've no idea if it's anywhere near enough to help Lucas reach his total.

'Thirty grand.' Chickie draws a line across his neck. 'Monty is officially cancelled.'

It's the start of the Easter weekend and the bar is heaving. I'm glad. After last night's burglary I've got two days to replace my stolen rent money. Seven hundred quid. Acquiring that amount of cash in such a short amount of time is going to be tricky but if I'm smart and choose the right targets I might be OK.

I move through the crowd, a stack of dirty pint glasses tucked against one arm, my other hand fanning people's inside and outside pockets and bags. I filter their possessions for wallets and purses, my fingers tracing the edges of phones, travelcards and lipsticks.

Every time I hit gold I store the booty in my front jeans pocket and then as soon as I get a chance I go off to the toilets to check my haul.

I'm doing well – three hundred quid and counting – when I open a brown leather wallet with a Met Police ID inside.

I drop it like it's hot, then immediately pick it back up. I pride myself on taking things without people realising, but there are no guarantees. What if the copper notices his wallet gone and decides to kick up a fuss? He could be out there now, accusing people, trying to figure out who did it. He might request the bar CCTV, see the moment I passed by.

It's not worth the risk.

I'll go out there now, put it back before he can clock it's missing.

Hannah

Queen's Crescent was quiet, the pavement deserted. Hannah headed toward the abandoned mansion, giddy at having made it there without incident. All she had to do now was get inside the grounds without being seen.

She'd spent the journey trying to re-version the second part of the plan. The guards would have put out an alert as soon as they discovered them both gone, their mugshots emailed to Customs and Immigration. It might make sense to hold off on the ferry crossing until things had died down; head out of London and then hang around in Kent for a while, somewhere near the port. They could lie low, sleep in the car, and then, when their faces were no longer all over the nightly news, make the crossing into France.

She reached the stone pillar that marked the entrance to the property and shrank back into the dim to consider her options. The walls were seven feet high, the iron gates even higher, a chain wrapped round their middle.

The bolt cutters she'd bought were waiting in the garage where they were no good to her.

She looked next door, at Maraschino's house. Every window was alight, the garden illuminated by a circular formation of white lanterns. Maybe she should try to access the mansion through it? She could manufacture some pretext for her visit and then, once she was in, try to find a way to slip out the back, through the hole in the fence to next door. But no, that was too ridiculous. Maraschino might not even be home and even if she were to inveigle her way inside it wasn't like they weren't going to notice if she suddenly vanished. Her only option was to scale the gates and drop down to the other side.

The front of the gate was covered in an elaborate spread of curlicued iron, designed to look like a tree branching out toward the edges. Hannah wedged her foot against the bottom-most flourish, grabbed the bars and pulled herself up to the next available toehold. Rust flaked off in her palm, the metal beneath freezing. She kept going but the higher she got, the fewer the points of leverage, until finally, a metre away from the top of the gate, she ran out of toeholds altogether. She decided to press the insides of her feet against the bars and propel herself up the rest of the way. Her technique worked and she scooched a few more inches without issue, but the rust here was much worse than below and soon her feet were scrabbling against the crumbling bars for purchase. One foot slipped and then the other. She dangled there a few seconds, hands burning with cold, then she fell to the floor, her rucksack breaking her fall as she crashed back against the gates.

Her hand went to her belly. From everything she'd read she knew that at this stage the baby would be fine, that it was too small for the impact to have caused it harm, and yet her instinct told her she'd be wrong to try to scale the fence, and possibly fall, again.

Brushing the frost from her knees, she was revisiting the Maraschino option when she noticed her tumble had dislodged the gates. There'd been more give in the chain than she'd realised and the force of her fall had shoved the right side open, creating a tiny gap.

She got down on the floor, took off her rucksack and threaded her arms and then her head and shoulders through the opening. Then she reached for her bag.

She was in.

The mansion lay ahead, dishevelled and rotting.

She got to her feet and jogged down the drive and round the back to the basement.

The steps that led down to the door were smeared with ice and so she broached them with care, but on the second step down her foot went out from under her. Flailing, her right hand collided with an old hanging basket and she grabbed it, her shoulder slamming hard against the brick. Breath ragged, she kept hold of it and slid down the wall until she reached a sitting position. Not wanting to risk another fall, she navigated the final few steps on her bottom.

The cold had made the door stiff and she had to shove her shoulder hard against it to get it open. She paused on the threshold, listening for any sound that might indicate she had been followed; then, closing the door behind her, she went inside.

The laundry room was dank, the air spored with dust. Something ran across her foot and she jumped. Then she laughed, her heart skittish against her ribs.

She got out her torch and turned it on. Light poled through the black, revealing a cupboard door swollen with moisture lolling from its hinges. A takeaway menu curled on the noticeboard. She followed the beam down the hall, past the chlorine reek of the pump room, toward the garage.

'Jem?' she said quietly and then, when there was no response, a little louder. 'Jem?'

Maybe he was hiding?

It would be the sensible thing to do, keep out of sight until he knew for sure it was her.

She opened the door into the garage and swung her torch around. The cars sat in their row, stately and silent. She licked her lips and felt grit, coarse as sand.

'Jem?' She strained her eyes and ears for any sign of him. 'It's me, Hannah.'

Maybe he was still trying to make his way across the ice? There was no knowing how long that would take.

She decided to head up to the first floor. The master bedroom overlooked the garden. She'd watch and wait for him to appear.

Her torch led the way, the beam dancing across bulging walls and piles of debris, to the entrance hall and the winding stair-case, blanketed with ferns. At night the foliage looked black, the furled leaves like tentacles, reaching. She edged her way up the stairs, the plants hushing around her knees. A frond tickled her cheek and she recoiled as if slapped.

In the bedroom she kicked her way through the pigeon bones and over to the window. The top pane was cracked and had a small hole in the bottom corner. She searched the dark below for movement but there was nothing.

Where was he?

Across the pond she sought out her house in among the others and saw that the guards had turned on all the lights. The curtains were open, the windows vacant holes.

Five minutes passed, then ten.

She'd just started to consider the possibility that the guards had spotted him on the ice and made pursuit when there was a beep.

A message on her pay-as-you-go.

Jem.

It was like someone had taken a bat to the back of her knees. He was OK, just delayed. Maybe a passer-by had seen him and he'd had to hide out in the reeds until they were gone?

She reached inside the backpack for the phone and her hand bashed against something sharp, a corner, hard and metallic. She opened the bag a little wider. Sitting on top of her things was a silver rectangle. The size of a paperback, it had white stickers printed with barcodes stuck to its outside. A hard drive of some kind? She delved deeper, searching for the phone, and landed on a jumper and a pair of jeans. Jem's clothes.

She'd picked up the wrong bag. Their packs were identical and so till now she'd had no idea. She looked again at the metal drive. She'd watched Jem place everything inside his bag, so when had this found its way inside?

Finally, she located the phone, Jem's phone, and read the text.

Don't worry. I have it.

She read it twice more, trying to make sense of the words.

'Have it.' Have what?

She clicked on the message and opened it full screen to reply. It was then she saw that this message was a follow-on from an earlier text sent by the same number.

I'll be there. See you in a couple of hours.

Her gut knew it first, that same ancient part of her nervous system that made her cross the street long before she heard the footsteps of a man walking too close for comfort.

She scrolled back up to the top of the conversation, to the first message in the sequence.

It's on. Leaving now. Cobham services, Esso forecourt. Remember, stay out of sight. I'll find you.

Sent 4.16 p.m.

4.16 p.m., a few minutes before they'd been about to leave. Jem must have written it when he went upstairs to use the toilet.

She looked again at the overgrown garden. The wind was getting up and with it came the odd flake of snow, sludgy and deformed.

Jem wasn't delayed. He hadn't been caught.

He wasn't coming.

Their relationship had been a ruse all along. A means of escape. A way for him to break out and take this hard drive, or whatever it was, with him.

She knew she should feel betrayed, that she should be angry at him and his lies, but right now in this moment, more than anything else, she felt sorry for him. Sad that he was the kind of person who felt able to do this to her, to their baby.

She turned off the torch and let the darkness cover her like a blanket. Outside, the pond glowed with reflected light. A sickly beacon; she couldn't tell if it was calling her home or warning her to stay away.

The snow was thickening, the sky a blurry mess. She poked a finger through the broken pane and caught the fattest flake she could. It was pure white but when she placed it on her tongue it fizzed like ash, dirty and grey.

Jem

The interesting thing about watching a magic trick is that you're agreeing to be deceived. You agree even though you don't really know when and where the deception might take place.

From the moment I was found guilty I began to plan. To plot. I had one goal: to access the money in time to donate it to the Tarkers and hopefully save Lucas's life.

Whatever it took to make this happen, I'd do it.

And so, from the minute I arrived at the house I started stealing – from the guards, from Mr Dalgliesh, even Hannah – taking anything I could because I knew that even the most random of objects might come in useful later, that I could use them to create opportunities.

I learned about the trick with the magnet while I was in the Holding Centre. If you placed it in a particular spot on the cell side of the door it would stop the electronic lock from functioning. But, as all those convicts would lament, you could use magnets all you liked; to get out you still needed the manual key. And even then, the electric fence made escape impossible.

But I didn't want to escape. What I wanted was inside the house.

If you don't know something is a magic trick, if you don't consent to the deception, then what is it?

I told Hannah about the call I overheard, the things her husband said, because I wanted to plant a seed of doubt. To make her drop her guard, just a little.

Uncertain people are easier to manipulate.

But then, as time passed things changed.

There were moments when I wondered if I should tell her the truth about what happened that night, if I should admit to what I did.

I always decided against it.

At first it was because I didn't know if I should trust her; later it was because I wanted her to continue to trust me. That's the thing with lying. If you do it for too long you reach a stage where it becomes impossible to turn the ship round. If I'd confided in Hannah, told her the truth about what was really going on, she might have changed her mind, turned her back on me. And so I made my peace with the deceit and held on to the notion that what she didn't know couldn't hurt her.

Or me.

Misdirection is the art of drawing your attention to one thing in order to ensure you are unaware of something else. It's about making you relax at a key moment, guiding you to look in the wrong place at the right time or the right place at the wrong time.

The clock was ticking and so the very first time Alina came to visit she made sure to carry things on her person she knew would be confiscated. The magnet I needed was inside a lipstick and when she knocked over the tray at the end of our session, she waited till Mr Dalgliesh was distracted and kicked it across the floor to the cell. It hit the bottom of the bars and I reached through and grabbed it. Mr Dalgliesh was none the wiser.

Once I had the magnet and could prevent the door from being locked electronically, I set my sights on the manual key.

I soon learned that Hannah rarely returned it to its hook straightaway; instead she'd slip it inside a pocket, only coming across it again later. The spare she kept in a tin on the windowsill.

To take the key from her unnoticed I needed bait. Something to move her attention elsewhere for a second. I'd stolen her engagement ring within minutes of my arrival and so I just had to wait for the right moment, to be ready.

That afternoon she was flustered, her mind elsewhere. I took my chance. I attached the magnet to the door, preventing her from locking it electronically, and then as soon as she turned the manual key and placed it in her front pocket, I tossed the ring at her feet. When she bent down to retrieve it I reached through the bars, dipped my hand into her dress and stole the key.

That night, while she was in bed, I unlocked the cell door, replaced the master on the hook (so that when she looked at it, she'd presume she put it there herself) and took the spare from the tin. There was a risk she might go there and find it empty, I knew that, but it was one I was willing to take.

After that, I could explore the house at my leisure.

Mr Tarker was an expert illusionist. Hannah is an illusionist too, in her own way. She takes eggs, flour, butter and sugar and turns them into something else entirely. Planets, buildings, animals, people. Love is another kind of illusion. Often, it's hard to know when it's real and when it's something else entirely.

I kept the key on me at all times – when I slept, when I showered, during my outside time – buried deep inside a pocket. Most days

I roamed around the house no problem, but there were a couple of occasions when I almost got caught. One night, Hannah came down to the living room for something long after I thought she was asleep and I had to hide behind the door. Then there was the time she saw me from across the pond and thought she had an intruder.

She did, in a way.

One evening, in my haste to get back to the cell, I knocked her wedding picture and it fell. The glass cracked. I was so scared Hannah would realise, that she'd figure out how it happened, that the game would be up.

After searching for weeks, there was still no sign of my brown paper custody bag. I tried edging around the subject with Hannah, encouraging her to tell me where she'd stored it, but whenever I pushed too hard she got suspicious and shut down.

Time was running out.

I used my phone allowance to call the hospital ward. Who I got on the line varied, as did how long they stayed talking once they realised the caller wasn't going to say anything, but I was sometimes rewarded with the odd snippet: Lucas's voice in the background, asking Mr Tarker about the Chelsea score or thanking the nurse for bringing his meds.

The day I heard Hannah scream, I didn't know what to do. If I came out of the cell I'd give myself away but if I stayed put . . .

In the end I told myself it was worth the risk, that I was only doing it to win her trust, to get her on side, that it would help toward my end goal.

That's what I told myself. Didn't mean it was true.

What does it take to hold a knife in your hand and drive it into another person's body over and over? The sheer physicality of it.

How do you know if you have it in you? Or do you only find out in the moment, when the other person is standing in front of you, the blade a weight in your palm?

The morning Hannah discovered my stash under the mattress I had to change my story, to offer her another version of the truth.

Truth.

When the police arrived in the bar that day I thought they were there to arrest me for the stolen bitcoin, that Monty had figured out it was me and called it in. I panicked. The drive was still stored with my things in Brixton, but the PIN and the fob were in my pocket. After the mix-up with the travelcard and the policeman I'd bought a cheap turquoise keyring, ceramic with a screw-off metal top. It had a compartment in which I'd rolled and stored the PIN.

Not wanting to be caught red-handed, I dropped the fob into one of the tiny wooden haberdashery drawers in the bar's window display, pushed it shut and was about to do the same with the keyring when I felt a hand on my shoulder. The next thing I knew my arms were being roughed behind me, my wrists cuffed.

In the police car on the way to the station my rational brain had kicked in. Of course they hadn't been there because of the stolen bitcoin; there was no way Monty would have alerted them. But by then it was too late.

At the station any possessions I had on my person were removed, logged and placed in a sealed paper bag. A bag that went on to reside somewhere in Hannah's house.

When Alina came to visit me at the Holding Centre I did ask if she could get the keyring for me. Once I and the bag were transferred to Hannah's house all it would take was a simple burglary, a trip to the bar and a visit to Brixton and she could bring the three elements together, access the money and hey presto.

She refused.

And so, together we came up with another plan.

I would find a way out of the cell, locate the custody bag and the keyring inside and then the next time she came to visit I'd pass it to her.

It was already tricky, unlikely to work. Then everything started to go wrong. To get complicated in ways I had never imagined.

To be a good pickpocket, to be good at misdirection, you need to know when the shift in interest occurs; better yet, you should control this shift.

That day with Pru. I could have swum her back to shore, turned round and got right back in that water. I know Hannah thought that was what I might do. But she didn't know about the PIN and the hard drive, the fact they were now under the same roof, her roof. That I had no choice but to return.

Alina had bailed on me. Lucas was getting sicker.

Everything seemed hopeless – and then, she kissed me.

Hannah

There was only one person who might be able to help her out of this mess. If he wasn't at the station she'd leave a message, ask him to call her on this number. She used the smartphone to search for the Scotland Yard switchboard. As it was, she was put through without fuss.

'Rupert.' She stopped, not sure how to explain. Should she start with the fact she and Jem had been in a relationship, that he'd played her like a fool or that she was facing ten years in a civic centre cell? 'Jem,' she said, deciding to start with the here and now. 'He's gone.'

She wondered about Jem's original plan, before they were derailed by the weather and Pru's fall. Would he have abandoned her as soon as they were across the pond, or would he have waited till they'd got to the Esso service station and ditched her there?

'Are you hurt?' said Rupert. In the background she could hear the trill of phones and the spike of laughter, like someone had just revealed the punchline to a joke. 'How did he get out?' There was a low rumble, like a chair being pushed back. Hannah imagined him on his feet, ready to run.

'I helped him.' Saying it out loud, Hannah cringed with shame. 'I'm in Queen's Crescent. He was supposed to meet me here.' The hurt was like a stone at the back of her throat. She tried to swallow it down.

'What? Why?' and then, as his brain caught up, 'You let him go?'

Hannah considered telling him about their relationship but she didn't know how. That story would have to wait.

'He didn't do it, he didn't kill John.' Despite everything, Jem's innocence was the one thing of which she was still certain. 'There's proof.'

A huff of air.

'Not this again.'

'There are witnesses, people who say it was a gang that had John killed. The Heppels. I know you don't want to believe it, but John was taking money from them, bribes. Somehow it all backfired and he ended up dead. It seems to be mixed up with the suicide of another officer, an undercover, but I've yet to figure out how or why.'

Silence.

'Rupert?'

She knew he was trying to be kind, holding back for fear of saying something he might regret.

'Come home, quick as you can. I'll blue-light my way through town, meet you there.' He spoke slowly, his tone thick with reassurance. The murmur of background voices thinned and she heard a click, a door opening and shutting. He was already on the move. 'Don't talk to anyone. And don't worry, we'll sort this—' He stopped and corrected himself. 'I'll sort this.'

Hannah said goodbye and made her way out of the mansion and back out through the gap in the front gates.

The snow had stopped. The flurry had been short-lived but it had left everything changed. She looked around, trying to get her bearings, no longer clear where the pavement ended and the road began. It was like the white sheet you throw over a corpse, the way you were still fairly confident what was where – there the prow of a toe, there the dip of a clavicle – but could never be sure unless you pulled it back to reveal cold, grey flesh.

She walked as fast as she dared, her mind whirring. Should she come clean with the DLO or should she concoct a story, something that, with Rupert's help, might keep her and her baby out of jail? Maybe she could say that Jem had escaped and so, afraid for her life, she'd run away from the house until she was sure things were safe?

She tried to weigh up the merits of each scenario but her mind was clouded with images of her and Jem together. His mouth on her stomach. Her legs round his waist. His hand trailing through the loose spill of her hair on the sheets.

A thousand tiny humiliations.

She'd spend the rest of her life wondering how she could have been so stupid.

She'd loved him.

The sadness pressed down on her from all sides.

Jem

Earlier

I pick my moment.

That fraction of a second when Hannah is too focused on making sure she's packed everything to question why I might want to use the upstairs bathroom.

She calls after me but I don't stop.

In the hall I pause, listening for any sign she might have followed me, then I head for the first floor and the airing cupboard.

For the last three and a half months I've passed it and its padlock twice a week on my way to the shower. Once I discovered this was where Hannah had chosen to store my custody bag and inside it the PIN, the item I need most – the entire reason I ended up here in the first place – the journey became torturous.

But these trips upstairs have had merit. A routine like that gives you the chance to properly take in your surroundings, to notice stuff that might one day be of use.

I go to the display cabinet outside the bathroom and open the door. John's vintage dart collection sits in a neat line on the shelf. The Kroflite darts are made of brass, the cardboard box they came in arranged behind them, small brown text boasting WITH FEATHERED FLIGHTS. I pick one up and weigh it in my palm. It's heavier than it looks, the pointed end sharp as a spear. It should more than do the trick.

Back at the cupboard, I bash the spike as hard as I dare into the tiny gap where the padlock's shackle meets the housing. Nothing. I try again, this time with more force. The lock stays intact but the screws holding the latch in place begin to loosen. I bring it down again and the wood splinters. A tug and the latch falls to the floor, the padlock still attached.

I wait a moment. I want to make sure Hannah hasn't heard, that she isn't about to appear at the bottom of the stairs.

Once I'm satisfied she isn't coming I put my hand on the door and pull.

The custody bag sits slumped against the wall. I rip open the seal and feel inside. The keyring is broken, the metal screw-top jagged with the remains of the ceramic holder – Hannah smashed it when she dumped it on the table that first day – the furled Post-it note littered with turquoise fragments. I open it out and there are the twelve digits and letters that form the PIN.

The slip of paper in my pocket, I go to the spare room. I find the hard drive in the middle box, pristine inside the plastic bag I put it in back in March. I place the PIN in with it, put them both in the rucksack and then I get out my phone.

I have Kenzie's number memorised.

I send him a text telling him I'm on my way.

We organised everything days ago, when Hannah gave me the phone to call Alina about the passports. I'm praying that this time he won't let me down.

Before I go, I try to tidy up the mess. I don't want to risk Hannah coming up and noticing it at the last minute. It would raise too many questions.

She calls my name.

I'll have to leave it as it is.

'Coming,' I shout. Then I scurry back down to the kitchen.

Pru has had a fall. Hannah goes to tend to her, only for the old lady to get confused and press Hannah's red button.

Hannah tells me to go, that she will follow after. Knowing the guards are on their way is frightening. Still, being separated will make things so much easier. I can send Kenzie another message, ask him to come and meet me in central London instead. He went to the bar earlier today, retrieved the fob from the haberdashery drawer where it's been hiding in plain sight the whole time.

I make out to Hannah like I don't want this, that I'm not happy, even though I know this is actually a bonus. Then I pull on my baseball cap and I leave.

I set off across the ice. My bag is full of the cash Hannah gave me to carry but my head is full of the money still to come. I imagine it as a pile of gold trapped inside a treasure chest, heavy and glittering. All I have to do now is place the key inside the lock and turn.

The night air frisks my lungs and I think back to the March night I followed John into that alley.

I remember it all.

The heft of his ribs against my palm.

The slow plash of his heart.

His yeasty breath, spreading across the cobbles like fumes.

Hannah has asked me over and over for the truth, to tell her what really happened. I did come close once, at Christmas. Lying there together in bed it seemed like a portal had opened up between us, a space in which I could finally say the words, explain what I did and why, and that everything would be OK. But then she got up and the moment disappeared.

I'm glad. No good would have come of it.

I reach the middle of the pond and pause. Looking back toward Hannah's house, I think of the months I spent locked inside her kitchen and then my mind goes back to the money, waiting quietly for me to come and collect.

The cage was a small price to pay.

I blow the house a kiss.

Goodbye.

Hannah

Hannah had expected an aftermath – guards clustered by the gate, police lights flashing – but the street was quiet, her front door open.

She went inside and called Rupert's name.

'Down here,' he said, 'in the kitchen.'

Passing through the hall, she noticed the door of the airing cupboard at the top of the stairs was ajar. Her first thought was that the guards had left it that way, but then she saw the gaping custody bag and the random things scattered across the floor. She remembered the hard drive she'd found in Jem's backpack, the way he'd dashed upstairs to use the bathroom at the last minute. More lies. Whatever the drive contained, the mix-up with the bags meant, on that front at least, his scheming had been for nothing.

Rupert was waiting by the cell in a tailored three-piece suit, with his yellow wool scarf tied round his neck. She went to him and they embraced. For the first time since Hannah had learned of Jem's betrayal she felt safe, like he would protect her from whatever might happen next.

'The prison service have been and gone,' he said quietly. 'There was a uniform stationed outside the house so I flashed my badge, told him to sweep this street and the next road over. Give us time to figure things out.'

Hannah set down her bag and was about to take off her coat when she stopped. There was something about the kitchen that felt different.

'Tell me what happened,' said Rupert as they drew apart, 'we'll go from there.'

She tried to order her thoughts, but her mind was slurry. She was about to put it down to the stress of the last few hours but then her lips began to tingle. Her sugar was low.

'Jem and I, we were going to escape, then Pru had a fall and she got confused, pressed my alarm.' Her hand fluttered against her stomach. She didn't feel able to tell him about the baby, not yet. 'I was thinking I could say I activated it, that Jem got out and so I ran?'

Rupert nodded, thinking. 'You said you had witnesses,' he continued, 'people who say they know who killed John?'

'Two people. I don't know if they'd go on the record but one used to work for the gang and one still does. Both of them mentioned the same man, Slig. Said there'd been talk that he killed a detective. I haven't mentioned anything about him to Mickey yet but I could, she'd get onto it immediately.'

Rupert took a breath and pursed his lips as if to stop the words he wanted to say from escaping. It was clear he was embarrassed for her, at the way she'd fallen for Jem's lies, that she was still clinging to a fiction he'd made clear he felt dishonoured his partner's memory, but he was too much of a gentleman to voice any of this out loud.

'I'm a fool, I know that. My husband was cheating on me with my best friend for years and I had no idea.' She pointed at the open cell door and saw a tremor pass through her hand. 'Now this. But when it comes to who killed John and why, I'm certain. Jem had nothing to do with it.'

The words felt stretchy in her mouth, the vowels lengthening and widening. Her heart began to pecker against her ribs.

'Your best friend.' He shook his head sadly. 'Terrible shame.'

Hannah tried to follow what he was saying but the ferocity of this low was frightening. She'd never had one come on so quickly and with such intensity; it was like being hit by a truck. She reached for her backpack and the dextrose tablets inside only to remember she had the wrong bag. Trying to stay calm, she reviewed her options. Her earlier clear-out meant the fridge and cupboards were empty, but there might be an ancient pack of tablets lurking at the back of a drawer.

She yanked one open, then another, rifling through cutlery, tea towels and tin foil in search of the packet's yellow and orange swoosh.

Rupert moved closer.

'What are you doing?'

His fingers hovered near his breastbone, as though he was about to reach for his badge.

'Hypo.' She showed him her wobbling fingers, then pushed them into another drawer. This time they landed on the black canvas of her old insulin kit. 'I need sugar.' She hadn't used the kit in years, not since she'd traded it for her clicker pen, but she'd often kept a stash of dextrose in the pouch at the front.

Empty.

She unzipped the rest of the kit, hoping to find a half-eaten packet inside, but there were only syringes, pristine in their plastic packets, and a vial of insulin, long past its expiry.

She looked up and there it was again, that feeling, like a speck of grit in the corner of her eye. She scanned the kitchen for something out of place. Then she saw it.

The fridge magnets.

They'd been rearranged.

NOT THE DORMOUSE BUT THE BEAR

Her first reaction was annoyance – someone had destroyed John's last message – but that soon changed to confusion.

The words were strange, the sentence nonsensical.

She read it again, trying to understand, but her sugar was falling fast. Her knees seemed to be dissolving, the structure that kept her legs upright crumbling. She swayed briefly and then sank toward the floor. Rupert caught her just in time and helped her to a dining chair but she was too weak to sit upright.

'Here,' he said, bending low and placing her arm tenderly across his shoulder. He guided her into the cell and onto the bed. She slumped back against the wall, in a half-sitting, half-lying position.

'Fruit juice,' she mumbled, her lips numb. 'Ask next door.'

He didn't move. He seemed preoccupied by some other task, as though he was plucking up the courage to ask her a question he didn't know how to phrase.

'Go,' she shouted, trying to snap him out of it.

'Yes, sorry,' he said, heading toward the stairs. 'On it.'

She looked again at the magnetic letters on the fridge, trying to understand their meaning. Not the dormouse but the bear.

Her brain was foggy, her thoughts as lumpen and shifting as the green algae that carpeted the pond at the start of summer.

No sooner had Rupert gone than he returned.

'No joy,' he said, showing her his empty hands.

She tried to speak but her tongue was numb. It lay in her mouth, thick as a piece of meat.

He spotted her old insulin kit, still open where she'd left it on the table.

'Is this what you need?' he asked. The elation at having found a solution made his voice jump an octave. He held the vial up to the light and smoothed his thumb across the metal seal.

'No.' It was more of a sound than a word. What was he thinking? Rupert knew how diabetes worked from his experience of it with his father.

He opened the packet, took out the syringe and removed the cap. His hands were shaking and he had to still them before skewering the vial. Slowly, he drew back the needle. The syringe full, he came into the cell, to where she lay slumped.

'No.' This time Hannah managed to articulate the word. She tried to lift her arm in the air, to push the needle away, but it refused to budge. The insulin was out of date and so its potency would be low; still, even a little would push her sugar danger-ously low. It could harm the baby, maybe even cause her to miscarry.

He lifted her top and once he'd exposed a small area of skin he brought the needle close to it and – jab – it was in. He pushed his thumb down onto the plunger, withdrew the needle and stepped back.

Hannah thought again of the pond algae. On the May Day Bank Holiday the entire surface had been covered in the stuff. In the late afternoon she'd been at the French doors when she'd seen a tourist in shorts and sunglasses mistake its green spread for grass. He'd stepped out onto it with the absolute expectation it would carry his weight. Bobbing back up to the surface with clumps sliding down his cheek, he'd been aghast, incredulous that something so solid-looking had swallowed him whole.

She willed her eyes to stay open, to find the energy to ask Rupert to call for an ambulance. To find a way for her and her baby to survive.

He watched her for a minute, then leaned forward and, after brushing her hair behind her ear, kissed her tenderly on the cheek.

He reached his hand back toward his badge in his inside jacket pocket.

She couldn't fight it any longer. Her head lolled heavy to the right, pulling her down toward the bed. The thought of the pillow was a comfort. She wanted somewhere soft to rest her face, to sink her skull into the cotton and surrender to the black flooding in her brain. Instead her cheek hit damp, foam-like material, more cleaning sponge than bedlinen. Mesh chafed her ears and ballooned up around her face. Unable to lift her head, she opened her eyes and saw red, bright and artificial as a clown's nose, and white geometrical peaks, the tail feathers of a rooster.

Jem's baseball cap.

He left it on the pillow so that even if she couldn't see him she would know not to be afraid.

Rupert retracted his hand from his pocket as if he'd decided he didn't need what was in there after all, and his yellow scarf swished against his suit.

'When you ignored Aisling's calls she contacted me. She'd remembered something, from one of her and John's hotel trysts.' He sneered. 'He wasn't above accepting free rooms in which to meet his mistress.' He stood up straight, cracked his neck left and right. 'One night, waiting for him in one of these rooms, Aisling saw an envelope pushed under the door. It wasn't addressed to anyone so she opened it. It was a graduation picture, police officers outside Peel House in Hendon, their names below. One of the officers had been circled, as had a name. Looking more closely, she realised it wasn't a picture but a screenshot of a message with the picture embedded. A message from me to someone she didn't recognise. She thought nothing of it, that maybe we were organising a college reunion of some kind. But then that day when you confronted her about the affair you mentioned a name, Roddy Blessop. She couldn't place it at the time, it was only later she remembered. It was Blessop's name that had been circled and, she presumed, whose face had been picked out. She didn't know what it meant but she was sure it was important. She was desperate to tell you, to see if it might help.' He took the end of his scarf and pressed it against his mouth. 'John had secretly been investigating what he'd heard was the murder of an UC, trying to find out who helped tip off the gang he was infiltrating. Someone provided him with a copy of that screenshot to help him on his way.' He dropped the scarf to his chest. 'Her memory of that message, that picture. The fact I sent it.' He paused. 'Very incriminating.'

Not the dormouse but the bear.

She looked again at Rupert's scarf.

Rupert the Bear.

She understood now. Who had changed the letters on the fridge and why.

A knock.

Someone was upstairs in the hall.

'Hello?' Their words funnelled through the air. 'DS Cammish. I've finished the street search.'

'Sorry,' said Rupert, backing toward the stairs. 'Really, I am.' He couldn't bring himself to look at her. His face was grey and he thrust his hands into his trouser pockets. He nodded at the discarded needle and vial. 'But you've made this easier than it was going to be, for both of us.'

Jem

One Hour Earlier

I'm a fifty feet from the ladder when I hear it. A polystyrene squeak that sets my teeth on edge. I look down and see a line between my feet. It forges forward, splitting and branching across the ice, and then it fissures, revealing a stripe of black.

Water.

I switch to a fast tiptoe movement but every time my shoe impacts the surface a new explosion of cracks appear. The sound is getting deeper, like the grumble of an approaching storm, the gaps arterial, veining out toward the shore.

I look to the ladder and the back of Queen's Crescent, the mansions fortressing up into the night. It's still a good fifty metres from here to there and the ice is becoming ever more fragile.

The thought enters my head like a bullet.

You're not going to make it.

I keep going, my brain scrapping around for a plan B: maybe I should lie flat, spread my weight like a seal and slide the rest of the way on my belly? Or, if the ice is that weak maybe I should get into the water and try to swim through it? Other ideas come, each more stupid than the last. Despite the temperature, beneath my clothes I'm hot, sweat fanning across my shoulders. I'm starting to think I should turn back, that all this has been for nothing, when the ice thickens. Soon the floor is solid again, the ice grey and dense as rock.

Being able to move through such wide-open space is dizzying, the expanse of sky and Heath overwhelming, and so I try to keep my eyes forward, my gaze narrow. I hate that I have to fight the impulse to scuttle back to the cell, that the impulse exists at all.

I distract myself with thoughts of Lucas after the treatment. The nurses unpicking the wires from his arms and chest, him getting up out of bed and walking to the lift, waving goodbyes as he goes.

Mr Tarker always said it was just as much of a skill to return an item to a person without them noticing as it was to take it from them in the first place. He's right. This has been the most difficult thing I've ever done, but I'm almost there. The secrets I've had to keep from Hannah stick to me like burrs but I tell myself that soon they won't matter.

The thought of us as a family of three makes my heart light.

A hiss, like a freezer being sealed, and the ice yawns open.

There is no time to run.

I drop like a stone, my clothes and backpack speeding me toward the muddy bottom. Water fills my mouth, the cold a jab to my throat.

I bob back to the surface, scrabbling for traction on the sheared ice, my fingers slipping and sliding, useless against the wet. I try to pull myself up but my body is freighted with saturated clothing, my arms numb. In the distance I can see someone on the Heath, walking a dog. I open my mouth to shout for help but then I stop. No one can know I am here.

My teeth bounce against each other and my breath huff-huff-huffs faster than my lungs can bear, my heart stunned.

I think about Hannah and our baby. The names we liked for a girl.

Audrey, Holly, Grace.

For a boy.

Jamie, Ben, Christopher.

I try again, pushing down and then using my natural buoyancy to launch myself up and onto the floe. Legs kicking, I manage to propel myself out of the water. I reach back to retrieve my baseball cap floating on the surface, and then I roll toward the solid section of pond from which I came.

Drenched and shivering, I try to figure out what to do. The hard drive and PIN were sealed in plastic; they should be fine. My phone on the other hand . . .

Close to the ground I can see how the ice toward Queen's Crescent is sheened with water. It's the same toward the Heath. The route back toward the house is more stable, but I can't return there – I'd walk straight into the lap of the guards who must surely have arrived by now.

I haul myself up to sitting and my eye catches on a sliver of sodium light, ten or fifteen houses down from Hannah's place. A tiny gap in the terrace. If I could get to it and cut through the garden I'd come out onto her road, well clear of the electric fence, then I could try to find my way to the Crescent on foot.

Upright, the water that had collected in my lower back rushes into my jeans. I walk, favouring the greyer-looking sections of ice as this seems to indicate thickness, and every time I step forward I do so carefully. The ice moans a little here and there but I make it back to the opposite end of the shore without incident.

Wooden steps lead me up to a gate, unlocked. I go through it into a garden and the security light comes on, washing me blue. The property itself is dark, no one home. I head for the gap at the side and the security fence dividing back from front. It's high, seven feet, and so I pull one of the lawn chairs over, clamber up onto it and heave myself over. I drop down onto gravel on the other side with a thump.

The street is speckled with frost, the street lamps hazy. I make my way onto the pavement and slink into the shadow of a tree. Up the road, outside Hannah's house, I see a van but no guards. They must be inside.

My body is still juddering with cold and water drips from the peak of my baseball cap but I'm triumphant. I'm going to do it, I'm going to get to the mansion, to the money.

I want to call Hannah, to let her know what happened, that I'm going to be late. The phone is almost certainly toast: still, I check it just in case. The screen is dead.

A hand grips my shoulder.

'Got you.'

They sound happy, like they just won a prize.

I go to run but the guard jerks me back.

'Not so fast.'

He has a lisp, like there isn't enough space for his tongue to form the words. I turn round.

He grins and his metal braces twinkle in the street-light.

'Hello sailor.'

Monty.

He nods at Hannah's house.

'You got out of your box?'

I pull away but he grabs my arm and twists until it feels like my wrist is going snap. He brings his face close to mine. Food, some kind of leafy green, is stuck in the metal barricading his right incisor.

'Where is it?'

I think of the PIN and the hard drive in my bag. I worry he somehow knows they're there.

'Where's what?'

He tightens his grip and my wrist strains against the torsion, the slim bones close to breaking.

'I don't have it,' I say, trying not to whimper.

'Cut the bullshit. I know it was you. I went through the CCTV. Took me days but I found it. How'd you get if off my neck like that?'

Down the street a radio scowls to life. A guard searches for something in the front seat of the van. Monty shoves me deeper into the shadows. It starts to snow, the flakes thin and watery.

'I've been hanging around this posho street for months,' he hisses, 'trying to figure out where you might have hidden it, who you might have given it to for safe keeping.'

I think about Pru and the person Hannah told me she claimed to have seen hanging around. We thought she was imagining it.

He nods at my backpack and I flinch, terrified my fear was correct, that he knows what it contains.

'You're obviously on your way there, your hiding spot. Tell me where it is and I won't hurt you too bad.' He looks down, assessing my knees. 'Just enough to slow you down.'

I say nothing.

'Look,' he says and I'm surprised to hear a wheedle in his tone, 'if I get them their money there's a chance they'll take me back.'

The guard slams the door shut and Monty's eyes jerk right, toward the noise. I take my chance and throw the phone hard in his face. He recoils and lets go of my arm.

I run.

At the end of the street I turn a corner and find myself at a crossroads. Whatever happens, I can't let him follow me to the Crescent, to Hannah. I look for a wall to hide behind or a car to slide under, but everything is too exposed, he'll spot me in an instant.

I'm starting to panic when I see something.

I think I'm imagining it, it makes no sense, but when I look closer I find I'm right. In the front garden of the corner house on the opposite side of the road is a dome tent. Pitched under a tree, it is furred with snow, its guy-lines baggy.

Maybe some kid had a camp-out and never put it away? I don't care why it's here, just that it is. A hiding place.

In the garden I zip open the front, crawl inside and try to still my breathing. The air is stale, the floor littered with books, pillows and a single sleeping bag, curled on its side like a discarded cocoon.

Outside I hear footsteps and someone hoarsing swearwords under their breath. Monty. He stops and I imagine him scouring the crossroads, peering for any sign of me in the distance, trying to work out which road to take. He makes a decision and the footsteps start back up. When I can't hear them anymore I peep outside.

The pavements are empty. I crawl into the garden, but no sooner have I set foot back on the street than I hear the dull thud of boots against snow.

Our eyes catch and he smiles.

'Surprise.'

Again, I run. I'm doing well, lengthening the distance between us, when I realise I've gone the wrong way. The crossroads confused me and I've doubled back onto Hannah's street. I twist my head, trying to work out what to do. If I turn round I'll run straight into Monty but if I keep going I'll hit the electric fence.

The pond. It's my only choice.

I head for the gap in the terrace, heave a wheelie bin over to the fence and clamber up onto the lid. The snow stutters and then stops as I pull myself over the wall and onto the lawn chair.

I'm at the bottom of the garden when Monty appears. He lumbers over the fence after me, misses the lawn chair and lands badly. A crunch and his knees go out from under him.

I head toward the bottom of the garden and down the steps to the shore.

I decide to stick to the pond's perimeter. The freeze here is thick and I figure that, even if it breaks, the water will be shallow. I'll fall in up to my knees, my thighs at most.

My plan works and I'm twenty metres from the ladder when Monty appears on the shore. He's limping but he sets out onto the pond without hesitation. He keeps looking over to where I stand and I realise that he assumes I got here in a straight line, that it's safe to retrace my route.

I stay put. I don't want him to know where I'm headed; whatever happens, I mustn't lead him toward Hannah.

When he makes it all the way to the middle without incident I start to panic. I'm wondering if I should try to skirt my way round to the Heath, lose him there, when there is a creak, like someone opening a door.

Splash.

He bobs back up and tries to pull himself out, but the ice where he fell is mushy and everything he grabs falls apart.

'Help me,' he screams before going back under.

I think of the time he pushed Chickie down the stairs, the bruises on Maya's face, her teeth like rubble.

He resurfaces gasping and coughing, but the icy water is like a lullaby and after another minute he quietens. Slowly, the water takes him.

I wait – I need to be sure – and then I walk the last few steps to the ladder. My wrist is sore, bruised from where he twisted it, but I climb and climb.

The door to the basement is wedged open.

Hannah, she made it.

The stairwell is dark, the steps slippery, but I leave the torch in my rucksack. The pond water will have done for it the same way it did my phone.

Inside I use my hands to feel my way through the gloom. I call her name as I go but every time the word leaves my mouth it stalls and fades to nothing, as if the air here is too stale to carry the sound.

I open the door to the garage expecting to see Hannah, torch in hand, preparing the car for our departure, but I am greeted by darkness and a silence so complete I know at once she is not here.

Still, I call her name.

I stay there a moment more, hoping she will appear, but the silence persists. Moving back through the house, I shout for her again as loud as I dare.

Nothing.

Back up the basement steps, I bristle against my damp clothes and pull at the jumper yoked round my neck.

Then I see them.

Footprints in the snow.

The narrow part of the foot is directed away from here, toward the front of the house. I follow them round the side of the mansion to the stone fountain. The trail continues on to the gate and the street beyond.

Hannah has been and gone, of that I'm sure. The question is why?

Did she get here and, finding no sign of me, assume I'd been caught? Has she gone back to hand herself in? Did she think I'd got into difficulty on the ice?

Then another thought emerges, one so horrible I won't acknowledge it at first, and try to swing my brain toward other more palatable scenarios. But it won't go away and prods and pokes until I turn to face it head-on.

Did Hannah get here and then turn on her heel because she had second thoughts?

About me?

About us?

I worry someone will walk by and see me here, so I return to the back of the house.

If Hannah has gone back home she'll be in trouble and, no matter what lies she tries to tell, most likely charged with aiding and abetting my escape. If I return too I could tell a different story, vouch for her innocence, keep her and our baby out of a cell.

But then Lucas.

I'm so close.

This has all been for him, to save him. Without the money he won't be able to access the treatment. He will die.

The car is sat downstairs in the garage, the tank full of fuel. I could get in, put the key in the ignition and drive. I could save Lucas and then I could be free.

I think of Hannah. The tiny babygrow she brought back that day. The way we held it up in the air and imagined feeling our child's hands and legs inside.

I make my way back toward the hole in the fence, to the pond.

Hannah decided not to wait. Whatever her reason I need to make sure she is OK, to keep her safe.

Jem

I rush back out front, to where I last saw the policeman, by the cigarette machine.

He's not there.

Pushing through the crowds, I scan the room, the hot thump of panic in my chest. I'm too late; he's gone. But then I see a flash of white hair by the door. He's on the phone and, judging by the way he's draining that glass, getting ready to leave soon.

I'm just in time.

A couple of empty wine glasses sit on the sill behind where he's standing and so I approach from the side, angling myself toward the front part of his body, and then, as I reach across to scoop them up I use my other hand to replace the wallet in his inside jacket pocket.

It isn't difficult. He's too busy issuing ultimatums to whomever he's arguing with to pay me any mind and I slip away unnoticed.

In the staffroom I find Maya on her break, crouched over a compact, make-up sponge in hand.

'I'm off,' I say, undoing my apron. She nods and I see purple on her cheek. A tinge, just below her eye socket. She retouches it gingerly. Every dab makes her flinch. 'You OK?'

'Fine.' Her upper lip is swollen, the right corner bisected by a thin red line. I remember the way she hid her mouth with her hand earlier. 'I'll be fine.'

Monty has spent most of the evening on his mobile offering impassioned denials that seemed to fall on deaf ears, or stalking around his office, no doubt trying to figure out how he might have mixed up the fobs, PIN and drive, why they don't work like they're supposed to. It's yet to occur to him that they might have been switched, that someone else is involved.

I look again at Maya's bust lip and the guilt settles on me like dirt. In the past Monty has done this and worse, but tonight I know these particular bruises are on me.

I put on my coat and as I head out to the corridor I feel inside my jeans for my travelcard.

Empty.

Trying to stay calm, I stop and check each pocket in turn, pulling the cotton out by the seams.

Nothing.

It must have got dislodged while I was working somehow, fallen on the floor. I'm about to go and scour the bar when I realise.

The policeman's wallet.

Before I gave it back to him I had it in my jeans. What if the travelcard got caught inside? It's happened before with my own wallet; it slides into the fold and the thin plastic cover gets hooked.

I need to find him before he goes, to somehow take his wallet from him for a second time, retrieve the travelcard and with it the PIN.

But when I get to the bar he's gone.

Outside I look left and right. The pavement is busy with people, the air clouded with steam from nearby food trucks. I look and look, and then I see him. A hundred metres away, he's trying to navigate his way round a lamp post but he's so drunk he misjudges, clips it with his shoulder and lurches forward. I break into a sprint and once I get close I start shouting, trying to get his attention, but there are so many people and it's not like I'm calling his name and so he keeps going, then he turns right into a cut or a back street and disappears.

I reach the opening and squint into the gloom. It's an alley, a dead end, lined with commercial waste bins. The ground is cobbled, the walls high. The policeman has stopped halfway along and has his hands on his hips. His head bobs left and right. The alley seems to have been a mistake, a wrong turn, and now he's figuring out what to do next.

Seeing me, he startles.

'Hello?'

'Hi.'

Slowly, I make my approach. I don't want to spook him.

The alley is murky and blotched with yellow light, overspill from the closest buildings.

I decide the best thing I can do is disarm him, to let him know right from the off I'm not a threat.

I hold out my phone.

'I work in Fleece,' I say, making sure to keep my distance. 'You dropped this on your way out.'

As he steps forward, I pretend to fumble and the phone drops to the cobbles.

'Sorry.'

I move in close, let him reach for it, and as he comes back up to standing I take my chance. For the second time tonight, I smooth my hand inside his jacket and take his wallet. While he presses at my phone, turning it this way and that, I swish the wallet behind my back and run my fingers over the leather. Just as I guessed, the travelcard is caught on one of the inside folds. I rip it free as he returns my phone.

'Not mine.' He sways a little and then he straightens and shakes his head, like he's trying to sober up. 'Thanks though.'

As I take it from him, I lean forward and replace his wallet.

The exchange is complete.

I wish him a good night and head off.

Back on the pavement I turn and look back. He's standing where I left him, studying the walls, as if he's expecting a doorway to magically appear. He moves toward the brick and his white hair catches on the light. It looks like a dandelion clock, soft and fragile.

Jem

I circle back round the outer edge of the pond to the shoreline and climb the steps to Hannah's garden. At the top I brace, certain I'm about to be intercepted by a guard or a roving torch, but the lawn is empty. Every light in the house is ablaze and yet there is no sign of anyone in the kitchen or in any of the other windows.

The French doors are unlocked. I come inside and close them behind me.

'Hannah?'

Nothing.

Maybe she didn't come back here after all? Or maybe she has been and gone, the guards having taken her off to be questioned and charged? The thought of her in an interview room leaves me short of breath, like someone has taken a fist to my stomach.

I'll call the police, turn myself in. Tell them she had nothing to do with the escape, that it was all me.

I'm headed upstairs to the living room landline when I hear something. A man on a phone. He sounds like he's in the hall near the front door and he has this way of pronouncing his words, his mouth cupping the vowels as if to protect them from a bitter wind, that makes him hard to understand.

Rupert.

Hannah must have called him, asked for his help, or he heard what happened and came to check things out.

Not wanting to startle him, I hold up my hands in surrender and slowly climb the stairs. I haven't gone far when he says something that makes me take pause.

'We have a problem.' He takes a breath, like he's trying to find the courage to say the remaining information out loud. 'John's wife. The dead undercover, she knows.' He exhales hard but his respite is short-lived. 'Don't you think I realise that?' he hisses, his anger tinged with fear. 'Look, she says she has proof.' His tone steadies but retains a certain amount of grit; he's still annoyed but trying to hide the fact. 'I'm meeting her now. I'll sort it.' He goes quiet and I think the call is finished, but it seems some accusation has been levelled against him, some question of doubt, and he retaliates, whiplash-fast. 'I got rid of the friend, didn't I?'

Mind reeling, I retreat into the kitchen, trying to make sense of what I've heard.

Rupert was involved in or knew about an undercover officer's death?

Roddy Blessop?

Who is the friend?

Aisling?

Rupert said Hannah was on her way back here. I need to talk to her first, to tell her he can't be trusted. This could be the final piece of the puzzle. But the moment Rupert sees me I'll be arrested and once I'm back in the system who knows how long it will be before I can talk to her again.

I try to calm my breathing, consider my options.

I could hide out, hope he leaves her alone at some point and then take my chance, tell her what I heard before I'm whisked away in a van. I scan the kitchen looking for a spot. There's only one place I know I won't be seen. In the cell, under the bed.

I want to let Hannah know to be on her guard, but I can't text her and if I left her a note Rupert might see. I'm scanning the kitchen for something, anything, when I land on a flash of colour in the corner. The fridge magnets. Hannah freaks out if anyone even so much as brushes past them.

I rearrange the letters into a warning, a message only she will understand. Then I slide myself and my backpack underneath the bed. The sugar figurines I've collected these past months sit lined in a row on the skirting board, like old friends waiting to greet me. I twist to flatten myself against the wall and the peak of my baseball cap knocks against the underside of the mattress. Thuds on the stairs. Rupert is on his way down to the kitchen. At the last second I take off my cap, reach out my arm and place it back up top on my pillow. I slink back under the bed just before Rupert appears.

He paces up and down, opening and closing drawers, turning the tap on and off. He doesn't seem to know what to do with himself. Then I hear her.

Hannah.

She comes down to the basement. They talk.

She left the mansion because she thinks I lied about my feelings, that our relationship was a con. She's so sad.

Rupert presses her for more information on the dead undercover and she tells him what she discovered. I watch their feet, see Hannah move away, and then I hear drawers being pulled open and the clatter of cutlery crashing back and forward.

She tells Rupert she's having a hypo and he rushes toward her, guides her into the cell. The mattress lumps toward me as she lies on the bed. She asks him to go next door to ask for fruit juice and he complies.

I don't understand why she doesn't take the dextrose in her backpack. Has she lost it somewhere along the way?

I wait until he's gone and then I slide out from under the bed, but before I can get to my feet I hear him returning. He must have had second thoughts; there is no way he's gone next door in that time. He seems to think he has something that will help but Hannah is against it, she sounds distressed.

The mattress above me flattens, like Hannah has fallen onto her side, and I hear someone calling for Rupert upstairs.

Hannah is quiet. Too quiet.

Once he's gone I take my chance. I don't care if he comes back down and sees me. Something is wrong.

I find her lying on her side, eyes closed. By her feet is a syringe and a vial of insulin.

I understand then.

All the things he's done and why.

Her backpack is nowhere to be seen. I open the fridge and the cupboards only to remember she cleared them out. The delicate metal tools she used to sculpt fondant lie in rows, like surgical instruments.

The figurines.

What was it Hannah said? They should come with a health warning because they're nothing but pure unadulterated sugar.

I duck back under the bed and reach for the last character she gave me, a man with a tiny swaddled baby in his arms.

I grab a mug and teaspoon and dissolve the man's feet in a small amount of water. Then, after propping Hannah up on the bed, I drip tiny amounts of the liquid onto her tongue. Her breathing is shallow, her skin pebbled white. I keep going, drip, drip, drip, and under my breath I tell her that I love her, that

I'm sorry, and pray that enough of the sugar dissolves into her bloodstream in time.

A shadow rises onto the wall in front of me.

Before I can turn round something stamps hard into my lower back and I lurch forward. My head hits the wall. Thud. I ricochet back to the floor, my arms sprawled. The spilt sugar water puddles by my wrist, sticky and wet.

Rupert

Something's up, I know it.

After a week of gruff one-word answers and a refusal to look me in the eye he's asking if I want to go for a drink after work. It's something we do all the time but today it feels wrong. Like getting on a plane the morning after you dreamed it would crash.

Symeon wants to see me later and so I suggest we head east, to the bar. John isn't keen and asks if we can go somewhere else. That's when I know.

He wants out.

I persuade him to come to the Kingsland Road and we order drinks. His pint arrives and he takes a sip, then straightens. He's yet to say the words but he already looks relieved, like a rock has been lifted from his shoulders. He's going to tell me he's had enough, that he doesn't want to do this anymore, that it's too stressful, that he once had an idea of himself that was good and decent and that he wants to be able to think like that again.

I've never had the luxury of choice. I'm trapped, have been for some time.

'It's over,' he says and gestures to the bar. 'All this. I'm not doing it anymore.' He sups at the lager. 'Neither are you.'

All this.

It started small. A blind eye here, a tip-off there. Payment in kind. But snowballs get big quick and as my debt grew so did the favours. You blink and a tiny sphere that can fit in the palm of your hand is suddenly a boulder, big enough to crush you and anyone who gets in its way.

'You know it doesn't work like that,' I say, quietly, 'once you're in, you're in.'

'That's just it,' he says and I realise that what I thought was a burden being lifted was actually him bracing. 'I've never been "in", as you put it, not really. I only made it seem that way.'

When I was seven I managed to follow my father up the Orange Wall at Symonds Yat. He was aghast I'd managed it, full of praise, but then, as we made our way back down, the belay failed and ten feet from the bottom the rope holding me went slack. That's how this feels, like that moment before I started to fall, when my toes still bobbed against the dry rock and I moved past trees slowly, leaves tickling my cheek.

He tells me he suspected I'd started taking bribes a while back, but he didn't want to believe it. We were friends, partners. I was a good man, the best. He wanted to be sure and so, before he made any kind of accusation, he set me a test, told me about his credit card debt, showed me the statements, said how much he and Hannah were struggling to make ends meet.

I took the bait.

'I had no intention of reporting you. I wanted to find out what you were into and then help get you out. But then in that first week I heard a rumour. The Heppels had murdered an undercover officer, made it look like suicide.' He drains the last of his pint, orders another. 'I needed to find out if there was any truth to it, and if so, who was responsible. So I kept going.'

Lying in a heap at the bottom of the wall, ankle broken, I had tried not to cry while I waited for Dad and Hugo to reach me. Hugo got there first. 'You mustn't let this spook you,' he said, taking my hand in his, 'you mustn't let this stop you from trusting the rope.'

John lowers his head, fixes his eyes on the battered wood table.

'You tipped them off,' he says, his voice cold. 'Told them he was a UC. Signed his death warrant. Why?'

There are many answers to this question.

Do I tell him about after my brother died, how all I could think about was his frozen corpse at the top of that mountain and the people stepping over him in their quest to get to the summit?

Do I tell him about the money, the car, my house, how it's all gone, how even now I can't stop? How when I'm playing I feel better, separate from what happened and the thought of Hugo's body lying there like litter, his face furred with ice.

Or do I tell him how when you're caught like I am, caged by your own need, you find yourself capable of things you never thought possible?

He's already figured out the bare bones. Has already imagined how, as soon as I got wind a UC had been placed into the Heppels' network, I panicked they'd learn I was dirty and expose me. How I ultimately decided this was a risk I wasn't willing to take.

'He had a wife and children,' he says and he can't hide his disgust. 'A baby on the way. I've been to see them. Tried to make reparations.'

I found out about the undercover by accident. Mickey had started drinking again, often at work, though most people had no idea. Me included. There was a crossover with an armed robbery we were working on. I stumbled on something I shouldn't and Mickey, worried I was going to jeopardise the operation, warned me off. At the time she was a bit worse for wear, let slip his codename. After that it didn't take me long to figure out who he was. It takes one to know one.

'Why are you even here?' I say, suddenly furious. 'If you're going to report me, just do it already.'

'I wanted to give you the opportunity to turn yourself in.'

I laugh.

'And ruin my whole life?'

'Prison,' he says quietly, 'is being trapped inside something you can't get out of. If I'm not mistaken, you're already there.'

He tells me he hasn't spent a penny of the thousands he's been paid, that he's kept it all secure, evidence, ready for when the time came.

I head for the door, expecting him to come after me. I try my hardest not to turn round and check, to trust the rope, but when I get to the exit I can't hold out any longer and look back. He hasn't moved. His head is still down, his gaze fixed on the table.

On the street I get out my burner and call Symeon. Tell him about John.

'You need to change his mind.' He's cavalier, straightforward, like I've just asked advice on how to change a tyre. 'Get him to see sense.'

He doesn't need to say it. This will be worse for me than them. The person they got to kill that UC is long gone, they made sure of it. Pinning anything on anyone will be impossible. I on the other hand— In the old days bent coppers had a terrible fear of going to prison. There was nothing the other convicts hated more than an ex-pig. Now those found to be corrupt serve their time in a cell installed in their old nick. Their ex-colleagues become responsible for their care. I saw one once at Paddington Green. There was no abuse, no nastiness, they just never spoke to him. Ever. He sat on the bed watching them work, a mushroom of a man, fleshy and white.

I think it's worse.

The thought of that happening to me.

The shame.

The humiliation.

I feel like I'm in a collapsing building, the fear pushing down on me like broken brick, the sheared concrete squeezing and pressing, crushing my lungs, making it hard to breathe.

I walk the length of Great Eastern Street, toward Hoxton, trying to work out what to do. I think of my father's face once he hears the news. His brow will not be furrowed in disappointment, his mouth will not drop open in shock. There'll be one quick nod, as if to say, 'Of course,' and he'll go on with his day.

I imagine sitting in the dock in court. The judge's gavel sharp in my ear.

I need to find a way to convince John to keep quiet.

I call. Ask if we can talk some more.

'No point.' His words are thick with drink. 'Never mind all the other stuff, what happened with Marzipan Rain, what happened at The Warlaby. We have to tell her.'

Mickey. What will she say when she realises what I've done, who I've become?

'Please,' I say. 'Five minutes.'

'My mind's made up. Tomorrow, I'm going to tell her everything.'

'Come meet me on the Coal Board roof,' I say, desperate now. Halfway down Rivington Street, the roof is one of the places we like to go when we need to puzzle out a case. We stumbled on it a year ago when we were investigating an attempted murder. The victim, a chef, worked in a restaurant at the bottom of the building and had been found beaten half to death in a stairwell four floors up. The roof was supposed to be secure but we'd discovered

that if you went up to the restaurant toilets and then kept going you'd reach a metal door that opened onto the top of the block with a city skyline view. A short walk from the bar, it will give us the quiet we need to talk properly. More than this, I hope it will remind him of our friendship, our bond. 'Please, ten minutes, that's all I ask.'

Finally, he agrees.

'I'll head now.'

Tears blur my vision. Relief.

'See you up there,' I say and use the heel of my palm to wipe them away.

I go in through the restaurant and to the toilets out back. There, I launch myself at the stairs, taking them two at a time until I reach the top floor and the metal door. A shove and I'm on the roof. The air up here is clogged with meat smells from the food trucks below, the night sky studded with light. Shoreditch High Street sits diagonal to here, one block back, but its traffic smog travels well. One breath and I feel it hit the back of my throat.

Five minutes pass, then ten. I go to stand at the top of the stairs and listen out for footsteps. He should have been here by now.

My burner buzzes with texts from Symeon wanting to know how I'm getting on.

I've almost given up and am working out whether to call Mickey now instead of waiting for the morning, to confess and get it over with, when I hear something.

Voices.

They're coming from below, somewhere back toward the high street. I lean over the barrier, squinting into the gloom. The Coal Board sits next to a much shorter building and beside it there seems to be a cut or some kind of alley. Long and thin, large industrial bins lining its walls. Then I see him. John. He's talking to someone but I can't see their face.

He must have got lost, or maybe he stopped to relieve himself?

The man he was talking to walks away, back toward the high street.

'John,' I call down to him, 'John, up here.'

He staggers left and right, his shoulder bashing against the wall as he tries to locate the source of my voice.

'Rupert?' he says, once he has me in his sights.

'The entrance is one street across,' I say, sketching the route in the air. 'On Rivington, remember?'

He sways, like he's trying to orient himself, then pushes his hands up and away in defeat.

'I'm going home. I've had too much to drink to talk properly.' He turns.

'No.' I think of the convicted copper I saw in Paddington Green. Think of myself sitting there. Reviled. Ignored.

He can't leave, he mustn't.

'I'll come down. Wait.'

I'm about to head toward the metal door and the stairwell when I see that he's already walking away. By the time I get downstairs and run the length of Rivington and round to the high street he'll be long gone.

I assess the drop to the alley. It's at least fifty feet but if I clamber down onto the squat building that adjoins this one, then boulder the rest of way to the alley, it won't be so bad. I could be there in minutes.

I swing my legs over the barrier and twist, then I lower myself down, my toes searching out footholds in the brick.

'Rupert?' I've got his attention. Good. He won't leave now, not till I'm on the ground.

I jump down onto the adjoining building and then I tackle the wall.

My driving gloves protect my hands from the sharper bits of masonry and slowly, clinging to the tiny, almost imperceptible bulges and crevices, I descend.

I jump the last few feet and land awkwardly.

John stands back, hands on hips.

'Jesus, I knew you were a climber but,' he blinks, trying to focus, 'that was some Spider-Man shit, right there.' A whiff of his breath. After I left the bar he must have moved on to spirits.

'Please don't tell Mickey.' I hold the tops of his arms, trying to stabilise him. 'It will be bad for both of us.'

'You want to know about bad?' He reaches inside his jacket. 'Let me show you a picture of the man whose kids no longer have a dad because of you.' He fumbles, searching for his phone, and the contents of his inside pockets fall to the floor.

He crouches, patting the cobbles for his wallet, and I go to help collect the other stuff.

My hand lands on a length of black and silver. I think it's a corkscrew at first, then I feel the weight of it in my palm.

'A knife?'

He tries to take it from me and so I pull it back, out of his reach.

'Unless you've forgotten already, this gang you're in bed with like to kill coppers.' He nods at the weapon in my hand. 'That's for my own protection.'

I press the button on the handle, out of curiosity more than anything, and the blade flicks out. The steel edge is curved, the bevel dark grey.

'I used to think you were a good man, the best,' he says and the sadness in his voice gives me hope. He cares about me too much to throw me to the wolves. Then he sneers. 'Turns out you're just like the rest of your family, a spoilt rich twat who does what he wants, no matter the cost.'

Its then I realise. He's going to go through with this. No matter what I say, no matter what I do. Tomorrow he will expose me, tomorrow I will be ruined.

I come toward him and he laughs.

'Seriously, so what, now you're a killer too? Come on. The game is up.' His whisky breath makes my eyes sting.

A shove and the blade goes in. Cutting through the muscle and tissue is harder than I thought, like that first jab through a chicken's spine before you spatchcock it flat on the tray. His eyes widen and then he blinks, shock turning to acceptance as he realises how much he has misjudged this, how he got it and me so terribly wrong.

I stab him twice more, pushing the blade deep into the barrel of him, until he topples forward onto his knees. My hand is getting tired now, but still I stab him twice more in the back, the blade struggling against bone and cartilage.

He lists, collapsing onto one hip, and then, slowly, he lurches face-first onto the cobbles.

Felled.

I reach in beneath where he lies and slide out his burner. Wipe my gloves on my trousers. Then I assess the scene, forcing my brain into gear, trying to work out what else I need to take, to wipe, so that I leave no trace.

Shouts and laughter. People. They sound like they're approaching the alley.

I panic.

They're going to come in and find us. I need to leave now, quickly, before they catch me here. I square up to the wall, wedge my foot in a gap where the pointing had come loose, reach up my hand to grab a slightly distended brick and then I climb.

I'm almost at the top and getting ready to swing myself onto the small squat building that will lead me back to the Coal Board roof when I lose my footing. I scramble and curse, my hand grasping for a hold, and the knife falls from my pocket. In its descent it bounces against the wall and then disappears. I consider going down to retrieve it, but the voices are getting louder, and besides, I'm wearing gloves, there will be no prints.

I keep going, reaching and pushing until finally I pull myself back onto the restaurant roof.

I lie there starfished on the floor. It's cold and before long I start to shiver.

Jem

Rupert stands over me, his foot pressed against my chest.

'You came back?'

I try to get up and he pushes down harder. The pressure on my lungs makes it hard to breathe.

'Why?'

'Hannah.'

He rolls his eyes.

'Sure.'

'Call an ambulance.' I twist my neck, trying to see her. 'She'll die.' I wriggle harder. I need to get to her, to give her more of the sugar water.

He removes his foot from my chest and I think he's going to let me up but then I see his leg, lifted in the air. The sole of his shoe is beige, the section near the toes scuffed black. He brings it down hard on my face and then he does it twice more.

When I come to, my eye is swollen, my lip cut. I think he's gone but then I see him, over by the bars. His shoulders jerk up and down, his hands busy.

'It was you,' I say, the words muffled by my broken mouth. 'You killed John.'

He stops.

'He was your partner, your friend.'

He turns round. His face is drawn, his features trapped behind his skin.

'He was going to report me,' he says, and I understand that it's not me he's bargaining with but himself.

He steps to one side and I see that he's tied something blue and white to the bars. Hannah's apron.

He steps back to survey his handiwork. 'I've looked up how to do this so many times since John died.' He yanks down on the material hard. 'Never had the courage to go through with it.'

It's then I realise.

He's made a noose.

Is he about to hang himself?

He comes over to where I lie and hooks his hands under my arms.

'I still don't understand how your fingerprints ended up on his things, the knife especially, but I stopped questioning it during the trial.' He drags me across the floor and over to the bars. I struggle as much as I can but my vision is blurred, my head light. 'It meant the investigation had no interest in looking for a suspect elsewhere and for that I'm grateful.'

He looks from me to the apron and back again, his eyes narrowed, like he's assessing something.

Even in the fog of my concussion I understand.

The noose isn't for him, it's for me.

I try to crawl away but I've barely got going when I feel his shoe connect with the back of my skull. Crack. I hit the floor and he drags me back over to the bars.

After placing a chair beneath the noose he lifts me onto it into a kind of slumped sitting position, and then, keeping one arm round my waist, he hoists me up and reaches for the apron.

We're close – it's like we're hugging – and even though I can't see straight, on reflex my hands start to roam, across his shirt, inside his jacket, the muscle memory a comfort, my own personal catechism. I take something and pocket it but I'm clumsy and, although he doesn't understand what I've done, he's suspicious and uses the other apron tie to fix my hands behind my back.

He places the loop over my head and I try to imagine what scenario he thinks will explain the scene the police will inevitably come upon. Once I'm dead will he untie my hands, wipe his prints from the syringe and place it in Hannah's grasp, make it look like some strange double suicide? How will he explain my other injuries? Maybe he's so desperate, so fraught with fear and panic that he's no longer thinking straight, just hell-bent on trying to silence anyone that might expose him, with no real thought to what comes after?

The cotton is already close against my throat when he kicks the chair out from under me. The band clutches at my neck, the fabric squeezing my windpipe. I gasp for breath and the sound is raw. It scratches at the air and then wizens to nothing.

Rupert faces me head-on. It seems that watching me die is a punishment he has decided on for himself. The veins in his neck twitch and strain, but he stands stock-still. He will not let himself look away.

Hannah

I open my eyes a crick. On the other side of the cell I can see a shape. Grey and white, it jerks up and down like a fish on a hook.

A grunt, bovine-deep, and then I hear shallow breaths.

I blink, trying to bring the cell into focus, and the moving blob sharpens into a person. Tall with shoulders that hover up near their ears, they are busy heaving something onto a chair.

Rupert.

Even in my post-hypo blur I know to be afraid and push myself away, toward the wall. Something red and white unsticks itself from my cheek and, free of my weight, pings back into shape. The baseball cap.

Jem. He came back.

I lick my lips. My tongue is sticky, my mouth glazed with a sweet, powdery substance.

Then I see him. His chin is wedged against Rupert's neck. The skin on his left cheek is flayed, his nose bloody. Both eyes are swollen shut. Another grunt and Rupert shucks him over his shoulder like a sack of wheat.

I try to push myself up to sitting, but my arms are weak. I flex my fingers, trying to coax them back to life, and watch as Rupert brings Jem to standing on the chair.

A flash of something white round Jem's neck but I don't understand what I'm seeing until Rupert draws back his leg and, with a push of his heel, kicks the chair away.

Jem slams his legs against the bars, his feet searching for purchase on the steel. He gargles and spits, his face purpling under the pressure.

My rage is like a shot of adrenalin.

This cannot happen.

I will not let someone I love die again.

I spread my fingers against the bedspread, tense my forearms and will my muscles to work. My head spins and vomit lurks at the back of my throat but this time I manage to bring myself up to sitting. Jem is making too much noise for Rupert to notice any rustling I make and I manage to stagger upright and over to their side of the cell before he turns round and with a quick shove pushes me away, back onto the bed.

I land in a heap and my hand brushes against something sharp. The syringe he used to inject me earlier.

Jem is quietening, his breath no more than a wheeze.

I grab the syringe, haul myself back up to standing and launch myself toward Jem. This time when Rupert tries to block me I'm ready.

I lift my hand in the air and stab the needle into a spot just below his eye socket.

A scream and he recoils, eyes focused on the object lodged in his face he tries to pull it out, only for the needle to snap. He ogles the steel spike now protruding from his cheekbone and then turns his focus to me.

'Bitch.'

He pats at his pockets, searching for something. When he can't find it he comes toward me. His hands are on my throat when he stumbles and falls back.

A flash of grey. A yowl, strange and pitiful, like a baby's cry. Poobah. He must have slipped in through the open front door again.

For a moment Rupert shifts his focus to the animal slinking through the steel bars. I take my chance and, with all the strength I can muster, push him toward the kitchen. He tumbles back, out of the cell. I pull the door shut and press down on the black button round my neck.

As soon as the door is secure I run to Jem, dangling against the bars, and take the weight of his body with mine. I pull and tug at the apron strings, trying to free him or at least relieve the pressure round his neck, but they are tied tight. Jem's body mass is too much for me to handle. A wave of dizziness and I stumble. I can't hold him much longer.

A clank.

Something has landed on the floor.

I must have dislodged it from his trouser pocket.

Rupert's red climbing knife, gold initials embossed on the handle.

H.C.

Hugo Cammish. Rupert's brother, the one that died.

Jem must have taken it from him before he got him into the noose.

Once a thief, always a thief.

I reach, grab it and flick it open. The blade is pristine, the steel polished. I hack at the apron strings but the canvas is thick and pulled taut. There is no give. Desperate, I hack even harder, bringing the blade against it in a downward motion. The material begins to fray. One last hack and Jem drops onto me, so heavy that I collapse with him to the floor. A red line circles his neck, the welt deep and wide.

I tilt his head and breathe into his mouth, then I cross my hands one on top of the other and press at his heart. Rupert watches me for a while and then he takes himself away from the cell, over to the French doors. Looking out at the snowy Heath, his shoulders drop. He seems relieved.

Free.

I perform CPR for as long as I can but I'm so wrung out from my hypo that I soon become dizzy, my hands flapping uselessly against his jumper. It's over.

I lie down next to him and place my head on his chest.

I'm a pond-skater again, but now I feel like I'm sinking through the surface to the world below.

Footsteps on the stairs.

'Hannah?'

Birkenstocks followed by the swish of cerise and yellow kaftan. Kiki.

'Poobah,' she trills. 'Poobah, are you in here?'

Entering the kitchen, she sees me first.

'The cat,' she says, too caught up in her own drama to process the rest of the scene. 'I saw him in your garden, then he snuck inside.'

Her view broadens. She registers I am locked inside the cell with Jem. Looks from us to Rupert.

I close my eyes and listen for the bob of Jem's heart against his ribs.

'Come back,' I say.

Two syllables. Monogamous as lovebirds.

They hit the air and, in an instant, they are gone.

One year later

Hannah waited until the verdict had been delivered and then, shivery and exhausted, she stumbled toward the exit and down the Old Bailey's deserted corridors.

The trial had been held in Court 3. A modern extension, it housed twelve courtrooms, but these days only a handful were in use. The surrounding empty rooms and dust-grimed witness boxes shouldn't have made a difference to the trial acoustics – the walls were well insulated – but they did. Every word that had come out of the barrister's mouth seemed to reverberate through the building.

Outside, she stood on the pavement and lifted her face to the sun. It was early spring and the trees were dormant with buds biding their time, the mud in the flowerbeds dark and sloppy.

She'd thought that seeing Rupert get what he deserved would make her feel more at peace – the Met and Aisling's parents had pressed charges and so, as well as Aisling's murder, Rupert had also been tried on multiple counts of police corruption and bribery, not to mention the conspiracy to murder Roddy Blessop, an undercover officer killed in the line of duty – but she found her fury was worse than ever. Her insides felt scorched, wildfired by a rage that kept finding ever more ways to burn brighter and hotter than before. Justice had been served but it wasn't enough, it would never be enough.

Jem had been waiting for her in a cafe opposite. He crossed the road, one hand pushing the buggy, the other clutching the baby to his hip.

'So?' His expression was drawn, his skin pale.

'Guilty,' said Hannah. She remembered the barrister's closing statement. The way she'd described how Rupert had strangled Aisling with such force he'd fractured two of her cervical vertebrae.

The baby screwed up his face and took a breath, readying for a crying jag, but then Jem bent in close, reached a hand behind his ear and produced a silver coin. He twirled it from thumb to finger, making sure to go slow enough for the infant to follow, and then, with a flourish, made the coin disappear.

A giggle.

Jem performed the trick again and the giggle grew.

'You've got the knack,' said Hannah.

'Smoke and mirrors,' said Jem and kissed his son's head, his nose lingering in the downy white hair.

It was true what they said. Having a child made it feel like you were walking around with your heart outside your body. It left you vulnerable to grit and knocks but it also meant you experienced the rainbows of the world unfiltered, that you felt the comfort of a lover's hand at your waist more keenly, the joy of a newborn's mouth against your collarbone in your marrow.

'No regrets?' said Jem, strapping the child into the buggy. They'd decided not to take action for John's murder and their respective assaults – they didn't want the burden.

'None.' Hannah tried to take comfort in the fact that Rupert would spend the decades to come in the cells at Scotland Yard, being tended by his ex-colleagues, and would see out his twilight years with a Foster Host.

'Me neither,' said Jem quietly. 'About any of it.' His foster-brother Lucas had responded well to the gene therapy and although there were no guarantees, for now at least his cancer was under control. The Tarkers still had no idea as to the identity of their last-minute benefactor and Jem and Hannah planned on keeping it that way.

'Home?' said Hannah, searching for the nearest bus stop.

'Home,' said Jem, linking his arm through hers. In the buggy the baby gurgled, a golden hiccupy sound that sunshined the air.

Acknowledgements

This is a pretty crazy idea for a novel. I will be forever grateful to my editor Sophie Orme and my agent Madeleine Milburn for taking the leap and for their faith in me to pull it off.

Katie Lumsden, Felice McKeown, Clare Kelly and all at Zaffre.

Hannah Chambers and Jeremy Austin, for having a house that helped inspire my plot and for giving me permission to use it and its geography as I saw fit. Hannah and Jem are named for them, although anyone who knows the real couple will know that they bear zero resemblance to every aspect of my fictional characters, all except for one thing, their love is also fierce and strong and built to stand the test of time.

Janet Oakes, who came to my rescue and rallied the troops on one of the worst days ever. I am lucky to have had someone as kind and smart as you in my corner.

Murray Boland, who takes leaps on my crazy ideas on a weekly basis and who didn't hesitate to give me the time to finish this when I needed it the most.

Chris Sussman, my earliest and best cheerleader. Thank you for the comments, thoughts and questions, all of which helped shape this book and the world it inhabits.

Shameem Sangha, for the decades of support, friendship, laughter, and steak and chips. Your Fleabag pencils and WhatsApps are responsible for my completing at least three chapters of this book.

Steve Roche, for always being at the end of the phone to answer anything police-related.

Irene Wong, for your friendship and for helping with a character backstory that (although it didn't make the final cut) did mean we got to have a lovely dinner together.

Danny O'Connor and Kirsty Walsh, for the childcare, moral support and family group chat. You've never known true love unless you have a sister-in-law prepared to drop everything, travel 300 miles and look after your kid for a few days so you can finish a first draft.

Alan and Dorothy. My lobsters.

If you enjoyed *The Captive*, why not join Deborah O'Connor's Readers' Club by visiting www.bit.ly/DeborahOConnor?

Dear Reader,

I got the idea for this novel after our flat was burgled. The police caught the culprits and we were contacted and asked if we would like to meet with them as part of a restorative justice programme. I think restorative justice is laudable. Turns out I only think that in theory. In reality my response was instant no. There was no way I wanted to meet the people who had broken into my home. The prospect of seeing them up close, of them knowing who I was, terrified me.

Shortly after the burglary I watched the film *Capote*, the story of how *In Cold Blood* came to be. Part-way through the film there was a scene in which the two suspects are shown locked inside prison cells that were situated inside the sheriff's actual house (this was common, being such a tiny Kansas town the local police often situated the holding cells in their homes). This image, of a prison cell inside a domestic setting (in one scene the wife is shown at the stove, frying bacon) collided with our burglary in my head and I started to wonder. What if restorative justice was taken to its most extreme and logical conclusion?

Everyone knows prisons don't work, so what if there was a new form of justice, one in which, if someone commits a crime against you and they are found guilty, you are responsible for their prison time? A cell is built somewhere in your home and you are responsible for overseeing their sentence – the food they eat, the comforts they do or don't get. How would that work?

And then I started to wonder, what if your prisoner turned around and told you they didn't do it, that they were innocent. Would you believe them?

If you would like to hear more about my books, you can visit **www.bit.ly/DeborahOConnor** where you can become part of my readers' club. It only takes a few moments to sign up, there are no catches or costs. Zaffre will keep your data private and confidential, and it will never be passed on to a third party. We won't spam you with loads of emails, we'll just get in touch now and again with news about my books, and you can unsubscribe any time you want.

And if you would like to get involved in a wider conversation about my books, please do review *The Captive* on Amazon, on Goodreads, on any other e-store, on your own blog and social media accounts, or talk about it with friends, family or reading groups. Sharing your thoughts helps other readers, and I always enjoy hearing about what people experience from my writing.

Thank you again for reading *The Captive*.

All the best,
Deborah